SANGUINE MOUNTAIN

Book One
Camazotz Trilogy

By Jennifer Foxcroft

Sanguine Mountain
Jennifer Foxcroft
Copyright © 2015 by Jennifer Foxcroft

First Edition III. February 2015.
Published in United States of America

Written and published by Jennifer Foxcroft
Cover design by Cate Pepper 2014

Print ISBN: 978-0-9909895-0-9

Acknowledgments

To my beta readers: Jen, Lynda, Betsy and Sandii. Thank you from the bottom of my heart. You made handing over my manuscript to be seen by the outside world for the first time so easy. Thank you for your honest opinions, asking questions that made me think, and holding my hand when I needed it. Not to mention spotting the million typos my brain just refused to see.

To Betsy, the best line editor a girl could wish for. I cannot thank you enough for the support, help and friendship you gave me through this entire process. You have the most amazing eagle eyes that spot the wrong word time and time again. I don't know how you do it, but thanks to you my manuscript looks like a bought one.

To Mel, Lynda, Corrie, Stacey, Misty, Jen, and the LAMBB crew. Thank you for being the best cheerleaders a girl could have when I started my writing journey. I will never forget the time you gave up happily for me, or your ceaseless patience in my experimental writing days. I know for a fact that I wouldn't have even attempted to follow my dream if it wasn't for your encouragement and friendship.

To my critique group at The Writers' Collective: Kathy, Jennifer and Megan. Thank you for helping turn my manuscript into a better story. I appreciate your raw, open honesty more than I can tell you.

To my family and friends. Thank you for not laughing at me when I first told you I had written a book. That alone will forever mean the world to me. Stepping out of my comfort zone was scary, but knowing you were all there to catch me made it easier. Thank you for your faith, courage, belief, and excitement. I love you all dearly.

1
Vanish

EVERY TIME I watch a horror movie, there is that moment when the young, sweet girl is faced with imminent doom and bloodshed. Every time, I find myself screaming at her to run and hide or at least arm herself to the brink, but she never listens.

Right now, I could be Horror Movie Girl's twin. I'm not listening to every ounce of logic telling me to stay in the car and lock the doors. Telling me not to get out on the dark and definitely creepy road to nowhere and go walking through the forest away from my car and the safety of being locked inside of it.

But it's my best option considering my circumstances.

My old, faithful Honda has steam hissing and spurting in great wafts from under the hood. I don't have the faintest clue where I am because my dad's satellite navigation system—which he doesn't know I'm using because he thinks I'm at Tiffany's house—told me to turn left fifty feet ago when there was nothing but giant oak trees lining the road.

Rolling down the window, I hear the faintest whisper of music in the distance. For a second, the breeze carries a brief murmur of voices that makes me believe there's a party nearby. That is, if I wasn't sitting in the middle of a forest where such a thing would be utterly absurd.

Who in their right mind would hold a celebration out here? Hippies celebrating the end of summer? Or axe murderers luring stupid, lost girls to the slaughter?

Locking the car seems redundant, but I do it anyway. The night is peaceful, but the absence of the moon makes my skin crawl. The twinkling stars blink down at me through the sliver of open sky the road cuts through the thick forest. They give me a hint of courage until I focus on dozens of winged shapes flying low.

Bats.

Dozens of bats are headed in the same direction as me. The animal lover in me is curious about what kind they are, but being alone out here in the forest their numbers are freaking me out.

Again, if I were watching Horror Movie Girl, I'd say she was a definite goner to follow a colony of bats. Surely it's just a coincidence that they're headed toward the music too.

Two steps off the asphalt and I'm ankle deep in cold, shoe-swallowing mud. Guess the sandals weren't the best idea, but then again, I thought I'd be in the middle of suburbia, laying eyes on my real mother for the very first time. Instead, I'm following the devil's minions to what I hope will be my savior who can fix my car, reboot the GPS and point me back to civilization.

Dead bracken crunches under my feet. The darkness swallows my path with every step. If I had breadcrumbs, I'd leave a trail. I should have stayed in my car. Pine needle fingers caress my body as I push through the dense branches. I can't help but glance over my shoulder to make sure it's just the trees touching me and not some beast lurking in my wake. My white Capri pants, baby-blue tank and striped summer scarf don't exactly scream forest hues. I feel as obvious as Cinderella's phosphorescent fairy godmother gliding through the air—well, except for the gliding. I'm stumbling, tripping and fumbling my way along and feel as though every nocturnal creature for miles around knows my exact location. Shame I don't know my exact location! I flick the end of my blonde, high ponytail over my shoulder and pray I can find my car again.

"Ouch."

Something sharp has pierced the side of my foot. Collapsing to the ground, I gingerly find the source of the pain. Dropping my phone into the engine when I opened the hood wasn't my finest moment. I'm blind without my flashlight app. Prickles—I think. I begin pulling them out one by one. I shouldn't be here. This is all wrong. Tonight, I told my parents the biggest lie of my entire life. Tears well up just thinking about them—the people that I used to trust. My perfect—generous to a fault, bake queen extraordinaire—mother who lets me paint the most outrageous designs on her fingernails regardless of whether she is working the next day or not. And my father—the man I admire for his wicked rappelling skills rather than his current affairs and news obsession—who always comes to my rescue. Except for now.

I think about my three-legged chinchilla, Feathers, and how Dad supported me regardless of the cost. Pet stores and me are like magnets to metal. Last year while perusing the chinchillas for sale, I saw one get it's leg caught in her exercise wheel. After alerting the store clerk, I was appalled they were going to break its neck when they confirmed the leg was broken. To save its life, I purchased the poor creature, and instead of my parents grounding me for the subsequent astronomical vet bill, they understood my passion for animals and were proud I'd rescued another one. I doubt they'd be proud of me now.

Wiping my tears, I focus on my surroundings. The music is clearer now. I get up and follow it. The underbrush lessens. A banjo, fiddle and bass beat—along with the undertone of mingling voices—sound close, and there's a warm reddish glow winking through the trees ahead. Somewhere along the way, I've lost the bats or I simply can't see them amongst the canopy of tree branches hiding the starry sky.

The twisting tree roots beneath my feet become lush grass. Emerging from a clump of pine trees, I find myself on the edge of a clearing that holds a carnival. The red paper lanterns, hanging from the outer branches of enormous trees, barely light the scene. Carved skeletons are nailed to gnarled tree trunks. Red streamers and paper bat cutouts flutter and sway in the breeze. Ahead, people mingle in groups around sideshow stalls that could have been transported out of the 1920s—miniature fishing poles dangle to catch garish floating fish, darts with red feathered ends are aimed at origami balls containing a prize, large golden hoops are thrown over handmade treasures sitting on antique octagonal boxes. It screams turn of the century and doesn't in any way remind me of my local county fair.

In fact, nothing about this carnival nestled in the treelined boulevard is normal. Maybe I'm overreacting because I'm not supposed to be here, but something isn't right. I close my eyes and sniff the air, hoping the familiar smell of fried carnival treats will calm me. The air is crisp and clean. It chills my nostrils and the forest fills my senses. The kitchens must be downwind. No carnival is complete without food stalls to tempt the revelers.

The absence of loud neon rides that the Georgia State fair takes great pride in draws my attention, but an occasional chilling scream fills the air nonetheless. I can't quite describe the feeling inching up my spine as I leave the safety of the trees. The warm family atmosphere isn't present. I want to leave, but can't say exactly why. It's as though a thousand eyes are watching me. I look over my shoulder, but nothing is there except the blanket of darkness I just escaped.

Crunching twigs and movement to my left leaves my heart trying to beat right out of my rib cage. I can't shake the feeling that I'm about to be mugged or something worse. Squinting, I spy a couple amongst the trees—young lovers kissing in the darkness. I find romance when all my senses are telling me to run. I need to get a handle on my nerves, but they're buzzing with adrenalin. I shake my shoulders out and fill my lungs.

Then I notice what's different about the carnival goers milling around the attractions. I'm the only one present not clad from head to toe in dark denim, black lace, leather, satin or velvet. The occasional splash of blood-red fabric catches my eye. I think I've stumbled across a Goth Kids Central Casting secret meeting.

Glancing around, jet-black, straight hair is the norm. Why do all these people look the same? I run my hand down the length of my golden ponytail and hold it to my neck. The feeling I'm glowing in the dark fills me once more as eyes start to track my progress. Even the little kids running around are mini Goths in the making in their medieval dress. Halloween has arrived early.

Down near the band, several lit braziers seem totally unnecessary on the first Saturday in August. I head to the adults warming themselves and away from the overly amorous, staring teens. I sense a crowd gathering in my wake from the whispers catching up with me. Where did these people suddenly come from?

"You lost?" A gruff male voice asks out of the darkness.

Turning around, I discover a crowd has gathered and they don't look pleased. "Yes. My car broke down—"

"So you just wandered in here?" Mr. Dark and Grumpy interrupts.

It's hard to make out clear features in the half-light from the lamps, but I don't miss the creepiest face tattoo I've ever seen. Two black, pointy fangs dominate his lower lip and chin. I force my eyes up to his, but they're drawn back to his ink.

The group edges closer, and my body stiffens. Horror Movie Girl is shouting at me to run for my life. I bounce on the balls of my feet but looking around the circle I'm surrounded by leather, inked skin and dark, dead eyes.

"Naughts aren't allowed," someone murmurs behind me.

"You shouldn't be here."

"I'm sorry. Listen—" I don't know who to face and feel like I'm being corralled away from the adults I was aiming for. Suddenly, sleeping in my car doesn't seem like the worst idea.

I make eye contact with a girl who has to be close in age. She's probably a senior too. "Please," I say, extending my hand.

She pulls out of reach and sneers. Her teeth look menacing, but I tell myself it's just my eyes adjusting to the dark. There's a thick feeling in the back of my throat that I can't swallow.

My fists curl at my sides, but before I can do or say anything, the angry mob parts and the whispers and jeers aimed at me are now aimed at the tallest boy I've ever seen. He's wearing a scarlet waistcoat—complete with a silver chain that disappears into his pocket—over a black, button up shirt, and he's actually smiling. Not a creepy I'm-going-to-cut-you-up grin but a true, friendly smile.

And it's for me.

I know because I look over my shoulder and the kids are speaking in hushed whispers amongst themselves.

"Good Evening. May I help you, Miss?"

Now that he's stopped in front of me, I'm aware of our ridiculous height difference. I admit I'm on the short side, but I barely come up to his chest. He has to be over a foot taller than me at least. His straight, ink-black hair is so long at the front that when he looks down at me it falls over his eyes. He flicks it to the left—in a gesture I get the sense he does a million times a day—and smiles again.

"Do you need assistance?"

"Um, my car." I point over my shoulder.

He looks at the crowd. The smile has vanished. "Go. I've got this," he commands.

"Trust *him* to show," a voice behind me sneers. My skin prickles once more. I can almost taste their disgust. "Just like his sister. You should be ashamed."

"Rocks, don't waste tonight of all nights on a naught," a guy to his right says, dressed from head to toe in leather.

"I said GO!"

I jump at his command, and his eyes look gentle and apologetic when he smiles at me again. It's a cute, almost shy, smile that guys who don't know many girls wear. The thing is he is cute—super cute—in a Goth way. I'm sure in the light of day he's rather good-looking.

A guy who's barely taller than me comes up and grabs his arm, pulling him closer. "You don't have the time." Their eyes meet for a moment and hold, but the animosity from the earlier exchanges is gone.

"Decker, I'll be fine," he states, shaking him off.

The crowd slinks back into the shadows, and he steps in to offer me his elbow. At first, I don't understand until he takes my hand and places it in the crook of his arm. It's a gesture my grandfather would have done back in his day. The boy's fingers are warm and rest over the top of mine.

"May I escort you to your vehicle?"

My brain is short-circuiting, and my tongue has forgotten how to form words. He chuckles quietly and leads the way back into the looming forest, but this time I don't trip once.

"Everyone calls me Rocks," he says in my ear.

I want to look up at him, but I focus on the trees he's guiding me around. The engulfing darkness has awoken my sense of hearing, and it makes his voice sound so alluring. I hope my car is this way.

"Contessa Phillips. But everyone calls me Connie."

"It's a pleasure to meet you, Miss Connie Phillips." His tone suggests he's smiling.

I'm sure it's just adrenaline that's making my heart beat out a drum rhythm I can feel in my toes. My muscles gradually relax with every step away from the creepy sideshow and leering tattooed faces. I'm sure it doesn't have anything to do with the guy I'm clinging to in the dark.

Walking at his side, I'm suddenly aware of my appearance. He seems to be so comfortable in his own skin as he guides me through the dark woods with ease. I'm pretty according to my dad, but now I know he's a liar.

Those girls in the forest had a dark, mysterious, gypsy kind of presence. Under other circumstances, I know I would have been mesmerized by their haunting looks. I'm not sure a guy like Rocks would think of me as pretty when velvet corsets and leather surround him. My growth spurt missed my legs and unfortunately hit my chest instead. My boobs are too big. They make the boys stare and the girls glare. It's not my fault, and I certainly didn't wish for them. Gym is just plain humiliating because I need NASA to design my sports bra to keep those suckers comfortably bound and holstered.

When we reach the side of the road, Rocks places both hands around my waist and lifts me with ease back onto the asphalt. My spine tingles and my ears burn. Thank God, it's too dark for him to notice.

"It's muddy. I didn't want you to ruin your—"

"Yeah, too late. But, thanks." My ankle-length mud boots are sure to impress him. "How did you even see that? I can barely see my own feet."

"So what's the problem?" he says, walking to my car.

The steam eruption has ceased, and I'm not sure why, but I'm suddenly embarrassed. I can't imagine the guy standing before me ever getting flustered. He's the personification of cool, and I'm the damsel in distress. My stomach churns. I hate being helpless. Standing on a deserted road with no clue as to what's wrong with my car or where I am makes me feel as helpless as a girl can get. I focus and explain what the car was doing when I left.

Lifting the hood, he looks around, poking a few things. His long arm reaches my phone with ease, and he smiles handing it over. I study his lean frame. His body is covered in muscle, but with not an ounce of fat. I can't stop the smile that forms. Walking next to him arm in arm made me feel like a lady from one of the plantation houses around here. His waistcoat takes me back to another time and era. But I shouldn't be daydreaming about older guys. He could easily pass for twenty-one or two.

My smile fades when I remember the hate filled sneers from the other carnival goers. Just because he's being nice doesn't mean I should trust him.

"Give it a go." He peeks out from the under the hood.

The motor turns over, but doesn't spark.

He frowns. "I think it's still too hot. I recommend we wait before adding some water. Your radiator appears to have overheated. What are you doing out here?"

Leaning against my car door, I look anywhere but at Rocks. The darkness helps me hide my secret. Like he's going to know from looking at me that my parents are traitors and that I'm a liar—like them.

"I'm sorry. I shouldn't pry," he says. He steps backward, but I don't want him to leave.

"No, I'm sorry. It's just, nobody knows."

My brain races through the possibility of finally sharing the biggest secret I've ever had to hide from my parents, my friends—everyone I know. I'm going to burst if I don't tell someone soon. My eyes scan him from head to toe. He's the perfect stranger that I'll never see again with no ties to my parents or friends.

My parents.

Not really my parents, and the betrayal of discovering that secret has had me in knots all week. How do you ruin the last week of your summer vacation and your eighteenth birthday in one easy step? Open a letter with no return address that tells you your whole world is not what you thought, and the people you called your parents are big, fat liars.

The letter revealed that I'm adopted and crushed my belief in who I am and what it means to be part of a family. I had no idea—not even the faintest clue. The letter was signed 'your birth mother' in neat cursive script. It warned me against searching for my parents' identities because I'm apparently better off without them. What. Ever. Since I'm officially an adult now, I have the right to know.

Before my brain can make a calculated decision, my mouth has spewed all of this and more at this stranger in the darkness. It feels amazing. The weight on my shoulders has lifted. I can breathe again. The only problem is that the floodgate is now open and it's hard to hold anything back. My eyes twitch. I blink rapidly.

They lied.
They have lied to me my entire life.
And I don't know who I really am.

"I just don't know what to believe anymore. But it kind of all makes sense. My blonde hair and brown eyes don't match their brown and blue," I say, indicating my features. "In fact, I've always felt like I must have been some genetic throwback in every family portrait. I'm all round. They're all long."

That's when the traitorous tears fall—just two. I never trusted my own instincts, and now I don't know who I am or where I come from.

"Hey, now." Rocks moves swiftly forward and lifts me up onto the trunk of my car. We are closer in height now. "Shhh, it's okay."

He rubs my bare arms, and even though I feel like the biggest loser for crying, he doesn't seem to mind. Most guys my age would head for the hills at the first sign of tears. Rocks pulls a linen handkerchief from inside his waistcoat with a smile. His hair flops over his eyes again, distracting me. Does he hide behind it? I wonder.

"You're the only one I've told," I confess quietly. I've never known a guy to carry a handkerchief before. I smile as I wipe my cheeks. Talking to him is easy. The guys at school must be another breed. I usually choke when I interact with them, but Rocks is so calm it's contagious.

He takes my hand in both of his and just holds it. I know in my gut I can tell him anything. He doesn't seem the type to judge, which is more than I can say for my school friends. What will they think? Maybe they already know I don't belong to Chad and Kelly! Maybe I'm the only delusional one who hasn't noticed.

"Do you think you should tell your parents you know?"

"What? *They* kept my identity a secret. *They* lied. How do you expect me to trust them?"

I'm hurt. He might not be on my side after all. Maybe he is judging me. Maybe I shouldn't be sitting alone with this stranger in the woods. I try to pull my hand away, but he holds on tight. He studies my face until I look away.

"I understand." He pauses, and I look up at him once more. "You can't trust them because you don't know what their motives are. They don't want you to be the real you," he states. I get the impression he's not talking about me anymore, but it's exactly how I feel.

"That doesn't explain how you ended up here," he continues. "This is wild country. Nobody for miles around."

"Yeah, I'm pretty sure the GPS thinks I'm in Kentucky." I shrug. It's not like I can talk to my dad about it. "I was looking for my mom. My real mom."

This evening is hands-down the stupidest thing I have ever done. The adoption news sent me into a whirling downward spiral of emotions and confusion. The words in the letter hid something. Something dark and that makes me uneasy about who the heck I am. My birth mother said I was a gift that she hated to part with, but did anyway, for a better life. *For me or for her?*

Why warn me to stay away and not look for them? *Yeah, right.* And since my adoptive parents think it's fine to lie to me, I'm not going to worry about lying to them until I get some answers.

"Hidden in my parent's safe was my birth certificate, and I'm not gonna lie that it didn't break my heart to see the name Josie Hendersen typed under mother. This was her address when I was born." I hand over the scrunched piece of paper.

Rocks studies it, and I'm amazed he can read in the dark.

"You know you aren't even close." He smiles again, making my heart stutter. He flicks his hair back and I can't look away as his eyes meet mine. We just stare at each other for a moment.

"Really?" I finally say.

"Really." He's quiet for a bit and rubs a hand up the back of his neck. His hair is short at the back and kind of at odds with the front but it works on him. "I coul—"

"Do you—" We both speak.

"Sorry," I say. "You go."

"Um, if you want. I mean … I don't know, but, I could go check this out for you."

I have no idea how to process his offer. It's too kind, but I don't know this guy. He's supposed to be the stranger that keeps my secret and doesn't know me. Horror Movie Girl floats into my head. Would I be screaming at her to get the heck away from him if I were watching from the safety of my living room? If the boy with the tattooed fangs had offered to walk me to my car, would I be this open with him too?

Rocks immediately backtracks, and I worry my face has betrayed me again. "I mean, just, you know, to see if anyone lives there. I wouldn't knock or anything, but I don't have to." His hair shield slips back into place.

Help is what I need, and it might loosen the anvil that's lodged in my stomach, but that's not what grabs my immediate attention. Something felt off about that carnival and feeling so relaxed now has made me forget that fact. My brain can't quite pinpoint what's not adding up.

"Hey, where are all the cars?" I look up and down the pitch-black road. Not one vehicle has driven past or has even been heard around here, and there are hundreds of people just behind those trees. "How did you all get here?"

Shock crosses his face for a fleeting moment. "Um, another mode of transportation," he says from behind his hair.

"Such as?"

"I got a lift." He looks at me now, flicking his hair back, but his eyes have a hard look to them.

I squint at him. I sense I'm missing something, but considering I've missed what has stared me in the face my whole life in my own family, my radar isn't the most reliable.

"Why were those guys so aggressive back there? I didn't mean to crash your party." I watch him closely. There are more secrets here than just mine, and I've shared way more than I should have already. The darkness I had forgotten is creeping back around me.

Rocks looks over his shoulder. He looks up into the stars. I count the seconds. He's buying time. My hackles rise, but finally he speaks.

"It's not you. Ash hates everybody." He still won't meet my eyes. "It's complicated."

I snort and wait.

"You're not the only one who feels like they don't belong—with their family." He looks at me and I almost wish he hadn't.

Pain.

Hurt.

I don't understand what else I see, but I have no doubt he's feeling as lost as me. I want to offer him the comfort that he has shown me, but I don't know how.

"Parents?"

"Yeah, them. Siblings, friends, it's … " He kicks my back tire and meets my eyes for a second before his hair falls over them, shielding the pain I just glimpsed. "You ever feel like destiny is dragging you one way, but it's all wrong. You want to dig your heels in and escape, but you don't know how? You don't even know where to begin."

I'm not sure I understand, but then maybe I do. I didn't know where to begin a week ago. Until recently, my whole life seemed to fit, but now I find out it doesn't. Maybe that hole in my chest is what he's describing.

"Yeah. It sucks and you feel helpless like someone else is pulling your strings. It makes me want to scream."

"I've got nobody to talk to about it."

"Me too," I say, suddenly understanding why I feel so calm with my midnight stranger.

He nods and takes a step closer to me—almost between my legs. He looks down. I cringe hoping he's not staring at my disgusting muddy feet. His long fingers run up the seams of my pants on either side of my knees. He looks as lost and as sad as I've felt all week. The urge to hug him surges through my system.

So I do.

I've always ignored my gut—my sixth sense—and look at where it has gotten me. After opening that letter, I vowed to trust my intuition more. My gut told me to hug this boy and holding him isn't weird or freaky. It's calming and lets me breathe again. I pull him in closer and wrap my arms around his neck. His head falls to my shoulder, and he sighs. Maybe he can breathe again too. His hands stay at my legs, tracing patterns on my thighs, but he relaxes into me. The night surrounds us— and our secrets.

We stay holding each other for a while and it's nice. He's warm. It's so easy being with Rocks even though I barely know him. He smells of the forest or the moon. It's weird to think he could smell like the moon, but his scent is clean and fresh. I bite the inside of my cheek and pray he can't read my mind. The last teenage boy I was this close to didn't smell this good.

Rocks suddenly jerks back. He's out of my reach. His eyes are giant and dark, full of fear and something I can't describe. He grabs the fob watch from his waistcoat pocket and the silver lid clicks open. The noise seems loud against the night.

"What's wrong?"

"Shit."

"What?" My blood pressure is suddenly at 'run, girl, run' level again. Regardless of the connection I feel, I don't know this boy at all.

Anguish is the only word that I can use to describe the look contorting his features. I want to tell him he's scaring me, but I think he knows.

He grabs the back of his neck with both hands and looks up at the sky before squeezing his eyes shut. His muscles are taut in his arms as though he's trying to hold on to something invisible I cannot comprehend. What the hell?

He twists at the waist left and right, repeatedly. He's breathing loudly in through his nose and out through his mouth. He folds his bent arms around his head, but the tension is still visible. Then he doubles over and takes a loud deep breath. When he stands, he flicks his hair back and looks deep into my eyes. I can't breathe.

"I'm sorry," he whispers, and then he's gone.

2
Bats

ROCKS HAS VANISHED.

He was standing in front of me a second ago; now he's gone. Simply vanished into thin air before my eyes.

I look around. No hot, Goth guy to the left, or right. Jumping off the car, I peek around the bumper, expecting to see him crouching in the darkness. But he has simply vanished—without a trace. This isn't possible.

Am I losing my mind?

I'm suddenly aware again of the isolation of this dark stretch of forest road. My parents think I'm at Tiffany's house painting our nails, and I just revealed a hell of a lot of personal information to a complete and utter stranger, regardless of whatever my gut was telling me. I can almost feel Horror Movie Girl's disapproving glare.

My chest tightens indicating a need for my inhaler, but my lungs aren't wheezing. Where did he go? How could I be talking to a six-foot-whatever giant boy and have him disappear INTO THIN AIR?

"Rocks? Rocks, please."

An owl hoots overhead.

The cool air chills my skin. All I can hear in my ears is the hammering of my heart. I close my eyes and focus on my breathing. Something isn't right. I need to take control, fill the water tank, start my car and get the hell out of here. Now that I'm still and a smidgen calmer, I swear someone is watching me. Spinning around, I'm convinced I'll come face to face with Rocks. Mere inches from my face, movement catches me off guard and I scream.

It's an Academy Award winning performance.

In fact, I didn't know that my body was capable of making such a shrill, earsplitting noise. Horror Movie Girl would be proud. But the animal lover in me is devastated.

Instead of coming face to face with Rocks, a flying bat was about to collide with me, and in my panic I screamed. What I didn't expect and what never happens to poor, doomed Horror Movie Girl is that, about half way through my lungs and vocal cords alert the world to my predicament, the bat drops to the ground like a lead weight. It's lying on it's back, wings spread wide at my feet, completely still.

Could my night get any worse? I wonder.

Where the *hell* is Rocks?

My unconscious night visitor is too much for my brain to process. I need to get my car started and then I'll work out what to do with it. Opening the door, I root around, collecting the half drunk water bottles that have been rolling around the backseat. For once, my laziness is paying off.

Stepping over the bat, I fill the radiator bit by bit and slam the hood. Every noise I make echoes through the dark forest. The surrounding darkness that was giving me the creeps almost feels like it's inching back away. Having a furry friend—even an unconscious one—is lowering my blood pressure back to a healthy level. I'll be fine. I was just letting my crazy imagination get the better of me. Although, having a giant boy vanish didn't exactly help. I push the thoughts of the strange boy I was hugging aside, but there's something I'm missing, I know it.

The bat is my next dilemma. I'm convinced that it's not dead and that my scream knocked it unconscious. I don't know how or even if that's possible, but my gut says so. I need to listen to my intuition. Years ago, I noticed that I don't resemble my parents, but I brushed aside the little voice asking why. My gut is telling me to rescue the bat, but should I start trusting it now?

The bat hasn't moved. Its wingspan is enormous, and I wonder, peering at its still body, what sort it could be. But the darkness doesn't help me find any clues. If I leave it, some fox or coyote will discover this juicy meal before dawn. If my chinchilla, Feathers, was lying on the road unconscious, I'd call animal rescue if someone noticed and didn't help her. I can't leave the bat defenseless. My Animal Planet heroes would be ashamed if I drove off. It's not like it actually tried to attack me. And if I'm being really honest, it's my fault the poor creature is flat on its back.

My purple cardigan becomes a makeshift towel that I wrap around its body. I hope I haven't crushed its wings when I tie the sleeves together loosely. The last thing I need on the strangest night of my life is for it to awaken and start flapping around trapped in my car on the highway.

Taking a deep breath, I buckle up and turn the key.

THIRTY MINUTES later, the reset GPS has finally realized I'm in Georgia, and I'm back on a highway that actually has other vehicles on it. I'm headed home, but I don't feel the triumph and exaltation I'd imagined I would be feeling driving home from finding my real Mom's house.

Deflated.

Lost.

Confused—even more so now, if that's actually possible. Maybe I should just come clean to my folks at home.

No. I need answers.

To distract myself, my mind goes over the crazy events I've just witnessed: a medieval/Emo carnival in the middle of nowhere, a boy that I told my biggest secret to before vanishing faster than David Copperfield, and my snoozing bat passenger.

Movement above catches my eye. Dark shapes are winging it across the sky.

Bats.

There are hundreds of bats flying overhead and my guess is that they're buddies of the guy on my front seat. They're gliding over the highway, and I wonder where they're headed. The bright red glow of taillights illuminates the darkness and catches my attention. My brakes engage. The car stops with just enough space to avoid hitting the pickup truck I'm following. The other vehicles have noticed the swarm of creatures flying overhead and are rubbernecking too. A faint screech of tires comes from behind. After a few seconds, the bats all pass and the traffic returns to normal. This fella had better be able to find his friends when he wakes up.

I don't know a single thing about bats—except they come out at night and hang upside down in caves—or wherever they live. Are there colonies near my home? Animal rescue will know—but I can't give them the exact location I found him or *they'll* know I wasn't at Tiff's. I didn't think this plan through. What the hell am I going to tell my parents? Not my parents.

Those people who raised me.

Lying is harder than I expected.

Turning off the engine, I sit and stare up at my family home. Family. I just wish I knew who mine really were. My crazy trip and break down took way longer than I anticipated, but I've made it just before curfew. I want to crawl into bed after a long, hot shower, but I have a bat to take care of.

"Hi, um, there," I call toward the family room before climbing the stairs.

The words 'Mom' and 'Dad' have caught in my throat all week. I hear the late news on and picture my dad in his leather chair with the remote in hand and the newspaper spread across his knees. My heart breaks a little. I want to run in and tell him about my latest rescue, but I have to keep my distance, otherwise I'll blurt out the truth for sure.

Since I can't come clean about the bat, I'm forced to take it up to my room. The smart move would've been to set it on our back porch—safe from predators until it wakes up. I wonder briefly if all lies lead to limited options.

In my room, I close the door and gently deposit my cardigan on the bed. Throwing my handbag on the scruffy wingback chair, I round the bed to turn on the lamp that's bent across my desk. It's in the far corner of my room, and I push the head down and toward the wall. Maybe bright lights will hurt the bat's night vision?

Untying the cardigan, I open it and wait. The girl-scout-wannabe in me pushes up the large window opposite my bed that faces onto the street and removes the fly screen. There's a small section of red tiled roof that runs out from the windowsill to cover the porch—plenty of room for a bat with that wingspan to escape into the night. My white lace curtains are a potential snag. I tie them out of the way. Operation Bat Wake Up—all set.

Without bothering to remove my old nail polish, I start Operation Cover Up. My black and white panda nails need to go. I grab my go-to shade of Berry Cherry red and sit at my desk. As each chipped panda face disappears under the thick red liquid, I feel my heart settle and my pulse slow. Nail art is another happy place for me. The smell of fresh polish is my version of sitting on a porch swing with a chamomile tea.

A quick trip to the bathroom to remove my mud boots, and I'm back at my desk monitoring the bat. Feathers is waking up for the night and is squeaking at me from her cage in the corner.

"I'll let you out later. Shhh."

I won't risk an interspecies freak out, as I'm sure the bat's going to be disorientated enough. Resting my feet on the wingback, I inspect my toes. Operation Cover Up must include a pedicure as well. I just might have a real knack for this lying game I think, as I rummage through the endless number of polish bottles in my carry-on suitcase.

THUD!

Rocks' enormous black army boots hit my bedroom floor, and he is standing on the other side of my bed near my built-in wardrobe. He blinks several times. Flicking his hair out of his eyes, he's frowning, but his eyes aren't quite focusing on anything in particular. He looks around slowly and spies the window. His dark, almost black eyes find mine. I can't move my arms, my legs, or my body in any way. I'm a frozen statue. A deer caught in headlights is how I feel right now—they see the twin lights speeding toward them, but they inexplicably can't move a muscle. There is a boy in my room that wasn't there a minute ago.

Not.

Possible.

"I'm so sorry," he whispers.

SWOOSH!

I'm looking at a large bat.

In the spot right where he was standing is a flapping black bat. My room being on the small side, forces it to flap a little closer to me as it tries to keep airborne in the confined space.

My mind pictures the tattooed fangs on that sneering boy's face, the bats flying overhead toward the music, the red streamers swaying in the breeze, the Gothic old world feel of the carnival, the lack of fried food…

Rocks is a VAMPIRE!

I scream.

I scream and scream and scream and scream. It's the only thing my brain seems to know how to do anymore. And just like earlier this evening, the bat that's flapping in midair, drops like a bomb onto my bed unconscious once more.

I have brought a vampire into *those people who raised me's* home and even *they* do not deserve to be feasted upon. I thought only things like this happened in movies.

Maybe I could chuck him out the window? Does bringing an unconscious vampire into your house count as an invitation? Heavy footfalls thunder up the stairs.

Dad!

No!

I grab my crocheted blanket from the chair and throw it over the unconscious bat—Rocks—bat! My father bursts into the room with a baseball bat over his shoulder. My mother is hot on his heels. She's by my side and giving me the once over. I know she's looking for blood—ugh, don't think about blood—because my scream probably measured on her injury scale as having clipped an artery. I swallow as her eyes land on my face, and she gives me a murderous glare.

"What's going on?" she spits out. "You scared the life out of me."

I know she hasn't missed the intensity of my snarky attitude this past week. Dad, meanwhile, has made a full sweep of my room including looking in my wardrobe and under my desk.

"Um, spiders—"

"Spiders?" My mom mimics me. She's watching me like a hawk.

Act normal. I try not to focus on the heat that wants out of my body. But what on earth is normal about what I just witnessed?

"And mice." Maybe I'm crap at this lying game after all.

Her BS radar clicks on. I wonder if I told her that I was protecting them from a bloodsucking monster that I found in the middle of the forest if her radar would turn off, or permanently go on the fritz with a crazy notion like that.

"Where?" My father asks. I hear the utter disbelief that such vermin could have breached his outer defenses and exist in his pristine, pest-free castle.

"Under the bed," I say, jumping onto it with my feet spread wide on either side of the crocheted heap concealing the creature that was the real cause for my vocal siren.

Mom narrows her eyes at me. "Well, you, the spiders and the mice keep it down. If you wake your baby sister," she pierces the air with a pointed finger, "you will be rocking her back to sleep for the next two hours. Got it?" She gives my dad the evil eye on her way into the hall.

"What did I do?" he mutters. "If it was a mouse, tell me you're cleaning out Feathers' cage regularly?"

If?

My eyes narrow. He doesn't believe me. I know I'm lying, but I've never been a liar before so why wouldn't he believe me? Maybe liars have a secret code and can recognize each other on sight. Awesome.

All I have to do is work out what to do with the shape-shifting vampire on my mattress.

It's been forty-seven minutes. I'm sitting cross-legged in the hallway outside my room. I need an emergency exit if he doesn't leave. The drive home and nail painting, I've guessed took about an hour and twenty minutes. In the time since *those people* came to check on me, I've done my best to vampire proof myself.

I'm wearing all the silver jewelry ever given to my mom or me. I have to keep still because the bracelets and bangles jingle loudly in the silence of our house each time I rearrange the Children's Bible and the kindling I found in the fireplace. The kindling looks as though the only damage it's capable of inflicting is splinters, but it's the closest thing to a stake I've got. My parents—God, that's hard to say—I mean, *those two* are in bed, and I'd prefer them to stay there.

The air is thick with the smell of garlic. I've used the entire jar of garlic powder to make a protection ring. I got the idea from one of my favorite TV shows as it's saved some witches once—but not from vampires and it wasn't garlic—but who cares. It can't hurt. Sitting inside the garlic powder power ring, I focus on my bed.

I wrap my fingers tighter around the cool metal handle of the meat cleaver resting in my lap. Just for added protection, I pinch some garlic powder from the thickest part of the circle and sprinkle it all over myself. If none of this works, there's a chance he might not attack me because of how utterly ridiculous I look—and smell.

This is not how I imagined the last weekend of my summer would go. I didn't really have any idea what would happen if I had found my real mother earlier, but I never expected to be bracing for a supernatural attack. The idealist in me imagined her inviting me back for afternoon tea while we flicked through old family photos of my real relatives. Then I remember her warning.

Stay away!

My mind moves to the carnival and the aggression I faced encircled by those freaks. Are they *all* vampires? Were they pushing me into the darkness to feast upon me? I think of Rocks appearing dazed in my room and the bat appearing a second later, and play this over and over again. It's just not possible.

But, I saw it.

Twice.

Holy crabapples!

The worst thought yet about my real parents suddenly occurs to me.

They're complete and utter nut cases!

I'm insane—like them. I'm having hallucinations of mythical monsters. Maybe I'm not supposed to look for them because they're locked in a creepy asylum for the deranged and delusional? Oh my God—

Breathe.

I saw him in my room. Rocks was definitely in my room. My lungs start to wheeze. That's impossible. Is hallucination a hereditary brain disease? Could my real parents be unstable maniacs who were forced to give me up? No wonder *those two* never mentioned it.

I'm staring at nothing, trying to calm my breathing, when two heavy boots hit the floor in my line of vision with a thud.

The darkness of his clothing seems at odds with the paleness of my room. Before I can raise the cleaver or brandish the Bible at him, his tight denim clad legs take two large steps toward my window. Without even looking back at me, he leaps out headfirst.

I brace myself for the crash of his body hitting the tiled roof, but there's nothing. Not a sound.

It's three a.m. by the time I finally get into bed, but my lamp stays on. I spent a ridiculous amount of time scraping up garlic powder with pieces of paper to reinforce my windowsill, and the front door handle is securely wrapped in silver. Google has not been very helpful. In fact, I'm not sure I'm ever going to sleep again. Almost two million results come up when I typed in 'protection against vampires.' Maybe it's a very realistic hallucination that includes a conversation and a hug, but maybe it's not. I can't take the risk.

My problem is that I know some of these Internet crackpots have never encountered a real bloodsucker. Now that I have unfortunately discovered their existence is very real—I think—I can't work out which of the websites to believe. So I've taken a little from each.

My mom is going to have a fit in the morning because I've sprinkled poppy seeds all over the porch and at each entrance to the house— inside and out. The fact that vampires love to count things and get distracted by seeds or grains and stop to count them seemed so utterly absurd that it just might be true. I can't trust Hollywood's version in case it's purely about box office sales. And my mind can't let go of the fact that the Count on *Sesame Street* is a vampire obsessed with counting.

There is even such a thing called an 'energy vampire.' Well, energy isn't what I'm worried about Rocks sucking! I cover my eyes with the heel of my palms. *Rocks*—the boy that I chose to share my secret with; the boy that I hugged after knowing for less than an hour; the boy who seemed to understand me until he turned into a freaking monster!

What I'm freaked out about the most is that I can smell him. I can smell him in my room and I can't sleep. That cool, clean, moon smell still lingers. I want to open the window, but that's not going to happen. Each inhalation soothes me until I remember what I saw.

"CONNIE," *SHE* SAYS, barging into my room. My new vampire tactic is to stay up all night and sleep all day. I won't fall to a surprise attack. Horror Movie Girl would be proud and never this prepared. "Is that *more* garlic? For Heaven's sake, what's gotten into you?"

I peak out from under my covers and watch as she screws up her nose, looking for the source of the offending smell.

"Garlic? What is going on, sweetheart?" The disappointment I hear in her tone stings. For the first time this week, I'm actually doing something nice for them. I'm protecting them. Regardless of our bloodlines, they protected me my whole life and I owe them, not to mention loving them dearly which is why I'm so twisted up to begin with.

"Nothing."

"Your attitude this past week." She sighs and looks at me, hoping I'll come clean, but I stay silent. It's Monday and she's working so if I keep tight-lipped, my plan will work. "Please clean this mess." She unlocks my window, dislodging the carefully balanced silver items and pushes the window up. "Vacuum this sill. The muffins cooling on the rack are plain orange. When you go to the store, I need more poppy seeds. I'm all out."

"Oh, I'll be buying more poppy seeds. Don't you worry." I should have kept my mouth shut.

She comes to the side of my bed. "Connie, sweetheart, if there's something going on, you know you can trust me?"

Trust!

Is she really going to talk to me about trust? How about trusting me with who I am? I bite my tongue because I'm going to find out who my real parents are alone. If I told them that I know I'm adopted, they'd probably just lie about my real parents anyway—particularly if they were committed psychopaths.

No.

I'm not crazy.

"Is that the time?"

Mom looks at her watch. "Oh, dang. Listen, Connie, we need to talk. Clean your room," —she's heading for the door— "stop at the market, pick up Mini before three. Don't forget your father and I have that fundraiser tonight so we'll see you around nine. Be safe." She doesn't close my door on the way out.

I have my own agenda, thank you. My plan is set, but first I need sleep.

Mini, formerly known as my eighteen-month-old baby sister Jasmine, thankfully has fallen asleep after only twenty-four minutes of rocking chair time. It's eight p.m. and I have just enough time to finish fully vampireproofing the whole house before the adults return. Vampireproofing a house takes time and effort I've discovered.

I had to visit three different grocers before I found enough fresh garlic to keep Italy going for a week. The wooden crosses were easier to come by, and the lovely lady I met at Christian Supplies threw in two sets of rosary beads for free. I tuck Mini into her crib and arrange her bear. I can't really blame her for not being my real baby sister.

That fateful letter explained so much that I just hadn't put together. Two years ago when they announced they were pregnant, my mom kept bursting into tears. I thought it was just crazy women's hormones, but now I know she spent that nine months waiting for something to go wrong. "This was a gift we never thought we'd receive. I just can't believe it's really happening," she used to say.

Why they adopted me in the first place is another question to add to my list. Dad was only twenty-five and Mom twenty-three. From what I know about adoption, that's awfully young. But I've currently got a little too much to deal with to even go there.

It's not that my parents—I can't believe how much it hurts to say those two familiar words. Anyhow, it's not that *Parents Version 2.0* have treated me any differently, but there was a slight shift. I realize now that I am no longer the *only* precious gift they've been blessed with.

To say they were strict when I was growing up doesn't even come close to describing my life. I didn't learn to ride a bicycle until I was twelve. That should be counted as abuse. Do you have any idea how embarrassing it is to not be able to ride a bike? "It's too dangerous," they would both chant. You name a childhood activity and it was too dangerous—until Mini entered our life. I guess I should thank the kid.

Tip-toeing back into her room, I slide the ten-inch cross under her bear. There's a silver bracelet securing her window lock and two long ropes of garlic, each containing over a dozen full cloves, hang from the top of the sill.

The roof outside her window is covered in confetti. Count them, you jerk! At least, the squirrels won't eat them during the night.

Knowing Mini is secure, I settle on my bed with my surprise find for the day. I stopped off at the Fulton County library on the off chance they would have some literature on killing creatures of the night and to my utter delight, they did. I turn to page one of *The Monster Hunter's Handbook: The Ultimate Guide to Saving Mankind from Vampires, Zombies, Hellhounds, and Other Mythical Beasts* and am immediately impressed by the fact that the author is a professor.

Page one hundred and sixteen shows my mortal enemy number one. I really need to write to the illustrator and describe Rocks to him. As much as Rocks scares the life out of me now, I can't help but think about how he made me feel two nights ago. I hugged a guy I don't even know. I told him everything. Vampire mental mind tricks maybe? I prefer that to hereditary insanity.

A swoosh and a thud and the object of my obsession is standing on my rug once more. Without hesitating, I scream. I grab the cross and hold it in the space between us.

"Stay back!"

He flicks his hair off his face and smiles. If I didn't know better, I'd say it was his cute, shy smile that he probably reserves for girls, but I now know this is his trust-me-I-am-about-to-drink-you smile.

"I'm armed and fully prepared to stake you," I say, almost falling out of bed in my rush to get under it and retrieve the stakes I got from Home Depot. "Back up, Drac!"

Rocks throws his head back and laughs. His eyes are scrunched shut from mirth, his whole upper body shakes, and it takes him a couple of seconds before he looks at me again. By this time, I've got my trusty Children's Bible, the cross, and two stakes at the ready. Taking it all in, he bites his lip, shaking his head. The smile he's fighting is even cuter than the previous one, but I'm not going to fall for that trap!

"Connie, what are you doing with all that?" I do not appreciate the humor in his voice.

My death is not a laughing matter. But it confirms I'm not insane. Hallucinations don't talk right?

It occurs to me the garlic is useless. He's just flown in my open window—damn you, Mom—past the confetti, garlic and silver. Fudge! I don't like the fact that I'm cornered. Rocks is near the door and I'm stuck near my desk and bookshelves. He takes a step closer to my bed and my heart rate spikes. I panic and start throwing everything I've got at him.

First, I aim the Bible. That just hits him and falls to the floor. No flames at all. I'm disappointed because that was my big gun. He picks it up and puts it on the bed. No evidence of burned fingers whatsoever. The flying cross zooms past his head as he ducks and laughs again. Stake one and two, at least hit the target, but he just flicked them aside with his arm. Let's face facts; I'm no Buffy. I can't risk getting within grabbing distance so I can ram those babies into his heart.

His grin widens and his eyes are twinkling with joy. He's enjoying this, the sick sucker.

"That all you got?" He crosses his arms over his chest. He's wearing another vest. This one is shiny, black silk over a dark grey, long-sleeved shirt, but I can't let him distract me. "Connie, I'm not going to hurt you."

"Said the spider to the fly."

I hurl my last cross, which he grabs midair and starts inspecting. "Double fudge! They told me they were blessed." Desperate, I open my desk drawer and then the next one. "It's here somewhere." I can feel my pulse pounding in my neck.

I need to calm down because I'm sure the pumping blood is only making him enjoy this game even more. Movement in my peripheral vision makes me begin throwing anything I get my hands on. My new textbooks, two photo frames, hairdryer, stress ball—it's all airborne and being dodged. Then I remember, it's on my shelves.

"God Bless you, Great Aunt May." I swivel and grab the tiny bottle from the back of my bookshelf covered with knickknacks. "HA!" I yell. "Prepare to burn, demon!"

The stopper is wedged good and tight on the Virgin bottle, obviously for international travel. Rocks, at least, isn't smiling now, and I'm sure I've got the upper hand. My fingers fumble as he leans closer to get a better look at what I'm clutching.

I hold the blue bottle between us by the feet, brandishing it like a miniature sword. "No closer."

"What is that?"

"Great Aunt May visited Lourdes before she died," I state and pull my best 'gotcha now, Vampire' face.

Rocks laughs so hard he needs to sit on my bed to stop from falling over. Hysterical doesn't even come close to describing his rib-holding guffaws. How dare he.

"Don't you care about whether you live or die?" I never realized how much arrogance comes with being immortal.

"Holy water?" He's laughing hard again. "That's a good one." He wipes his eyes like he's crying.

"Get off my bed."

"Make me." He's stopped laughing, but is still highly amused and stretches back on my quilt with his hands behind his head. He owns my bed.

"Oh, that's it, buddy. You're done for." I wrestle some more with the tiny stopper until it pops free and rolls under the bed. The look on Rocks' face tells me he knows I don't want to get any closer. I only have one splash of this sacred, life saving water.

Deep breath. Breathe.

I lunge forward and upend the tiny Mary shaped bottle. It takes several shakes before maybe a tablespoon of water dribbles over his chest.

"Owww, ohhh, argh," he moans. Trust *me* to meet the only vampire with a sense of humor. That smile is really pissing me off.

"Those bastards!" I shout, staring at the empty Mary bottle. Rocks looks at me confused. "They sold fake holy water to a senior citizen. How could they?"

Mr. Sprawled-All-Over-My-Bed rolls his eyes at me. "Are you done?"

I've exhausted all ammunition, but I'll be damned if I'm going to admit defeat. I'll be a goner for sure.

I stand tall—which is ridiculously short compared to him. Animal Planet *always* tells you to look big when faced with a deadly predator, so I put my hands on my hips to reinforce my stance. I'm trying to spy another weapon from my desk or floor, but he's watching my every move.

He sits up, and I back up against my bookshelves.

"You shared a secret with me the other night, and I shared mine with you, although I hadn't exactly planned on it. So now you know, I'm a vampire b—"

I scream again. I can't help it. Hearing the words from his mouth sends a shot of liquid nitrogen down my spine. I might actually be going to die for real this time.

He holds out both hands. "Shhh, Connie. You'll wake your baby sister."

"What? How do you know about my sister?" My heart can't possibly beat any faster.

"I've been watching you for two days." His honesty is freaking me out. "To make sure you hadn't told anyone."

I clutch at my head and then my stomach. My body has gone into full-blown overload, and I don't know whether I'm going to be sick, pass out, or spontaneously combust. "You leave her alone. She's just a baby." I stare at him. "How could you eat a baby?"

Rocks shoots off the bed. "You think I would hurt her?" He stares at me, and there is no sign of his earlier amusement. "What have I done to make you think I would be capable of *that*?"

He walks toward the window. His back is tense. I've pissed off the vampire.

Fantastic.

When he turns around and looks at me, I wish he hadn't.

Wounded. I can see it in his eyes. How is it possible for *me* to wound *him*? He shakes his head and his hair saves me from his dark stare.

Turning toward the window, he adds in flat tone, "The confetti was a nice touch. You clearly did your research."

WHOOSH!

He becomes a bat so fast that my eyes can't track the change. It's instantaneous. One second he's human, the next a flapping bat, and vanishes out my window.

I walk over to lock it and see that Parents V2.0 have pulled into the driveway.

3
Garlic

"CONNIE. TIFF. Wait up," Brandy calls out above the chaos in the hall. Since middle school, the three of us have been soul mates and inseparable. In junior year, Mary Lou Whitfield and her gorgeous flame-red hair turned our threesome into a foursome, and anyone would swear she has known us for just as long.

"Oh my God, did you see Paige?" Brandy asks, her Afro curls bouncing on her shoulders as she steps in line beside me. Just like I hate my boobs, Brandy hates her curls. If only teenage girls could swap and choose body parts until we were all happy. We're on our way to Mary Lou's locker to see if she's arrived. "According to Chrissy, Paige spent the summer in Cancun or The Bahamas or Puerto Rico or whatever, and let me say, orange is so not her color!" She grins.

"And that outfit," Tiff adds. "Didn't anyone tell her to hang her bikini up at the end of summer?"

My brain is not processing enough of these details to make sense. It's short-circuiting and making me yawn. The vampire plan is so not compatible with school. Thank God, the first week back is short, and I only have to survive two more days till the weekend.

"You okay, Con?" Brandy asks. The new lip-gloss she's sporting is the perfect shade against her skin.

"First day nerves, you know," I lie. Since when did my friends join the ranks of my parents?

"We're seniors, girl," Tiff says, her massive blue eyes sparkling. She's always reminded me of one of those anime girls with her perfect outfits, expressive face, and overabundance of confidence. "No room for nerves. We own these halls."

I spy Mary Lou's red hair through the crowds in the hallway. She's already stuck a giant red and black falcon on the outside of her locker. For such a dainty little wisp, she swears like a trucker, but only when absorbed in a football game. The last time we went together, my face was redder than her hair by half time.

"Oh, I'm so glad you found me. Have the guys suddenly gotten hotter this year? Taller? Broader? Just more?" she says, fanning herself. I bet she's imagining how well the school football team has filled out over the summer.

The first bell clangs, and Tiff and I head to English. We take our usual seats closer to the front of class. Most kids think the back is where to head to be further away from the teacher, but Tiff and I worked out long ago that spot is where the teacher assumes trouble is parked. If you sit closer, you're right under their nose. The perfect blind spot for gossiping and avoiding too many surprise questions.

"Hey, Connie, looking good." A student has just walked past my desk, headed for the back.

Tiff elbows me. Her anime eyes are showing a full circle of white around her stunning blue irises. It almost makes me laugh, but my curiosity wins.

Looking over my shoulder, Parker Reed salutes me with two fingers. Parker Reed just spoke to me. I know I can't be at home dreaming because my room still smells of garlic, but my nose is full of the stench of the musty carpet that covers our English classroom.

Parker Reed is on the wrestling team and has never once looked my way. Paige and her flying monkeys usually surround him, puffing up his wrestler's ego, so it's hard to get within talking range. I want to pinch myself, but I kind of like the tingle that finger salute released. Even I have to admit that the number of weird things happening is climbing dangerously high.

"Why didn't you say anything?" Tiff whispers. "Parker said hello!"

"I'm glad you were here to witness that. I thought I was hallucinating for a second there."

"I *knew* senior year was going to be our year." Tiff opens her notebook. "Do you think you could get him to introduce me to Tom?

Wrestler Tom, I mean. Not chess geek Tom." I look at Tiff. She's imagining our wedding; I can tell. Tiff is a planner, schemer, and fixer. She has a knack of making things happen.

"You are aware of the fact that I don't actually know Parker, right? He just spoke to me, and I'm confused as to why." I look at my outfit. I wonder if my ponytail is crooked or weird. "Is there anything on my face?"

Tiff rolls her eyes. "Like I wouldn't tell you? He likes you. Just deal."

"It's my boobs."

Tiff bangs her head on the desk. My chest hate drives her nuts. Tiff would kill for cleavage—any cleavage at all. The boob fairy obviously was tired and gave me Tiff's helping instead. We all joke that her flat chest is a sign that Mother Nature does screw up occasionally— otherwise she'd be perfect.

"Who cares? The point is he said hello, and he got your name right. If it was meant for 'the girls,' that's not the end of the world. Teenage boys aren't interested in brains."

I open my book and refuse to look at her.

"So where were you all weekend? I left three messages."

Sugarplums!

Secrets suck. "Oh, sorry. I was, uh, around and stuff. You know … on Mini duty. I didn't want you to feel compelled to join me or anything and ruin your last weekend of freedom." I swallow the acid in my throat.

I'm a fudged up liar. Maybe living with Parents V2.0 is exactly where I'm supposed to be.

Not telling Tiff, Brandy, and Mary Lou about the letter was nearly impossible. They'd all come over to help me celebrate hitting eighteen, and thankfully had buffered my dealings with my parents. That day wasn't my best where they were concerned. The day had started out perfectly—presents, hugs and kisses, and a massive slice of birthday cake for breakfast—and not just any birthday cake, but her triple-layered, death by chocolate. Mom and I celebrated with a trip to the nail salon where we got matching balloon themed nails. Then I got home, cleared the mailbox and lost my identity in half a page of type. Even I'm not proud of how I've treated them since, but I have to find the truth, and I have to do it on my own.

Tiff knows my Gmail password, how much money I have to my name, and the ugly details of both boys I've kissed. Secrets are deal-breakers, and all of a sudden I'm collecting them. The mystery letter is one thing, but the Rocks fiasco is a whole other level.

"Pfft, I love that kid." She looks at me. I face the board. Mrs. Yamaguchi—who is actually only a Yamaguchi after finding love in Japan—enters the room.

IN BED, WHILE I'm trying to stay awake, I think about Parker Reed. Everyone knows Parker. The way he dominates the wrestling ring has acquired him a legion of fans. He's not going to be Prom King, but he would romp in a vote in the top five without even trying. I imagine being levelheaded enough to have answered him in class.

'Hi, Connie, looking good.'
'Thanks, Parker, back at ya!'
I think I've had too much caffeine.
Take two. 'Hey, Handsome, how was your summer?'
Now I'm channeling Paige.
Take three. 'Hi Parker, do you need a pen or something?'

Guys to me are one of the mysteries of the modern world. I never know what to do or say and mostly end up a staring mute—like today. I just gape, freeze up and generally freak out inside my head. The brave voice commands I do one thing, while the super chicken says another, and the two voices end up arguing. By the time they have agreed on a response, the boy in question has usually walked off, thinking I fit the stereotype of my hair color. I wish my friends had brothers so at least I could practice not being an idiot.

But there is a boy I can talk to like a normal person. If only he was just a boy.

Sitting up, I re-arrange my pillows. Sleep is whispering my name, so I cannot afford to be horizontal. School is a good topic to occupy my brain. Tiffany has always been my go-to girl. She's honest.

'Con, that shirt's all wrong.'

'Don't ever get corn rows.'

'You have sauce on your chin.'

'I always knew you were adopted.'

I feel sick. I wonder how she'd cope with the truth. Has anyone else noticed I don't belong to *the people downstairs who have broken my heart?*

'Tiff, I'm adopted and have a vampire stalking me.'

'Oh, I love this game. Let's start with the vamps. The adoption one sounds like a tearjerker, and you know that's not my thing. Sexy or killing machine vamp?'

Everything in Tiff's world relates to a book.

'Pretty sure both.'

'Um, lone vamp or a coven?'

'Ah, loner with an alarmingly large coven waiting in the wings.'

'Can't say I've read that one. I give up. Sounds juicy though.'

'The Secret Life Of Your BFF.'

Fudge! That conversation is never gonna happen.

"I PREFER THE ones with poppy seeds in 'em," Tiff says, smearing vanilla cream cheese icing over her muffin. "God, your mom can cook."

I pour three lemonades and slide one over to Lou. The mention of poppy seeds makes my breath catch. *The woman formerly known as my perfect Mom* enters with a freshly changed Mini on her hip.

"What's with the garlic?" Mary Lou asks, looking at the back door that leads from our kitchen to a paved patio.

"I've been asking my daughter that for the last five days."

"You going all European on us?" Eyes are all on me.

"It's good for you. Kills cold and flu bugs." But apparently has zero effect on flying vampires.

"Ok-ay, Dr. Con," Tiff says. I'm not sure if it's just my guilty conscious or whether my friend is watching me closer than usual. She's commented on the amount I'm yawning, the bags under my eyes, and the fact that I jump every time someone comes up behind me. "Mrs. Phillips, can Connie come and work with me at the hotdog stand?"

I've been trying to convince my Parents V2.0 to let me get a part-time job since I was fifteen. The last two days at school, I've told Tiff to drop it. There's an opening at her work—which is weekends only—and she's decided the job is mine.

Kelly gives me the look. "Connie, we've discussed this, sweetheart." Her tone implies that they're doing this for my own good—keeping me safe and secure. Is that why they never told me? Them not knowing I know the truth sucks. I judge their every move and word now, searching for hidden meanings and clues. It's utterly exhausting. I miss the days when the words out of my mother's mouth made me smile instead of frown with suspicion.

"Mrs. Phillips, Connie needs to spread her wings," Tiff argues. She's never been afraid of authority. She's the only person I know who can get away with correcting teachers and still have them like her.

The last thing I need are wings. Sugarplums! He can't actually *give* me wings, if he bites me, can he? A rhythm starts to pound inside my head. I take a seat at the kitchen island and rest my cheek on the cool marble. There is no way I'm sleeping later.

"Hello, ladies," Chad greets, joining our party at the kitchen island. He places a kiss on Kelly's cheek and one on Mini's head. He pauses and eyes me, but apparently, he's all out of kisses after that. I'm just the stand-in kid.

"Mr. Phillips, nice tie." Tiffany starts her attack. For a split second, I almost feel sorry for him. I would wish him luck except I'm on Tiff's team—I want that job. "Let's talk about Connie coming for two trial shifts next Friday and Saturday night." She amps up her megawatt smile. "You know my parents are very safety conscious, and they never allow me to do anything remotely risky."

"Ah, well, yes, I do know your parents' values, Tiff." He looks at her and then at me. I'm still cooling my heated skin on the bench top, but I meet his eye. "Senior year is important. Connie—"

"Connie needs to learn some street smarts before she's shipped off to college and all alone in the big bad world. Trust me, I know her better than anyone. The hotdog stand is a perfectly safe environment for her to learn to deal with drunk idiots who lurk in every corner of college campuses these days. Seriously, she's got to learn to say no and mean it, Mr. Phillips."

Mary Lou swoops in for the kill. "Do you know the statistics on college attacks on female students these days? If you can't stand your ground, you're easy pickings. She does need the practice."

"Well, not all campuses have this sort of problem, right dear?" When Chad defers to Kelly, it's game over. *The woman who doesn't look like me* comes to my side. Mini is in her high chair, clapping her hands.

"Is this what you want?" She lays a tentative hand on my shoulder, and for a second I want to erase the past two weeks and go back to life in the Phillips' household the way it used to be. Being torn in two sucks.

But has she really forgotten my four thousand previous requests? "Yes, *Mom*." It's the first time that word has passed my lips in two weeks. I feel the knife blade slice open my chest and re-expose my heart. What I wouldn't give to really be her biological daughter. Why on earth don't they trust me? The anger rushes to the surface again, but I swallow it down.

Kelly shrugs at Chad.

"Oh, Mr. Phillips, you're doing the responsible thing. Friday night is eight to midnight. Saturday eight to one, and I'll make sure she gets home." Deal done and dusted. "I'll pick up a shirt and bring it to school next week."

FRIDAY AFTER SCHOOL, Mini and I are enjoying the sunshine in the front garden. She's running around on the grass playing her version of soccer with a handful of different sized balls. I watch from the porch swing, lazily painting my fingernails. The white base coat is dry and I'm hand painting pink, purple and yellow tulips on each nail. Parents V2.0 are bringing take out and will be home by Mini's dinnertime.

Mini manages to 'kick' the large pink ball under the trees that mark our fence line. A holly tree stands between two red cedars that are just taller than our house and have low hanging branches touching the lawn in places. Her sudden squeal of delight makes me look. She giggles and waddles to the next ball trying to send it under the trees. Her chubby leg misses the ball by a mile causing her to topple over. My nail art brush hovers in anticipation of a cry, but she pushes herself up into a seated position and claps her hands. Her squeals fill the air.

Our house faces west so the setting sun makes it difficult for me to see what's got her in such a good mood.

"Ball," she proclaims.

Next minute, the pink ball slowly rolls into her waiting arms from under the trees.

Oh, fudge no!

I'm on the grass and snatching her up in a millisecond. Mini protests at me for ending her game and struggles to get free.

"Down. Down." She might have missed kicking the ball, but she's making contact with my thighs now.

Rocks emerges from under the trees. I find it hard to believe how a boy so tall could fit under there. He unfolds like one of those Transformers to his full height.

"Get away from her!" I wrap my arms around Mini, cradling her head to my shoulder. My tone causes her to cling back for a moment.

The smile on his face vanishes. He huffs and looks toward the sun. "I wouldn't lay a finger on that kid."

Rocks is standing in full sunlight, looking into the orange glow. I notice that his black eyes are actually a blue as deep as the ocean. Only the reflected sun reveals their true color. After a moment, he squints and looks back at me.

"What are you doing here?"

Mini is trying to look at Rocks, but I don't want her to. I keep turning away each time she turns toward him. There is no way this kid is being corrupted on my watch.

"I want to explain now that you've calmed down. I hate seeing you scared of me." His hair falls over his eyes, which makes it hard for me to trust him when I can't see if he's lying or not. He can't seem to keep still.

"Ball. Down."

"Why should I listen to you?" Part of me wants to believe in fairy tales and discover this boy isn't an evil killer monster, but then I remember the fangs tattooed on his friend.

"You've got it all wrong. I want you to sleep at night. I'm not a vampire. That's why I'm here in broad daylight to fail another of your absurd tests."

My heart is beating so hard that I'm convinced Rocks can see it thumping against my ribs. I have to protect my sister. She can't get involved in my stupid mess, but my curiosity is piqued. Sleeping for eight hours straight again would be a dream come true. I turn and go up the three porch steps and leave Rocks on the lawn. He's in dark denim with a long sleeved, black Henley. Surprisingly, the vest's absence makes me sad.

"Connie, please."

My hand pauses over the door handle, and my eyes squeeze shut from the hurt in his voice. Each second I hesitate feels like a lifetime. I have no clue what to do and my gut feeling has left the building. Mini giggles, and I know she can see him over my shoulder. Her delighted squeal has me look as well. What the—

Rocks is juggling the three smallest balls. She's enthralled. She jigs up and down in my arms, cheering him on. The balls drop to the lawn the second Rocks notices me watching. He studies his boots and hooks both thumbs into his back pockets.

My brave side is telling me to give him a chance. "Wait there."

Once inside, I place Mini in her playpen. The Cartoon Network never fails to mesmerize her, so I flick it on and return to the porch. Before the door has swung shut, Mini is screaming at the top of her lungs. It's her I-want-to-play-with-the-big-kids-scream.

Crabapples.

"I won't hurt her. I swear to you." Rock is waiting on the other side of porch railing. He's closer, but I still have the height advantage—just.

I observe his body language to try and gauge his intent. "Don't mess with me. I'll kill for that kid."

"I know."

Once Mini is back on the porch, she heads straight to the wooden palings. Her chubby hands grip the beams as she play peek-a-boo with Rocks between the rails. He winks and clicks his tongue at her, which makes her jig up and down. The kid is smitten.

"Still got the garlic going on," he says, indicating to the cloves above the doorway. We both know it doesn't affect him, but every time Kelly takes it down, I put it back up. I know it's immature to taunt her this way, but I just can't get over the fact that they never told me the truth. God dammit. I want to talk to them. I really do, but I would never know if their answers were the truth. I can't focus on them right now.

"You have five minutes and counting." I have to be stern. I'm not going to be tricked with juggling and winking at babies. "I know what I saw and it's not normal."

He winces. "Not for you, but that doesn't make me a killer vampire either." He's ignoring Mini now. The softness on his features is gone.

"What are you?"

"A guy most of the time. And a vampire bat when I have to be." He flicks his hair back, and there is nothing jovial about the look he gives me.

My rocketing heart rate instinctively has me inching closer to Mini. "So you are a vampire then? And Hollywood just has all the wrong ways to keep you out of my house?"

"No, I'm not. Stop believing what you see on the television box. I'm not Dracula. Okay? I'm the Batman man."

"Oh, please." I stop myself from rolling my eyes because it drives Mom—Kelly—*her* nuts, but she isn't here so I let him have it. "You expect me to believe that?"

"Well, you seemed to believe I was a vampire pretty quickly. Why is it so hard to believe I'm not a monster?" His voice fades when he says monster, and he steps back from me.

I've got nothing. I focus on Mini. She's wedged her little arm through the palings and is reaching out to him. *Do little kids have better intuition than adults? Is she still in touch with her sixth sense or is she just naïve and innocent of the evil that lurks in the world?* Rocks raises his hand, one slender finger extended.

"Don't." It drops to his side, and the pain I just inflicted is visible across his features. How did I become the bad guy?

"Okay, let's say you are a bat and then a boy. What do you feed on?" I demand.

He swallows. "When I'm human, I eat regular food. I love it. There is so much to try." He cracks a tiny smile, almost to himself and his eyes are softer. "It's amazing. But I, I …"

"You what?"

"I don't know much about it. I haven't had that much until recently."

"Explain." I wince at my curt tone. I am not this girl, but I have to think of Mini.

"Where I live, um, with my colony, they feed as bats, so …"

"Sooooo? Rocks, you need to keep talking because in two minutes, I'm going inside and locking the door." I fold my arms over my chest. If I don't get the answer I want, I'm done.

"As a bat, I drink blood."

My stomach rolls as though I'm on a boat in bad weather. "Well, if you're coming around here to chomp on my sister and me, then you've got the wrong house." I half yell, aware of the neighbors. "We are *not* on the menu." I stand behind her, making a cage with my legs around her little body.

Rocks flinches at my words.

His wide eyes and open mouth tell me I've stunned him silent. Kneeling down on his haunches, he takes a moment before shaking his head. I don't understand why my words have struck a physical blow. When he starts to speak, I can barely hear him.

"Wow, to think I thought *you* were the one to trust. The one who would understand and give me a chance in your fancy world." He stands again, and I don't like the mask that has fallen into place. He slips out the biggest pair of sunglasses from his back pocket and slides them on. They cover half his face. "You were never a menu item. I'd like to think I have better taste in women."

Fudge me.

That missile hit its target, and now I want to jump the railing and slap him. There is no need to insult me when I'm just trying to understand and protect my family. "So why are you here then?"

"To help you find out who you are, but it doesn't matter."

"I don't need your help." Fudge you and your better taste in women.

"I can see that now." He spins around and walks a few steps toward the mailbox. Turning back, he continues, "That address. It's an abandoned house, but I guess you already know that. Decker was right. You naughts will only see what you want to see. I don't belong there, and you've made it pretty clear that I don't belong here, so I guess I'm on my own." His voice rises. "And I don't need the judgment in your eyes anymore than I need it from my own kind."

He marches off without another glance. My eyes water, and I struggle to swallow the bile in the back of my throat. Gripping the wooden railing, I resist the urge to scream like a wild animal because I don't want to scare Mini. I take her hand and encourage her over to the door. The sweet little imp is completely oblivious to the emotional storm raging under my skin. Reaching up, I grab the garlic ropes and pitch them across the yard.

4
Hotdogs

THE SAYING 'CAREFUL what you wish for' has never been more appropriate. I wanted to be left alone, and I have been. Rocks hasn't shown up since he stormed across our lawn. I swear I don't recognize myself anymore. I'm so full of anger these days, and I took part of that out on Rocks. It's not his fault my real mother wrote that letter. Why now? Why after all these years? If it was so important that I don't look for them, then why tempt me with contact? My fists ball at my sides as I try to imagine what she looks like. Maybe I'm channeling my anger at the wrong people. I wish for the millionth time that I resembled Kelly.

On the weekend, I slept day and night and removed all vampire wards from every nook and cranny that I'd crammed them into around the house. Parents V2.0 watched me but didn't say a word. Even though I have more than caught up on the sleep I missed, I still feel drained. The girls are starting to take my shopping refusals personally, and I can't afford for them to get curious. On the days that Mom V2.0 doesn't work, I usually hang with my friends at the mall after class. But I just haven't felt like going. There's an emptiness inside that I can't chase away. I stare at my chipped nails daily but can't muster the inspiration I need to cover them.

The other days of the week—which change depending on her roster—I have Mini duty, like today. Mini is strapped into her seat behind me and instead of heading home, we are zooming down the I-20 W. *It's an abandoned house, but I guess you already know that.* His words simultaneously haunt me and give me hope. I'm at war with myself. My goal is finding my parents. End of story! Bats and boys that can fly are not my focus, but my conscience won't let me forget the hurt in his voice when he said he didn't belong. I'm the monster. I know how that feels. I know what being alone all of a sudden means. Not gossiping daily with Kelly about her crazy work colleagues is killing me and refusing to paint her nails last week took me to an all time low I didn't think possible. But I want to know where I came from. I realize I know absolutely nothing about the guy I felt safe enough to share my secret with in the forest. Why doesn't he belong? Is he really alone too? All those other bats at the carnival …

Not wanting to end up in the middle of a forest again, I've printed out the directions to her house using Google maps. Sometimes the old fashioned way is best.

"Mini, my plan is find my birth mother. That's it," I say into the rearview mirror. She claps her hands together and smiles. "Maybe then I'll be able to say the words mom and dad again without choking."

Mini's eyes brighten. "Da-da. Mom-mom-mom." She's so lucky living in her little world of innocence. I used to share that space with her and miss it. "Dog," Mini says, pointing out the window.

"We're looking for four hundred and ninety-two. If the house is like Rocks said, then I know he's on my team after all." But if Rocks is telling the truth, then I'm back to square one on the hunt for my identity. I don't know what to wish for.

The houses I'm driving past don't look promising. In fact, the yards are getting more overgrown and uncared for as we go further long the road. Most of the houses have wide green areas surrounding them, no fences, and there's not even a sidewalk—the grass just meets the road. The area is pretty in a Southern way. According to my map, Josie Hendersen's house should be at the end of this dead end road. Pulling up outside number 492, it's obvious that the only residents are raccoons and squirrels.

"I am the world's biggest idiot, Mini." I look at her and her tiny brown pigtails in my mirror. "That boy has done nothing but help me and all I've done is throw things at him. What's happened to me? I need to apologize."

When I read that letter, it made me feel like a fool. Now I feel like a fool for completely different reasons. The black hole inside me is spreading. My identity search has hit a dead end, and the only person who cares enough to help me, I let walk away because I was convinced he was a liar and a monster rolled into one.

"Tree. Tree," says a little voice. Mini smiles when I turn around to her. At least there's one person in my world I haven't let down—yet.

The shirt I'm forced to wear is almost indecent. It's not that it's revealing but the bright red fabric with the cartoon picture of a hotdog stretched across my breasts looks all kinds of wrong. The wiener is wedged between two bulging sides of a pinkish bun and has very dubious-looking mustard spraying everywhere. Freud would have a field day. The words Bun Lovin' Barn are in puffy 70s writing, but the word 'Barn' is lost on the underside of my boobs, so all you can see is the Lovin' part—which makes the picture even worse. I can't let my father see me in this, or it's game over before I even clock in. I'll have to have a word with Tiff, but it probably looks quite tame on her chest.

The Bun Lovin' Barn is a food van that is permanently parked on Peachtree Road. It's the perfect location to attract drunks and hungry under 21s leaving the bars and dance club across the street. Tiff thinks it's the perfect job because it's easy, and she gets to flirt with hot college guys suffering from late night munchies.

"We," Tiff squeals, "are going to have soooo much fun!" I've just climbed into the back of the van. She's filling the giant sauce fountain that usually sits on the window counter with mustard, ketchup, barbecue and chili sauce.

"I still can't believe you got my dad to agree." Since school has been back, I've used the dreaded D and M words more than I cared to. What I would give to be able to talk to my friends about that fudged-up letter.

I point to my chest and ask her opinion. Her laughter tells me the shirt looks as bad as I suspected.

"Okay, the dogs go here, warm buns here, and we stock the warmer from the supply there." Tiff wastes no time. She lets me watch for the first few customers so that I know where everything is located by the time we get busy.

By eleven, I'm an old pro at slapping dogs into buns and loading them up to desired tastes. Tiff is right. The number of attractive guys that eat hot dogs after too many beers is outstanding. It's almost enough to distract me from my identity crisis and the guilt I feel over the boy with his own identity crisis, whom I pushed away.

"Connie, check this one out," Tiff says, pointing across the road to the narrow parking lot beside Wicked Beats. "Nice." She's been scoring the hotness level of the guys that come and go from the club. From her extensive experience, she insists that the dance club has the best eye candy. Guys that dance have much sexier bods than the ones that just sit around drinking in bars, she insisted earlier when I argued.

The parking lot has two dumpsters a little way in under a small streetlight, which belong to the row of shops that are closed at this hour. Hot sweaty bodies mill around the emergency exit by the cars, cooling down after the heat of the dance floor. This side door allows for easy access once they've gotten a stamp from the main entrance. In the glow of the streetlight, I notice a dark-haired woman wearing a sparkling dress. Movement in front of her reveals a guy dressed from head to toe in black, resting against the brick wall. Her hand is travelling up and down his chest. I squint. Impossible!

"Look at those tattoos. He's the real deal." Tiff is openly watching the couple across the street. Customers forgotten. "Oh. My. God."

I hand over the hotdog and change to the blond dude I'm serving and look again. Little Miss Glitterbug stands on tippy toes and pulls him down for a kiss. The guy—who looks alarmingly like Rocks, except the full sleeve tats that cover both arms mean it absolutely, positively cannot be Rocks—jerks back at first. Glitterbug knows what she wants and grabs his—oh, hell no—vest to pull him in for another go.

"Hot damn. You go for it girl!"

"Is he wearing a vest?" I blink my eyes. I can't be seeing this right. My body is reacting to the possibility that Rocks is in close range. My heart pounds hard knowing he's not a threat. A chance to make up for my bad behavior is all I'm after. He saved me that night in the forest, and all I've done is insult him.

"Yeah, leather too by the looks. Uh, I *love* guys in leather. Why don't high school boys wear leather? It's not fair." Tiff pouts. Tiff spends way too much time lost in her mother's adult fiction. I'm convinced she has a seriously screwed up idea of real relationships as a result.

Kneeling down under the counter, I grab the napkins and straws to restock the holders. I can't watch. That guy's body is so similar to Rocks' body. The idea of Rocks with another girl—stop! When did it become *another* girl? I was never *his* girl, but I was his human. Was. But I didn't want to be at the time. Oh, sugarplums.

"Get up here. You're missing all the good stuff. There's some serious grinding going on. What I wouldn't give for a bit of that action."

"Grinding? Grinding?" Even I can hear the touch of hysteria in my voice. Tiff's brow furrows. I'm on my knees clutching her leg with both hands.

"Settle, petal." Tiff looks back at the spectacle across the street. "Okay, so not really grinding. No grinding. Just kissing. Happy?" She pouts.

"I thought you were describing what was going on over there, and you're just describing what's playing out in your head!"

"So? If I described what is actually happening, it wouldn't be half as exciting. She's kissing him and he's kinda hesitant I guess. Hesitant ain't sexy."

"You need to stop reading those books." I let go of her leg and settle back down on the floor. She smiles and shrugs. That look in her eye indicates she's lost within the pages of one of them.

Tiff suddenly flicks her light brown hair over her shoulder. She straightens her shirt and puffs her chest up.

"Oh, God," I mutter. My fingers are shaking and I miss the container. The straws go rolling over the floor. I'm such a chicken. I want to see him but not with his new human. "Whoops. I'll just fix this mess." The unmistakable sound of stiletto heels clicking on the asphalt echoes in through our serving window.

"Two dogs with onions please," a chirpy female voices requests.

"Absolutely." Tiff is a smiling statue.

"Should I pay first?" the woman asks, trying to trigger some action. I imagine my stunned co-worker has confused her.

Tiff blinks. "Oh, no, you can pay Connie. I'll get the dogs." She knocks me with the side of her sneaker.

Fudge!

I take a deep breath, still out of sight. Tiff is away from the serving window and is gesturing wildly for me to look at the 'hottie' outside. It might not be Rocks. It might not be Rocks. It might not be Rocks. I take a deep breath. If it is Rocks, then I don't want to see the misery I witnessed in his eyes last time.

Popping up from my hiding spot, I spy the dark-haired woman in the shiny dress and Rocks. Rocks is standing in front of me. Fate has returned him to me. I need to raise my white flag and show him that I come in peace.

The fear I once felt in his presence has dissolved into curiosity at his supernatural abilities, and I have a chance to show him that I don't think he's weird. All I care about is making him see that he does belong in this world. And maybe we can find the answers together.

His hair is slightly damp and sticking to his forehead. It allows me to see his eyes. The touch of pink in his cheeks I assume is from dancing. The short-sleeved fitted t-shirt covered with a black leather vest outlines his chest. His bare arms look incredible. They're covered from the wrist up in intricate black and grey patterns and swirls. I find myself wanting to stare at them, but I can't resist his face.

The instant Rocks recognizes me his eyes light up for a second before he looks at his feet. But after a moment, he gives me his unsure little smile. My ears burn. I smile back, hoping it conveys how sorry I am. He's not angry. I could fly. This boy has every reason to be pissed at me, but he's standing there smiling.

Tiff is back at my side as I take the money. "So one for you." She hands the woman one hotdog. "And one for you." Tiff curls her index finger indicating for Rocks to come closer. The woman doesn't seem fazed by Tiff's interactions and squirts mustard on her hotdog before walking back toward the curb. He steps up slowly, his eyes staying fixed on mine. Tiff hands over the biggest hotdog I've ever seen. She must have gone digging through the mother lode for that giant.

I bite my lip to hold in a giggle as I watch Rocks' eyes widen in delight. "Wow," he says. "Thank you very much, Miss."

Tiff makes a revoltingly girlie sound, and I can only empathize with her. Rocks hasn't moved from the window. The feast he's holding like it's sacred with both hands mesmerizes him. He studies the hotdog closely, and I'm guessing it's his first one. When he licks his lips, I feel Tiff fidget.

I lean over the counter to get closer. "These sauces make it even better. This is ketchup—an all American favorite that's a sweet tomato flavor." I don't care if the people lining up behind him think I'm nuts; I'm going to help him discover a real American fast food, and I'm going to do it right. I describe the taste of the other three sauces and wish I had more to say when I'm done. It's not the apology that I wanted him to hear. "I like loads of ketchup with a bit of mustard."

Rocks' dark eyes never leave mine. "I appreciate the lesson. Thank you." He steps to the side so the next guy can place his order. I watch him douse his dog with precision. It's a work of red and yellow art by the time he's done. He follows the woman back over to the club. The last thing I hear is his delighted moan, and it leaves me grinning from ear to ear.

LATE SATURDAY MORNING, I float into the kitchen.

"Hon, did you hear that the police have arrested two key players in The Vipers gang. Doesn't say who they are yet. I doubt it will be their boss though." Dad is reading the headlines. Mom is placing the third layer of her death by chocolate cake into place. Before I started my mutiny, I often admired how easy they made marriage seem. "It says they've got a key witness to the murder of those two officers last year."

Mom V2.0 notices as I place a kiss on Mini's head. "Nee," Mini says, showing her gap-toothed grin.

"Hi, sweetheart. How was work?" I want to cringe. As awful as I've been to them, she seems like she genuinely wants to know. I look at her for a moment. This woman loves a child that isn't her own blood. Her generous heart makes me cringe, but I can't think about this because for the first time in weeks, I'm on a high.

"Awesome." I steal a massive finger load of frosting on my way to the fridge.

"You'll remember to lock that van door after you arrive, won't you?" Dad V2.0 has done recon. Impressive. Okay, so maybe he still is my hero. I smile at him, and for the first time in three weeks, I don't have to pretend. As parents go, or even as people who raised a kid they were given, I'm really lucky. That's what's making this deception so freaking hard.

"Tiff's gonna give me a ride home tonight. Parking sucks."

"Can't tell you how relieved I am that you decided not to walk at that hour. And it's probably a good idea that Tiff isn't alone when she heads to her car," he says. If it weren't so late I would walk home, as it's not that far. But if riding with Tiff makes him happy, I'm not going to rock the boat. I want this job.

I'M AT THE Bun Lovin' Barn before Tiff has had a chance to unlock.

"Someone's keen. You don't need to be here for another hour yet." I grab the top two trays of buns she's carrying up from her car and shrug.

"It was fun."

She grins. "I'm on to you, Connie Phillips. You just want to sit outside and enjoy the perv fest before you start."

I'm praying that Rocks comes back. He knows I work here, and if he's still in the market for a human buddy, then I want a shot at the title. Sitting on a crate at the back of the van, I scan the street for raven-haired, leather-wearing, lean giants.

Nothing.

Disappointment seeps through my system as I drag my feet up the steps to start a little early. Tiff is dog diving—there is no other way to describe it. With tongs in hand, she's fishing around the enormous pot, separating the wieners.

"What are you doing?"

She jumps. "Finding the prize dogs."

"For?"

"Hot guys. Didn't I tell you that yesterday?" She looks genuinely horrified. I shake my head. "This pot is for the guys you want to return. This pot is for everyone else."

"Aren't hotdogs the same size?"

"Surprisingly, no."

Tiff definitely gets points for effort. That girl doesn't do anything by accident.

An hour later, I'm zoning out while Tiff tells me about the hottest book she's ever read. It sounds very much like the last four books she described to me, but I refrain from mentioning that fact. I continue to scan the sidewalk since we don't have any customers and that's when he appears.

Rocks swaggers up to the van. He's dressed like I'm accustomed to; a dark grey long-sleeved dress shirt and vest, but the vest is one I haven't seen before. Thick, soft black velvet with antique silver buttons that set off the silver watch chain perfectly. Tiff has stopped speaking, and when I look at her, she's standing with her mouth hanging open. Rocks' mouth twitches a little and he flicks his hair out of his eyes.

"Good evening, ladies."

"Well, hello." Tiff recovers fast.

"I'm Rocks." He extends his hand up through the order window. Tiff shakes it with delight and introduces us. I'm glad he's playing along and maybe this is a new start for us.

"Are you hungry?" I ask after letting go of his hand. I'm giddy at the thought of getting a shot at the title after all.

"Famished. I want it all." He gestures to all the jars, condiments and toppings we have on the counter. His eyes seem to sparkle.

All these flavors are not a good idea. Tiff is confused. "All of it?" she confirms.

"Please." He nods.

"Um, if I may suggest something. That's a lot of flavors. How about we both make you our favorite combo to try." Rocks agrees without hesitation. Tiff is a barbeque sauce, bacon and cheese fan while I'm a sauerkraut, mustard and pickles lover. Since he's already done onions, I'm sure we'll create two delicious new feasts.

One thing I'm becoming addicted to is seeing the look on Rocks' face when he lays his eyes on a new food sensation and promptly devours it. Mini at Christmas time has nothing on him. It's pure untarnished delight. Eyeing both dogs, he's faced with a huge dilemma—which to taste first. When he goes to hand over a stack of wrinkled dollar bills, I shake my head.

"I must pay."

"Not for these. It's my treat." Tiff nods a little too enthusiastically. I know she's adding this to her list of how-to-get-hottie-repeat-business tricks.

Placing a hand over his heart, he looks at us. "Connie. Tiffany. Thank you ever so much. I will enjoy every morsel you have prepared for me." And that he does. Rocks repays our kindness by standing at the counter and letting us share his new appreciation for barbeque sauce, bacon and sauerkraut.

Once he finishes devouring them, he heads over the road to dance until one a.m. He's offered to walk me home, and if I thought Tiff was excited by Parker Reed knowing my name, that was nothing in comparison to Rocks offering to be my escort. When I catch her humming the wedding march, I punch her arm.

Tiff is looking at me with dreamy eyes and a smile that actually has me nervous. But on second inspection, she's not really focusing on anything. She sighs, "Oh, Rocks, just who is it you remind me of?"

Oh no, I know that look and can tell she's trolling through her book boyfriends.

"'Miss Connie,'" she imitates. "'Would you do me the honor of allowing me to escort you home this evening?' Bless the Lord up above! Even your cold heart had to have melted with that."

The rest of my shift flies past in a whirl of excited anticipation and slightly freaked out apprehension. Rocks is a bat, and it's easy to forget that when he's standing in a velvet vest eating hotdogs. And not just any bat, but a blood-drinking vampire bat. I take a massive sip of lemonade. Sugar is my friend.

Clean up is fast and easy with Tiff at the helm. She's so organized that her methods and precision would be a little daunting if she wasn't my best friend. The last thing she does is prepare two sweet iced teas. "For the walk." I love her work.

Rocks is waiting in the shadows of the trees that line the sidewalk when we emerge from the van. His hair is shiny and damp. He tries to brush it aside with his fingers. "Sorry, I'm a bit hot."

I can't stop my grin. I hand him the drink and receive the shy smile—my favorite. His eyes widen when the sweetness hits hit tongue.

"Sweet iced tea."

"New favorite."

I laugh as we start to walk along. His appreciation for things I take for granted is starting to warm my cold heart. I like it—a lot—but I'd never tell Tiff. "I think your list of favorites is getting pretty long."

He hasn't stopped drinking and nods, smiling around the straw. I'm aware of his height again and the distance between our bodies. I don't know what to do with my hand that's nearest to him. My body remembers our last walk in the dark. Almost as though Rocks can read my mind, he offers me his elbow. Without a word, I place my hand in the crook of his arm and exhale.

His straw sucking air is the first sound for a whole block. I hand over my cup and he graciously accepts it.

"You aren't scared anymore?" I can't figure out his tone. Guarded?

"You said you wouldn't hurt me and I believe you." It's not a lie. I don't ever want to lie to Rocks.

"But you're scared?"

"How do you do that? Special bat psychic abilities?" I half laugh. It better not be.

"No, I just listen. My senses keep me alive. I trust what I feel." The way he speaks with such earnest conviction makes me a little uncomfortable. I don't know anyone else like this, and I feel myself wanting to mirror his style—to tell only the truth. That thought pulls my gut in two different directions.

"I'm a little scared." I feel the muscle in his arm tighten. "But only of what I don't know. It's a lot to take in." He relaxes under my fingers and nods.

"You can ask me anything, Connie. That night I flipped—"

"Flipped?"

"It's what we call it when we change. I flip between human and bat," he explains. It doesn't sound so scary. "That night I didn't mean to flip on you like that. Sometimes, I can't control it. I want to apologize for frightening you and abandoning you when you needed my assistance." He looks into my eyes for a moment and we stop walking. "I'm truly sorry."

"Rocks, you have nothing to be sorry for. I'm the one that's sorry. I'm sorry I screamed and threw things at you and splashed you with holy water." Not one of my finest moments. "I'm sorry I thought you'd eat me and Mini." I can't look at him. My behavior was shameful.

"Please don't feel bad," he says quietly. I meet his eyes. They're so dark but look so gentle. "I don't have much experience being friends with an aeronaught—just a human, I mean. I'm just so grateful that you're giving me a chance. Helping me learn"—he gestures to the tea—"while you can."

"Rocks, listen to me. I'm in." Just like Mini, when I listen to my heart, I know he's a good guy, and I can't cope with all the secrets on my own. "Together we'll work it out—who I am and where you belong."

Rocks is the one to look away. His eyes begin to glisten and he shakes his head. I think he's trying to hide behind his hair, but it's still damp and stuck in place. We start to walk once more in silence. He drinks his tea, and I don't disturb him. What I'm learning about Rocks—the flying vampire bat boy—is that he's the biggest softy of all time.

When my house is within sight, I ask the one question I'm dying to know. "So you're a shape-shifter then? Shape-shifters are real."

Rocks turns and shakes his head. "No. Five hundred years ago, my ancestors were just human like you."

"Huh?" I can tell this conversation is going to take a while, so I tug on his elbow and pull Rocks back toward Garden Hills Park. There's no way in hell I'll sleep tonight without more answers. "What do you mean 'human like me?'"

"I'm not supposed to tell." He looks up at the sky with a wistful longing, and I wonder if he's wishing he were gliding past the stars instead of being quizzed by me.

I don't know this boy with abilities I thought were impossible, but the connection I felt to him in the forest stirs in my chest. "I trust you won't tell my parents I know I'm adopted."

He snorts and looks at me smiling. "Definitely will not be doing that." The smile fades and Rocks stares at me. I don't know what his searching eyes are looking for or what they're seeing. "I trust you. We both have secrets, and we both don't know where we really belong." He takes my hand in his and settles back on the bench next to me. "Back in the 1520s, my ancestors were simple villagers in Mexico—"

"Mexico? But you don't look—"

He laughs. "I'll get to that bit. Trust me." Rocks gives me a look that tells me he wants me to listen. I smile and pretend to zip my lips shut. "It was when the Spanish invaded. Unfortunately, we never kept a written history, so depending on who you talk to will depend on the version you get told. This is my leader's version. In a desperate attempt to beat the invading Spanish, a shaman invoked a charm and transformed the whole village into bats."

"Transformed?" Holy fudge, a man did this to Rocks. "Into bats?" Not exactly an animal I'd pick if I wanted to defeat an invading army.

"Yes, the village worshipped a Bat God."

I open my mouth to speak, but one of Rocks' eyebrows disappears under his hair. I close my mouth. He smiles, his eyes shining in the lamplight, and my chest tightens. He's sharing his deepest, darkest secrets with me. That level of trust is more than I've given him, and I can't help but feel secretly thrilled.

"The plan was to swoop down behind the enemy, return to our human form and slay the soldiers before they could even draw their weapons. The Camazotz—that's what we are—were literally to become what our name means—death bat or sudden bloodletter." I shiver, unable to stop myself. Rocks turns and pulls a leg up between us on the bench so he's facing me. He looks into my eyes. "You know that's not me. Right? I'd never hurt you."

I nod and swallow. Trust is something earned and so far Rocks has done nothing to deserve my dark thoughts. I'm letting Hollywood movies cloud my judgment. "Sorry. Go on."

"Even with the bat warriors, the battle was lost. The only survivors were those who were Camazotz and they fled. The shaman was slain during battle, and it was expected that the Camazotz would return to human form once his power ended in death. But, they didn't. We've been cursed in this form ever since. The others believe that being Camazotz saved us so that's how we're meant to exist. I disagree."

My mind is reeling. "So you're a bat, a Camazotz, because of a magic spell? Is that what you're telling me?"

Rocks swivels toward the gardens and sighs. His fingers trace patterns on the back of my hand. "Do you believe in magic, Connie?"

Now it's my turn to sigh. "Ahhhh …"

"Not even after you've witnessed me flip?"

"Oh, right. But …"

"I know it's a lot to take in. Makes you wonder about people being burned alive for witchcraft throughout history, doesn't it?"

I know my eyes must be the size of dinner plates. "Oh my God, they *were* witches? I just assumed they were normal people persecuted for being different or modern." I sit and think about what Rocks has revealed to me about history. Witches really do or did exist. Holy crabapples. "So if it's magic, then you can find a spell to get turned back to human if that's what you want. Right?"

He smiles again, but there's sadness in his eyes I don't like. "Know the address of a local witch I can hire?"

5
1982

"SO I'M AN aeronaught and you're a Camazotz?" My mind has been working overtime. My curfew on Saturday night cut my question time short, and it's tricky to know what's appropriate or inappropriate to ask about being a bat. "I've got so many questions it's driving me insane."

"You're not the only one."

Rocks—decked out in a black and grey paisley vest—was waiting on the porch swing when Mini and I pulled in after school. She practically leaped from my arms when we got within reach of him. Rocks hesitated, but in keeping with my new vow to follow my instincts and trust him, I handed her over. She snuggled into his chest like they were long lost buddies as we walked through to the kitchen.

"Aero is a prefix that means air travel and naught means nothing. So one of no air travel—roughly. That's you."

He seems excited. Mini is touching his nose, but he doesn't pull away. Rocks let's her explore his face. I bite the inside of my cheek. Seeing my little sister so enamored with this giant Goth boy is the cutest thing I've witnessed in a long time. There's a calm patience that seems to ooze from him. It's contagious and I like the feeling. I can't remember ever being this relaxed around a guy.

Rocks explains that the only vampire bats located in the USA these days are Camazotz. Plain old vampire bats that are simply bats are only located in Central or South America. Regular bats, with dark brown fur, are smaller and would easily fit in the palm of my hand. Rocks is bigger, longer and heavier with a wingspan of a foot and a half and has jet-black fur.

"So how did the Camazotz end up in Georgia?"

"Over the centuries, we've been persecuted. Feared. The remaining Camazotz migrated further and further north to find a place that didn't worship the Bat God. My colony has been in Georgia since just before it was founded."

"Your colony?" Every piece of the puzzle I get about Rocks makes me realize I need ten more. "Is there more than one?"

"The original Camazotz sought safety through integration with the early settlers. But it was impossible to hide their secret. If any Camazotz has a child, that child will be Camazotz even if one of their parents isn't. Makes life complicated. The integration caused a rift and three colonies formed as a result. My colony believes that the shaman gave us a gift, and that aeronaughts are full of fear and ignorance."

"What do you believe?"

"That we're the ignorant ones." He shrugs. "I don't know what's right or wrong anymore, I just know how I feel. And we've been so isolated that your world is a complete mystery to us now."

I walk around the marble island to stand next to him. I understand what it feels like to be the odd one out in my family. The difference is that I'm the one alienating myself. My parents love and believe in me. What I can't imagine is what it would feel like to have everyone else pointing the finger at my differences.

"I'm going to help you sort this out. I swear." His long hair shades his eyes and he doesn't flick it back. "I'm going to fix us a snack." He nods. "Can you strap her in her chair?"

Rocks goes to work, and I grab Mini a handful of raisins and a kid's sized yogurt. Without me asking, Rocks drags up a stool and assists Mini with her spoon. I pull Mom V2.0's baked beans from the fridge. Popping the microwave open, I load it up and start hitting buttons. Rocks is by my side and regarding the machine. When he notices my stare, his cheeks flush slightly.

"It's a microwave," I say hesitantly, hoping I'm not insulting him.

"Why did you put the food in it?"

"You don't have any stuff like this?" I indicate to all the kitchen appliances.

He shakes his head and looks away. "No need." I don't want to make him feel embarrassed about who he is, but then I focus on the 'need' part. *Ugh, blood.* As much as I'm cool with his magical powers of transformation, the blood drinking freaks me right out. Swallowing the lump in my throat, I pull him across the kitchen and show him the bread and the toaster.

"I want four slices toasted golden brown. Don't burn 'em." His eyes widen and a smile begins to form. "You can adjust the cooking time with this knob here." It's Christmas in August. He positively beams when the toaster pops up the golden hot bread, but the smile quickly fades and he walks back to sit with Mini.

"You must think I'm a freak on so many levels." The curtain of hair covers his eyes and he leaves it there. I'm beginning to see that he does hide behind it, and this boy shouldn't hide—ever. He continues, "I hate seeing that look on your face."

What look? God. "Rocks, this is really new to me. It's going to take some adjustment time for both of us. I don't mean to look at you funny. I … well, it's hard to believe you've never used a toaster before. Sorry."

I push a massive pile of beans on toast toward him. These beans are to die for. He's in for such a treat.

We both moan in unison and smile, savoring the first mouthful. It's a secret family recipe. I wonder if I'll have to steal Mini's copy. *Ugh, stop it!* Rocks is by my side, and I don't want to waste the opportunity thinking about my family crap. He continues to moan and groan and devours half the beans so fast that I'm not sure he even tasted them. I've hardly touched mine because I'm too busy sifting through the questions I want to ask and staring at the joyful expression that's back on his face. When Mini grunts at him and holds out her fingers, Rocks grabs her yogurt spoon and scoops up a mouthful of beans from his plate. It's like watching the Hallmark channel—my heart is slowly melting into a pile of pink goo.

"I've only just started discovering the gourmet delights you have to choose from. I don't have much money so I have to be wise. Your world, Connie, and the technological wonders it has to offer. You have no idea how lucky you are."

"Technological wonders?"

"At the colony, they abhor advancement. Technology—even electricity—is used sparingly. We live a simple life in touch with our instincts. Imagine being stuck in 1865. It's going to be our downfall. Our numbers are declining, and we need to modernize, but nobody listens to me." He stops eating. "Except you. That's why when I met you, I was so absorbed with how much alike we were that I forgot the time. I flipped."

The mention of us being alike sends shooting stars whizzing around my stomach.

"You said you can't control it. Is that why you flipped when I screamed at you? How on earth do you even do it? Does it hurt? Can you—" Rocks' fork has stopped mid air. I think I've stunned him with my curiosity attack. "Sorry."

He looks away and continues eating. "It's okay. I— I like that you're interested, but I, um ..." He takes a deep breath. "I'm just not used to talking so much about myself. Feels weird." He gives me a little smile and looks back at his plate. His quiet humility is endearing and is doing more strange things to my stomach. Imagine the football team being this humble—yeah, right.

I've only eaten half my beans; I'm too distracted, and push my plate to him. Rocks isn't at all offended at the idea of leftovers. He gives Mini two more spoonfuls and digs in, talking around chews.

"Okay—the screaming? Ugh, I'm gonna be in big trouble for that. I've given you ..." He's thinking. "What's that stuff that makes Superman weak?"

I laugh. "Kryptonite?"

"Yes. I've given you my kryptonite." I go to the fridge and pull out two cold sodas. I show Rocks both and when he can't decide between cherry and regular, I grab two glasses. "Most of the colony wants to be Camazotz. It's natural for them. I love being human, so I stay like this unless I have to feed. If I don't flip, after thirty-six hours my body forces a flip. The shaman must have done it to stop any of the villagers that didn't want to be bats from staying human. So that night, I was going to flip when I had to, but I hadn't planned on being with you when it happened and couldn't stop it." He smiles, but there's a trace of sadness on his face. "No, it doesn't hurt. And honestly, I have no idea how I do it. Magic."

I have a burning desire to whip out a notebook, but I'm sure that wouldn't be allowed. "And the screaming?" The look on his face tells me he likes regular cola better. Me too.

"That's our one weakness—nature's mistake. Bats rely on echolocation to hunt. Our hearing is key." Thank goodness I did well in biology.

Rocks explains that for some reason there is a frequency range that knocks them out, but wouldn't knock out a regular bat. And it just happens to be around the level of a woman's high-pitched scream of terror. "You can't tell anyone this stuff."

When he looks at me, my heart flutters in my chest. He's so vulnerable, trusting me completely. I feel the weight of the responsibility sink into my gut. He has just exposed his Achilles' heel. I trusted him with my secret, but it's nothing in comparison to his.

Up in my room later, Mini is emptying my nail polish suitcase all over the floor. Rocks is sitting with one leg folded underneath him in the wingback, flipping through *The Monster Hunters Handbook,* and I'm at my desk painting ladybugs on my nails. It occurs to me that I would never feel this comfortable hanging out with any of the guys from school.

"So you can be a bat forever and not flip, but you can't stay human forever without flipping. Why?"

"If I could have five minutes with that shaman."

I nod in understanding and wonder how many times he's thought that. As little as I know about my history, at least I'll get answers when I find my real parents. Rocks only has stories handed down from people he doesn't share beliefs with.

"Is it my turn yet?" he asks, looking hopeful.

I cringe. He's so interesting; I can't help myself. I haven't shown him anything since we left the kitchen. "Can you please show me the interweb?"

I bite the inside of my cheek. "Internet or world wide web." I pull out my phone. "Here."

"It's on that? I thought that was a cellular telephonic device." He's puzzled, but soaks up every word I say. I know by his focus that I'll never need to tell him anything twice. I explain the wonders of the smart phone and how many of us are completely addicted and totally dependent on them. The awe is apparent all over his face when I hand my phone over. Before I finish explaining the apps, engine noise floats in my window.

Rock is out of the chair and across my room before my eyes can focus. A quick peek shows Dad V2.0's van parked in our driveway. He works for a courier company as an accountant, but his company car is a delivery van—something about bigger, better advertising. It's so embarrassing.

I pick up Mini, smile at Rocks and leave the room. He understands that I don't want to draw Mini's attention to his 'exit' style. A second later, when I poke my head back in, it's empty. My lace curtains flutter in the hint of breeze. The awe I have for his ability is growing by the second.

THE NEXT NIGHT, Mini is in her high chair waiting for *her mother* to feed her. Kelly is at the stove and the kitchen smells very similar to my favorite Italian restaurant—there's still a bit of garlic to get through.

"Rocks," she says and looks at me. "Rocks."

Sugarplums. Rocks didn't stop by today so I don't know why she's thinking about him. Then again, he's all I've thought about so I can't blame the little tike.

"Connie, I hope you're putting her sun cream on if you're out in the garden," she admonishes.

"Yes. Cat." I walk the plastic cat figure across her tray, praying it distracts her. "Meow."

"Mmm-ow," she mimics.

"Honey, did you hear the NFL is asking for $765 million to settle the concussion lawsuit?" he calls from the adjoining family room.

"Con, go tell your father dinner is almost ready please?"

Well, I'd like to be able to tell him, but I don't know who he is, Kelly. I fill my lungs with air and remain mute as I go retrieve *Mini's* father from the other room. Not having answers is making me crazy. There's an anger constantly bubbling inside me like hot mud, and the only time I don't feel it is when I think about Rocks. I want to move past feeling pissed off with them but have a feeling it will linger until I find what I'm looking for.

Until I know who I am.

"Hello, sweetheart." He lowers his newspaper. "I was thinking. Do you want to come rappelling with me on the weekend?"

WHAT? I'm tempted to dig my finger around in my ear to dislodge whatever is making me hear ridiculous invitations to highly dangerous activities suggested by none other than *that man who wrapped me in cotton wool* for sixteen and a half years.

"Huh? Since when have I been allowed to go rappelling?" The only word to describe his look is sheepish.

"Your mother and I have spoken. This job made you so happy last week we thought maybe we've been a little, well, over-protective. Maybe it's time you tried some new experiences—before college. What do you think?"

Oh, I could kiss Tiff and Brandy. It's the remnants of the 'teach her to be confident and defend herself' argument they used to get me the job tryout.

"And ruin these?" I say, holding up ten hand-painted ladybugs. I can't believe I'm allowed to go rappelling *now*. The sad thing is that if he'd asked me before I read that stupid letter, I would have jumped at the chance to hang off a mountain ledge with my hero.

The hole in my chest widens a little, but I have a plan and I'm sticking to it. I have to keep Parents V2.0 at arm's length or I know I'll cave and come clean. Saying no hurts. If this is what it feels like to be an adult, then I want to stay a teenager forever. I wonder if this is his way of telling me he's noticed I don't hang out in the family room with him anymore.

"You can do them again."

"These are one of a kind original works of art." I wiggle my fingers at him and pray my face doesn't betray that I know how stupid I sound.

"You're being ridiculous, honey."

I know I am, but it's the best lie I can think of on the spot. I can't exactly tell him he's in the bad books for keeping my family tree a secret. Jeez, this lying game is a tricky business.

"No, ridiculous are those helmets y'all wear. Have you looked in the mirror? And dinner's ready."

I DITCH MY friends outside school with the lame excuse of Kelly teaching me to bake her death by chocolate. I cross all my fingers and pray they don't ask to join the lesson.

"Cooking lessons on a Friday night?" Mary Lou says with an arched brow.

"Only time she had. And you've gotta work, Tiff, so it's not like you guys will be at the mall long anyway."

They exchange looks, but nobody says anything when they face me.

"Tiff, can you ask your boss if I passed the trial and got the job?"

Back home, I head straight to my room and open the window. Not knowing when Rocks is going to show up is driving me crazy. I hope it's today because I can't imagine he'll come around on the weekend.

Homework done.

Glittery cupcake nails painted.

Dinner consumed.

Internet research on Josie Hendersen stalled. Peoplesearch.com has four Josie Hendersen's listed in Georgia. My Google searches aren't giving me the results I'd hope for. There is nothing concrete even though I know her date of birth from my birth certificate. Maybe I should try to find where she attended high school.

New Gmail account created.

Still no sign of Rocks.

I have to trust that Rocks will want to return to me. When he's not around, I miss his quiet calmness, and I'm not going to lie—it's super exciting knowing what he can do.

The weekend drags. Chad goes rappelling, memorizes the newspaper from cover to cover, watches the pre-season games, and works in his office. Kelly does gardening to prepare for the change of season that's coming, bakes dozens of goodies that we'll never eat, visits the neighbors to relieve us of said baked treats, and asks me thirteen times what's wrong. Mini does what eighteen-month-old kids do. Poops at the worst possible time, demolishes my room then leaves, and gets generally adored by all, including smothered with kisses.

I mope around looking at the clock every five minutes, sit and stare at the trees outside my window imagining what it must feel like to fly, make a list of food that Rocks absolutely must try, check my phone obsessively then remind myself he's not going to call, and try to speak to Parents V2.0 as little as possible.

Monday after school, I give in to peer group pressure and wander around the mall. I buy a large box of Milk Duds, and then want to hit myself with them because I have no idea if I'll ever see him again.

"So Tiff tells me that Parker liked your top." Brandy elbows me as we exit Hot Topic.

Parker Reed did in fact tell me he liked my top when he passed my desk in English this morning. This time, at least, I replied.

"Really?" I said to him, looking down at my chest to see if 'the girls' were on high beam or doing something equally as embarrassing that a boy would notice.

Tiff had jammed her elbow so far into my ribcage that I'm sure it will bruise. We then had a hissed argument for the first twenty minutes of class about the fact that when I don't talk to him, it clearly shows a lack of interest. She insisted I must be clinically insane not to at least be curious why he's talking to me—according to Tiff, the expert. I countered that if he wanted a conversation, he wouldn't speak to me on the run. He would stop and be polite, like another boy I know—but that I kept to myself—and I followed that up with why I should listen to expert advice from a single girl.

"Yeah, so polite to talk to someone without stopping, don't you think?" Brandy looks at me and then at the others. They're using silent girl code. I should have known they would have discussed my new freakish behavior by now.

"Maybe he's shy," suggests Lou.

"Are we talking about the same Parker Reed who ran around at the wrestling championship end of year party naked? Shy?" I don't even need to roll my eyes at that one.

Tiff sighs. " I just wish I'd seen it. Can you imagine that body?"

The girls go off on a naked, hot boys tangent and I monitor the minute hand on my watch.

IT'S NOT UNTIL I'm in bed and twist around to turn my bedside lamp off that I see the tiny blood-red velvet pouch. It's the same as the ones you get from a jewelry store with little gold ties and is sitting propped against my lamp base.

I sit up so fast I nearly give myself whiplash. I grab the pouch and my neck. Ouch. Rocks was here. At least part of my world rights itself, and I let out a breath as I lay down again with the pouch clutched to my chest.

I don't know why I'm nervous.

After a second—I can't wait any longer—I untie the loops. A pair of tiny silver earrings fall into my palm. Oh. My. God. I hold up a little silver girl dangling from the earring hook. The other one is a tiny silver bat. It's Connie and Rocks. I roll over and squeal into my pillow. Sleep is out of the question.

Inside the pouch is a folded piece of paper that reads—*Dear Connie, I'm sorry that I missed you today. It's terribly rude of me to just keep appearing without an invitation. I do apologize. If you are free, I will call on Thursday afternoon. If you have already made plans, please do not alter them. I understand. Yours, Rocks.*

The buzz I felt fizzles as I recall Mom V2.0's roster this week, and the fact that Milk Duds don't even compare to sterling silver earrings. Crabapples.

I leave school on Thursday faster than my Quick-dry nail polish hardens. I don't even have time to spin the girls another lame excuse, and I know my absence will come back to bite me later, but I don't care. Rocks is going to be at my house and Kelly is home.

Bursting into the house, I expect disaster but am met with the overwhelmingly sweet aroma that suggests *the woman that doesn't look like me* has made cinnamon buns. A quick scan of my room, and I'm back out on the porch in 3.6 seconds. Mini screeches from the kitchen, calling for me. That kid has supersonic radar or something because she's sitting two rooms away but miraculously knows I'm home. Before I can sit on the porch swing, a short, sharp squawk echoes from the trees. My grin is unstoppable. I race to the tree line and get as close as possible.

"We can't stay here so we'll go to the library because I think I'm onto something in my search. Meet me in my room in a second." I half whisper up into the branches. A squawk answers me. "One for yes and two for no, okay?"

One squawk.

I'm off.

"Hi Mini. Hi— Can I go to the library?"

She's drizzling sticky white icing on the warm buns on the oven tray. "Sure. Just don't be late."

"Yes." My fist pumps the air.

Mom eyes me and I know I have to tone down my excitement. I'm pretty sure they've been discussing my mood swings, and I wouldn't blame them. I hardly moved all weekend, and now I'm about to explode. "Can I have three of them to take with me?"

"You're going to eat three of these?"

"Oh, ah, not for me. I mean … the girls are going to the library too. So make that four."

This is Kelly's weakness—feeding others. She was born to bake and feed the masses and ended up with two girls to feed and a husband who couldn't care less about sweets. "Oh, honey, let me pack them up for you. I'll give you the biggest ones because I'm sure the girls will be hungry."

Must escape. When Mom is her super-awesome-best-Mom-in-the-world self, it makes referring to her as Version 2.0 sting. In my room,

Rocks is perched on the edge of my bed, looking ready to jump out the window. God, he makes everything seem so small.

"Okay, we're going to the library, but not my school library. Do you want me to show you on a map?"

He frowns. "Can't I come with you?"

"What?"

"In your car?"

Idiot. My ears burn. I know he notices because he's looking at the side of my face, but then he gives me a full-blown Rocks blissed-out-on-food smile. He's seen them.

"Thank you for the earrings. I love them."

"You're welcome." He looks away and stares at his feet, but due to our insane height difference, I can still see his face perfectly well. It's just that our eyes don't meet now, and there's some hair interference. It's hard to hide from a short person. "I wasn't sure—if—well, you're my only friend so thank you for wearing them."

Oh, Rocks, you have no idea how cute you are right now. I open my drawer and hand him the giant box of Milk Duds. "These in no way equal these, but I thought you might like them. It's caramel and chocolate together." Now it's my turn to look away.

"For me?" His excitement over a couple of dollars worth of chocolate makes me feel cheaper than my Great Aunt May at a bake sale. But just like when he walked me home, he senses my unease. "You were thinking about me. And the earrings didn't cost me anything but time. I made them."

"How? What?" I frown. "Don't you live in a tree?" My ears burn hotter than hell.

He pulls a face. "No! I do not live in a tree."

My cheeks come to the pink party too and when he notices my embarrassment, he smiles. "We have a market in the mountains to make money for essentials like clothing and stuff. I live there ninety percent of the time, but the others sleep in our roost."

"Oh." I touch the little bat earring and time stands still. Rocks is mere inches away from me. He *made* these for me. *Is there anything this boy can't do?* His eyes roam slowly over my face. I watch their path ... my eyes, my mouth, my hand playing with the bat, my mouth ... I wait ...

Mini squeals downstairs.

Rocks steps back as though I've electrocuted him, and now I want to scream.

"So will you drive me?"

"Yeah, sure. Meet me by the car in two."

As predicted, cinnamon buns are his new favorite. I can't wipe the smile off my face as I zip down the back streets to avoid the traffic. Having Rocks in my car is surreal. He can't leave the stereo alone. Much to my dismay, he settles on some techno beat, but I'd never tell him I hate that stuff. He's wearing those massive dark sunglasses again.

"The only other guy I've seen wear glasses that big is that dude from U2, and I think even his are smaller."

I'm not sure how much pop culture he's been exposed to, but he knows about Superman and Batman. He explains that his nocturnal vision is amped up so direct sunlight hurts him after a while. He hates the fact it confuses him about who or what he's supposed to be. If his human eyes can't take too much sunlight, then maybe he should be a bat.

"Do you like them?" He points back to the sunglasses.

"Oddly enough I do. They suit you. I bet you can wear hats too. Like any hat and it'll look good on you."

"I have a fedora. Does that count?" He grins. "I'll wear it one day." His smile is almost responsible for a traffic accident.

Focus on the road.

Focus.

Rocks winds down the window and the wind blows his hair back off his face. I wish I wasn't the one behind the wheel. Stealing quick glances, it's the first time I've seen his whole face, and to say he's good-looking is an understatement. He has the nicest cheekbones and jawline, a straight nose, and flawless skin. His hands are tapping out the beat on his knees that barely fit under the dashboard. There is just so much boy sitting beside me. I wonder if it's a side effect of the magic that is drawing me toward him or whether it's just that he's as lost and confused as I am.

"I love the bass beat," he says over the music. "It's what I love about that dance club. I can feel that boom boom in here." He's mimicking the bass line over his heart. "This is where I'm free. In here." His happiness fades. He lets his hand drop to his lap and looks back out the window. I wish I could see behind those dark glasses. "I'm me—without feeling like a traitor for picking one side over the other."

Rocks didn't speak for the rest of the trip to the library. It took longer than I expected to reach what I think is my real mother's old high school.

On my 500th Google search, I discovered a blogger reminiscing over her high school days. She listed the names of her softball teammates who helped win the championship her senior year. According to Josie's age, she would've graduated high school that very same year. I cross everything and pray that the Josie Hendersen listed looks like me. My gut thinks I'm getting warmer and I hope it's right.

Rocks follows close behind as we head down the stacks. He loved the brief tutorial on using library computers and the cataloguing system. I glance over my shoulder and see him trailing one long finger along the book spines. I must give him my membership to the county library. He won't know what to do with all that information at his fingertips for free.

The collection of yearbooks is way down the back. "We need to find 1982." I say, crossing my fingers.

The yearbooks aren't in any particular order. Dust and the smell of old carpet fills my nose while my eyes scan the shelves. Without thinking, I move closer to Rocks and take a deep breath. A crisp forest night and the moon overwhelm me. He smells so clean and fresh for someone who dresses so dark and mysterious. I freeze.

I just smelled Rocks. Slowly, my eyes drift up to my left and I'm met with two twinkling midnight blues looking back. I focus on the dimple starting to appear on his cheek as he bends toward me.

"Do I smell good?" His voice is lower than normal.

Holy Fudge Sundae.

"Mmm-hmm," I confess, swallowing.

The stacks are suddenly closing in on me. He's so close, so tall, so everything. Everywhere I look is—Rocks. I'm too hot and my skin feels too tight. I swallow the lump of self-doubt forming in my throat.

"That's what the woman at the club said too. What do I smell like?" My core temperature has gone from volcanic to arctic at the mention of the woman—he kissed.

The flame inside me has been thoroughly doused. What is happening to me? I look at my hand and it's shaking slightly. I make a fist and hide it behind my back.

"Who was she?" Rocks frowns. My voice sounds super weird even to me. "Camazotz?"

"Hell, no. Don't know." His eyes scan my face, but I take a step away and focus back on the yearbooks. The numbers are blurred.

"Connie." His fingers slide down my arm. I move it away. "She wasn't anyone special. I … I felt so—alone. You were *scared* of me, and I thought that maybe I was a monster." He slumps back against the bookshelf.

I lean back against the opposite one and study him.

"I just started walking after I left you. I wound up near the bars and went in. My plan was to try to get drunk, but that was way out of my budget. So I sat in a dark corner and let the music wash away my—my loathing."

"Of me?" I whisper.

His head jerks up. "No! Of me! Everything I do disappoints someone—either my family or myself." He taps the center of his chest. "Anyhow, I ended up on the dance floor. Connie, I've never experienced anything like it. Moving with the crowd was exhilarating. I just let the beat consume me. I'm not so different." His eyes look sad.

Rocks explains that he went back every chance he could to get away from the colony, and she danced with him the night I saw them in the parking lot.

"I wanted to see if all aeronaughts were scared to be alone with me. I wanted to see what her instincts told her without her knowing the truth. I wanted to know if I could find my place."

His words strip me of my own. Nothing I consider saying is adequate. I'm not adequate. I'm a selfish, cruel witch. I need air. The stinky carpet is constricting my lungs. I want to rip the skin from my flesh.

"Rocks," I can barely speak. "I'm so sorry I made you feel that way. So sorry."

He doesn't respond. His hair is blocking his eyes, but he hands me a yearbook. The class of 1982. On the pages of this old ratty book could be the answer I'm looking for.

I can't open it.

What are my problems compared to what this boy standing in front of me is feeling? I *know* I'm loved. It might not be perfect but they would do anything for me. I belong to them, and there is no question of that on their part. This search for answers is all me.

His fingers pry the book from my hands and he starts flicking through the pages. All I can do is watch. When he looks back at me his eyes are wide. The way he is studying the page and then my face makes me tremble.

"It's her."

There on the third row down, for the first time in my life, I look at a photo and see a family resemblance.

It's as though I've been punched in the gut. She is me or I am her. It doesn't matter because I've found my blood. Straight, long, blonde hair also worn pulled high, and eyes that crinkle at the side just like mine. The thing I never expected to learn from one glance is that she doesn't like having her photo taken either. I know because her ears are pink—the same shade as mine every class photo day.

I close my eyes to try to stop the tears. My body slides down the shelf until my legs crumple onto the carpet. I cry. What's wrong with me? I've never been a screaming, crying girl before, but I can't stop the flood of emotions. The letter. Rocks. My mom.

I finally found someone who looks like me.

"Come here." I hear Rocks in my ear and suddenly I'm warm. He's folding himself around me in the small awkward space and pulling me close. The forest. The moon. I sigh and open my arms enough to cling to him and cry out the nervous tension that's been bottled up inside.

THE FOLLOWING AFTERNOON, Tiff pulls up in my driveway. She's dropping me home because I was too tired to drive today. I stayed awake last night guessing who Josie Hendersen really is. I imagined Mom V1.0 in a pretty dress drinking sweet iced tea on the porch of her beautiful home. She'll cook up a storm to celebrate our first afternoon tea together while her loving husband gives us time to get to know each other. I thought the photo would make me feel whole, but it's somehow only added to the emptiness. I need to meet her.

Rock won't be back till after Labor Day and the thought of the long weekend ahead excites me.

"Do you think your mom has baked?" Tiff asks.

I smile. I've missed my girl time lately and hope that Tiff will forgive me. "Probs. Come in and see."

The house smells of melted chocolate and sugar. "Oh, God. I'd be enormous if I lived here."

The kitchen counter is covered in the remnants of her bake off. Canisters of flour, cracked eggshells, and spilled cocoa litter the marble, but right in the center, is a tray of cooling marshmallow brownies.

"Hi, Mrs. Phillips, have I told you lately how much I love you?" Tiff zeros in.

"Perfect timing, girls." Kelly grabs a second plate and beams at the idea of having another mouth to feed. We've made her day.

Tiff is on her second brownie when my day takes a wrong turn. A do-not-collect-two-hundred-dollars, go-directly-to-jail kind of turn.

Putting down her coffee mug, *the woman that I'd give anything to show the yearbook* speaks, "Did you like the cinnamon rolls, Tiff?"

Fudge me with a serving of crabapples on the side.

"What cinnamon rolls?"

THINK!

I get eyed from two angles. "Oh, I forgot. Yeah, I saw a homeless man on my way, um, to the library ..." I give Tiff the go-along-with-me eye as discreetly as I can. "Felt *so* guilty." Bit like I do now, I think, trying not to grimace. "I bet he enjoyed them though." I smile, but my face feels as though I forgot to remove last night's mud mask.

Tiff is a fixer even when I don't deserve her to be. "Oh, that guy. Yeah, so sad. He hangs around a bit, but I heard Principle Skenner say he's got to go."

Kelly then asks the appropriate questions that fit the sad tale, and Tiff soldiers on lying on my behalf.

I'm going to have to start keeping notes on who I have told what exactly and when. Alice was right about falling down the rabbit hole.

6
Fedora

TUESDAY AFTERNOON, Rocks is swinging on the porch when I get home. It's a black leather vest day befitting his Camazotz side. I wonder how similar to me Rocks would be if it wasn't for the spell. I notice his Camazotz senses in action. The way he'll turn his head to the side a little when he's listening to frequencies I cannot hear, how often he takes a deep breath scanning the air for information. Subtle differences that mark him as not just a boy.

"Where's Mini?"

"She's going to out us to my folks. I've left her at daycare till four thirty."

Rocks frowns. "No, you can't do that. I won't be responsible for her spending time away from you. I'll leave. Go pick her up." He's standing. What? The last four days without him passed slower than public transport in the South. I need my Rocks fix.

"She's fine. Really. She keeps saying your name, and Kelly thinks I've got her outside in the dirt every second." Please don't go.

We argue back and forth as we walk in the door, up the stairs to my room, back down to the kitchen—where he eats three cupcakes that have been decorated to Master Chef standard—and back to my room.

Rocks wins.

Saying no and meaning it when he looks down at me with that smile is harder than I ever imagined.

We're now in my car heading to collect Mini, and he's happy again. He didn't leave, so I'm happy. And I know Mini will be ecstatic when Rocks walks in to collect her.

The looks Rocks and I get when we enter the daycare center make me want to smack my forehead against the front doors. His six-foot-four frame looms over everyone and everything since it's designed for tiny, little people. His goth presence and black clothing are a wicked contrast against the pastels and teddy bears.

Mini spies us through the glass window near the office. Her tiny voice echoes through chanting his name. Rocks can't get to her fast enough and goes to collect her while I sign the checkout book.

"A new friend, Connie?" Mrs. Papadopoulos asks, with a knowing smile. I did not think this idea through. My palms begin to sweat.

"Yeah, he's a friend from, uh, work." Lie number one hundred and ninety-three.

Mini is singing her version of "Twinkle Twinkle"—which if you don't know that's what she's singing, you'd never guess because it consists of 'tar' and 'winkle' said at random. She's happy as a lark and her grin matches the smile spread across Rocks' face. Not wanting to tell any more lies, especially in front of him, I grab him by the sleeve the second he's next to me and pull them both out the door.

On the way to the car, he's frowning again. "What?" So much is unknown to him about my world, but I can't work out what modern problem has him perplexed this time.

"She hasn't been changed." The glares he gives the daycare center would melt metal. The group of drooling moms don't even notice. "I don't like that place. They should talk less and care more."

There is a tightening sensation in my chest. Mini has her own champion. I never would've listed maturity as a trait I'd find attractive in a guy. Seeing it in action though makes the boys at school look even more stupid. These moms will gossip about the leather, the vest, and those gigantic biker boots for days. I *must* talk to my legal guardians before this gets reported back to them.

Back in my bedroom, after watching him devour another cupcake, I hand him a bunch of printouts. Rocks quietly reads while I wait for the family laptop to fire up. Rocks has been patiently waiting to get his hands on a computer and learn about the power of the Internet. It will be the first time he's ever touched one and that's a concept that I just don't understand. How could the colony survive without these? When I ask, he frowns and shakes his head.

"Don't get me started." He sighs and returns to reading. "Where did you get this stuff?" His eyes are dancing with an emotion I can't name. It might be excitement. To think I've done something to help him makes me giddy.

Google didn't have much information on Camazotz legends, but what I found was interesting. The Zapotec Indians were the people who worshipped the Bat God. Their ancient civilization dates back to anywhere between 700-200BC. The half bat, half man was a deity they worshipped and revered. Centuries later, the Mayan people adopted the same God, but he was seen as a vampiric, winged demon of darkness and blood sacrifice. He was accused of committing genocide on the Mayans.

"This explains so much." Rocks shakes his head, then begins to massage his temples. "How is it possible you know more about me than I do?" he asks, nodding at the printouts as a smile creeps across his features.

"Welcome to the power of the world wide web." I bask in the warm and fuzzies from finally having helped him find a piece of his puzzle.

"This is huge, Connie." He grins. "One of our colonies clearly believes the Mayan side while the other two lean toward the Zapotec. One thinks we're cursed; the others feel blessed and *now* I understand why." His joy is contagious. He scoops Mini up off the floor and kisses her forehead before taking a seat by my side in front of the laptop. "Thank you. You found what your mom looks like and now I've found this. We're getting there, you and me. We're starting to find out who we are—together."

I feel so happy I could die.

"Hey, I forgot to tell you that I emailed that blogger who said she played softball with Josie in high school. I haven't heard back yet."

With Mini parked on his lap, I explain search engines, websites, email and have just started on social media when my phone chimes.

Rocks scrutinizes my every move. I remind myself he just wants to learn about the modern world, but I'm becoming addicted to his eyes on me, particularly when he's this excited.

"A text from Tiff." Opening it, I show him the screen.

"Congratulations." He smiles.

She confirmed I got the job. The Bun Lovin' Barn will have a new team member every Friday and Saturday night starting this week. I hit reply.

"I'll walk you home safely each night."

I love my new job.

"You'll meet me after work?"

"Every shift. Nights are good for me." He winks. The bat side of Rocks prefers the dark. His human eyes, ears, and nose are all more sensitive, and he feels more at ease after sundown. My job is the best thing that ever happened to me—guaranteed Rocks time.

My phone chimes a second later. Tiff is already making plans for better ways to lure hot guys to the van. According to her, I'm supposed to wear more eyeliner on Friday—her latest theory.

"Tiff again?" Rocks is astonished.

"Yeah, I replied and now she has."

He's awed by the speed of modern communication. He's used to snail mail and sending messages by wing. Once a month, Rocks and one of his colony elders venture into the town near their market to collect their postal orders. They aren't allowed to shop at the mall but have suppliers that will ship them the raw materials they need. "You should totally get online. Internet shopping will change your life."

Photo booth is my next gift. His level of awe at what the Mac can do rises exponentially. Mini got bored with computer lessons and is trying to coax Feathers out of her hiding hole in the corner of my room.

The tiny camera on the laptop means we need to move closer together to fit on screen. And I won't deny that my heart rate spiked when Rocks put his arm around my back. We snap shot after shot of silly photos. The sound of Rocks laughing—something he doesn't do often—fills me with a sensation similar to dentist happy gas. I suddenly don't have a care in the world, and I can't feel my lips from smiling so hard.

After twenty minutes, he's selected his favorites. A set of four pictures—us with alien heads, us with bug eyes, a sepia shot of me looking at him while he's laughing hysterically, and one of the two of us smiling. The photos show what a stark contrast we are together. He's midnight against my golden sunny morning. We are day and night—the sun and the moon.

I'm drunk on my own laughter, but I quickly sober up when two fingertips slowly run up the length of my spine.

"Thank you again." His breath tickles my neck. "I can't remember the last time I felt this good."

When his fingers reach the top of my spine, he folds them over and lightly drags the backs of them all the way down again. My heart is beating out a Morse code message. I'm sure it reads something along the lines of 'Tiff, what do your books say to do with hot guys and lingering fingers?'

I want to be calm and nonchalant, but instead I freeze. I can sense his eyes watching me, but I don't trust myself to risk a glance. I stare straight ahead at the screen and pretend to do more clicking for the print job.

"You're not breathing."

I let out the air that's been trapped in my lungs and escape to my desk. Distance is good. Distance lets my internal organs function. Heart palpitations cannot be a good sign in someone my age.

Rocks sits and watches me for another moment. I want to be inside his head more than anything. He returns ever so quietly to his spot on the wingback, and I breathe normally once more. I can't think about romance and Rocks. He's a vampire bat, and those Goth Camazotz girls are way out of my league. I just can't.

"I need to tell my parents about you, and I'm pretty sure they'll want an introduction. That cool?" My voice sounds off to my own ears.

"I'd be honored to meet your parents. Just tell me when."

Does nothing affect him? I wonder as I study his body language. "Aren't you nervous? *I'm* nervous for crying out loud."

"Of course, but if it means getting to walk in the front door." He shrugs like it's obvious. His sincerity hurts me sometimes. "Why are you nervous?"

"I've, um, never invited a boy home before. She's going to go nuts." I roll my eyes just thinking about how Kelly will react to this news.

"I'll be your first?" He's grinning.

Ears, if you are listening and I know you are listening because you are ears—do NOT blush. Please, I beg you not to turn red.

The traitors burn. I walk to the window and push it all the way up.

"Go. Get. Hit the air, bat boy!"

"Hmm, I like being your first."

His laughter fills my room and then he's gone.

ALL THROUGH DINNER I practice different ways of mentioning Rocks. When Kelly gets to daycare tomorrow, the bat will be out of the bag. The plates get cleared. Chad says a polite "no thank you" to the offer of pecan pie. My stomach churns.

"Where did all the cupcakes go?" It's not that Kelly minds what I eat, more that she loves to know who she's feeding and what they thought of her creations.

No time like the present. "Oh, um, I got the job at the hotdog stand." I look from one to the other.

A hint of a grimace passes over Dad V2.0's face before he regains his composure. He doesn't say anything. I imagine old overprotective habits die a slow death where I'm concerned.

"Oh, sweetheart, that's great news. I knew they'd love you. Congratulations." She's looking at the cupcake container again.

Breathe.

"So there's this guy who …" All the time I spent thinking about this and I don't even have a good lie, I mean, explanation. I swallow. "Well, he helps us lock up. Like security, sort of. Anyhow, he's promised to make sure I get home safe each night, and he poppedaroundtoday and loves your cupcakes."

"What was that last bit, sweetheart?"

"Who's this guy?" he asks.

It's an intensive sixteen-minute grilling. I feel slightly charred but alive. Rocks will come for dinner on Thursday night. Chad will give him the third degree and make sure he really is nothing more than just a friend—like I told him at least twice every minute of the grilling. The bake queen is floating across the kitchen with my pie and a dreamy look in her eye. Kill. Me. Now.

English is my last class on Thursdays. Dragging back her chair, Tiff takes a seat eyeing me. She's been trying to corner me all week, and I can't put this chat off any longer. Parker Reed enters and stares in a way that makes me sure he's got X-ray vision. He never looks away the whole time he walks toward me until he passes. Tiff missed it. Thank God.

"Are we good?" She has proof of my lying game. Knowing Tiff, the other afternoon was probably not the first time she's suspected me, but she's been too nice to say anything. Getting her to lie to mom for me is a whole new low for us.

"I'm sorry. We good?"

"Spill it." She deserves something, and if I tell her now, I'll save myself another Rocks related grilling when he shows up at closing time.

"I told Mom I was at the library with you, but I was with Rocks."

Her eyes widen and her jaw almost falls off her face. "OMG!" Tiff smacks her forehead. "I forgot to ask you how that 'walk home' went." Her eyebrows do a scary dance. But before she can take in my eye roll, she's a squealing mess.

She draws the attention of half the class. I'm so glad Mrs. Yamaguchi hasn't arrived yet. The squealing is followed by hugging, some bouncing up and down, and eventual begging for juicy details.

"We're not dating." I don't know why I bother speaking sometimes.

"Not yet."

"No. Look at me. Listen." I try to get in her direct line of sight. "We're not dating. Just friends, and he's going to walk me home after work."

The look on her face is starting to scare me. "First, Parker. Now, Rocks. Prom will be a hard choice!"

Oh good God.

KELLY HAS PULLED out all stops with dinner. It's going to be a three-course affair and since I told her Rocks has a sweet tooth, dessert is a platter of mini creations that rival anything I've ever seen on Master Chef.

At precisely seven, there's a knock at the door. Kelly and Chad position themselves on one side of the kitchen island—the perfect couple. When I open the door, my heart completely stops. Dead.

Rocks is standing on the porch and looks like he's just stepped out of a black and white mobster movie. Bonnie and Clyde would adopt him in a heartbeat. Forget the fob watch, the fedora has come to dinner. It's on his head at just the right angle to stop my heart. But the fedora is just the beginning. He's wearing a three-piece suit—dark grey with a super thin black pinstripe—and holding a bunch of wild flowers. The suit admittedly looks old, almost antique if that was possible for clothing. I'm guessing he's not the first or second person to own it, but regardless, I'm going to die the happiest teenager ever.

I want to bask in the glory of Rocks dressed for dinner, but now he could easily pass for twenty-five, and my father is going to have kittens at the kitchen counter, and I'm never going to be allowed to leave the house again.

Inadequate is the word that's playing on repeat inside my head. I never dress for dinner. I did change out of my cutoffs into a denim mini skirt, but I'd need to be wearing a twenties flapper dress to look the part on his arm this evening.

He's smiling. I can tell he's waiting for my approval. And I want to give it, I do. But ...

Stepping out, I pull the door almost closed behind me. Without saying a word, Rocks has read me yet again and is deflating before my eyes. I'm a giant pin at a balloon party.

"Too much?" He's staring at his shoes. It's the first time I haven't seen him in his giant boots. The hat rim completely blocks me. Oh, Rocks, what am I going to do with you?

I step in closer than normal to get under his hat. "Hey, you look amazing, but my dad is going to have a coronary."

He says nothing. "Rocks, I mean it. The fedora is *my* new favorite." That earns me a shy smile. So much of what he discovers in my world becomes his new favorite. It's our thing, and the fact that we have 'a thing' makes my stomach do a triple loop-de-loop.

"That good, huh?" He's back.

I'm about to head inside, but the look on his face makes me halt. His eyes are doing that slow roam that Rocks never seems to be embarrassed about. I wait.

"You look lovely."

It's the first time he's seen my hair down. It's my turn to use it as a shield—my casual outfit is not worthy of his compliments. A long strand slips over my shoulder as I look from his shiny black shoes to my tiny silver sandals. Two fingers slide into my hair near my crown, and I hold my breath. Rocks lets the strands slip through his fingers all the way down. At the bottom, he gently twirls my hair around his finger. "Your hair is spellbinding."

I meet his gaze. "Thank you." I'm not even sure if he's aware, but his sincerity has the ability to stop a healthy heart from beating. Rocks winks and I grin back. The spell broken. "Come on, let's go scare those two half to death."

Kelly is in love. The flowers were a massive hit, but it's the fact that Rocks is on his third helping of dinner that has truly won her loyalty. I'm safe. If Mom approves, Dad won't stand a chance.

For the first time in weeks, the two adults sitting at our formal dining table are my parents again. They're playing the perfect hosts and doing what all good, caring parents do when teenage girls bring boys home. I can't help but forget my anger and hurt and grant them a 'get out of jail' card for the evening.

I try to imagine Parker in Rocks' place. I'm sure he would know the exact things to say to concerned parents, but I can't imagine him making me smile the way Rocks is. Parker can sometimes be a dick, something I'd never say about Rocks.

Rocks is answering all their questions in his usual honest and sincere manner. And thanks to Chad and Kelly, I'm learning even more about this dark, bewildering boy.

Rocks is short for Rockland, an old family name. He was homeschooled—so that's how he describes it—in rural Georgia, graduated early and became a silversmith. He works in the family business at the historic town of Helen in the southern Appalachian Mountains and is one of eight children.

"Eight kids?" I screech, my mouth hanging open in shock. Kelly gives me her 'guest manners please' look so I close my mouth. A faint hint of pink creeps across Rockland's cheeks. At least he knows he's been keeping me in the dark. Sneaky bat.

Eight kids in one family, and he thinks he doesn't belong anywhere? We're going to have a serious discussion next time I get him alone. Rocks continues answering and says he has an extra soft spot for babies, and since his youngest sibling is now five, he wants to adopt Mini. Kelly gushes. Chad is a slow thaw.

At the mention of adoption—I could kiss Rocks for that one— Chad's eyes flit to his wife and then to me. He looks away, but I continue to hunt for signs. He meets my eyes a second time before straightening his already neat cutlery across his empty plate.

"How old did you say you were, son?" Chad fidgets under my stare.

"Turned nineteen on July first, sir."

"No way. I'm the twenty-sixth," I say. Dad visibly relaxes now that he's confirmed Rocks isn't an older man. And I bite my tongue to prevent my elated squeal from escaping.

The topic moves to him working 'security' at Bun Lovin' while Mom puts the finishing touches on dessert. I help clear the table but have one ear glued to the dining room.

"He's adorable, Connie. What a lovely young man."

I nod and smile. I can't help myself. He's bewitched us all—well, all the females. I wonder for a moment if it's Camazotz magic he's seducing us with.

Entering the dining room with the course that I know will blow his mind, they're still talking about my work. The spring in Kelly's step is starting to grate on my nerves. I guess there was a time limit on their reprieve after all.

"I worry about Connie at night, sir. So if I have your permission, I'll escort her home each evening to make sure she gets here safe and sound." Chad gives a curt nod. Kelly sighs.

Dessert is the highlight. Mini flatly refused to go to sleep and is currently bouncing on Rocks' knee while Kelly basks in the glow of

Rocks sampling new treats. She has thoroughly earned it—mini cheesecakes, raspberry chocolate mousse cups, and tiny lemon meringue pies. He might never leave.

At the end of the evening, Rocks has consumed a ludicrous amount of food and has a takeout container in a paper bag under his arm. Kelly is borderline giddy and insists that the door is always open and that pot roast is every Sunday. Chad shakes his hand and gives him a brief shoulder slap.

The night was a success because at least there's one area of my life that I won't have to lie about, but I feel torn. Rocks is not supposed to be Team Kelly and Chad. He's *my* support crew, and I don't need Kelly giving me *those* looks. The ones where, if I told her we were in love, she'd scream like a fan girl. It's bad enough that Tiff is marrying me off so young.

I imagine what it would feel like to open the door for a movie date and see Rocks in his suit. I bite the inside of my cheek. Those palpitations are back and doing the rumba. STOP! He's a Camazotz. It's too complicated. It can never happen. He's probably never even been to the movies. I sigh. My heart has relocated to somewhere in my lower intestines.

As I walk him to the porch, my mood darkens.

"Here's a tip. Let's call this Modern Girl Code 101. If the parents hate the guy, the girl is far more likely to keep the guy."

"What?" His eyes are the size of dinner plates. "You want your parents to hate me?" His confusion could be measured on the Richter scale. "You're not keeping me?"

"Ugh, no. Ugh!" I roll my eyes. I shouldn't have said a word. Kelly and Chad are my battle. It isn't fair to take this out on Rocks.

"No, you're not keeping me? Or no the parent part?"

I've scared him. Fudge my life! He just doesn't get it. He really is from 1865, and I am the only monster in this equation.

"What did I do to make you mad?" he asks.

"I'm not mad at you but at them. They acted like such perfect hosts tonight it makes me almost believe the lies, but they are lies." I walk to the railing and look up at the sky. "I'm going crazy trying to determine when to trust them and when not to. You know? I *need* to meet Josie."

Rocks nods and rubs my arm, but he doesn't looked very relaxed.

"I'm sorry I snapped at you. Of course, I want them to like you." He gives me his shy smile. "And, yes, I'm keeping you, but my mom is totally crushing on you, so cut it out." I punch his arm.

His shoulders ease and then his eyes light up. "Your mom really likes me?" His chest puffs out and he hooks his fingers into the pockets of his waistcoat. Rocks' moods are infectious. We end up facing each other and smiling like fools.

"Another aeronaught in your corner, huh?"

His grin widens. "Yes, ma'am." He flicks his hair back and places that killer hat on his head.

"Were you really homeschooled?" I whisper, glancing over my shoulder to make sure the folks are still cleaning up. He laughs.

"It's the response the Sire insists we tell any curious aeronaughts." He pokes my rib making me jump. That grin is going to be the death of me. "But it's near enough to the truth. Our mothers teach us to read, write, and basic math, but that's it from the human world apart from our trade for the market. The rest is Camazotz history, but now I know we're only told one side of it."

I wish we could take a seat and chat some more, but if I'm too long Chad will be spying through the window. "I'll see you tomorrow night." I turn him around and push him toward the porch steps before closing the door. Peaking out the curtains, I watch him stride across the yard, he's grinning.

Never in a million years did I think my senior year would involve dinner parties with a vampire bat boy as the guest of honor and my parents fully approving.

7
Beans

TIFF WAS NEVER so right than when she proclaimed senior was going to be our year. The year we take control. Rocks and I have a routine, and I love it. I know when my supernatural best friend is going to visit and it calms my heart. Monday and Wednesday afternoons, Rocks and I hang in my room. He takes over Mini duty if Kelly is working, and when she is here, she keeps Rocks in a permanent food-induced coma.

Friday and Saturday nights, he's always leaning against the back of the van when my shift finishes. Most nights, his hair is damp and his cheeks are flushed from feeling the beat across the street.

Our new arrangement leaves me plenty of mall time with my girls. Less lies are spewing from my lips, and that's definitely a good thing. My chest feels lighter, and I can honestly say I've never been happier. The last three weeks have been heavenly.

Parker Reed is still making comments in passing, and I must admit my curiosity is growing. At least now, I usually manage a response.

It's Wednesday. Rocks is in the wingback studying the Driver's Manual. He wants me to teach him how to drive. The colony surviving without a car just seems insane. Rocks explains that only one member is allowed to drive—another control mechanism—and the current member is Judge—a leader of sorts. Judge drives to Helen for the supplies the colony can't produce themselves, and the expression on Rocks' face tells me he wants that job—desperately.

"Can I see your tattoos?" I've only seen them that one night when Rocks wasn't expecting to see me. Since then, he's always in long sleeves.

He marks his page. When our eyes meet, Rocks smiles. So often when he's learning or studying technology that I take for granted, he seems to almost shine. I love the way he makes me look at my world now, and I appreciate how technology opens up so many possibilities with just a few clicks of a mouse.

"They don't offend you?"

Silly Camazotz.

"Nope. Tattoos are cool." Hot, sexy and yours look dark and dangerous, but I'd never admit that out loud. Rocks is thinking. He looks at the sleeves covering his arms. "I want you to be yourself."

He focuses on me. "I've never been more myself than with you." His voice is so earnest. The air that fills my lungs isn't enough. "Do you mind if I wait till I've got a short-sleeved shirt on?"

I can't decipher the look on his face. Surely, he isn't shy about his body. I try to imagine how many milliseconds it would take Parker to remove his shirt if I showed a smidge of interest. Rocks is like no other teenage boy I know. I smile and return to my nail art. Little hot pink bear faces are taking shape on the corners of my white nails. I hunt for the right dotting tool to make eyes.

"Well ..."

Looking up, I notice the frown pulling his eyebrows together. Sensing he's about to tell me something important, I wait.

"I get very cold ... um ... well, when I don't feed." His eyes dart away when he says the word feed, and the meaning becomes crystal clear. He's definitely not talking about eating Kelly's baked goods. I'm glad he isn't watching me because I'm sure my eyes are wider than normal, and I can't afford to make him feel bad. "If I just eat aeronaught food, I get cold. I didn't know this would happen. That shaman used some pretty powerful magic. And from a biological point of view, it doesn't make sense." Now, he does make eye contact, and the vulnerability I can see in his dark blue eyes almost wounds me. Rocks really is discovering who he is—just like I'm trying to discover who I am. We share so much in an unexpected way.

"But why don't you" —I swallow— "feed, um, more?" I force my face into a neutral position and pray he can't see the gooseflesh forming on my arms.

"I want to see if I can belong in your world. Just be human like I've always dreamed about." He smiles. "And I really couldn't do it without Kelly." He rubs his belly and I know he's remembering the pulled pork sandwich he just demolished.

"Just make sure you don't, you know, hurt yourself. Promise me?"

He nods and I know I've said the right thing because he relaxes. "I have to learn about myself though. The colony is on the cusp of ..." His eyes move to my open window.

I wait, but he doesn't speak. "Of what?"

"I don't know. It's just this feeling." He rubs his chest. "Some of the members—the ones that don't like aeronaughts—I don't trust them. Our numbers are declining rapidly, and if I can't find a way for us to integrate successfully, I don't know what's going to happen. If I knew more about how we were changed, I'd be better prepared."

"Do you want me to Google witchcraft or voodoo?" Oh boy, I can just imagine what the search results will look like.

Rocks shrugs. "Maybe all the real witches were burned alive? It seems like an impossible dream."

I can relate to impossible dreams. "I thought finding Josie was impossible at first, but I've got to believe it will happen. We can do this. I know we can get you the answers you need."

"Thanks, Beans."

"Beans?" I get the grin, and his eyes show he's highly amused. "As in green beans?"

"Baked. Your mom's actually." His grin spreads as he watches my face. Rocks loves to make me react. It might be his new hobby. And little does he know that, when he looks at me that way, my whole body reacts on the inside.

"You're nicknaming me after my mother's baked beans?" I exaggerate my enunciation of the last two words.

"Yes."

"No."

"Yes."

"Why?" I learned that the yes/no game can go on forever with Rocks. It's the only thing about him that reminds me he's my age. If it takes all day, Rocks will keep saying "yes" until I eventually cave. I suspect he's discovered my weakness.

"Because of the delicious sounds you make when you eat them."

I'm pretty sure I resemble one of Mini's cartoon characters when their eyes boing in and out of their head.

"I do NOT make any kind of sounds when I eat them," I snap.

"Do too."

"Not!"

"Too."

He just grins and sits back in his chair—like he completely owns it. I'm trying to figure out how to wipe the shit-eating grin off his face.

"Those moans and groans. It's almost R-rated stuff."

"I wouldn't know how to be R-rated if I tried," I say, completely aghast.

I watch as one of his eyebrows disappears under the jet-black hair that hangs too low over his face.

Wanting to dislodge the numbness in my toes and the weird flutter my heart, I continue, "The first thing I think of when someone says 'beans' is, well ..." My brain has been disconnected and is not helping. Maybe if I reconnect it, I could win this argument, but looking at him sprawled all over my chair being ridiculously alluring isn't helping me focus.

"Yes ... is?"

"Bad gas." The tips of my ears start to heat.

The laughter that erupts from Rocks makes me jump. I'll never tire of watching Rocks lose control and laugh. But maybe less so when it's at my expense. When did he get so bold? I'm starting to prefer polite, proper Rocks. I look out the window and then check the cuticles on each finger until the laughter subsides into shorter bursts.

"Farting is the last thing," he says, before letting out another half snort, "that I think of when I think of you, Beans." His eyes are full of mischief, and it's increasingly difficult not to give in.

"So what do you think of?" My throat is tight.

Rocks stills and holds my gaze until I look down at my hands again.

"Hunger," he says in a soft even voice. "A hunger that makes me want to devour—my Beans."

Flames are shooting out of the tips of my ears. I know it. I need Tiff. I don't know how to process that or what it's doing to me. Is he joking? I can't look at him.

FUDGE ME!

"Weirdo," I mutter.

"CONNIE?" Kelly's voice echoes up through the house. Saved. "Can you please come get Mini?"

The Driving Manual is discarded, and Rocks is down the stairs before I can even put the lid on my polish. When his favorite little human needs looking after, nothing will keep him away. When I get to the kitchen, Mini is in his arms, sharing his marshmallow brownie. Where does he put it all?

"Would you say beans are Connie's favorite?" he asks.

You did not bring *her* into this, bud! Even though I'm trying to ignore him, his eyes are glued to me as I make my way around the kitchen island.

"Without a doubt. She begs me to make them."

"Mrs. Phillips, I feel a hug coming on."

I'm going to be sick. That woman is a traitor, and he is joining her side. I have a new enemy.

"Speaking of names, *Mom*. Why did you and Dad decide to call me Contessa? It's not like Contessa and *Jasmine* really match." I watch her for any sudden movement the same way a hungry hawk scans the forest for prey. I pick at the crumbs crumbling off Rocks' next brownie.

Calm as always, my mother concentrates on arranging the left over gooey chocolate squares in a container—no doubt for Mr. Hollow Legs Traitor Boy to devour later. "Oh, well, I thought it suited you."

The fact there are no baby photos of me until I'm at least six months old has been playing on my mind. I want to ask so badly what age I was when they adopted me, but I can't—yet.

Back in my room, Rocks enters with Mini and her Duplo blocks barrel and settles on my bed.

"Connie." He's watching me.

"What?"

"They love you. We'll find Josie. Why are you taunting them? They *are* your family."

How dare he. "Excuse me?"

"Beans, calm down." I hate that he's so levelheaded sometimes.

"No, let's talk families, shall we?" I swivel my chair to face the bed and rest my feet on the edge near his leg. "Let's talk about the fact that you feel like you don't belong, and yet you have SEVEN siblings. I've seen you with Mini. She adores you. Are you saying all your siblings can't stand you?"

He hangs his head down and pulls two red blocks apart, handing them to Mini.

"Why don't you explain your family situation to me for once?" I get so focused on finding my parents and teaching him about gadgets that I get sidetracked from probing him for more Camazotz information. The last thing I want to do is make him uncomfortable because I can't control my face. Having him think I find his ability weird is worse than not knowing the answers to my questions.

"It's—"

"Do not say complicated," I cut him off. I know that look.

"You won't understand." I haven't seen him this upset since we first met. When he admits bat details that he thinks will bother me, he fidgets. Right now, he's putting two bricks together and pulling them apart over and over. I wait.

"My Mom, Zada, I lived with her."

"Your Dad?"

"He's around, but …" He covers his eyes with a hand for a moment. "I only have two full-blooded siblings—my sisters. The others are half brothers and sisters. The name Zada means prosperous, and boy, did she prosper. Most females only have two or three pups."

Fudge! David Attenborough springs to mind, but Rocks is describing his family, not some animal behavior. My room is suddenly a hell of a lot hotter.

"Pups?"

"Bat young." His hair flops down. "We breed as bats. But without modern medicine, we're dying out."

Pups? Breed? If he weren't on my bed, I would lie down. It's so easy to forget that Rocks isn't just a guy. He's an animal and his colony prefers to be that way. Rocks always comforts me when I need him. Didn't I just tell him to be himself? I take a deep breath.

"So your Mom's remarried. That's cool. Half the kids at school have divorced parents."

He looks through his hair at me for a brief second. "She's not exactly remarried and ..." He sighs. "She has kids with three men, and Dad's got another woman too."

Holy smokes that's one fudged up family tree. My nerves do react better to him referring to everyone in human form.

"That's way too many surnames for one school to handle," I joke. Mini is on the floor with the animals Rocks has built her. I silently pray she won't interrupt this chance to find out about him.

"We don't have surnames." His voice is so soft.

I try to keep my eyebrows in place. They have a tendency to shoot into my hair at odd information. Rocks explains that kids are named for their father's clan—or what they call a wing. His sisters are Celand and Graceland of the Land wing. He also talks about the Fold. It's their council or government of sorts and they rule the wings. Of the seven Fold members, one gets voted into power—The Sire—and rules the colony. The Fold members are usually the seven strongest bloodlines from the dozens that make up the colony. Judge—the Camazotz that can drive—is a Fold member.

Bloodlines freak me out a little. The mention of blood makes me think of sucking, and I don't want to imagine him that way. I make a mental note to really work on putting a lid on the giddy feeling I get when Rocks smiles at me. If he doesn't belong in *his* world, then why would I? There is absolutely no future for us *as an us*.

"So why don't you belong?" I move and sit on the end of the bed. The leftover colored blocks are separating us.

"I'm a bad example to my siblings. I'm always human. They ask questions." Rocks flicks his hair back and stares at me. "You coping with this?"

Oh, Rocks. Don't worry about me. "Yeah." I reach and take one of his hands.

"I was born human."

I'm not following. Why does he make that sound like a death sentence?

He continues, but his body language is closing up before my eyes. "We breed as bats. I'm one of three offspring alive to have been born while my mother was human. I was born a human—like my ancestors all were—but I'm judged for it. Flipping sometimes causes females to lose their young, so they stay as bats throughout pregnancy. The pups remain in bat form until around three years old."

He explains that the shaman probably never thought past the battle. He probably thought they'd succeed and turn them all back again, but never got the chance.

I stare at Mini on the floor. His obsession with her and what she can do is finally making sense. With all those siblings, he's never witnessed the baby years.

"I was the opposite. I didn't learn to fly until I was three. And with so many siblings, well, my mom's not been around much. She chooses to stay a bat like my father. I pretty much raised myself."

I will not get upset when Kelly dotes on him ever again. He's never known what it feels like to be coddled. Rocks. Alone. Abandoned.

A misfit.

"Mom was forced to remain human until she got pregnant again. Then I was handed around to any adult in human form—the colony leper so to speak. Zada would check in on me and get upset once I was older when I wouldn't want to flip. That's why I'm too skinny, well, not so much now." He gives me a brief smile. "I only ever fed when I absolutely had to. I've been a disappointment my whole life. The human freak. My interest in modern ways is seen as a defection. Some of the other wings want me gone."

"Gone?"

"Out. Away from them so I can't gain support, but I'm determined to find a way to ensure our future."

I need to cheer him up. I grab a paper and pen. "Draw your family tree."

"No way. It's too fudged up." Rocks has adopted my allowance-guaranteed vocabulary of curse words. If Mini ever utters one single curse, I'll never see another cent of my allowance.

"Teach me your siblings' names. Please." There is no way he doesn't love them all as much as he loves Mini. "Are they all as cute as you?"

I get the smile I was hoping for as he takes the pen and paper. "I know you want to be human, but is there anything about being a bat that you love?"

Head down, he continues to work on his family tree but answers. "Flying."

"What's it like?"

He looks up with the biggest grin I've seen on him yet. "Like nothing on earth. I can't describe the sensation of gliding high on a moonlit night and do it justice. It's freedom. It's heaven. It's more fun than you can possibly imagine." His eyes are full of sparkling life. It's the first time I've seen him so animated about his Camazotz side. "The boys and I play death drop. There's a sheer cliff face we go to and hang off the top. In unison, we drop off the edge and free fall—no wings. We just plummet down, the air whistling past us, and the last one to extend his wings is the winner."

"Oh my God, that sounds crazy dangerous."

He laughs. "It is. I've never seen Zada so angry in all my life when she caught us one night."

"I can't believe you play chicken."

"Chicken? Chickens can't fly."

On Saturday night, the Bun Lovin' Barn is dead quiet. There's a massive football game on so Tiff and I decide to close early. I can't let Rocks know so I wait on the steps to the van. Tiff says she'll stay, but I wave her off.

It gives me a chance to think about the colony and his family. He told me that since he's the first-born male to his father—his sister Celand is older but can't be voted in—he's expected to lead the wing in the future, but because of his human weakness, he's a disgrace to the blood in his veins. The wings all vote, and if he's not careful, they'll vote him out of the colony rather than into leadership.

I would only complicate his life in ways he doesn't need. For the past few weeks, I've been trying to ignore the flutters and giddy feeling Rocks ignites as he slowly opens up and shares his secrets. I haven't wanted to name it but since the dinner party I know I've got feelings for him—more than 'just friends' feelings. But Rocks and I will never be. I'm human, and I'm not going to add to his list of problems.

"You're done already?" His voice interrupts the conversation in my head.

I look up and—BAM. My heart has exploded and my mouth has gone dry. What was I just telling myself?

Rock is wearing a short-sleeved, blood red t-shirt. His gloriously inked arms are on display.

I want to punch the universe in the nose. Why tonight? Why now? He looks edible. The ink is black and grey with tinges of red. The pattern swirls up his arms, and I can't decipher the design. I push aside the fact that he has fed in order to be wearing this. He did it for me.

"Connie?" he asks, smiling. I shut my mouth.

"Hi." I'm breathless and want to smack myself. "Your arms ..."

"Surprise." That's an understatement. "What do you think?"

He holds both arms out straight in front of him and slowly turns them over. If you can imagine a design that hints at wrought iron filigree work found on the gates of fancy mansions and ancient stone carvings, then that's what covers his skin. It's hypnotic.

"Amazing. Beautiful." He stands tall. I hate how little it takes to make Rocks' day.

He pulls the fob from the front of his black jeans. "We have some time. Wanna dance?"

"What?"

He gestures to the club across the road, the move flicking his hair across his face.

"I'm the worst dancer." I can't. No. That's not going to help my 'Rocks is off limits' plan.

"It's pretty dark. Nobody will see and I'm not one to judge. My moves probably went out of style with horse-drawn carriages."

"Haven't you had enough for tonight?" I have an urge to sniff my armpits. I'm sure I smell of wiener and don't look anything like the girls I see in the parking lot dressed to impress.

"Just got here. Had some colony stuff to do," he explains. "I'm—I'm not going to be able to see you next week. My father's asked me for help which he usually avoids at all costs. I have a responsibility to him. It will be our last time together for a bit."

Oh, crabapples.

The club is dark, loud, and crammed to capacity. I only agreed because I was convinced I'd never get past security. Rocks bumped fists with the bouncer and announced that I was with him, and we were let through. Easy-peasy.

Thin neon tracks mark out the dance floor and bar space—both a writhing tangle of body parts. I understand how Baby felt in *Dirty Dancing* when she entered the staff club. My heart feels like it's beating in the back of my throat. Are we going to dance like that? The crowd sways and pumps with the music.

Rocks blends into the dark, and I'm reminded of the night in the forest. The blue lights make my hair glow brighter than a nuclear reactor. I'd let it down to get in, but now I pull it back up into a high ponytail. Rocks takes my hand and pulls me further into the sea of gyrating bodies. We stop in the back corner, and I try not to look at what the couples lining the edge of the dance space are doing in the dark. I'm nervous enough.

Rocks turns and faces me, towering over my short frame. Leaning down, he says above the music. "Put your arms around me."

I can't control the shiver that runs up my body, sizzling every nerve ending with a tingle that I never want to end. He doesn't hesitate and takes both my hands and loops them around his neck. We're close—too close. Too close for my brain to remember we're 'just friends.' His body starts a slow sway as his hands rest on my hips. I'm hyperaware of all the places our bodies are connecting right now—particularly my chest.

Parker Reed constantly talks to my breasts. I'm convinced of it although Tiff thinks I'm insane. But Rocks is different. I know I'm sensitive when it comes to the size of my chest, but in all the time we've hung out, I've never once caught him checking them out. He's never made me feel self-conscious—until now. It's hot. I'm hot. He sizzles under my fingers. I stop playing with the short edge of his hairline the second I realize that's what my traitorous fingers are doing.

He pulls me closer as the tempo pounds out from hidden speakers above us, rattling my ribs. I feel the primal beat he talks about, and my mind wanders to other primal things. My chest is against his, and the feel of our bodies together is making it hard to keep my distance. The song changes, and Rocks spins me around and pulls my back to his chest. His inked arms wrap around and hold me tight. I let my fingers trail down the patterns as he uses his hips to keep me moving with him. The parts of his tattoo design that are bare skin glow gently in the blue light. I can't stop touching him.

He bends over and I feel his breath on the exposed skin behind my ear. I should have left my hair down! I don't know if it's the dancing or Rocks that is driving my heart faster and out of control. All I can think about are his lips and the urge I have to spin around and climb him. Rocks can dance. Nothing about this reminds me of 1865. If I didn't know better, I'd say he watched MTV every week to learn his moves. He's agile. He's graceful. And he knows how to lead.

The music changes to a calmer pace, and we slow along with the rest of the crowd. I see grinding and lazy thrusts and close my eyes to block out the sensual display that is only making everything more intense.

His nose skims the shell of my ear, and I hold my breath in anticipation.

"We better go."

The feeling that was building inside me collapses, and I squeeze my eyes shut.

No kiss. No parking lot make-out for me. The disappointment is burning behind my eyes and tearing my chest in two.

"I could move with the beat and you in my arms all night, but I don't want you in trouble." His breath tickles my damp skin.

The trance I was under has lifted; I straighten up, shake off the lingering tingles and push toward the green glowing exit sign.

It's an hour past my curfew. Somehow I've been sliding against Rocks for two full hours, and I thought it was just a couple of songs. He offers me his elbow, but I can't touch him—skin-to-skin is deadly.

It's never going to be. We are never going to be. I feel stupid. I fold my arms across my chest under the pretense that I'm cold.

The cool night air is clearing my fogged up brain, but I'm still not paying attention. Thinking I'm cold, Rocks wraps his arm around my body, tucking his finger into the top of my jeans, pulling me in to share his warmth. I grit my teeth to stop the tears that threaten to spill. I need to get a grip on my emotions. I had lectured myself about not getting involved and immediately ignored my own advice. I'm acutely aware of him next to me. I don't know if he can sense the war that is raging inside of me, but if he can, he doesn't mention it.

Neither of us says a word for the entire walk home. On the porch, he pulls me even closer against his side and gently kisses the top of my head.

"I'll see you when I can." And then he's gone.

8
Market

I CAN'T SHAKE the feeling that his parting words rang with an echo of goodbye. It's been two weeks and no sign of Rocks. The more time that passes the kiss on my head becomes a figment of my imagination. The only consolation I have is that I'm not the only one feeling his absence.

Kelly continues to bake up a storm every Monday and Wednesday and then is left knocking on the neighbors' doors. Tiff said if she sees another marshmallow brownie, she's going to turn into one. The weird part for me is they simply don't taste as good without him around. How fudged up is that? What's happened to me? I never thought of myself as being one of those girls that gets turned upside down by some boy.

The dance club haunts me. When I close my eyes, I can almost feel his body against mine. My brain knows that we can never be together, but my heart is longing for him. I can't deny any longer that I have feelings for Rocks—stupid, illogical, inconvenient feelings. I wanted him to kiss me so badly at the club, and the thought sends wave after wave of nausea through my system. I know why he didn't. I'm not bat enough for that boy—and I never will be. I'll never be able to fly on a moonlit night by his side.

Google informs me that there are half a million search results for 'shape-shifting spells.' Plenty of sites are claiming it's possible. I *know* it's possible, but I'm stunned that others out there are telling the world so.

My chinchilla, Feathers, jumps from my desk onto my shoulder. I tickle behind her ear while scrolling down the pages. Entry after entry mention this is dark magic and to stay away. But if there really was a way to make Rocks just a boy …

"Oh, Feathers, this is crazy!" She squeaks in my ear. "I can't imagine finding another guy that understands me the way he does. He gets my need for answers and supports me—no question."

I pick her up and stare into her adorable little face just inches from the end of my nose. "Don't bad boys get the girls? Who knew the sweet one with the kindest soul and most generous heart would steal mine." I glance at the door before whispering, "And as clichéd as this sounds, that little shy smile makes me totally weak at the knees."

At night, I stare at the family tree he drew. It's stuck on my wall—a reminder that he is real. I wonder about his father and the responsibility he said he couldn't ignore. I have no idea if he's ever mentioned me, or if the colony thinks that the aeronaught who crashed their forest festival is long gone. Any food I consume sits in a lump in my stomach. I try not eating as much, but it doesn't help.

I think about secrets—their cause and effect. I'm keeping secrets so I have no right to expect Rocks not to keep secrets too. It's just that I'm pretty sure that *I'm* his secret. That hurts. Yet, I understand. It leads me to think about my parents—not my biological parents—but the ones that on a good day I can't help but love and on a bad day I'm still annoyed at for lying. How would they feel if they knew the secret that I'm holding deep inside? I guess they'd be disappointed, just like I am in them for turning my adoption into a secret.

Nights are the worst. As darkness sets in my mind imagines slinking shadows, winged creatures, moving bodies, and spilt blood. I toss and turn and confuse myself. I don't know what to think or feel anymore because all I know is that I'm a traitor. I'm lying to people who love me, and the sooner I get some answers, the sooner the lies can stop. I need to focus on finding my real parents with or without Rocks. My anger is the only thing helping me distance myself from *those two* and I'm exhausted. I just want the truth and to hopefully return to my old life of a carefree teenager.

My mind wanders to the start of last summer when I'd hit the mall with Mom and Mini as often as I'd hit it with my girlfriends. I miss our time together, and it's taking a toll on me. I think that's why the letter cut me so deep to begin with. I never used to tell Mom everything—a girl's gotta have some teenage secrets—but we used to share so much, and I certainly never ever lied to her. And to think she's lied to me all this time just adds to the giant hole in my chest.

Tiff has been my anchor. She understands why I don't care about walking around the mall or gossiping about who's hooking up with whom in senior year. She leans over closer to me. We're in English, watching the minute hand get closer to lunchtime.

"Do you think he'll show up tonight?" she asks. It was such a relief to share the reason for my glum mood with her.

I shrug. I've been trying not to think about when or *whether* I'll see Rocks again.

"Maybe tomorrow night then?" She's ever the optimist.

The bell clangs, signaling our release. Before I've packed up my books, a body stops next to my desk in the aisle. When I hear Tiff's breath catch, I know immediately whom that body belongs to.

"Hi, Connie," he says. Parker Reed is channeling the Cheshire Cat. His body language mirrors that of every high school student that only has two more classes to survive before the weekend. "It's Tiffany, right?"

Tiff shoots out of her chair, her books forgotten and offers a hand. "Hi Parker." Her tone makes me want to gag.

"Walk with me, Connie … alone?"

My eyes plead with Tiff to stay. As my best friend, she knows perfectly well what my face is asking so she ignores me. I stand up to get between them, trying to catch her eye, but it's pointless.

"See you in the cafeteria." And she's gone.

Crabapples.

Parker helps me collect my books, and we head to the cafeteria at a speed even a garden snail would find amusing. "Looking forward to the weekend?"

Not what I was expecting, but I honestly don't know what I'm expecting at this point. It's an innocent question and not at all boob related. "Sure. I work so that takes up a bit of it." Be polite. It's not his fault I feel cut off from a boy I wish was my other half. "You?"

He smiles. "Training" —he flexes his bicep and grins— "and study. Got my eye on a scholarship next year."

Two of the cheerleaders pass us going the opposite way down the hall. I can feel their eyes burning into my skull, and when I look to see if I'm right, my suspicions are confirmed. I bet they're wondering, just like I am, what Parker Reed is doing talking to me.

"You see the pre-season wrestling competition coming up? Coach is arranging it."

The halls are lined with posters advertising the event and predicting our team's victory. "Yeah. You nervous?"

His snail's pace is killing me. I ignore the urge to sprint to the cafeteria for cover and safety.

"Nah, can't wait. The season never seems to start fast enough for me. Wanna come and watch me rule the mats? It's in November." Finally, the cafeteria materializes.

There is no way I'm eating lunch now. Parker seems like a nice guy. A guy doesn't get this popular and not have loads going for him. Maybe the universe is giving me a sign, but I'm suspicious.

"Sure. Why not."

"Awesome." He smiles and it warms my insides. It's not the shy smile I'm used to seeing, but it's genuine. Parker is confident and it shows in everything he does. He holds the cafeteria door open. "See you in class." He heads to his table, and I prepare for imminent squealing and speculation.

I KNOW WHERE Josie Hendersen lives.

Finding out took my lying abilities to the next level entirely, but I'm fairly confident that this address is the one. According to the white pages, a J. Hendersen resides there, and it matches the address my alias—the sports journalist for FASTPITCH magazine—received back from the softball blogger. Yeah, I'm a liar and an imposter these days. But who would honestly believe an email from FASTPITCH @ gmail.com wanting to organize a 1982 winning team reunion? With the amount of spam these days, it amazes me that people are still being conned, then again, I'm not about to start complaining.

Josie Hendersen lives in Watkinsville. It's a bit of a drive so I'm going to need plenty of time to get there, introduce myself, and hopefully sit down for a nice glass of lemonade on her porch. The image of the pretty house with manicured flowerbeds and my elegant blonde mother out front thrills me.

My excitement is short-lived though. Try as I might I can't actually visualize myself walking up to a strange house and knocking on the front door—alone.

That's what Horror Movie Girl would do, and we all know what happens to her. Knowing my luck, I'd probably find myself locked in some psycho's basement, and nobody would have a clue about where to even start looking for me. Somewhere between getting lost in the forest, driving to the abandoned house and finding this new address, I've lost my bravado. Or maybe it's just that I've lost the six-foot-four guy who worries about my safety.

After a whole weekend of thinking about what my mother looks like in her forties, I decide I can't do this alone.

"Hon, listen to this," the news addict calls out to the bake queen. "The Vipers leader, Mitchell 'The Finger' Jones and his right hand man, Raymond Ramirez are to stand trial. Bet that witness is praying for his or her life." I guess he saves her from having to re-read the day's top stories. "Who in their right mind would admit to witnessing those thugs kill two cops? Jones and Ramirez run half the drugs through the south. Everybody knows it. Not exactly the kind of folks you want as enemies."

The woman whom I never thought capable of lying is perusing her cookbooks at the island. "I'd rather take on Jones than that Enzo Ascari character."

When I'm sure news hour is over, I speak. "Make lots of something that doesn't need to be refrigerated."

"Hmm?" she questions, not bothering to look up.

"I'm driving up to Helen tomorrow to visit Rocks."

That gets her attention. "You are not on a school day, Missy."

I roll my eyes deliberately, although I don't know why I'm trying to annoy her when I really do want to take Rocks some baked goods. "It's Columbus Day." I reel back my tone before adding, "Teacher planning or whatever, but it's pupil free. Remember?"

"Oh, sorry, sweetheart. How can it be Columbus Day already? This year is flying, and we've hardly spent any time together lately."

I study my nail polish and shrug. If I look her in the eye, she might see how much that hurts me as well, and then I'll be done for. I'm not mentioning adoption to them until I have my own answers. Having given her a purpose, she opens the cupboard and starts pulling out canisters. I take this as approval for my trip and retreat to my bedroom. I have a gift to prepare myself.

TELLING THE TRUTH has advantages. Chad has set up his GPS in my car, and he's assured me that it's set to Georgia. He did look at me like I had lost my marbles, when I asked, before I remembered he doesn't know about *that* night. I don't know how people manage to lead double lives. I'm barely in control of one with a few secrets, but having a second family or something crazy that you see on news.com must take some serious preparation and planning.

Once I get north of Atlanta, I realize I've never driven up this way before. It's only a couple of hours away from my home, and I wonder if Chad knows these roads well with his rappelling trips. The roadside is filled with little vendors selling boiled peanuts, fresh picked apples, and pumpkins. I notice that folks seem to plant corn in tiny patches wherever they can. It's not something I would think to produce in my garden even if I did live on a couple of acres.

Helen is a small historic town on the edge of the southern Appalachian Mountains. Way before I was born, the town was redesigned as a replica Bavarian Alpine village. Some architect thought it was funny to build an alpine town in the Appalachians instead of the Alps. If you imagine a main street lined with steep-roofed, brightly colored, gingerbread houses, then you've seen Helen.

The knot in my stomach vanishes once I pass through Helen. I would dare anyone to drive through there for the first time and not smile. I feel as though I should have gotten a stamp in my passport because I've been teleported to Germany or Austria or somewhere gorgeous in the Alps. My neck hurt from turning this way and that repeatedly while I drove down the main street. Even creeping at twenty miles per hour due to the other drivers doing the same thing, it's too fast to take in all the little stores.

Helen is just too cute for words. The ironic thing is that a man wearing lederhosen wouldn't cause anyone to blink, but all that Camazotz leather and black velvet must really turn some heads.

The drive takes me way longer than the GPS originally predicted due to traffic. Weekend trippers are clogging the highway to photograph the beginning of fall. The leaves are turning from green to yellow, orange and red. The road is bathed in a golden halo and showers of leaves rain down on the breeze. In the coming weeks, the mountains will be congested, and that's got to be good for the Camazotz market business.

Rocks had told me about the market the colony owns on the outskirts of Helen in the mountains. Open on weekends, the small historical market caters to the passing tourist traffic. When I asked him why they run it, Rocks said that even though they shun modern society, they still need cash to buy clothing and other essentials they can't procure from nature. Just the bare minimum, but they need an income source nonetheless.

The trees are magnificent and a nice distraction. The leaves fluttering to the ground in bursts mirror what's happening in my stomach. I'm getting closer.

The GPS tells me to turn around because it was set for Helen. I silence her annoying voice and keep my eyes peeled for any break in the trees to signal an entrance. Up ahead, there are two motorcycles and a huge pickup truck on the side of the road. I automatically slow, but when I get closer, I see that there isn't a gate or driveway. The pickup truck has the National Park Service logo on the door. The Ranger is pushing one of several huge metal cages along the truck bed to the tailgate. A massive, dark bird—about two-foot tall—sits glaring out at the world.

The car behind is getting impatient so I speed up a little. A hundred or so feet later, a gate with a large carved wooden sign emerges. Sanguine Mountain Market. I turn off the highway and into the gravel drive before I see the smaller sign that reads CLOSED.

Sugarplums. All this way and Rocks probably isn't here. Determined not to give up so easily, I follow the road through the trees until it opens up to a small parking area. There are two gleaming motorcycles and one really beat up van. I park next to the van and sling the overstuffed tote onto my shoulder. Outside the car, the crisp pine air circles my bare legs, and I want to hit myself for my outfit choice. Why didn't I wear black? In my excitement at seeing him, I put on a sunshine yellow dress with a white cardigan. Idiot. Maybe I should just go home? Getting him into trouble is not part of my plan, and his words about some members wanting him 'gone' come back to me. A creeping sensation floats up my spine.

It's now or never. Walking around a massive tree the path curves around, I spy two guys having a hushed conversation ahead. Camazotz. My blood pressure soars. The sunlight gives me a chance to drink in all the details of other colony members. It surprises me to know I'd recognize one anywhere. Despite the sunlight, they seem to ooze shadows dark as midnight. The caramel color of their skin tone shows their Mexican origins three or four generations removed just like Rocks said. Their movements are graceful—almost fluid.

One of the guys, in his early twenties, flinches and I know he's sensed my presence. He steps away from the other. The expression on his face, as he turns, is feral. I feel so insignificant, and that feeling is confirmed by the reflection I see in his mirrored aviators. I do not belong here. He's taller than me but short in comparison to Rocks.

"Can't you read?" His voice is void of emotion and slices through me with the precision of a newly sharpened blade. This man is harder and colder than steel.

The lies are starting to come without much thought. "I'm here on personal business."

The way he stares at me and the memory of Rocks talking about judgmental looks makes my blood begin to simmer. If this dude has been making Rocks doubt his place in the world, then he can talk to me about it.

"Feisty," his partner comments.

I've taken a step toward him and am glaring at my own reflection in his glasses.

"Business with whom?"

"Rockland, the jeweler. Special order."

They look at each other briefly. He stands down and gestures for me to walk on ahead. "Lead the way then."

"Thought we were going to see the tanner?" the other one mutters.

Lying gets you nothing but trouble. This has been proven to me ten times over. I don't let the fear inside show as I stride up the path. I fill my lungs with as much pine air as I can inhale. Visiting a friend should not be classed as a crime. The guys are talking in hushed voices behind me, and I resist the urge to give them a rude sign over my shoulder. They could be relatives. I don't want to push my luck.

Ahead, a wooden welcome sign appears, and the universe is again on my side. I have to act like I know where I'm going. Thick arrows made from gnarled tree branches are carved with locations and point the way. The jeweler is left, along with the candy store, apothecary hall, candle works, and museum. The blacksmith, tanner, dairy and tinsmith are down to the right.

"This is me," I announce, pointing left. I pick up my pace without stopping in case they grill me again.

The path opens up into a circular area that reminds me of a tiny replica Western town. The buildings are small and roughly constructed. Felled trees have been carved into picnic tables and benches for shoppers to rest at, and old-fashioned equipment for photo opportunities is scattered here and there. The only people I see chatting at the storefronts are definitely not aeronaughts.

A large group of guys and girls are gathered around one of the picnic tables opposite the apothecary shop. The conversation stops dead when they spot the only blonde. I stare back. Rocks is not the only man to wear a vest, or maybe I should call them waistcoats. I have a sudden urge to act proper and dignified. The girls—holy sugarplums—wear a mix of proper 1865 and modern Goth-burlesque-sex shop ensembles.

There's a familiar closeness about them as many of the girls are sitting on boys' laps or leaning close. Bodies touch bodies with an air of intimacy that makes me look away. I think of bats huddled together on the ceiling of a cave and understand their need to touch each other in human form.

One girl leaves the group and cuts me off, just as I spot the sign for the jeweler's shop. I'm so close. Her blood-red velvet corset has leather highlights and is showing way more of her breasts than I'm comfortable looking at. The skirt of black satin falls almost to the ground, but as she moves I notice there are four thigh-high slits in her dress, and the lace-up boots she's wearing go up past her knees. Her wavy hair frames her angular, hard features, but the jagged scar that joins her lip to her chin is what I focus on. Until I notice the half-inch wide tattooed eyeliner that surrounds her eyes in thick bands. The whites of her eyes are a stark contrast to the dark pupils and black inked lines.

"The village is closed." If she relies on tips from her amiable customer services, then I'm convinced she's penniless.

"I'm sorry. I know, but I just need a minute with the jeweler."

Her eyes narrow, swallowing the visible whites, and she bares her teeth. If I thought she was prickly before, she's downright lethal now. "You have no business with him. Leave." She starts to walk toward me, and I instinctively step backward. I can't stop looking at the angry puckered scar on her face, and I'm sure that's not helping with her attitude. "He needs to be with his own kind at a time like this."

"What? Why?" The lead weight in my stomach starts to roll about.

A guy approaches us, scowling. I clench my fists and take another two steps back. His ink-black hair is super short and draws attention to the fact that half his ear is missing. Fudge me. The tattoos and scars are starting to get under my skin.

What on earth does Rocks see in me?

"Zabreena, leave her alone." He's standing behind her but is looking at me and jerks his head toward the jeweler's shop. "I'll take you to Rockland."

He moves quickly and I half run to keep up. The words "naught lover" echo from the group as we leave. He steps onto the old-fashioned shop verandah and into the open doorway with me hot on his heels. Two figures are standing together in the dimly lit shop. From his height, I know the guy is Rocks, and as my eyes adjust to the dull light, I can see he's rubbing his hands up and down a girl's bare arms. She's resting her forehead in the middle of his chest. Her hands grip his waist.

I've been sucker punched. A jarring sensation slams through my whole body as my brain processes the closeness between them. His head is bowed and he's whispering to her, but he looks up when he registers our presence.

A wooden workbench and heavy anvil are behind them. The heat on my cheeks is actually coming from a corner pit fire, but my insides are burning too. The oven reminds me of the pizza oven at Giovanni's, but the oversized leather bellows at the opening confirm it's far too hot for cooking. Two long, mismatched counters line the walls on either side of the oven. Pliers, hammers, tongs, and sheets of metal litter every other surface. A barrel of water stands next to the smelting tools resting near the fire. Not only have I stepped back in time, but I would swear I've stepped right out of my own body. I do not belong here.

"Connie?" My eyes close for a moment at the sound of his voice.

I'm backing out the door. "I'm sorry. I shouldn't have come."

"No, wait."

The girl in his arms turns her head my way. Her eyes are red and puffy. He leans over and speaks softly in her ear. The guy that brought me here tries to get past, but I'm blocking the doorway. I go left; he goes left. I go right; he goes right. We pause. I back out and wait on the porch. Witnessing what's happening in there will end me. My guide follows and stands near the door. I curse my stupid sundress yet again. I can tell he's trying to not stare, as am I. Each time I chance a quick look at him he looks away, and we continue our silent parley until Rocks appears.

The girl is against his side. Her black dress is a lot less sex shop and a lot more burlesque. There is a sensuality to her darkness that makes my eyes burn green.

"This is Jeremiah and Rebekkah," Rocks says, looking at me. "This is my friend Connie Phillips." Jeremiah says a quiet hello and nods. Rebekkah flicks her waist-length hair over her shoulder, acting like she hasn't been crying and walks off. "Keep an eye on her for me," he says to Jeremiah.

I wish I'd never gotten out of my car. My stupid sundress. My stupid golden hair. The stupid cookies. And my stupid idea. I honestly need my head examined. I'm frozen, staring into his midnight eyes.

"Come in." He waits for me, but I can't seem to get my feet to move. I want to know the significance of Rebekkah, but I also don't. Part of me wants to erase today and be left with the memory of him kissing my head and never seeing him again. He lifts a hand and gestures for me to enter. I know he won't go first—ever the gentleman.

I find the motivation to move when I notice every single person in the street is gawking at us. Rocks is close behind me and half shuts the glass-fronted door. He takes my bag and places it on the thin, wooden pew style seat near the entrance. My eyes drift over his workspace—the place where he created my earrings. The place he spends his nights in human form—alone. Or is he?

"What are you doing here?" My back stiffens. His tone isn't angry, but I know I've caused him grief by visiting.

"I wanted to give you this." I spin without looking at him and dig down the side of my tote. I hand over the out of date phone.

"What?" Rocks cradles the ancient technology like a baby bird. "For me? No, Connie. I can't accept this. It's too much."

I look at him now. My emotions are bubbling up inside, brewing and ready to spill over. I need to get a lid on them. I can't have him reject my lifeline.

"It's an old piece of shit! Take it." He looks at me and frowns. I never swear and he knows it. "I'm serious. I can't contact you and it's driving me crazy. It's got plenty of credit. Look, it's just an old model. No Internet, but we can text." I will get down on my knees and beg if I have to. I've finally found a good use for my Bun Lovin' wages.

Rocks looks out the door window. The group is still hovering in the distance.

"I can't." He hands it back to me. "I can't afford this."

"But, I can. We just buy minutes when you run out. It's simple."

He shakes his head.

"Rocks, please let me do this. I miss you, and I feel like everything's broken." I swallow back tears. He's slipping through my fingertips, and I'm not ready to let go.

Rocks pulls me into the circle of his powerful arms. I pull away, fighting him. I can't get that close after what I just witnessed, but he won't let go. "Hey, it's me." His voice is solemn and lets me know he can see the turmoil inside me. "Please."

I can't deny him and collide heavily with his chest. He engulfs me while I struggle to keep the tears at bay.

"Shhh. It's okay." The smell of his leather jeweler's apron calms me—it's him. I rest the side of my head against his chest and listen to his beating heart. I don't want to let go. After a minute, Rocks pulls away and studies me. "Let's see what's in these containers that smells so good, huh, Beans?"

The Rocks I know is back. The tears have been chased away by the protection of his arms and that stupid nickname I'll never admit to loving. The lead weight is vanishing, but I still feel a heaviness on my shoulders. We need to talk.

Rocks brings each of the three containers to his nose and takes a deep breath. His smile is wicked, and he decides to sample the chocolate chip macadamia cookies first. While he eats one of everything else, I show him how the phone works. It's pretty old and there's not much to it. He can call or text. The end. I sit on the edge of the bench and let Rocks play with the phone. I've missed the joy on his face when he eats, and the phone is only adding to it. He's smiling at the glowing green screen and nearly explodes when he hears my phone chime. He's sent his very first text.

"Oh fudge me!" I exclaim.

"What?" His glow fades.

I pull out the power adaptor and want to strangle myself with it. What part of 'we don't use electricity' did my brain not comprehend? I hold the offending cord in the air.

He laughs a little. "Don't worry. I'll sort it out. You're not taking this back." He slips his hand behind the apron and slides the phone into his front jean's pocket.

"But ..."

I could stare at his smiling face all day. Rocks hasn't lost his ability to read my every mood and thought. "Zola runs the dairy. She sells cheese to the tourists, and I keep goats so I'll swap her some goat's milk for a charge up."

He keeps goats? I don't know this boy I spend so much time thinking about at all.

"Goats?" I can't help myself.

Rocks rolls his eyes. A habit I know he's learned from me. "I'm pretty sure you didn't come all this way to talk about my goats." He raises an eyebrow. I keep staring at him and he sighs. "We keep animals here, Connie."

I don't understand and my frown gives me away. "To feed on," he explains, not meeting my eyes.

Oh, good God! Right. Okay. I swallow. His stance weakens.

"Right, so you look after them and in return …" I suck at being a supportive friend, and my issue with his need for blood has to end.

"Yeah." He doesn't offer any thing else.

"You okay? Is everything around here good?" The tears cried onto his chest have to mean something. He shrugs. "You help your dad?"

"Still am."

I can take a hint. I'm not going to beg for details. I walk to my bag and stack the food containers on the bench. Rolling up the electrical cable to place it on top.

"There have been attacks," he says, quietly.

"What?" I shout. Rocks frowns and looks out the door again. We have more attention than before. "Sorry. Attacks on the Camazotz?" I whisper. My heart rate has skyrocketed.

"You don't need to worry. I'm fine. It's …"

"If you say bat business, I'll punch you." I glare.

"Well, it is. It doesn't concern you." He flicks his hair in a move that feels like he's daring me to argue.

"Fine. I won't worry. Just like I'm sure you won't worry when you know that I've got a new lead on Josie, and I'll be checking that out without you since you're so consumed with secret bat stuff."

"No, you won't."

"Yes, I will. I want answers. You know what this means to me."

Rocks rubs his face and sighs. "I admire your independence. I really do. But I have way too much going on here to add worrying about you to my list. You were *warned* to stay away. Warnings usually equate to danger. We're doing this *together*."

"Together? I don't see you asking me for help here—to sort your problems out TOGETHER."

The muscle in his jaw ticks and he leans over to whisper yell at me. "You know damn well I can't."

My eyes begin to water and I blink rapidly. "But you can share it with Rebekkah."

"That's different and you know it."

Yeah, I'm the one who's different and after today, boy, do I know it.

Rocks takes my hand in his. "You mean the world to me. Please. Please don't go alone. Just wait. You know how fragile my place is here."

The crowd that has gathered outside suddenly focuses on something else, and the movement draws both of our attention. A middle-aged man, in full leathers with thick band tattoos circling his forearms, has entered their circle. I watch as the group step back from him and lower their gazes.

Rocks tenses. "Shit. That's the Sire."

"Oh my God, the dude that runs the whole freaking colony?" My voice has risen in my panic.

"Shhh. You have to go. I'm sorry."

By the time I gather my bag and am out the door, the Sire is standing on the porch. Waiting. Watching. Judging. His gaze follows me as I try to slip past without a fuss. I don't know whether to talk to him or not. He's their king—of sorts. I have the urge to curtsey but don't want to risk embarrassing Rocks any more than my visit already has. I break into a half run and scurry through the Goth honor guard toward the path. Nobody says anything and a quick glance over my shoulder shows he's still on the porch watching. Fudge sundae!

At the signposts, my 'friend' from the entrance is talking to Scarface—about me. I know because I'm pretty confident I'm the only 'naught bitch' for miles around. I think I'm going to be sick, but when I get closer, they don't do or say a thing. He steps back, forcing me to run the gauntlet between them. When the Sire is present, order ensues.

Back in my car, I lock the door. I take a moment to calm myself and check my phone. The text from Rocks is waiting.

My head hits the steering wheel. I don't understand. Seeing those Goth, gypsy, emo girls has left me even more lost and confused. There is no way in this world that Rocks could ever be attracted to my sunshine yellow self. We are night and day. Dumping my phone in my bag, I start the drive home—the words of his text echoing the whole way.

You're my first too.

9

Visitors

THE VISIT LEFT me trapped on a seesaw of emotions. The colony is not at all what I imagined. One look at the Camazotz and it's obvious they worship the night. Seeing them talking in groups during daylight is similar to seeing a family of polar bears without snow or ice. The Camazotz belong in the shadows and their love of darkness almost oozes out of them. When Rocks and I are in our own little bubble—just the two of us together in my room— the sense of midnight around him lessens. Maybe my light evens up the contrast. Maybe together we find balance.

Maybe I'm delusional.

The glares, whispers and sneers echo in my memory. My golden hair couldn't be more of a target. I bring attention to Rocks that he simply does not need. My stomach churns. An eel or something equally as disgusting has taken up residence inside me since the visit. Those girls hate me, and my gut completely agrees.

My mood overall hasn't exactly lifted. *That woman who might adopt Rocks next* won't leave me alone. She hovers and questions, and innuendos linger in the air. Like Tiff, she has come to her own conclusions regardless of my answers. I'm tempted to leave a note on the fridge in block capitals. WE ARE NOT FIGHTING. IT'S NOT MY FAULT HE ISN'T VISITING.

The exact words haven't been said but her eyes tell me she's convinced my attitude has sent the polite, well-raised boy running for the hills. Mini is my only solace. She distracts me from the urge to text him every ten minutes. There has been no contact, and in a moment of clarity, I realized a chiming gadget would only push him further into their bad books. Cell phones are probably highly illegal contraband in the colony. I must show him how to silence it.

It's Wednesday and my school day is finally done. During lunch, I continued my hunt for Parents V1.0. The image of Josie's house on Google Maps must be the universe's way of giving me the finger. A ginormous removal van completely obscured any and all views of the home—just my luck. If the house had matched what I've imagined, then I was going to plan a visit.

"Rocks with you?" Mom V2.0 inquires.

"My day was great. Thanks for asking." I walk back out of the kitchen without even getting a drink. Maybe she's right. I'm one enormous pile of human baggage. My technology lessons can't possibly be worth putting up with the love-hate relationship I get lost in with my parents, and then there's the whole adoption hunt on top of that. Why would he bother?

It's late when I pull my window closed and switch off my lamp. Closing the window seems as though I'm shutting him out, but leaving it open only leads to more disappointment the following morning—not to mention mosquitoes eating me alive since I've removed the screen.

But the disappointment is momentarily chased away when I shut off my alarm. My screen shows a text from Rocks.

Open your window.

He's here! I fling the bedcovers off and race across my room. The wooden frame protests with the speed I shove it open. Grabbing the sill, I lean out into the morning air and look toward the trees.

The air is still. No sound of flapping wings or shrill calls.

Then, I notice the tiny velvet pouch sitting on the red roof tiles.

My shoulders sag and the wings my feet had a moment ago have fallen off. I stumble back to bed. Up. Down. Up. Down. My emotions are an elevator that can't make up its mind. He visited. The window was closed. He left a gift. I'd rather *he* was my gift.

The silver hairclips have a little metal bow on the end. I immediately slide them into my bird's nest hair. I need to feel him close. I risk a text.

Thank you so much.

After breakfast, his reply flashes across my screen.

No, thank you for my gift.

I hesitate, chewing the inside of my mouth.

You should have tapped on the glass.

I imagine the ding of his phone echoing through the empty market.

Would never wake you. You need your sleep.

I need you more.

But I don't hit send on the last message.

ARRIVING AT BUN Lovin' on Saturday night, I find Tiff inundated with hungry, young boys. A busload of boys in Tennessee colors has stormed the van. I had asked the universe for a distraction, and it appears to have answered. This starts off a run of unexpected rushes, and it isn't until half way through the shift that Tiff and I get a chance to chat.

"Is he coming?"

I shake my head, pouting.

"For sure?"

"He texted and ordered I get a lift with you." It's the first I've heard from him since our morning conversation a couple of days ago. He apologized, explaining he had hoped to see me tonight before telling me to stick close to Tiff. He also requested Josie's new address. Just like I never seem to win an argument with Rocks face-to-face, texting is no different.

I look at Tiff's sad face. "I'm just gonna walk. Make the most of these nights before it gets stupidly cold." Tiff eyes me. "I'll be fine. I promise to keep my phone at the ready." I draw a cross over my heart.

"He's so hot," Tiff adds. I shrug.

"Oh, come on, Connie," she admonishes. "Are you kidding me?"

"What?"

"Do you think he's good-looking?" Her eyes narrow. I don't want to risk any kind of move or she'll be onto me.

"Not sure." I don't need to look at her to know she's giving me the biggest eye roll.

"You are so full of it." She shakes her head. "There's something about him that I just can't put my finger on." I stiffen. Looking at her face, she stands tapping a finger on her lips. "Don't take this the wrong way, but it's, um, almost animalistic or something."

The room spins. I need to sit down.

Tiff is still dubious about my decision to walk when we close up the van. We linger for a few minutes, planning a nail afternoon with the four of us soon. Tiff suddenly puts her shoulders back, adding an inch or two to her height.

"What's wrong?" I look around and see dark shapes moving just out of the streetlight near the trees. Sounds like a few teenagers but when I squint harder, I recognize those clothes. "Crabapples."

"Sure you don't want a ride?" Tiff asks, watching the group emerge into a sliver of light.

"Um …" Lie number two hundred and forty-nine? Or the truth? "Um, they know Rocks." The truth lightens my load, but watching them in the shadows fills me with dread simultaneously.

"Oh?" Tiff doesn't look happy or even curious like I thought she would be at the mention of Rocks' friends. Her erotic romance-addled brain would normally have been imagining equally hot, available best friends. "You never told me you'd met his friends."

"Can I get that ride after all?" She nods and I know she's sensed their Camazotz side. "I just need to talk to them first."

She goes to say something but then stops and frowns. "I'll get the car." She sighs and walks off before I can respond.

The fact that the bat gang has found my place of work has the eel slithering about inside of me. Rocks said he wouldn't be here, and I know he wouldn't send my cheer squad instead.

"Hey, naught, we need to talk." I'd recognize the acid in that tone anywhere.

Stepping further into the light, I see Scarface leading the group. There are four girls and two boys lingering behind them. The hairs on my neck prickle when my eyes land on the boy with the fangs tattooed under his lip. He's not my biggest fan, and the disgust in the eyes of his friend is crystal clear. Message received.

I stand, tight-lipped. My eyes scan each face, soaking up details. Rebekkah—with no red eyes—I hate to admit is really pretty. Her features are elf-like in the dim light. Another girl around our age, who has a burst of delicate stars tattooed around her eyes, holds the hand of the girl farthest from me. It's impossible not to notice how young she is—barely even a freshman—or the angry oozing gash above her eye. It's a fresh wound and turns my stomach. Scanning her body, I see a long cut down her forearm, but it isn't as deep as the eye wound. Finally, front and center and looking as ghoulish as I remember is Scarface—Zabreena.

"How dare you mess up his life!" Zabreena spits. She steps forward, but this time I hold my ground. This is my territory—my neighborhood. Locking my jaw, I refuse to show her how much her words scare me.

"Cat got your tongue. Don't you care that his father's about to disown him after your little stunt?"

"What?" I've made his life worse.

Rebekkah lets out an ugly laugh. "You think you know him because he flipped by accident. Remember, that was an accident. He would never have revealed himself to an aeronaught if he'd fed like he was supposed to." Her stare reminds me of frozen ice.

My heart is thundering inside my rib cage. She continues, "He's going to be our Sire, and nothing you show him about this corrupt world will change that. Stay away. You will never understand him like I do—like we do." She looks for support at her sides. They all bristle in agreement. "We're his. Not you. Celand and her pathetic human phase was one thing and look where that got her. But you … you need to stay away and let him take his rightful place."

"Wait, I haven't seen Rocks since I drove up to visit."

Rebekkah looks disgusted. "Don't try to tell me you haven't been in contact using that device you gave him. Trying to lure him back with your technology. He admitted that he's been helping you. I know so don't lie to me."

I would kill right this second for a puff of my inhaler. Instead, I concentrate on my heart rate. It needs to slow down and more oxygen needs to get into my lungs. I open and close my fists behind my back. My mind is reeling from her words. I *was* his secret and now that his secret is out, it's putting his position at the colony in jeopardy.

The little one with the head wound speaks. Her tone is harder than steel. "Rockland doesn't need to be out alone risking his neck for a naught. He needs the protection of his wing. You want to see him dead like the others?" As tough as I can tell she's trying to be, there are tears welling in her eyes.

What is she talking about?

"I told you he isn't visiting me so how can he be risking his neck? And what does 'dead like the others' mean?" I demand. I look at the gashes on her head and arm.

There are rumbles of disgust from the group in front of me. I've shown them my lack of knowledge. The boys at the back aren't focused on me but seem to be watching the sky. I automatically look around myself, but what I'm scanning for I have no idea. Are there real monsters that come out at night?

"Six dead," Scarface informs me. The starry-eyed girl slips her other hand into Rebekkah's. "And eight wounded. No member goes out alone from now on. You want Rockland to become a number flying to Watkinsville? Your pathetic crush worth his life?"

I gasp and they hear it. My eyes dart back and forth. Even I can't really name what I feel for Rocks, and "crush" seems so simplistic. But what rips through me is that he told them my secret. I can't focus on that now. "You don't know anything about me." It sounds as weak in my ears as I'm guessing it sounds in theirs.

Rock is risking his life by helping me find Josie. I have to put an end to that.

I can almost feel the chill of her eyes on my skin. Rebekkah frees her hand, her gaze narrows. "You don't know anything about *him*. You think you do, but you're totally blind." Her smile makes my heart rate spike. "How pathetic. Hairclips and earrings do not mean he's yours. Rockland and I have grown up together, and our union is expected— it's a given. It's the way nature intended. He doesn't get to pick and choose like you naughts and your fleeting love affairs."

I know Rocks cares. I'm learning that he probably shouldn't, but I won't let her tarnish our friendship. When I make him laugh in my room, that is real.

"*Nature* has nothing to do with y'all. I know so don't lie to me either. Rocks is free to be friends with, or date, whoever he wants." I match her scowl. He wouldn't give me hairclips if he didn't want to be my friend. I have to believe in him and ignore these girls. "His mother chose who to marry." The second I finish speaking; my gut knows I shouldn't have mentioned that.

"Oh, isn't she sweet," Starry-eyes says. "She thinks we fall in love and get married."

Scarface swoops in. Her face shows smug triumph. "Newsflash, naught. Camazotz don't mate for life. They fuck the strongest, hottest male. It's about blood and keeping the colony strong. Rocks has got a lot of females waiting in the *wings* for his special attention." They all laugh at their little bat joke.

I'm going to hurl. I sense the hotdog that I shouldn't have eaten at the back of my throat. All I can taste is sauerkraut.

"He's ours, bitch," Scarface announces before licking her lips. "Last full moon, we hit it so hard. Tell him to stay away if you know what's good for you."

Ours? Hit it? Hit what?

Oh!

Fudge me inside out!

He can't possibly be dating all of these girls, and that little one shouldn't even be thinking about this kind of stuff. Even for a guy that looks and smells as good as Rocks, he can't possibly be juggling four different girls. The ice hockey team at school isn't even that adept. My gut is screaming that he isn't one of those boys, but that's the kicker. He isn't just a boy—he's a bat.

I stay in bed all day Sunday. Parents V2.0 take turns checking on me, but I groan and burrow further under the covers. The wounds on that little girl are nothing compared to the ache in my chest.

Rocks and Zabreena. I swallow bile.

Rocks and Rebekkah. *Our union is expected.*

Girls waiting in the wings. I can't breathe.

He shared my secret.

Has he been to Watkinsville yet?

He could get hurt or …

Sleep evades me. I'm sure my brain resembles one of those plasma globes—glowing tendrils of electricity buzzing out from every side of my head waiting to make a connection on the outside. Each time I rub my head, it only seems to focus the ache.

I trudge back over every single interaction between us—his looks; his shy smile; his gentle touches; his gifts. Never once did he take it that step further. Rocks has never crossed that line between us. We're just friends. I can't be angry with him because my feelings have changed. The tidal wave this is causing inside me is too much. I don't know what to do. Whatever I'm feeling for him must end as of now. He's not allowed to fall in love. He has responsibilities to ensure the survival of his colony. And his life is at risk every time he visits me. I can't do much but I can control one of those things.

His blood will not be on my conscience. Now that I know what he's risking, I'll do the right thing. He's always taken such good care of me and it's my turn to return the favor. My hand shakes when I reach out to grab my cell.

I can't be your friend anymore. Keep the phone.

I would never have believed that a text could end a life. That text has ended the only part of my life since the letter that felt right. But was it ever right? Or was it all in my head?

It takes me until Monday morning to finally name the emotion that has confused me.

Hope.

I had told myself repeatedly that Rocks and I were nothing more than just friends, and it's the absolute truth. We were great friends, and I liked him a lot. What my heart had recently admitted to my logical brain was that it had hope. Hope for us. Hope that one day we would find a place where we both belonged—together.

The girls and I are on our way to the parking lot. I've called an emergency mall trip as my Monday/Wednesday routine has ceased. Mary Lou is coming in my car, and Brandy is heading over with Tiff. Half of the wrestling team is loitering three cars away from mine.

"Testosterone overload at 2 o'clock," Lou says, smiling.

Parker makes eye contact and gives me a quick head nod. The guy standing with his back to us, in front of Parker, turns around.

"Hi, Tom," Tiff greets. Now I know who Wrestler Tom is.

The dark-haired boy smiles and opens his mouth to speak. Parker lunges from behind, and suddenly we're all staring at Tom's bright red boxer briefs. Parker has dropped the guy's gym shorts to his ankles for the world to see—or is it for me to see? He gives me a double finger salute as I continue past them. Lou is trying to stifle her giggle. Wrestler Tom's cheeks match his underwear, and a punching match begins against the hood of the jeep.

Brandy has to grab Tiff's arm and pull her toward our cars.

"Didn't I tell you," Lou says.

My lungs constrict. Before I can stop myself, my brain compares the midnight boy that bounces Mini on his hip to the jock, who just pantsed his friend, whom I have a date with.

WEDNESDAY AFTERNOON I stop at Sephora. The girls have commitments and new polish never fails to cheer me up. I know protecting Rocks from killers is the right thing to do, but I'm a little crushed that he never replied to my text. It stings to know that he never really believed I was going to keep him after all.

Six dead.

I can't comprehend the chaos amongst The Fold. Do the police know? I must pay attention to *that man who loves to read the headlines.*

Three bottles of glitter and four new season metallic colors later and I'm pushing open our front door.

"It's my pleasure, you darling boy. Have more." She practically sings from the kitchen. "See," she laughs, "I'm not the only one who thinks you look hungry."

My heart stops, then starts, and stops all over again. I eye the stairs and wonder if I can sneak up.

"Nee!" Mini announces. Blast that kid and her radar. She can't even see me. Her highchair is two rooms away around the corner of the doorway to the living room. I shake my head.

Entering the kitchen, I soak up the details. Mini is not in her highchair. She's in his arms, feeding Rocks fistfuls of carrot cake. Her chubby little fingers are covered in cream cheese frosting and she misses his mouth more times than she gets it. Cake is everywhere, including down the front of his vest but nobody, least of all Rocks, seems to mind.

Rocks' hair is covering his eyes. I never anticipated how much it would hurt laying eyes on him again. God, I've missed his calm spirit.

"Hi," I say. Kelly gives me her evil eye. Please tell me he didn't blab that I told him to stay away. "I'll meet you upstairs."

The ten minutes it takes for Rocks to join me is agonizing. My hands are sweaty. He walks in but doesn't sit in his chair. He leans against the window frame and crosses one heavy, unevenly laced boot over the other.

"I want to know why."

"Why what?" The tidal wave is about to flood the shore. I want to keep my friend, but I want him alive and well more. The Band-Aid must be ripped off.

He huffs but plays along. "Why you can't be my friend any longer? What's going on?"

"Where's Jeremiah?"

That catches him. His face contorts in what I can only guess is confusion. "Jeremiah?" he confirms. Rocks has no idea about my visitors.

"Your bat buddy."

Rocks narrows his eyes at me. I wish I could do this without hurting him.

"I know about the buddy protection program. If you're here alone, you're breaking new rules," I state.

He groans, rubbing his forehead and moves to sit on the bed. Once he's facing me, he asks, "Who told you?" His voice is quiet.

"Oh, your girlfriends!" I pull my best not impressed face. I know I'm acting less mature than Mini, but it cut deep that he never told me himself. He never really explained that marriage wasn't a colony option. It made my hope seem stupid—not that marriage ever crossed my mind—but where Rocks is concerned, I already feel stupid enough on my own.

"I don't have a girlfriend."

"No, not just one from what I can gather."

"What is that supposed to mean?" His shoulders sag a little. There are dark shadows under his eyes that I've never noticed before.

"Your obscene little harem. You know the ones or are there so many that it gets too confusing for you? I know for a fact that you have a Camazotz-friend? Lady? Whatever! I know. Okay."

"Well, can you inform me of the identity of my new love? I'd sure like to know who she is."

"Sca—Zabreena."

Rocks winces. "She is *not* my girlfriend." He actually looks genuinely disgusted by the concept. "Is not and never ever will be." Disgust is morphing into anger.

"I don't believe you. She told me you two were practically … bumping uglies on the last full moon." My ears begin their burn. Thinking about him having sex is not helping.

"Bumping what?" His voice has risen to that 'I have no clue what insanity is passing through your lips' level.

FUDGE!

"You know?" My vague hand gestures make him wrinkle his nose and frown.

"No."

"Sex." Ears—flame on. Not only can I feel them burn but his eyes flick to the tips of them and then back to my eyes, but what I don't expect is that he smiles—his really cute smile. The one I love that makes me want to say yes no matter what he asks. The one that makes the betrayal I felt at him sharing my secret vanish. The one I'm going to miss so much when we're done.

Rocks looks at his feet before flicking his hair out of his eyes. "Connie, you gotta believe me. I'm not having sex with Zabreena. Will. Not. Happen. Okay?" Then his smile widens even more, and his eyes sweep briefly down my body. "Can't understand why it's called 'bumping uglies' though. There'd be nothing ugly to bump on you."

My jaw has dropped wide open, and I'd bet my eyebrows are high enough that I could add them to my ponytail. How did we get here? I don't know what that's supposed to mean, and I can't think about it with him sitting on my bed, looking and smelling the way he does. This is not an even playing field.

He reaches over and runs one long finger over my knee. It tickles through the denim. "Please don't believe a word Zabreena tells you. I'll tell you anything you want to know. You have to trust me." He gaze is intent. His joke from earlier forgotten.

"I did and you told them all my secret. How could you? My best friend doesn't even know about Josie, and you told the Camazotz that hate me?"

He pales. Another secret I wasn't meant to know. "I didn't tell them about Josie—" I turn my back on him and walk to Feathers' cage.

"Do not lie to me."

"I'm not. I swear to—"

"They know you're planning a flight to Watkinsville for me."

He breathes out heavily. "Yes, I told Rebekkah about my plans. She's worried. It's chaos. But I didn't tell her why. I would never betray you—ever."

Crossing my arms over my chest, I turn and watch him. He flicks his hair back and meets my eyes. Nothing to hide. I nod, relieved that he didn't sell me out. He holds out a hand, and I take it sitting back at my desk.

"She said there were six deaths."

"Seven now. One of the injured died yesterday." My mind flits to that little girl. How could anyone hurt her?

"I'm really sorry. Did you know them?" I can barely hear my own voice.

He winces and nods. "We're one big family. The whole colony feels every single loss."

"How?"

"Owl attacks."

I lurch back. Not witches or werewolves or any other dark, sinister monster my imagination had conjured up. "Oh, like mother nature?"

"Connie, the owls that are attacking aren't usually found in our area in those numbers. That's why we settled here. The Sire is trying to get to the bottom of it. There's no doubt this is an assault on the colony."

This information makes my blood boil. "And you're not supposed to be out alone anymore," I yell. "What are you doing?" He's not going to get attacked because of me. He said I can trust him, but can I really?

"I can take care of myself."

I tear my hand away from his. The contact is fogging my brain.

"Just like Celand?" I checked his family tree the second I got home last Saturday night. Celand is his oldest full-blooded sibling. Rocks never mentioned any of his siblings being dead.

Rocks sucks in a loud breath. He stands, walks to the window and scans the sky. "That has nothing to do with this." He still isn't facing me. He is keeping secrets from me just as I suspected.

"Tell me."

"No." He turns. The hard look from when I accused him of being a monster is back. "I said it's got nothing to do with this."

Just like his sister ... the jeers from the carnival night come back to me. *Her pathetic human phase* ...

"How about us?" My voice is louder now. I can smell a rat or in this case, when a usually sincere bat is hiding the truth. "Why are you risking your life to be here with me?"

"Drop it." His eyes are hard and void of emotion.

I stand and try to puff myself up. I want to tear out my hair. "Fine. I don't really care because I'm dating now, so whatever." When the words are free, I'm shocked. It's the closest thing to a lie that I've ever told him.

It's technically not a lie, just a version of the truth, but I want him to think I have a secret too. My hand settles over my stomach, and I try not to grip it too tightly. I don't know how much longer I can prevent myself from collapsing onto the floor.

"Connie, you're not listening to me. I'm not dating those girls. I, we, I thought we …. You're dating?" He drops onto my bed, confusion replacing the anger in his eyes.

"Whatever, Rocks. Yes." Looking at him makes me want to cry. I look away.

"Yeah, well, I guess what I thought doesn't really matter then." His fingers twist together and it reminds me how my intestines feel.

I don't see why I should be the only open book. I can't stop him from keeping secrets, but I can stop him from putting himself in danger. When I see his current body language, I wonder if my hope wasn't that stupid.

After a silence that is thick with tension, he speaks. "Can you do some research on the portable lap computer regarding the owls?" His eyes are blank.

Deep breath.

"So that's why you hang around with a naught? I'm just an information source, aren't I? Is it really worth the risk?" I want to stab myself for being a bitch, but I'm cornered. He says he's not dating them, but I know he's keeping secrets.

The emotion that burns in his eyes can only be one thing—anger. Rocks glares at me like I've just turned into the wicked witch and eaten Mini whole.

"Do not use that term in my presence. Aeronaught is fine, but you are NOT NOTHING." His raised voice echoes in my room. The movement in his jaw shows he's grinding his teeth. I want him to tell me what's going on. I don't want him hurt—ever. But my gut is telling me that this isn't the first time he's argued that point. I'm desperate to reach out and hug him, but I need the truth about humans, the colony and his sister.

Rocks walks to my open window. He rarely leaves that way, especially when Kelly knows he's in the house. He speaks without looking at me, "You'll always be worth the risk."

But before I can blink, he's gone.

10
Enemy

THAT NIGHT I cry silently into my pillow. Fighting with Rocks makes me hate myself. I know he isn't entirely innocent but I regret saying some of the things I did. He's keeping secrets; secrets that I know are related to humans, but he didn't deserve my snarky attack. He also didn't deserve the jealous undercurrent of my tone when I confronted him about the Camazotz girls.

I ignored my instinct to trust him and hurt him again. He's not telling me everything I need to know. There's a history that involves his sister, the colony, and humans. Until I know what that is, I can't shield myself from the Camazotz girls properly. Information is power. They know it—and have it.

The hole in my chest just seems to vary in size these days. It's a permanent fixture I'm learning to live with. It's currently a bottomless abyss. I don't want Rocks to risk himself Friday night, but I can't stop wondering if he'll show up or not. Logic tells me I pushed enough buttons to send him packing, but his parting words haunt me; I know I'm not worth it.

Lunchtime Thursday my phone vibrates with a text.

Your mother does lives in Watkinsville.

My hand flinches around the juice box and sends OJ shooting across the lunch table. Brandy ducks but luckily the juice runs out of momentum before it gets that far.

"All good?" she asks.

My heart is beating in my throat. My mother has been located. That address really is hers. She's real. I'm so close to getting the answers I need. I can't speak. The floodgates have opened.

My reply is quick.

You saw her?

My lungs feel like they are refusing to let air in.

Yes. Briefly.

My real mother has been located—at long last. I don't know whether to laugh or cry. Then my guilty conscious forces me to send another text.

I hope you took Jeremiah with you.

Nothing.

Is your phone on silent?

That gets a response.

No. Sounds like a woodpecker is living in my pants.

The mention of woodpeckers reminds me of the owls. Fudge! He risks his life to check whether my mother lives at the new address and I can't even do a simple Internet search on killer owls.

What sort of owls?

My study hall is spent on Google learning about the Great Horned Owl. Reading that they *eat* bats almost sends me to the bathroom to be sick. Their yellow eyes give me the creeps. I'm sure Horror Movie Girl could describe the exact owl that is staring at me from my monitor. They appear in every classic horror film to witness her demise. Think classic creepy owl with a wingspan of over four feet and you've got our assassin. Tufts of feathers stick up to form eyebrow horns, arching over their deadly yellow eyes, giving the impression of a permanent angry scowl. Regardless of whether it's Mother Nature at work, that's our enemy.

Mini is out of sorts when I collect her. Her little face is red and sweaty. She cries for no reason when I strap her in the car, and big fat tears accompany us all the way home.

She won't eat. She doesn't want a bath and hurls the books I open to read across the room.

Kelly finds us rocking quietly back and forth in the wooden rocker when she gets home. Mini isn't sleeping, but she's resting comfortably using my chest as a pillow. My homework hasn't been touched, and my human brain can't work out how Rocks knows the owl attacks are on purpose.

In the quiet of Mini's room, I spend the hours trying to work out the constant churning in my gut. Conflict, I've decided is my new soul mate. One text from Rocks sent my emotions into turmoil. This can't be normal or healthy. The emotional elevator that leads to the hole inside of me is no fun. My mood is up or down, or waiting for the next up or down. I need to get a grip. I list my lunchtime elevator rides in my head. The rhythmic back and forth of the rocker helping me think.

Your mother lives there—Josie is real—I'm elated, eager, nervous. The elevator is up.

Your mother lives there—Josie warned me to stay away—I'm apprehensive, annoyed, unsettled. Elevator down.

Your mother lives there—Rocks hasn't abandoned me—I'm stunned, relieved, ecstatic. Elevator up again. I was so worried he was upset about my stupid dating remark.

Your mother lives there—Rocks risked his life for me—I'm worried, frustrated, angry. The elevator plummets down.

Your mother lives there—He thinks I'm worth it—a good dash of awww, along with honored, and weepy. Up, up, up it goes.

One text caused fifteen emotions to be dumped into the swirling tidal pool. It's no wonder my chest aches, and my inhaler's almost empty.

Mini has a temperature, and *her parents* can't decide whether to take her to the urgent care medical center or not. Dinner is freezer foraging for me and caffeine for them.

The English assignments I've been ignoring get pulled out and stared at some more. Thankfully, I'm up to date on Economics. Circling the essay questions with my red pen, I focus on nothing in particular.

I wake with a gasp.

My neck aches from using my desk as a pillow and my lower back agrees. I know about the owls. My dream was filled with dark wings and strange cries from the trees and low growling rumbles. I was crouched down looking through bars at the surrounding forest—caged.

The caged birds. Those mammoth winged monsters the Park Ranger was obviously about to let go. These aren't colony attacks. There's no mystery to solve. The colony has just been given new neighbors. Part of the hole in my chest cavity lessens. There is nobody out to hurt Rocks. It really is just nature at work.

Park Ranger released owls. I saw it.

The reply is instant. Guess he's not winging it through the forest.

When. Where.

A second later…

Cannot find the question mark. Sorry.

I bite my lip.

Day I visited. About 150 feet from your front gate.

Does not make sense. Keep looking. He replies.

I thump my forehead against the desk. If Rocks isn't happy, then I keep digging. He has never questioned my methods or hunches in relation to my parents, so it would be unfair for me to call him on his feelings regarding the birds. I roll into bed fully clothed and drift off with the promise of continuing the Great Horned Owl hunt when the sun is up.

I SCAN THE entrance to Wicked Beats between customers. With the worries of the colony going on, I know he won't have time to dance, but I can't help myself. Tiff is floating around our tiny space due to the fact that not one, but two college guys handed over cell numbers scrawled on napkins. They were both giant wiener winners.

Wiping mustard from my forearm, I peak out the van door. I didn't really expect to find him waiting, but I'd hoped. I'm about to ask Tiff for a lift, but she's texting wiener winner number one, and her smile is blinding. There's no way I'm going to be a third wheel.

I start my walk home and pull out my phone to text Rocks. Before work, I located an email contact at the National Park Service and sent them an enquiry about the release of owls in the Helen area.

Cutting through the parking lot gets me home faster; I scan the dark spaces between cars. Walking home alone after midnight isn't my favorite thing to do, but sometimes it can't be helped. Confirming I'm alone, I focus back on my glowing screen to finish my text.

Umph!

Something whacks into the back of my head. "Ouch." My hair is pulled as whatever hit me gets tangled in my long strands. I spin around and feel little bursts of air against my face. Looking up, I can't see anything. There's no moon. My spine tingles. Humans are so dependent on their eyesight and yet our night vision is a joke. I twist and turn trying to find whatever slammed into me.

"Rocks?"

A loud screech echoes from above. He's here. Another screech, higher above this time. But instead of the calmness I feel when Rocks accompanies me home, a spike of adrenaline surges through my veins. I fill my lungs to capacity and let the air out slowly through my mouth. Maybe it's just being out alone at this time of night. My gut is telling me something isn't right. I hurry, crossing the street and heading away from the shops and into suburbia.

Before my eyes can focus properly on the shadowed sidewalk, Camazotz-Rocks collides with the side of my face. I resist my urge to scream and duck down, crouching on the grass. He swoops past my head, repeatedly dipping and rising and I feel the wind from each pass move my ponytail. I turn my head this way and that, trying to catch a proper glimpse of him. He's too quick.

He won't hurt me, I chant inside my head.

His flying form flashes before my eyes, and I stand up not wanting to lose sight of him. Whack! He's slammed into the side of my head again. I raise my arm to protect my head, but he whacks me from the opposite direction.

Whack! Whack!

"Stop it. Ouch! Rocks, don't." I really want to scream.

Fur and wings and claws all blur in front of me. Rocks is screeching at an earsplitting level. A wing wraps around my head, claws tangling in my hair. Trying to protect my eyes, I stumble, and his claws rip open the flesh above my eye. The shooting pain makes me gasp. Before I can register why Rocks would do this, more wings and cries and flapping surround my head. I'm hit again. I lurch back and warmth trickles down my face. Bright blood drips from my hand when I pull it away. Seeing the blood somehow amplifies the sting from my eyebrow.

In front of my face is a jumble of leathery wings, fur and biting heads. The screeches intensify, and I freeze. There are three—no—four bats all caught in a tumbling ball of wings and chaotic movement. Almost in slow motion, I watch one bat chomp down hard on the neck of one of the others.

Eeek!

I recognize that call.

Help me!

Two words echo in a man's voice inside my head.

"Shit!" Doubling over, I cover my ears. I just heard a man's voice crying out for help inside my head. "What the hell?" Standing up, I feel dizzy. *Great, now I'm hearing things.*

The tumbling quagmire of bat limbs dips before one bat breaks free, pumping its wings to gain height. Two others break apart in chase. I'm left holding my eyebrow trying to stop the constant trickle of blood and facing a lone bat at eye level.

Rocks.

The other bats screech and tumble onto someone's lawn and to my shock are very agile on the ground. They jump and wrestle with wings catching on limbs and I worry about deadly tears across the fragile membranes. The bats launch themselves into the air and the three of them take off across the sky.

When I turn back, Rocks is standing before me.

"Oh my God, are you all right? Why didn't you scream when he attacked you? You should have defended yourself." He's moved my hand and is fussing over my eye. His handkerchief covers half my vision, and the applied pressure is oddly comforting.

I'm quivering worse than the abused kittens I've seen at the shelter. It hurts. Rocks grabs me. "Connie?"

I focus on his face. He's bending down still holding the handkerchief but pushing my head back. "I thought it was you."

The pressure on my forehead vanishes. I blink. Rocks is standing before me holding the bloody cotton, his mouth ajar. "I would *never* attack you!" The tone of his voice cuts me, and the look in his eyes hurts more than the wound above my eye. "Why would you think I'd attack you? God."

Blood dribbles down my cheeks. Rocks tips my head back and applies pressure again.

"I'm sorry. I don't know, it all happened so fast. Last time I saw you, you were pretty mad about me and the whole dating stuff."

I want to take the words back as soon as they leave my mouth. The eel is doing gymnastics or something crazy in there. I'm an idiot who never learns.

"Come on, I've got to get you home." I'm walking, being supported by Rocks. His body is stiff against my side, and looking up, I notice blood trailing down the side of his neck.

"You're hurt."

"It's nothing I'm not used to."

At my house, Rocks leads me up the porch steps to the swing. The bleeding has slowed from the pressure he's applying. Head wounds suck. I swap my hand for his, and he kneels in front of me with his hands on my knees.

"Are you okay?"

I nod. "Who was that?"

"I don't know, but I hope Jeremiah and Decker caught him. I'm so sorry." Moving my head hurts. I wince. "Easy. Don't move."

"Sorry, I thought it was you. I'm so confused these days I don't know what I'm thinking, and it's always the wrong thing no matter my intention. My instincts were telling me to scream, but I didn't want to knock you out again. I never listen at the right time. I just ..." Tears join the streaks of blood on my face. I'm pretty sure I now resemble Horror Movie Girl at her finest.

"We have to work on that, Beans." I can't even muster a smile. "Listen. You need to recognize me as a bat. Why didn't you look for my tattoos?"

I frown and wish I hadn't. "Ow, what? You think I can see black tattoos on black wings that are moving rapidly toward my face in the dark?" I stare at him with my good eye. He shrugs. "Yeah, you obviously have no idea what aeronaught eyesight is capable of seeing."

He's in a t-shirt tonight and holds his arms out straight between us displaying his tatts.

"You can see these clearly when I'm a bat."

I roll my eyes and regret it. "No, I can't."

"Shit."

Crouched in front of me, I notice every muscle in his body is hard with tension. I've never seen him this on edge. His bat senses are on high alert. At the slightest noise, his head jerks and his eye dart away. I'm not used to seeing a Rocks who isn't calm and at ease. The animal within him is barely being contained.

"I'm sorry. First, the owls and now you. I don't know what's going on. Or who's behind this."

"The girls?" I suggest. Rocks meets my gaze. Instead of dismissing my accusation, he rubs his finger along his lip.

"I don't know. Better not be." He shakes his head. "They wouldn't dare. I didn't recognize that male, but they do know plenty of other Camazotz."

Rocks stands and eases me up with him. He knocks on the door, and when Dad V2.0's eyes land on the bloody freak show on his porch chaos ensues as my attack become a storm in a teacup.

"Connie, what …" His hands are on me much the same as Rocks' before, examining every inch of my face to assess the damage.

"Sir, it's my fault." I flinch. He can't possibly be going to say what I think he is. "She was attacked by a bat. I'm sorry I couldn't prevent it, sir."

The woman who has patched me up over the years has joined his side in her nightgown, and the pitch of her voice, I'm sure, is going to make my ears bleed as well.

"Oh, Lord, the blood. What. Oh honey. Chad, get the car." It's an endless stream of mostly nonsense.

"I take full responsibility." I hear Rocks continue.

Chad allows Kelly to take over first aid duties and glares hard at Rocks. "A bat did this you say." The rise of his eyebrow shows he doesn't believe us. Ironic that when I actually tell the truth it sounds more like a lie.

"Guys, he saved me," I add. I've been pulled into the living room and am resting on the love seat with my head forced back to stop the bleeding.

"Bats? Did you say a bat did this?" she asks, looking frantically between Rocks and I. He nods. "We're going to the hospital. Rabies!"

Rocks lets out a strangled laugh before ducking his head. It's every girl's dream to spend her Friday night in emergency getting *unnecessary* rabies injections. Right now, if I could punch Rocks and get away with it, I would.

THE NUMBERS ON my alarm clock show it's three in the morning. The painkillers the doctor gave me have worn off. Two neat stitches sit above my eyebrow. Now who's going to be called scarface? I wonder. My head is pounding and it's not from the wound. No matter what I said to any adult present, none listened. I was given the first of four rabies injections. My arm is red and a little swollen; my stomach is trying to revolt, and my head is thumping. The worst part is that I'll have to go through this again in three days time. The lecture I received from the doctor about never touching a bat is still ringing in my ears. If only they knew.

After grabbing a drink of water in the bathroom, I push my window up. The darkness obscures my vision, but the cool night air helps my face relax. I rest my hand lightly on my forehead. The bandage is annoying and looms as a dark spot in my vision. I need to lie down. Before I make it back to bed, I hear three loud thumps and a cool hand from behind covers my mouth. My body is pulled back against a hard form. I try to suck in air in preparation.

The familiar voice whispers in my ear, "It's just us. Don't scream." My pulse throbs in my neck.

I turn my head and see two more dark human shapes in my room. I jerk in his arms. "Shh …" Rocks removes his hand but keeps me flush against him. My hand moves to pull at the hem of my cotton nightshirt. Not exactly what I would have chosen to wear if I had known I was going to have two strange boys in my room.

Rocks closes my door before turning on the lamp.

"You remember Jeremiah?" he asks, helping me back under the covers. "This is Ezra, his half brother."

I get a nod from Jeremiah and try not to stare at his ear. "Nice to meet you, Connie." Ezra's voice is low and really deep. It seems at odds with the short boy, fidgeting in the corner of my room. His hair is longer than his brother's, but I can see they share the same shape nose.

I look to Rocks. He places another pillow under my head and moves his body between me and the lamp. My squint vanishes.

"I wanted to make sure you were okay," he says. "Your mom didn't bake by any chance, did she?"

My good eyebrow rises before I can stop myself.

"I promised the boys food if they would leave me here with you."

"Rocks—"

"Please."

I nod. Rocks disappears, leaving me staring at the boys. I pull the covers higher. "Did you catch that Camazotz?"

Jeremiah is obviously a talker. He shakes his head.

"He got away," Ezra confirms. "I'm sorry about that." He indicates with his hand to his own eye. "It's not right to attack an aeronaught no matter what."

Rocks is back loaded with goodies. Two sets of eyes widen and the smiles that follow make my lips automatically lift.

"Promise me you'll never leave the van without me or one of these two at your side." There is no room for argument in his tone.

The three boys exit my room to sneak out the front door. It's not possible to carry that much food and fly at the same time. When Rocks returns, he sits on the edge of my bed and plays with my hand. We don't speak for a while.

"I had to see you. I'm responsible for this." One finger lightly brushes my forehead. "I shouldn't have left you alone. I just don't know what to think. Why would they attack you? It doesn't make sense." His brow is marred by a deep furrow. It's not often I get to see his forehead with his long hair. "I can't rule out that this wasn't someone from my colony who arranged this. I haven't exactly been popular since they learned we're friends."

"Why would the other colonies care?" The pounding inside my head increases. I wince.

"It's complicated." The second the word leaves his lips that gorgeous shy smile I love appears, but he continues. "Inter-colony relations are dicey at best. We take a vested interest in who gets voted in as Sire."

My brain isn't following why that could have anything to do with me. I frown. Rocks tilts his head to the side. His eyes are sad. "My association with an aeronaught makes the others nervous if I do become Sire one day. If one Camazotz colony gets discovered, it affects us all."

"Holy sugarplums."

"But I don't want you to worry. The others—they don't live in this area. We don't have much interaction so I can't work out how they would connect you to me." His long leg bounces up and down.

Hateful, despising stares fill my mind including the judgmental glare from the Sire—there are a number of candidates in the running. If they can't get rid of Rocks, then maybe they can get rid of me.

"Maybe at the carnival," he says almost to himself. "Can't be."

Rocks explains that the carnival in the forest was an invitation from their colony to the others to strengthen bloodlines. New blood. Visiting males and females—a chance to better strengthen and widen the colony's gene pool. I grab my already upset stomach. This Camazotz dating game is getting worse by the second.

Rocks' frown deepens when he notices.

"Connie," he says softly. "About the other day. It's not what you think—the girls," he explains. "I want to kick myself for not sitting you down and explaining everything from the start, but … there's stuff. You know my whole world is a secret, and my survival depends on it, right? There're lots of reasons we keep to ourselves and avoid the aeronaught world. Apart from the vampire confusion and fear of blood drinking, we avoid mixing because my colony has chosen to live by Camazotz lore—not human morals." His voice sounds urgent like he's running out of time.

I bite the inside of my mouth. His hair flops down. He flicks it back and continues. "I'm not saying we don't have morals, but we also have an animal instinct that rules us as well. A duck can't ignore the need to fly south for the winter. A bear can't decide not to hibernate this year just for fun. Salmon automatically know how to get upstream. It's nature."

"I understand." I'm trying at least.

"Do you? This is really hard to explain. A bat doesn't know how to get married. I do as a man, but my Camazotz side just wants to protect the colony. It's what I was designed for long ago. I know I told you I want to be human, but at the same time I have to protect the colony. It's why I'm so lost."

I nod. This is part of Rocks, and I have to learn to accept all of him if I want him to ever feel like anything other than a misfit. It starts with me.

A question is hovering in the back of my mind, and if I don't ask him now, I know it will fester. "Do you have kids?" I blurt out and hold my breath.

"No. No!" He shakes his head. "Although that's a sore topic with my father."

"You're so young. Only nineteen."

"I'm the freak that stepped out of 1865 remember." I wish there was some way I could lighten the load that is pressing down on him. "I'm supposed to set an example."

He's quiet for a minute or two before meeting my gaze.

"You're the only girl I have ever trusted. I care about you and admire you so much. I hate seeing you hurt. I …" He swallows. My eyes narrow when I notice the slightest hint of color appear on his cheeks. "I've never had sex as a human. Okay? I've never wanted to be that intimate before. Those girls aren't *my* choice—as a man."

Before I can stop myself, my hand flies over my mouth. He gives me a little smile and a half shrug. I can't stop the strangled laugh that escapes. Taking his hand, we both smile. Rocks is dead sexy when he's embarrassed.

"I hang out with you Connie Phillips because just like at the dance club, when I'm with you, I feel free. You make me believe that my desire to be human is a normal, natural part of me. The other Camazotz have just forgotten that side of themselves."

I wrap my arms around his neck. He laughs and hugs me back just as fiercely. "Forgive me for being such a jerk?" I say against his chest.

His lips move against the top of my head. "There's nothing to forgive."

MONDAY, I DITCH school. I feel fine but when I winced at the kitchen island—remembering I have sport today—Kelly insisted I return to bed. She wrapped me up in two blankets before leaving the phone by my bed to call her if I feel, well, if I feel "any odd feeling at all" according to her.

All weekend, my Parents V2.0 wouldn't leave my side for a second. I'm a lab experiment they're monitoring for signs of foam at the mouth or fear of water. Mini was not left alone with me all weekend, which suited me fine since I felt rotten.

My eyebrow has a nice solid scab beneath the stitches so I'm bandage free. I'm waiting in my car for Rocks. Since the attack, he's visited me late each night, and between visits I know there are aeronaught-friendly Camazotz babysitting me from the trees. His schedule is so busy at the colony that he can't get away enough and absolutely insists that I can't go find Josie alone.

I text Tiff to let her know I'm fine even though I'm not coming today. I don't want my bestie to panic. Rocks jumps in next to me, smiling. I'm a little disappointed his arms are covered up but he still manages to mesmerize me anyway. I shake my head to clear the spell his animal magnetism puts on me.

Half an hour later, I'm quizzing Rocks on road rules when my phone chimes in the center console. His eyes light up. Even though Rocks is a very proud phone owner, he isn't a smart phone owner.

"Go on."

He grabs the phone and reads the text from Tiff. As predicted, my absence sent her into a tailspin of worry. Rabies isn't a laughing matter but I can't explain to her how I know I don't have it. She's glad I'm resting up.

"Text her back." I had anticipated a happy grin but get shot with pure ecstasy instead. "Don't deviate from what I dictate, Mister!" He receives my own version of the evil eye.

Rocks bows his head over the screen and types away. It takes way longer than if I had done it, but I know the punctuation will be perfect and no horrid text spellings will be used.

He carefully places the phone back in the console and grins. When I glance over, both his eyebrows wiggle for a second.

"What?"

He looks out the window, smiling.

Josie Hendersen's house is on an extra wide block of land surrounded by trees. I pull up outside her place and just stare. Mom V1.0 cannot call this place home. The white paint is peeling off the wooden boards. The two-story house could use an urgent dose of TLC. A bucket load of money wouldn't even come close to turning it into the home I'd dreamed about. House-proud, baking Josie can't live here. Being confronted with reality I wonder why my mind had painted the perfect picture. This is a woman who gave away her baby. This is not a fairy tale with a happy ending. I'm not sure I want to get out of the car. Maybe the parents I've given myself in my imagination are the better ones to keep.

Rocks takes my hand. "You don't have to do this, Beans."

I try to smile.

There's a beat-up, faded green sedan parked under the crooked carport. The lawn could use a mow. It's now or never.

Rocks stands a little ways from the door, behind me. We wait an eternity for her to answer. When the wooden door swings back, I can't make out her face clearly enough through the heavy screen. She pushes open the screen door.

My hands fist at my side. I clench my teeth. An urge to touch my own living flesh and blood surges through me. This is where I came from. I must not hug her—unless she initiates it first. I drink in every minuscule detail about *my mother*.

There is no mistaking the fact that she is my flesh and blood. I get the first ever glimpse of how I'll age. I scan her up and down, trying not to miss any detail. Her hair is less gold since it's tinged with the first signs of grey. It's shoulder length and her skin is makeup free. Her denim shorts and baggy t-shirt are not the pretty floral dress I'd imagined. Her feet are bare, and the glossy red nails call to me.

Josie's eyes move from me to Rocks and back again. She frowns and squints—the same way I do even though I have perfect vision. I can't even imagine what she's seeing standing on her doorstep—the giant Goth boy and the tiny golden girl. We sure do make a pair.

"Can I help—" she gasps. Her hand covers her mouth. "Oh, no."

The elevator momentarily skyrockets at the fact my birth mother recognizes me, but then it plummets to a record low. "Oh, no" weren't the words my vivid imagination had convinced me she would say. There's definitely not going to be any hugging.

"I told you not to look for me." The fact that she hasn't slammed the door shut I'm taking as a positive sign.

"Mom?" The word feels wrong and doesn't fit the way I thought it might. I've hardly used it in the last three months, but my brain is refusing to label this woman as such.

"No, call me Josie," she says in firm tone. She allows us to enter.

The furnishings are rough and plain. Old furniture, threadbare carpet, and peeling seventies wallpaper are all that I can focus on. The shallow side of me is glad this isn't my home. I wince when the thought crosses my mind, but it's the truth and it's about time I started telling the truth—even if it's just to myself.

"I came to find out who you are, why you put me up for adoption, and who my father is. What's with the warning?"

Rocks and I are seated squashed together on a large armchair. It was this or he'd have to stand, and I need him close. Josie is perched on the very edge of her chair, nursing a chipped coffee mug. There are no baked goods on offer—in fact, no food at all.

"Contessa—"

"Did you name me?"

She nods. "I kept you for six months before …" Her voice fades.

So the story of the burst water pipe soaking my baby photos was the first lie of many. "Why give me up then?"

She swirls the coffee around before taking a sip. "You shouldn't be here. You might think you want to know who your father is, but I assure you—you don't. You're better off without him in your life, as am I. I won't tell you anything so ask a question I can answer while you have the only chance you're going to get."

My heart is thundering in my chest. The door I thought was opening is sliding shut, and there's not a damn thing I can do to stop it. Every angle I try is blocked. She's tightlipped about my family tree and every detail of her life.

"Fine. Are there any hereditary diseases I should know about?" I huff.

Rocks extricates himself from the chair. I grab his arm. "Just going to smoke," he explains to Josie, pulling himself free and leaving without acknowledging me.

"I'm sorry, Contessa. But this is for your own good." She smiles, but her eyes seem sad. "You've grown into such a pretty, young woman." It's the first time the tension leaves her slender frame. I wonder whom she sees before her.

"You know I didn't know I was adopted till your letter."

Her head drops onto her chest; her eyes squeeze closed. "Oh. What did your parents say?"

"They don't know."

She stands up. "Right, you're going. Now. They don't know you're here, do they?"

"But, I want—"

"You need to forget me and that letter. I mean it, Contessa." She heads to the front door. "Burn it and move on."

"I want answers, damn you!" I yell. "For three months, I've been a raging, confused mess. I've been a complete bitch to my parents while trying to find out who I am, and after fifteen minutes of your precious time, you're kicking me out. That's it? We're done?"

She stands still as a statue by the door, not one single emotion showing on her face.

"Why write to me then?" I can feel tears filling my eyes, but I won't show her how much this hurts.

"Since you're an adult now, I wanted to cut you off before you began your search. I see it was a mistake." She gestures for me to leave.

"This is bullshit!" I grab my bag and stop just over the threshold. "You're such a disappointment."

"Forget about me," she says, locking the door.

Through my tears, I make out Rocks leaning against my car and head that way.

I want to destroy something. Anything. "Fudge. Fudge!" If her garden was the manicured picture I had imagined, I'd be squashing and stomping across her flowerbed. But all that lives here are a tangle of weeds. This was supposed to give me answers. The emotions that have been added to the tidal pool inside are violent and disillusioned ones.

"Since when do you smoke?" I snap. Stopping, I let the air whoosh from my lungs. "I'm sorry. This is about her." I swipe at the falling tears. "I'm just—ugh! I'm no closer to knowing. But that woman" —I point over my shoulder— "is not my mom."

Rocks steps up next to me. Two fingertips slide up my spine from waist to shoulder. At the top, his fingers fold over and he glides them back down. The knot in my neck fades. "Get in. It's not over yet." He glances back at the house.

Rocks insists we move before explaining what he's talking about. He keeps looking at the house, and I realize that guilt is a new look on him. I turn the car around and drive a couple of blocks before he asks me to pull over.

He lifts a hip and pulls something from his back pocket—a tattered, old Polaroid. The couple, standing together, are obviously at the beach. Turquoise ocean meets a vibrant sky behind their heads. The woman is a very young Josie Hendersen. The man has his arm slung around her shoulders and a smile that doesn't show his teeth. But that's not what grabs my attention; it's the tiny baby in her arms.

"How?" I can't form a sentence. My eyes are filling with tears once more.

"I stole it." He bites his lip. "I don't smoke. I noticed humans at the club always go outside so … I flipped and went snooping upstairs. I could sense she wasn't going to help you. It was on her mirror." He admits. "It might not be your dad, but—"

"It's the only lead we've got." I finish for him. My blood is pounding and I can't look at him. He was a bat—just moments ago. I touch my eyebrow and shiver before starting the car. Rocks watches me.

Guilt doesn't suit him. "You just borrowed it. That's not stealing."

"Turn it over."

On the back written in faint pencil is the best clue we've got.

Forever, my Love.
E.A.

11
Halloween

THE THOUGHT OF driving home on an empty stomach after meeting the epic failure that is Mom V1.0 is too much for me to bear. Lunch is my treat—pizza and a hot fudge sundae. Rocks has been curious about hot fudge sundaes for a while since it's one of my favorite non-cuss phrases. Hot fudge sundaes are his new favorite.

Back in my room, we have a few hours to kill before I need to see the doctor. Mini is staying longer at the center thanks to Kelly. My anger toward Kelly has fizzled since laying eyes on Josie. I feel like a deflated balloon, and that's not how I thought I would feel after coming face to face with my own flesh and blood. The more I compare the mother I imagined to Josie, the more I realize I invented a blonde version of Kelly. Kelly is the floral-dress wearing, house-proud, gardening, bake queen. The mother I dreamed of is the mother the universe gave me. As much as I want to tell her this, I'm going to hold off until I track down E.A.

Rocks and I are sitting on my bed, and I'm memorizing every detail of the man in the photo. It's the only lead we have and in truth, it's close to useless. My first task is to get hold of the 1982 yearbook, but my gut is telling me I won't find answers there.

"I need to try something." Rocks' eyes dart to mine and away, and his Adam's apple bobs when he swallows. "I'm not sure it will work, but it's worth a try."

I don't like it when Rocks is nervous. "What?"

"I'm going to flip." I flinch. He notices and frowns.

"You're scared of my Camazotz side again, aren't you?" His hair flops down over his eyes.

"No." I can't lie to him. I just can't. "Um, yes, a bit." How does he know?

"Connie, I would never hurt you. You know I didn't attack you." I touch my eyebrow. The stitches are starting to itch.

Rocks explains that he's going to flip and land on the bed. He wants to try communicating with me telepathically. The shaman that evoked the original spell allowed the bats the ability to communicate with him and each other. It's presumed this ability was to help coordinate their surprise attack, but he doesn't really know.

"You can talk to me as a bat?" My mind flashes to standing, bleeding on someone's lawn as the words *help me* reverberated between my ears.

"Apparently." He shrugs. "Never tried with an aeronaught before."

The Camazotz talk to each other mentally in bat form. Rocks said that since he spends so much time in human form his family often fly past and give him messages. Bat to human and bat to bat works.

"Fudge me," I whisper.

"What?"

"You can. I've heard you before. I just didn't know it was you."

I explain as fast as I can about the attack, and what I heard that I had convinced myself was impossible. He sits wide-eyed in awe. "You should have told me. This is going to be fun."

I swallow, not convinced.

Rocks flips, and I can't stop myself from scooting back against my headboard. It's the leathery wings and claws that I never really noticed until the attack. I realize Rocks hasn't really been a Camazotz around me since we met.

He flips back. "I'm sorry," I whimper.

"It's okay." He grabs a piece of paper and draws a wing. His biology lesson is an attempt to convince me that his wing is not a danger to me, but all I can remember is the feeling of a claw slicing open my eyebrow. About halfway down the top of a vampire bat's wing is a large protruding claw. He points to the claw and calls it his thumb. I don't feel any better.

He flips again. I stay perfectly still, and his little bat body lands silently on the bed. Vampire bats are very agile on the ground. He tucks his wings up and squawks once. I try to clear my mind. Seeing his bat body is making my palms sweat. I close my eyes.

Nothing.

He flips.

"Did you hear me?" His eyes are dancing.

"Nope."

"Maybe empty your mind. It'll take practice." He flips.

Nothing. Three times we try, but I can't hear anything other than my internal arguing. I'm trying to convince myself not to be scared. The fear is completely irrational, but I just can't put a lid on it. If only we knew who was behind that attack.

Rocks flips back and watches me for a moment. "I want you to pick me up."

"What? No way." As an animal lover, I'm ashamed of my sudden stupid behavior.

"Connie, it's the best way to get over your fear of me. Just hold your hands like this," he says, holding his first two fingers out horizontally, "and I'll hook my 'thumbs' over here. Pick me up and have a look. I swear I won't hurt you."

I can't speak. My mouth will not open. Touching him or his claws is out of the question.

"I'm the same. It's still me, and if anything, I'm the one who's nervous here." He says, looking away. "I know that bat hurt you, but it was superficial." He holds out two placating hands, so I let him finish. "I'm not saying it didn't hurt you and wasn't terrifying, but it's just a scratch. A bat could never do you serious harm. We simply aren't built for it. My wings are my life, and you're a giant, super-strong human in comparison, who could snap them without even trying."

"Rocks—" I would never hurt him. My stomach rolls at the mention of snapping anything. Animal cruelty has always left me totally flummoxed.

"I know. But just so you know, you're not the only one who is scared. I've never let an aeronaught touch me, and I never imagined that I ever would."

Rocks sits on the bed and takes my hands. His eyes are so dark and when I look into them, I see his fear. My fear might be superficial in comparison but that doesn't mean it is any less real.

"Remember, you know my weakness. If you're really scared, just scream. You control this."

His logic helps me to find my courage. I take a long deep breath. Rocks is trusting me with his life. If I feel scared, I can end this experiment. He has given me the power.

Rocks flips and lands on the bed. I wipe my palms before placing my hands as he instructed. In two little jumps, he's next to my hands. He waits.

"You can touch me," I tell him.

He hooks his wing claws over my fingers, and I use all my self-control not to rip my hands away. My skin crawls. Slowly, ever so slowly, I raise my hands and stretch out his wings to their full wingspan. His little body hangs between them. The sun is arcing its way across the sky, and I hold him up in the light coming through my window. My breath catches.

When the sunlight hits his wings, it's magical. The dark swirls and lines of the tattoo design pop out against the paler leather of his wing membrane. The only way I can describe it is stunning. He's stunning in the sunlight.

The patterns on his arms finally make sense. In the center of his wing is a baroque style bat with its wings spread wide. It's magnificent. The filigree pattern swirls up, down and around making two gorgeous curlicue wing shapes. The remaining space along the curved edges of his wings is filled with twisting lines and swirls. The red I noticed on his arms highlights the flying bat image, making it pop.

"Oh my God, you're beautiful." My eyes roam back and forth over every detail of his wing art. "I can't believe it."

Rocks makes a little squawk, and the sound brings me back to reality. The art on his wings had totally distracted me from the fact that I am holding a real live vampire bat. I freeze.

"Do you want me to put you down?"

Two squeaks.

"Is this okay still?"

One squeak. I take another deep breath.

I don't want to hurt him, but I'm not finished studying his tattoos now that his wings reveal the design. The swirls are perfect, the detail so fine and intricate. The tattooed edges of the little bat's wings are as fine as lace.

Beans.
Beans.
Beans.

"Holy crabapples!"

That voice inside my head—again.

Without thinking, I launch Rocks into the air and cover my ears with my hands.

THUMP!

"Are you okay?" Rocks rests a hand gently on my shoulder making me flinch. "Tell me what you heard."

I'm out of breath, bending over. "Beans."

Looking up, I watch the smile spread over his face, right up to his eyes. "We did it." He hoots in celebration. I jump from the loudness echoing in my small room. "Sorry. This is massive."

Straightening up, I study Rocks' face. The fear and worry from earlier are gone. His eyes sparkle in comparison. That is absolutely the weirdest thing that has ever happened to me. Witnessing Rocks flip had previously held the title, but this is way weirder—a *male* voice inside my head I cannot control.

"Let's do it again. You were focused on my tattoos so your mind wasn't blocking me. Can you relax like that again?"

"What? Um, it's weird. Like really freaking weird."

He stills. "What's wrong?"

"It might be normal for you hearing other voices in your head, but man, that's freaky!" I wrap my arms around my body. I don't know why this is freaking me out but it is—it most definitely is.

Rocks pulls me into his arms with mine pinned between us. His body is warm, and I swear his arms can wrap around me twice.

"You're the first. I've never heard of us trying to communicate with aeronaughts. I mean, our colony—now. I didn't really believe the story. This is huge. You're helping me discover myself." I can almost feel his excitement passing from his body to mine. I sink into him. He's right. I'm not the only one to learn something about myself today, and that finally makes me grin.

"You ready to try again?" he asks quietly. I have to try—for Rocks.

A moment later, I'm standing by the window again looking at the ink work adorning his wings, but my heart is pounding. All I can hear is my own panic. I try closing my eyes, but that just makes the blood pounding in my veins sound even louder.

"Can you flip back?"

Rocks appears. I can't look at him. I don't understand what's wrong with me. This should be amazing to have my friend be able to communicate with me telepathically.

"You're still scared of me." There is no judgment in his voice.

"I don't know …" I shrug. The doctor that continues to jab me with rabies shots would have a coronary if he knew what I was doing.

"I want you to lie on the bed. I'm going to flip but not yet."

Following his instructions, Rocks sits close and requests I close my eyes. Taking a deep breath, I focus on the scent of a forest at night. He starts talking about my pet chinchilla, Feathers. He reminds me of how cute Feathers is, and how fluffy her fur feels against my neck when she sits on my shoulder. He describes the trust Feathers has in me to care and love and protect her. He asks me to visualize Feathers sleeping cradled in my arms.

I feel a small weight on my stomach. My brain knows that it isn't Feathers, but I focus on the visual. I lift my hands from my ribs and feel a little jump. It's definitely not Feathers, but I cling to the calming memory of holding her. My shirt ruffles slightly and then he's still. Lowering my hands, they fold around a warm bundle. It could be Feathers. I gently stroke two fingers down his back—that's Feathers' favorite. The fur is rougher than what I'm used to and the body shape is wrong.

Opening my eyes, I see the bat resting on my tummy in my hands. Rocks is really cute now that I'm calm. His leathery wings are folded in under his body mostly. I know that's what freaks me out, but now that I can't see or feel them, he's kinda cute. His pointy ears are hysterically large, but somehow aren't out of place on his little head. I lift one hand. His beady bat eyes dart to it immediately.

"I won't hurt you. I just want to touch your ears."

Slowly, my index finger closes in and I touch the tip. It flicks immediately. Next I study his nose. It reminds me of a little pug my great aunt used to have. There are two folds of skin like a nose on a nose. I touch it ever so lightly.

Ffffttt!

Rocks shoots backward half a foot. He sneezed. My giggle escapes, which turns into laughter that only increases every time I look at him because he is now on my stomach bumping up and down with the waves of my guffaws. His claws dig into my t-shirt so that he doesn't fall off. The claws get my attention, but he's not trying to hurt me. I place a hand around his body to secure him.

"I don't know why I was so scared of you," I admit. He crawls back up to rest on my ribs again.

I touch his nose and another sneeze shoots him backward. It's so freaking cute it surpasses Mini wearing Rocks' enormous sunglasses. I bite my lip to ease my laughter because my stomach rolls are causing him grief.

Rocks.
Tickles.
Beans.

That kills my laughter. Trying not to panic, I keep still.

"Holy crabapples, Rocks. I heard you." My heart is pounding. I heard him—a voice that's not exactly his but close to it—inside my head. "Say something else."

I stroke two fingers down his fur and empty my brain.

Cupcakes.

Laughter fills the air. "How could I have been so scared of a cupcake, sugar-addicted bat?" A floating sensation eases through my system. I'm sure it's just an overload of adrenaline, but it's pleasant. Carefully picking him up, I place him in the middle of my chest. The calmness I'm experiencing allows my animal lover curiosity to take over. I hook a finger under each main claw and open his wings. They are slightly wider than my shoulders. With his wings outstretched, they cover my chest. Two dark beady eyes follow my every move.

"I just want to touch them," I explain. It's now or never for me to get over my wing fear. "Your wings are what freak me out. All that flapping around my head the other night."

The membrane is incredibly delicate. It wouldn't take much for me to rip it. Rocks is trusting me more than I can comprehend. I run my fingers, ever so lightly, down the length of his open wing. There is nothing sinister about it. The thin rubbery surface reminds me of popped balloon pieces; it's stretchy almost. Rocks shifts and his claw brushes over my nipple.

My eyes widen. He is lying on my boobs!

"Get off, you little boob grabber," I say, trying to sit up but not wanting to hurt him. I scoop him up faster than a hummingbird's wings flap and put him on the bed. I cross my arms over my chest.

In the blink of an eye, the boy appears, his cheeks the brightest red I've ever seen them.

I scowl.

"You put my hands there," he protests. "I didn't. It wasn't me." His hands go in his front pockets. When he removes them, his thumbs are wrapped inside his fists. He shoves them in his back pockets next.

"Well, you could have moved them." I huff. He's right, I did put his hands, no, wings, fingers … Ugh! "You could have moved them."

"Hello, I am a guy. As if." One side of his lip twitches, but his eyes stay fixed on the floor.

"Oh" —I point to the window— "get out, you fiend. Out."

The following afternoon, Tiff comes home with me. She's been quieter than normal lately but is desperate to find out how my day with Rocks went. I knew I shouldn't have told her we were hanging out while I ditched, but ever since she caught me lying, I feel compelled to tell her as much of the truth as I can.

Picking Mini up from the changing table, I help push her little feet through the legs of her shorts. Once she's fully dressed, we return to my room. Tiff has a pile of six different shades of pink nail polish that she's trying to choose from.

"So you just went for a drive in the country together and nothing much happened?"

I nod, hoping my face doesn't scream that I'm lying again. Tiff studies me for a moment.

"So you absolutely aren't dating?"

"No!"

"Well, why do you hang out with him so much? What about me? If he's your secret boyfriend, then I get it, but if not, this sucks."

Holy crapabbles with sugarplums on top.

"Tiff?"

"Do not tell me you don't know what I'm talking about, Connie. You're keeping secrets from me. I know it. You know it. You thought your best friend wouldn't notice? You've been all weird and mysterious for months now."

Fudge. Fudge. Fudge. I shouldn't be surprised, but I am.

"With Rocks around there's no room for me, and like I said, if he's your boyfriend, then I get it, but ..."

My heart sinks. Never in a million years would I have guessed that Tiff felt replaced by Rocks, but when I think about it, I tell him everything. And that used to be Tiff's job.

"I'm really sorry. I know we haven't hung out much, but it's just nice to have a guy that understands me so well." I will not lie to her again today. "Don't you agree that it's good for me to have a guy to talk to?"

She looks at me from under her frown, but her lips are starting to lift at one corner. Eventually she smiles. "Shit, yeah."

"Want me to paint cupcakes on your nails?"

Tiff nods her head slowly. She's not *happy* happy, but she's accepting my raised white flag as a sign that I still love her.

An hour later, Tiff's nails are gorgeous, and she wants to say goodbye to Kelly.

"See ya, Mrs. Phillips."

"Wait. Show me your nails." Kelly grabs her fingers and inspects my work. "Lucky you. I know my daughter's artwork when I see it. My nails have been sadly neglected for months."

Good God, is it guilt trip day or something? But, Kelly's right. I haven't sat down long enough with her to paint her nails since that letter.

Dad V2.0's voice calls from his spot in the living room. "Hey, Hon, did you see the headlines? 'Mob Daughter: Authentic Witness or Rival Shutdown?' Are the police really going to take her testimony seriously?" He appears, shaking his head.

"I saw an interview this morning. The Mayor wouldn't comment on whether the Ascari girl really witnessed those murders or not. To be honest, I don't think they care. They just want to cut the drug supply off at the source and by any means possible."

I pull Tiff toward the door and away from death by parental news hour.

"HEY—THERE," I yell as I push through the front doors. The word 'Mom' still doesn't feel right even though I'm painfully aware that Josie Hendersen isn't my mom. She's my birth mother, but that's it.

The house smells amazing.

"In the kitchen, darling, is Rocks with you?"

My hands fist at my side. "School was great. I'm fine. Thanks for asking," I say as I walk into what was previously known as my kitchen which is now something closer to a French patisserie.

"What the ..." I mutter in disbelief.

"Is Rocks with you?"

"Tell me this isn't all for him?" I ask, pointing to the three different kinds of baked goods. "Mo-om, you know he isn't like my boyfriend or anything, right? Like, do you actually get that? Him. Me. Just. Friends.

And that's not 'special friends' with single quotes like I know you think in your head."

The crazy lady in my kitchen looks at me like I'm insane. Kelly had mentioned wanting to say thank you to Rocks for "rescuing me from killer bats," but this is ridiculous. How am I the insane one here? I'm not a crazy baking wacko.

"I know. I know," she says, sprinkling tiny colored sugar stars on cupcakes that would put those cupcake-baking sisters on cable to shame. "He saved you."

I raise one eyebrow.

"Oh, and he walks you home at night, and he's too skinny. He needs feeding up. He's a growing boy. His poor mother has all those mouths to feed. And you're the only one in this household that appreciates my baking."

When Rocks enters the house five minutes later, I feel like shoving my hand down the garbage compactor—not that my *mother* would notice.

"Mrs. Philips," he says, absolutely beaming at her, as he walks around the island to envelop her in an enormous bear hug. It's positively obscene. Frilly aprons and all that leather should not be seen together.

"You have outdone yourself today." He kisses the top of her head. I'm having trouble looking at him because the last time he was here, he touched my boobs. Okay, so I made him touch my boobs, which is even worse. I want to cover my ears.

My mother coos like she's turned into a freaking pigeon, handing him a plate as she dons oven mitts and reveals yet more. No, the marshmallow brownies, cinnamon rolls, and otherworldly cupcakes were not enough. She adds a tray of piping hot mini quiches to the spread.

Savory—how could the hostess in me forget?

"What are these little numbers?" He points to the quiche, and I can tell that bat nose of his has already got him excited about what they are going to taste like.

I shouldn't be mad at him. Am I mad? Jealous? No, embarrassed. Embarrassed is what I'm feeling. And maybe a little jealous. Kelly would adopt him in a flash. She didn't even bake this much for my eighteenth birthday, and that was a planned event with my friends. There were plenty of mouths to feed that night.

I want Rocks to experience all of this. I do. Of course, he's never seen a handmade quiche before, and of course, their buttery goodness melts in your mouth, but …

I don't know what I'm supposed to feel where he's concerned. He touched my boobs, but didn't really touch my boobs, and now all I can think about is him actually touching my boobs, and that night we danced. What's wrong with me? I slump on a stool and watch the show—the blissed-out Rocks show. He passes me a plate of handpicked delicacies. I want to scream and cry. He's given me the largest cupcake, the corner brownie—he knows I love the chewy edges—and a perfect quiche. His thoughtfulness makes me look like the worst friend in the whole wide world—and if you asked Tiff, she'd agree.

"Connie, your father and I received the McNamara's invitation. It's going to be between Christmas and New Year and—"

"I'm not going. I'm staying here." I cut her off.

I know where this is headed. Each year, my folks reunite with their college friends who are now scattered across the east coast. Last year, we hosted and the three other couples, along with their kids, came to stay for the weekend. Attending their reunion is worse than having unnecessary rabies injections.

"Oh, honey, please. We want you to come. Next year, you'll be goodness knows where. This will be the last time we're all together."

Rock is giving Mini bites of his quiche after blowing on the filling for her. How could his father possibly be disappointed in him? He's the most caring, responsible boy I know.

"You only want me to come so I can be the day-care supervisor while you all get drunk." It's true.

I'm the oldest by nine years and am expected to monitor the other kids. The girls are fine, but I'm convinced the twin boys, who belong to the McNamara's, have suicidal tendencies. Either that or they're going to grow up to be daredevils.

"I bet Rocks would go if his mother asked him to," she says.

Without a word, I stand and head to my room.

"YOU'RE HER NEW favorite." I'm swiveling around on the office chair when he enters seconds later. I can't be angry at Rocks for Kelly adoring him.

"No, I'm not."

"You are."

"Nah-uh." He slumps in his chair and hooks a long leg over the arm.

"Uh-huh!"

"She likes me, but she *loves* you, Beans." I glance at him on my way round. "Nah-uh." He finishes.

I smile and stop spinning. Being in his presence has a funny way of calming me down. He controls the elevator better than I do. "I have a question."

Since holding Rocks in bat form, my mind has been working overtime. I've tried to understand why the colony is so upset with him. Being a bat or a human are both parts of being a Camazotz. Technically, they were designed to be both to succeed—a bat to fly over the invaders and a human to kill them. I might not like their mistrust of me in his life, but it's really starting to piss me off that they make him feel guilty about what he wants.

"Does it hurt when you flip?"

Rocks smiles. "No, can't feel a thing. All I know is for a second my mind is blank, but that's it."

I douse a cotton pad in nail polish remover. "In movies, shape-shifters are naked." I focus on removing the miniature pumpkins that adorn my nails to celebrate Halloween. I want to redo them for the coming big night.

"You disappointed?"

My eyes snap to his. "No!"

Rocks laughs and scoots further down in the chair. He sits smiling with his fingers linked over his stomach.

"Soooo, why aren't you naked?" I know he just wants to hear me say naked again. My ears burn.

"Because that wouldn't be appropriate while your mom's home."

"Ugh!" I scan my desk for something to hurl at him. "Boob grabber!"

"What?" His voice is high enough to be a girl's. He sits forward. "Am not!"

"Boob grabber."

"Don't. I didn't. You did that." He swings his leg off the arm of the chair and leans forward. "I didn't." He pleads. The look on his face is priceless. It's what I like to call his earnest face and is my favorite because it makes him seem more of a teenager than the responsible boy he usually is.

I can't hold my laughter in any longer. The one thing I have always known about Rocks, right from the first minute I met him, is that he's an absolute gentleman. He makes a growling sound and sits back in a huff, his hair flopping over his eyes.

"Tell me how, BG," I tease.

"I will if you swear you won't call me that again."

Rocks explains that the reason he isn't naked when he flips is because of his blood. Their whole world revolves around blood—it's their life force. He says that the villagers were splattered with blood from the attack when they were cursed, so anything that has his blood on it when he flips will appear when he flips back. His clothes, boots, sunglasses, wallet all have a smudge of blood on them. There're limitations though. As a bat, he must physically be able to carry everything he has on him when he flips. If he wears too many clothes or has too much stuff, he finds it draining to fly a long distance.

"That's incredible. Don't you think?" The more I think about what Rocks can do, the more I'm blown away by it. "Both parts of what turn you into a Camazotz work together as one."

"Why is it that you see it, but the Sire can't?" he asks. "I get so frustrated with the colony for ostracizing me. I'm me—I'm one of them—one way or the other."

"Do you think they're afraid?"

"Maybe." He sighs. "No matter what I say to them, they just won't listen. I would do anything for the Sire. I do. And indulging in my human side doesn't change that, but—"

"But he's scared he'll lose you to my world."

Rocks shrugs. "And I want more choice."

"Should I paint skulls or ghosts on my nails for Halloween tomorrow?" All the bat decorations hanging from neighborhood houses have been keeping Rocks constantly on my mind.

"Connie." His flat tone draws my eyes to him.

"Yeah?" I hate it when he looks serious. "Skulls or ghosts?"

"It's about tomorrow." He flicks his hair back, and I wait. "Don't go out trick or treating. Just come straight home from school and stay in."

I frown. Kelly got Mini the cutest little pumpkin costume, and we were planning on heading out.

"Please. Just stay home." I watch Rocks twisting his fingers, and a chill runs up my spine.

"Why?" I barely whisper. My gut tells me I don't want to know, but I can't help myself.

"I can't visit. And it's not safe—for you."

My heart rate spikes. "Why, Rocks? I'm taking Mini."

That gets his attention as his eyes snap to mine. "No, you can't! She's too little and ..." He sighs. "Halloween is the only night the Sire won't punish us for—"

"FOR WHAT?" I whisper yell, leaning over the corner of my desk, aware that we aren't home alone.

"Drinking from humans."

I'm trying not to let my face show the horror that I'm feeling. Why have I never asked him about drinking from humans before? The pressure in my jaw is almost hurting. My teeth grind together. I just assumed because he kept goats that they wouldn't do that.

Rocks shifts in his seat. "I better go. Just remember, I won't be coming by. If a bat comes near you, scream as though your life depends on it."

12
Bird Lover

LIES NUMBER FOUR hundred and two through to four hundred and six—my head is pounding; I'm going to vomit; I'm too sick to trick or treat; I think those rabies shots aren't working. Parents V2.0 eye me closely, but the final lie sealed the deal. The mention of the R word and Kelly announces all festivities for the evening are canceled, and I'm on bed rest with hourly parental check ups. Mini and I are safe. I weigh up the cost of the lies and decide they're worth it.

No bat is drinking from my little sister on Halloween.

The thought of him drinking blood from any human makes me shudder. All I have done since last night is go over every conversation. Thinking back to our first interactions and the way I freaked out, I understand why he never told me this—but he should have. I believe he won't ever hurt me and making sure Mini and I aren't out tonight is proof, but I need to know more.

Are you planning on drinking to the occasion?

He answers almost straight away.

What does that mean?

Halloween and humans?

I resist the urge to cringe when I press send but I need to get this straight.

No! I don't drink from humans. You should know that by now.

Now I cringe. It's funny how you can tell tone from just little words on a screen. If Rocks knew about emoticons, I'm sure I'd be looking at a red angry face.

The added bonus I never saw coming from my fake Halloween sickness is that I'm allowed to stay home on Friday too. Kelly is so concerned about the previous evening that she takes me to the clinic herself for my third rabies injection and consults the doctor about my reactions. In her mind, my body must be infected to be reacting so severely. Once the needle has stabbed me, the lies to convince the doctor flow a little easier. He frowns. She bites her nails while rubbing my arm and soon I'm back in bed with a new book.

The downside is there is no Bun Lovin' allowed all weekend, but I feel rotten from the shot, so it's not the end of the world. I'm also not overly keen to be out past midnight until all signs of Halloween are long gone so that any rebellious Camazotz won't be tempted. I'll miss Rocks, but again I've been saved. I won't have to face him after the wrestling date. How did that come around so quickly?

I DIG AROUND in my bag for my inhaler. My lungs are wheezing, and even though I'll just be sitting in the bleachers with the girls, I don't want to cough and splutter all day. Before sucking on my puffer, I pause. Does Josie suffer from asthma? Or my father maybe? Asthma is often genetic, and Josie never did answer my question about hereditary diseases. Think that had something to do with my sarcastic tone. Maybe my father will answer my questions—when I find him.

Brandy—who is sporting her home made cheerleader costume that she wears to all the football games—knocks me with her elbow. "Lover boy is waving to you," she says, securing the second pigtail of tiny short curls with ribbons. She can do anything to her hair and still look gorgeous.

"He is not my lover." I see Parker standing at the bottom of the bleachers in his wrestling spandex. How those outfits are considered manly I'll never know.

"Go say hi," hisses Tiff on my other side.

I don't know where to look. One thing about those costumes is that they don't leave anything to the imagination. Parker is muscled in all the right places. It's suddenly a lot warmer in the gym as I descend the stairs.

"Hey Parker, good luck today." I smile and focus on his face.

"I won't be needing luck. I'll pin those girls before they know what hit 'em. We'll go grab a soda to celebrate our win afterwards, okay?"

I nod. The emotional elevator dings as the door opens. I remind myself that I'm not doing anything wrong by hanging out with Parker. The coach's whistle startles me. I smile again and head back to my inhaler.

"Do you think Parker's good-looking?" Tiff asks.

"Um ..." I watch him rooting for his teammate from the side of the ring. His hair is always painfully neat even now after two warm up matches. "Yeah. He's good-looking."

"Wow, so that makes two."

"Huh?" I eye Tiff.

"Two what?" Brandy asks.

"Who else is hot?" Lou pipes in.

Tiff smiles. I stiffen. I know that smile—the one where your secret is about to come out because the 'relationship expert' thinks it's time or this could be payback for ignoring her so much lately. "Connie has another guy that she thinks is good looking."

Banana fudge sundae!

I close my eyes as the questions start firing.

"I never said he was good-looking!" I grit out between clenched teeth. She means no harm, but I don't need any more people asking me about Rocks and especially, not today when I'm watching Parker get way too close to boys from surrounding counties. Parker's next. He struts across the mat and waves one arm in the air while the official gets ready to start their match.

"Contessa Phillips," Brandy announces. "Have you been keeping secret hot guys from us?"

"Yes, you did." Tiff grins.

"I did not!" I know I have never said those words out loud. Admitting Rocks is attractive is a slippery slope, and there are too many obstacles—blood-drinking relatives being the main offender.

Tiff rummages through her backpack. Mary Lou and Brandy are still firing questions that I'm ignoring. Parker hits the mats with a resounding "oofff," and the school supporters boo and hiss at his opponent. I try to focus on what's happening in case I'm cross-examined later. He gets to his feet and shakes out his shoulders before circling the ring. His opponent is getting an earful from our coach.

Tiff retrieves her phone and brings up her text messages. "You did," she says, triumphantly shoving the phone at me. My name and some of our recent texts fill the screen. Scrolling up the words hit me harder than Parker just hit the floor.

Have I mentioned that I think Rocks is SO good-looking? Wow.

That sneaky little bat! At the end of the text I dictated to him in my car is the extra line. He's going to pay. I just have to work out how. My ears are on fire, and I can practically feel the burn of three sets of eyes boring into me.

Tiff can't take the silence any longer and proceeds to fill the girls in on my Bun Lovin' Barn escort. She goes into great detail regarding his appearance, and I can't argue with a single description. Rock isn't just good-looking—he's gorgeous, and the shy sexiness—that Tiff tells the others he's oozing—is what makes him so appealing. The real kicker is that he has impeccable manners, a quiet maturity that I admire, and a heart of gold unheard of in a teenage boy—but he isn't just a boy.

"We're just friends."

"But do you want to be more or has Parker got your attention?" Brandy asks. She always cuts to the point.

My mind flits to the times I thought Rocks might kiss me, or when he's hugged me so tight the whole world disappeared. I remember the feel of his fingers stroking up my spine, or worse the feel of his whole body dancing against mine. Or watching him discover new food, or when he entertains Mini. I want him so badly it's ridiculous. My heart pounds as the words echo in my skull. I want Rocks. I really do, but I can't have him—it's way too complicated.

"I have no idea what Parker is up to," I admit. Tiff huffs. "Tiff, I know you think he's into me, but that doesn't make sense. He doesn't know me."

The girls go into detailed analysis of the dating game, signs a boy is interested, and tests to really make sure he likes you for the remainder of the wrestling competition. I sit and munch on the leftovers from Kelly's 'Rocks is my new favorite' feast until Parker is again waving up at me.

The girls wish me luck and send me off armed with dating game experiments. I don't even know where to begin. I have the ability to screw up simple biology labs so no way I'm getting these right.

Parker drives to his favorite hamburger diner. They make to-die-for thick shakes, which I know is all my stomach can handle. Parker orders what I would describe as a week's worth of food. I try not to think of Rocks and how many burgers that boy could inhale in one sitting if given unlimited funds. Thinking about him isn't helping.

Parker wipes his mouth and takes a break from his burgers. I sip steadily on my berry magic shake.

"I hear you're acing Economics," he says with a smile.

Penny. Dropped.

Parker needs outstanding grades to have a chance of chasing his full scholarship.

"I need a tutor," he continues. "Since you're so good at it, I thought you could help me out." His eyes flick to my chest. I casually fold my arms on the table in front of the girls.

Much to my own amazement, I can't feel my ears at all. They're not even a little bit warm. "Sure, I'll tutor you, but Economics isn't really that hard." Boring maybe, but difficult not so much.

He focuses on his fries and dollops ketchup everywhere. "It's more the assignment."

Unlike Tiff predicted, the planets have not aligned, and Venus is not in my sector. Parker just needs someone to write his paper. Mystery solved.

I ARRANGE THE last marshmallow brownie on the center of a white oval platter. It looks delicious. My payback plan for him telling Tiff I think he's good-looking is set. I wait. Thankfully, I'm home alone.

Right on time, Rocks pushes through the front door and enters the kitchen. It's become the routine—he doesn't even knock. Kelly was a hairsbreadth away from giving him his own key until Chad stepped in. As Rocks rounds the doorway, I set my laser to stun, or should I say payback.

"Hey, Mr *So Good-Looking*, see this brownie? It's the last one."

His eyes focus on the gooey treat, and that's when I pounce and shovel the entire chocolaty mess into my mouth like a sea monster eating little children in a horror movie. The effect is startlingly similar. Rocks looks as though he's witnessed a massacre. He raises both hands in a feeble attempt to stop my attack but gives up as the brownie is demolished in half a second. Crumbs litter the kitchen counter, as I struggle to close my mouth and chew. Kelly would pass out. I'm fairly certain I have chocolate on my face.

"Was that really the last one?"

He's failed to notice the fact that I called him good-looking.

Abort. Abort.

Plan backfire.

"You didn't want to share?"

Fudge!

My mouth is too full to speak.

He goes to the fridge and makes a brief inspection, but I know for a fact that nothing compares in his mind to mom's famous brownies. His shoulders slump and by some miracle, I've actually made him shrink in size. He usually takes up too much space, but my laser didn't stun him, it pulverized. I've hit hard and low—maybe too low. I remember him telling me how they share everything at the colony in order to survive.

When I've chewed and swallowed enough brownie to semi talk, I start my backpedaling.

"You texted Tiff that I think you're good-looking."

"You obviously don't think so, do you?"

His eyes meet mine for a brief minute, before he lets his hair fall over them to block me. He turns and heads to the stairs.

HOLY FUDGE!

By the time I get to my room, he's in his chair and is too quiet. I crack. Did I seriously think I could be hard-core and win? I never win against Rocks. I should know this after all our mini disagreements.

"I'm sorry I ate all the brownie." But I'm not sure that's all he's upset about.

"I'm sorry I deviated." He opens his Driver's Manual and starts to read. On my way to the desk, I shove my unlocked iPhone under his nose with my games folder on the screen.

He shakes his head and buries his nose further in. iPhone refusal is a disastrous sign.

I survive all of twelve minutes of silence, more excruciating than lemon juice in a paper cut, before completely caving like the wimpy peacekeeper I am. I can't hurt Rocks.

"Follow me," I say, exiting my room.

Knowing his biggest weakness will allow me to redeem myself spectacularly, if he'll give me half a chance.

By the time he enters the kitchen, I have the biggest, glossiest photo cookbook on the bench.

The kicked puppy watches with suspicion.

"Pick whatever you want, and I'll make it for you."

He slides the cookbook over and flicks page after page. Rocks pays special attention to each recipe and studies the photos in a way that suggests they contain the ancient spell used to change him. Four minutes later, I'm forgiven, and I know this because he gives me the shyest of smiles—just one little corner of his mouth curves up—as his long finger taps a winner.

I can breathe again.

Just to prove that I'm extra sorry for the brownie eating incident—I think I'm understanding "the punishment doesn't fit the crime" slogan

NBC was going on about the other day—I let him take full charge of the KitchenAid, but he's still too quiet.

Like always, he seems to realize I know he's not just upset about the brownie, and after the butter and sugar are creamed to perfection, he speaks. "So *do* you think I'm good-looking?"

My joy is short-lived, and suddenly I feel as though my lungs are full of all purpose flour. He catches my bug-eyed look before I can control myself, and his shoulders slump to post-brownie-gobbling level once more.

"What?"

"You heard me." He still won't meet my eye and I'm kind of glad. It's uncanny how, when you need to be at your most quick-witted and intelligent, your brain seems to short circuit.

"Look. Just wait till mom gets home if you're fishing for compliments. She's practically ready to adopt you, she loves you so much," I say, trying to make light of the heaviest situation we've crossed that doesn't involve blood or Camazotz girls.

"I'm serious, Con. I want to know what you think. You mean the world to me. You're smart, and funny and fiercely independent—"

"No, I'm not."

"You don't see it, do you? The Camazotz girls travel in packs. They never do anything on their own or think for themselves, but not you. That night we met, you got lost" —he starts ticking things off on his long slender fingers— "you broke down, you were stumbling around a dark forest alone, you discovered the Camazotz—you took it all in your stride because of your need to find answers about who you are. I don't know any girls that would do that."

I shrug. "I don't remember taking all that in my stride. I was a screaming lunatic."

"My point is you set goals, and you don't give up. You have this quiet determination that I admire, and I wish I were more like you. I know how many times you've wanted to cave and tell your parents. But you haven't. You've kept your eye on the goal. Don't you think it would have been ten times easier to just ask them? But you don't care if the path is hard or not." Rocks stands stock-still waiting for me to respond.

I can't. I don't know how to process what he's said.

"And you're prettier than all the stars on a moonless night," he whispers. "Tell me. Am I acceptable, or do I stick out like the crazy turn of the century freak that I feel like most days when we hang out? I get the feeling I'm never gonna fit in anywhere. Not here and not there."

I'm such an idiot. Rocks thinks I'm pretty, independent, and strong. He sounds so sincere that it sets off a jackhammer inside my chest. I rest a hand over my heart. He's hurt and lost and giving me a moment of honesty that I don't know what to do with. I stand before him a mute idiot and try to focus on sifting flour and adding vanilla. I will not add a lie to my collection today.

Rocks is desperate to belong. His reaction to me eating the brownie did seem a bit over the top, but he's always comparing what he knows at the colony to my world. He's trying to find a place and teasing him isn't helping. It just leaves him feeling the gap is too wide to bridge.

"You're not a freak." I kill the mixer and grab his hand between both of mine. He meets my gaze. "Honestly, you're the strong one. Trust me. I wouldn't last five seconds if I thought my family was trying to get rid of me." His frown doesn't lessen any.

"The boys at school are immature losers compared to you. So where do you belong, Rocks? You belong wherever you want to be, and if it's here, with us, then I'll teach you all you need to know. And if you think for one minute that Parker Reed could make a vest and fob watch look cool, you're completely insane."

Rocks leans over and places the tiniest kiss on my forehead. His lips hardly touch me, but the spot where they make contact zings to life. He flicks his hair, returns to his full towering height, and the mixer whizzes to life.

I gobbled his favorite food, and he told me I'm independent and strong. I think he's insanely good-looking and failed to tell him when he needed to hear it. Creepy Ursula from *The Little Mermaid* could pass for the Fairy Godmother if she stood next to me.

The next morning, I wake to find a tiny silver hair clip with a shiny cupcake on the end. My heart does a somersault picturing Rocks in his old-fashioned workshop up half the night creating my gift. But it quickly sinks when I remember I didn't give him the comfort he deserved.

A TEXT FROM Rocks arrives just as I pull into our driveway. Seeing his name on my screen always makes me smile because I know how excited he gets when he has a reason to use his favorite gadget.

Connie, I won't be visiting today. Colony business.

Our Wednesday visit is cancelled and before I have a chance to ask, I get another text.

Please don't worry. There have been more attacks. No deaths. I'm safe.

Not seeing Rocks gives me the chance to follow up on my E.A. lead. I return to Josie's old high school to scour the yearbooks.

The class of '82 doesn't contain a single E.A. student. Neither does '81 or '83. In 1980, there's an Evan Alder, but his photo is nothing like the guy in the Polaroid. No high school romance in my family tree. On my birth certificate, the box under father's name is blank. Without a name, I have no clue how to find him. I stare at the webpage offering free family searches, but without his name, I can't fill in half the form. And the only person who knows is dead set against telling me.

When I arrive home, the news is blaring from the family room. Sneaking upstairs, I log on and check my email. Nothing. My search has stalled and so has Rocks'. It's only been two weeks, but the colony needs answers pronto. It occurs to me a lie will get their attention so I open my Gmail impersonator account. Curious teenager wanting information on owls got me nothing.

Let's try annoyed, irate, local bird lover a hairsbreadth away from complaining to some higher body about pesky new owls she saw released in the area that are killing her homing pigeons. Lie number four hundred and twelve is a good one. I almost want to pat myself on the back for this stroke of genius. Send.

With nothing to do, my mind wanders back to Josie. Could I trick her into telling me his name? No chance. Josie is one tough nut. Rocks said I was strong, and even though I imagined Mom V1.0 as an almost carbon copy of Mom V2.0, I now know I get my determination from Josie.

I head for the family room to watch Chad while he watches the news. "Hi, honey," he says, without looking up from the newspaper spread across his lap.

I collapse in the chair opposite and study him. The disappointment of Josie has made me hesitant about imagining my real dad. I don't want to make the mistake of taking the best parts of Chad and giving them to the grainy face in the Polaroid. Chad turns the page of the newspaper and simultaneously flicks the remote. The opening credits of the international news hour begin—his timing perfect. How does he focus on the TV and read at the same time?

"Whatcha reading?"

He looks up and smiles. "About the crazy crime rates that are skyrocketing. You need to be careful coming home late at night. Drug-related muggings are getting out of hand. Police are at a loss. Taking down organized crime is one thing, but how do you trail after the ever increasing number of cocaine addicts in the city?"

I blink so my eyes won't have that glazed over look. Josie turned out to be the opposite of Kelly. The thought that Dad V1.0 won't care about drug addicts, crime statistics, and police man power problems makes me smile—but not for long. Chad is my hero, and he's never let me down until the whole adoption secret.

The first time I volunteered at the dog shelter, I had no clue that my four-hour shift was solely going to consist of picking up dog poo. Chad had walked me in to make sure all was safe. When he saw the look of disappointment on my face that I wasn't going to be playing with puppies the whole time, he rolled up his sleeves, swapped his shiny leather shoes for the hiking boots in the trunk and grabbed the pooper scooper. Two hours later, I was swamped with puppies vying for my attention.

If there's one thing that I learned from finding Josie, it's that the blank father box on my birth certificate doesn't hold much promise.

Friday brings more disappointment. Rocks texts again to inform me to wait for an escort home from work, but that it won't be him.

Tiff is wiping out the wiener pot. Tonight will go down in Bun Lovin' Barn history as the night we ran out of wieners. It's the first time we've ever sold out of hot dogs.

"Rocks coming tonight?" Tiff asks.

I shake my head. "Why did you tell Lou and Brandy about him?" I send a quick text to Rocks explaining why I'm heading home early. To say I'm nervous about 'the escort' is the understatement of the century. If any of those girls show up, I'm sleeping in the Bun Lovin' Barn.

"'Cause I can't work out if you *like him* like him or not. And I still think you're up to something."

Nothing gets past Tiff. I miss honesty. I know all the lies are the reason I'm so confused and pissed off half the time. Her comment about feeling replaced echoes in my head. I did that to my best friend and she isn't mad. She isn't ignoring me in the halls. She's just waiting patiently for me to return to her.

"It's complicated."

The dishrag flies at my face, but I duck with plenty of time. "We're teenagers. How complicated can it be?"

"His family doesn't approve of me—like can't stand me complicated."

"Well, that sucks," she says, making a sad face. "It's not exactly the end of the world though. You wouldn't be the first couple who've dated behind their parent's backs. If you like him and he likes you, do it."

"That's just it. I don't know if he *likes me* likes me." Can I trust my gut? Are my instincts right where Rocks is concerned? A kiss on the cheek instead of my forehead would've been a sign. He does want to know if I think he's hot though. But admiration? Admiration and attraction aren't the same thing.

"Sometimes you've just got to stick your neck out. If you're not living life on the edge, you're taking up too much room."

We close up and Tiff heads to her car. There is no boy or bat waiting. I check my phone. I just want to go home, but Rocks made me promise. The memory of blood trickling down my face makes me shiver, and I rub my scar. Owls aren't going to attack me, but Camazotz might.

I pace back and forth behind the van. If I run, I'll be home in half the time. I text Rocks again.

Nothing.

Promises suck. The old crate behind the van digs into my thighs. I'm not going to do anything stupid. I keep screwing up where Rocks is concerned, and my gut is telling me not to walk home alone. I'm going to trust my instincts for once. I need the practice, and Horror Movie girl would be proud.

An hour later, two dark figures instantaneously appear a foot away causing a small shriek to escape before I get control. The last thing I want is to embarrass him.

Jeremiah is unmistakable, but the guy next to him is not Ezra. I don't move a muscle.

"Connie?" the new guy asks. He bends down to crate head height. "I'm Decker, Rockland's coolest brother. He has entrusted me with your safety and wellbeing for the evening."

I smile. His eyes remind me of Rocks when he's high on technology. They're kind. The tension eases out of my neck.

Decker is seventeen and not only Rocks' half brother, but also one of his best friends. His grey t-shirt shows off full arm tattoos that match his brother's tatts. Rocks and he obviously visit the same artist.

Jeremiah pulls a pocket watch from his vest and clicks it open. He looks at the van.

"You're not late," I explain. Jeremiah makes me nervous. "We closed up early. I tried to tell Rocks—" Stop talking now. That phone is top secret. I slide mine into my bag with as little movement as possible and stand.

"I know you gave him one of those telephonic devices." Decker smiles. "It's his pride and joy, but the Sire probably wants to flog you with it."

Holy fudge, does every Camazotz know?

Decker laughs and I squint. Is he joking, or am I really enemy number one?

"Anyhow, Rockland is—" He lifts both hands and makes little flapping motions. "On patrol."

Confirmation that Rocks is a bat when the owls are still attacking makes the pit in my stomach deepen. He said he was safe. I can't panic. I have to trust his judgment.

"Rockland tells me you make a 'mean dog,'" Decker says. A distraction is exactly what I need.

"Oh, really?" I smile. I haven't given Rocks a free hot dog in ages and make a mental note to bring him one next time he walks me home. "Ah, I don't actually have any dogs for you guys tonight."

Sugarplums! The last time Rocks' friends helped him we paid them off in baked goods.

I look back and forth between the boys. "We sold out."

Jeremiah's mouth twists, but Decker breathes an audible sigh of relief.

"I'm sorry, Jeremiah." He shrugs and starts to walk in the direction of my house. I know it's shallow, but I'm relieved to be on his good ear side.

"Don't be sorry," Decker says, gesturing that I should go before him. "I'm a vegetarian."

"Really? How does that work?" My brain can't grasp that concept. Isn't blood a protein? Or does he not drink from meat eaters? What?

Jeremiah stops dead and turns around. "You're a *what*?" His voice is loud and unexpected. So he can talk—just not to me.

"I don't eat dogs."

"Since when?"

They stand face to face. "Since I knew Connie cooked the poor creatures up and served them in buns."

"Oh, no—" I say.

"You would so feed off a dog, Decker. I know you would. Maybe not a cat … I'd draw the line there unless I was desperate, but definitely a dog." Jeremiah crosses his arms.

I watch the conversation go back and forth. Rocks is open, but at the same time I never get free information without donning my Spanish Inquisition hat. I wonder for a second if I make Rocks doubt who he is. Is it me that's making him feel ashamed of his world?

"'Maybe not a cat?'" Decker repeats. "Are you planning on losing the other ear? That's a death wish dinner if ever I heard of one." Decker mirrors Jeremiah's body language and crosses his heavily tattooed arms as well. He's only a few inches taller than I am, but there is something in the way that he moves his body that reminds me of Rocks.

"You just got to be quick," Jeremiah shrugs.

"And get your wings shredded. No thanks."

"Hot dogs aren't dogs," I state. Both boys focus on me. "It's not made from dog meat."

Decker frowns. "Well, why are they called dogs?"

I laugh. "I don't have the faintest idea." So many things in my world must seem ridiculous to them.

"Well, you're not going to get employee of the month, are you, Beans?" he asks with a wide smile.

Beans.

My heart flutters. Maybe I'm not such a dirty little secret after all. Decker doesn't seem as though he wants to do away with me and hide my body. Jeremiah I'm not so sure about, but Decker is without a doubt friendly. They walk on and I follow.

We're silent for a few blocks, but my mind is screaming a thousand questions.

"So everyone's okay?" I look at Decker. "You know, from the recent attacks?" I don't want to get Rocks into any more trouble. I'm not sure what I'm supposed to know.

"Sort of," he says quietly. "Bailey might lose her eye, but she's alive so that's good, right?"

My blood runs ice cold. "Bailey?" I half yell. "Little Bailey? No. She's what … five?" The dog I ate earlier rolls around.

Decker looks at Jeremiah and back to me. "Yeah, she's five. I'm impressed you know who my little sister is. What else has Rockland been telling you?"

I know Bailey is the reason Rocks is so Mini obsessed. He misses his baby sister because she's mostly a bat due to her age. I have to keep reminding myself that the owls are just owls and don't know they are attacking five-year-old girls. They're just trying to survive in nature. It's not personal.

"I'm so sorry, Decker." I raise my hand to touch his arm, but catch myself. I drop it back to my side and look away. Aeronaught germs probably wouldn't go down well.

"Thanks. She'll be okay. I hope." We continue on.

I want to text Rocks and tell him how sorry I am, but I know he's busy. He must be devastated. I wish he'd told me.

"Is there anything I can get her?" I have no idea if this is appropriate or not, but I want to help.

Decker laughs. "Nah, she's got Zada doting over her, but that's very kind of you, Beans. You're alright for an aeronaught." I look up in time to see him wink.

I stop again. At this rate, it'll be dawn before I'm home. "You don't, um, hate me?"

Jeremiah snorts and continues walking. Decker answers, "Nope, I can't. You make my brother smile in a way I've never seen before. He's been sad for a long time. I worry about him out here for sure, but I don't hate you."

Decker could answer my questions about Celand, but he's being so nice I don't want to push my luck. Not belonging might make Rocks lonely, but sad?

"Do you approve?" If I can gauge how he feels about humans in general, it might help me understand something about the mystery of his sister.

He shrugs and pulls a face. "I'm not gonna scare you away like the others would, but, I don't know. It's fraught with danger, Connie." He points to the red scar above my eye. "And not just that kind either."

13
E.A.

DECKER TURNED OUT to be the chattiest bat I've met. He's a sweet boy, and I like him a lot. He prefers savory snacks to sweet, and while sitting on the porch swing, devouring the leftover mac and cheese, he told me about the new job Rockland has been given by the Sire.

Apparently, Rocks is part of the official envoy to visit one of the other colonies in the coming week. The other colony had ordered some goods from the market that are ready for delivery, and the Sire thought it was a good opportunity to see if they are also under attack. Decker wouldn't tell me where Rocks was headed exactly, and he bristled when I asked him, leading me to think the colony locations are a guarded secret. I know Rocks has said their colony roost is highly classified, but why would they care about the other colonies? I guess bats of a feather—wing—stick together.

The down arrow chimed on my emotional elevator when Decker confirmed I wouldn't be seeing Rocks for a while.

It's Monday afternoon and instead of quizzing Rocks on his Driver's Manual, I'm in the library with Parker. He was serious about the tutoring, and after brushing him off twice, I figured I might as well just get it over with. I do feel traitorous spending time with him on a Rocks visit day, but colony business still has him absent. I haven't had a single text in ten days.

Ezra and Decker were on escort duty this past weekend, and those two bats are fun. I almost feel as much at ease with them as I do with Rocks. The two of them are best friends, are the same age and hero-worship Rocks. This information surprises me since Rocks thinks everyone is trying to vote him out. But the boys insist they aren't the only ones at the colony who feel Rocks is destined for leadership. I had to bite my lip from saying that the weight of impending leadership is nearly killing their friend.

Poor Rocks.

Parker has decided to write his paper on the pros and cons of building stadiums with government subsidies. I can guess already what side he's going to take, and I have to restrain myself from yawning. This should be almost comical, but the annoying part is that I'll have to help him with his research.

"Did you do this topic?" Like he needs to ask.

"No."

He watches me and I imagine Tiff bruising me tomorrow if I don't report having played nicely. "I discussed how effective cigarette taxation is and whether or not the amount collected offsets the increased pressure on our health care system."

Parker's eyes glaze over. It's going to be a long afternoon.

I seemed to have found more information and highlighted more points in fifteen minutes than Parker has in the entire hour we've been here. I mark two more sections and slide the journal articles I printed earlier across to him.

When I stop, Parker is just sitting and watching my methodical research methods.

"What?" I lift my copy of *Essentials of Economics* and block all sight of my boobs. I'm not in this library because I want to be, so I don't want to make the experience any more pleasurable for him.

"Got Thanksgiving plans?" he asks.

"Yeah, family stuff. You?" The ease with which I talk to Rocks has abandoned me.

"Same. Dad's taking me hiking though so that'll rock." He flips his pen over his thumb with his index finger. "Can I take you to the dance?"

Parker's eyes scan my face, and I bet he's seeing the shock and horror written all over it. I thought this was about grades—him and me. "Don't look so scared, Connie. I don't just want to study with you."

Huh? Are my ears working properly? "Say again." It's a struggle to fill my lungs with air. Shallow breathing will have to do for now. "The dance?"

"Yeah, we could go together." He frowns. "You haven't been asked already, have you?"

I shake my head, blinking.

"Well?"

The reappearance of the girl who goes mute when talking to boys couldn't be timed any worse.

"You really thought I just wanted to study with you, didn't you? I know my wrestling doesn't impress you. In fact, the stuff I do that leaves the cheerleaders crying for more, you ignore. So I went for the study angle."

Parker Reed wants to impress me. Me. Parker Reed! And me!

It's the first time a guy has ever admitted to trying to impress me. I smile. "Okay, yeah, let's go to the dance."

Parker will never be Rocks, but I can't have Rocks the way I want him. Maybe dating Parker and being friends with Rocks is how the universe thinks it should be.

I'M DISTRACTED AND my Hemingway essay is getting worse by the second. Thanksgiving is a week tomorrow. My vacation will officially start in two days. I want to get a bit of work done before it starts so I can slob around the house for the whole nine days.

Rocks is supposed to be sitting in his chair. He's back and I can barely contain my excitement. He's supposed to be helping me because he loves anything and everything related to literature, but he's been lured to the kitchen. Kelly's trialing new dessert ideas for Thanksgiving, and Rocks is the judge and jury—or the pig in mud, as I prefer.

My sister is chanting, "Rocks. Rocks. Rocks." Which in two-year-old speak—that Rocks is fluent in—means again. I have a funny feeling the thubalup, thubalup, thubalup sound effect that is echoing up the staircase is supposed to be a horse mid gallop. And if I was a betting girl, I'd put it all on the fact that she's currently slung across his back and doing laps around the island bench while mom plates up the next morsel. They've missed him. We all have, and since he won't be able to join us for Thanksgiving dinner, Kelly is going to stuff him full this afternoon instead. I'm actually looking forward to watching him taste his first pumpkin pie.

Tiff thinks Rocks is emo cool. Big freaking marshmallow is what that boy is. He's left his jacket on the chair, leaving his tattoos proudly on display. The effect on my internal temperature reminded me of Fourth of July bottle rockets. His arms are glorious now that I understand the pattern, and the bands of ink make his muscles pop. Without thinking, I pick up his jacket, hug it to my chest and take a deep breath. *Rocks*. The smell of a cool moonlit forest night fills my lungs. His wallet falls to the ground and pulls me from my temporary moment of insanity. If he found me sniffing his clothing, I'd die. Sniffing him that one time was bad enough.

Picking up his wallet, my curiosity wins. I can't help it. The heaviness makes me wonder what could be in there since every item has to come in under a total weight. I don't know what I'm looking for, but I wasn't prepared to find the picture of Rocks and me. Where his license should be is a picture of us. The quality isn't great as it just ordinary paper. We look happy.

I remember the afternoon in my room when we played with photo booth. I'd printed those shots, but don't remember him taking them. He must have swiped this one when I wasn't looking. Back then he hardly knew me. Back then I hardly knew him—or anything about the Camazotz. I didn't understand what the colony meant, or how he fit into that life and to some extent, I know I'm just scratching the surface.

I replace the wallet and jacket on my way to retrieve the laptop from my parents' office. Hemingway can wait.

Firing it up, I check my email. The search for my father is dead in the water, but I'm hoping to get a response for Rocks.

"ROCKS!"

They've replied, but it can't be right.

Rocks tears into my room and stops behind me. His hand slips over my shoulder. "What's wrong? Are you okay?"

"Read this." I point to the email reply we've been waiting on. "You were right."

Rocks leans over and his scent distracts me.

"Shit!" He slumps into the chair. "Sorry, sugarplums," he corrects, looking toward the door. "I just can't work it out. Ugh! What am I missing?" he says in a louder voice than usual.

The National Parks Service has confirmed that no owl relocations or releases have occurred in the Appalachian Mountains this year. The email informs bird lover that she must have been mistaken in seeing their logo, but they would greatly appreciate any and all details to track down who is responsible. It does not miss my attention that lying gets better results than telling the truth. Is this what I need to learn in order to be considered an adult? Is this how all adults operate? But I have a more immediate issue to focus on.

"Someone is targeting your colony. But why? Do other aeronaughts know about you?"

"A few. Like you, sometimes the secret gets out."

"Could it be one of them?"

"Don't even think that." He sighs. "Please no. That's trouble that *we* don't need."

"The other colonies?"

Rocks rubs his temples. "The Sire suspects so and that's where I was last week. We went to take a look around. We had an order to drop off so it was a good excuse. They said they've been under attack as well."

"Really?" Does this mean all the Camazotz are under threat?

"I spoke with one of their Fold members—Océano—she seemed nervous. She … I can't describe it."

"Of course, she's nervous. If they're being attacked and killed too."

He shakes his head. "I don't know. They had a new truck."

"So?"

"We have an old beat-up van to get supplies when we need them, but they have a brand new one. That's a lot of cash for a colony to lay down on one purchase."

The Sire and their Sire—Saturno—had a long meeting, Rocks explains. The topics were Sire to Sire only, but afterward his Sire seemed convinced that Saturno isn't behind the attacks.

"They explained the new leather harnesses we made them were designed to carry a large number of bats by other bats."

"Huh?"

"Strong bats fly connected to the harness carrying the elderly and young pups. They're gearing up for a colony move." He steeples his fingers and rests them against his lips.

"Why don't you all move?" The thought of Rocks moving away sets the eel loose.

"Not possible. It's a huge undertaking. We live under the radar to a certain extent and that many people suddenly showing up in a new town would bring attention we don't want or need. Finding a suitable location is extremely difficult. There just aren't that many places for us away from aeronaughts. Setting up the marketplace? No, that's a headache we don't need."

Opening the bottom drawer, I pull out the purple sparkle gift bag and hand it over. The contrast of color against his dark leather is a little frightening. Rocks peers inside slowly, and his frown is replaced with a cute smile.

"They're called Beanie babies."

"Bean's babies?" His face lights up.

"Almost." I smile. "They're for Bailey, but I didn't know if …"

The pain I was sure he had been hiding flicks across his features for a split second. "I'm sorry I didn't tell you. She's … well, it was so close. I don't know what I would have done. I should've been there."

Oh Rocks. I want to slap my forehead for not connecting the dots correctly. Of course, Rocks would feel responsible for not protecting his littlest sister. "It's not your fault."

Rocks nods, but I know how that brain of his works.

"Will she be allowed to have them?"

"I'll make sure of it. She'll be the envy of all the pups. You might be able to sell these next time you visit." He smiles, but it doesn't reach his eyes.

Rocks sits the dark magenta wooly mammoth on one knee, the pastel tie-dyed peace bear on the other knee, a hot pink seahorse joins them, followed by a dark brown moose and that hardest one to find—

the little black bat with orange lined wings covered in gold stars and moons.

My selection, at first, only included bright colors, but remembering the mini Goth kids in the forest, I added the two in earth tones.

"This is too much, Connie." His head falls to one side, and I watch his gaze roaming over me. Warmth bubbles up inside my chest, lighting the next rocket for launch.

"No, it's not." I touch the cupcake clip in my hair. "But don't let Mini see those, or you'll never get them out of here."

Rocks folds himself into the chair. I know he needs time to think. The email changed everything. He was counting on the National Park being responsible. The alternative is far worse and sinister. I open Google but am stumped on where to start. Owl sightings? I stare at the screen.

After a moment, Rocks speaks. "Why don't you search for your dad? I want to talk to the Sire about that email."

Every search on Josie Hendersen I did never had any links to a person with the initials E.A. I hate to admit it, but the sinking feeling deep inside my gut is telling me the search for my real dad is over.

I retrieve the Polaroid from my bookshelf and study it some more. There's absolutely nothing in the photo to give me any clues. The beach is generic and could be one of thousands. Is this Georgia or some place way more exotic? I contemplate going back to Josie and quizzing her on holiday locations. The problem is I know she'll have missed her photo by now and will be onto me.

My eyes wander to the boy in the corner. He's reading about wireless Internet from information I collected at the mall. He thinks the colony should connect to the modern world, even if only by the Internet at first.

Sometimes the things that I notice in detail disturb me. Do I notice and remember the headlines of the morning paper? No.

Do I notice the price of gas so when I have to fill up I get a bargain? Nope.

But do I notice that Rocks' eighteen hole gigantic boots are never laced correctly and are also laced differently every time? Hell, yeah.

He has one leg hooked over the armrest so his boot is easy to study.

"What's with your laces?"

"Hmm?" His eyes are soft. I'm hoping that means he's been distracted from thoughts of Bailey.

"Your laces are always wrong—but different wrong."

He straightens his leg a little to stare at his foot.

"Taking notes are we? Surprised you'd notice." He grins.

Notice?

I notice every darn thing about you, bat boy!

I lean toward him and whisper at the same volume that Mini does. "I can teach you how so you can be like the big kids."

He grins, but before it turns into my favorite one, it fades. Sadness fills his features instead. "Can you teach my baby sister? She helps me get dressed if she's around. She thinks I need help because Zada doesn't live with me like she does with the little ones. Bailey worries. Acts like she's my mother." He looks at his laces again. "Once I re-tied my boots at the shop, and she noticed and cried. With her eye gone, they're getting worse." He focuses back on the paper in his hands.

Fudge!

I know he's thinking about her, and I hate feeling so useless. "Will she lose it?"

He nods.

"The doctors couldn't do anything?" The thought of explaining to a five-year-old that she's lost an eye makes mine fill with tears.

"Don't make me laugh." He stops and takes a breath. "Sorry. I'm sorry. The Sire won't allow it. There's a woman at the colony we go to if we're sick."

"Tell me she's not a witch." I need a distraction because the thought of them not taking her to get proper medical attention when her eye was at stake is making my hands shake.

"No, I guess you would call her a medicine woman. She collects herbs and roots from the forest, but what use is that to save an eye?" His voice is loud again. "Sorry. It's another sore point between the Fold and I. We're dying, and they won't seek help that's available."

"I'm so sorry, Rocks. I really am. Can she reverse the curse?"

He frowns and shakes his head. "That power's long gone." He sits forward and takes a deep breath. "But I do think that's why the Fold keep her around. They like to believe they have the power to change us back, but choose to stay as Camazotz. It's just ignorant Camazotz superiority if you ask me. But enough of that. Distract me with your evil modern gadgets, will you?" He smiles.

"Um, we could watch some TV?"

He grins. "Yes! I've been dying to watch some of that."

"Why didn't you say?"

He shrugs. "I'm happy no matter what we do. It'll be another first." He winks.

Chad is perched in his chair, bent over his newspaper. The remote balances on the armrest.

I'd explained how the remote control works while we were still in my room. Since I have no clue how the remote actually 'talks' to the television, I told Rocks it was aeronaught magic. Seeing his wide-eyed awe made me laugh.

On my way past, I casually nab the remote. With my back toward Chad, I present the Instrument of Power to Rocks. He gingerly accepts and I mime pointing it at the TV and show him the channel change button. Taking a seat, he aims and fires. The channel flips up one station and Rocks is spellbound. I can't decide if he's more impressed with the animated bumblebee buzzing across the screen, or the feeling of authority that possessing the remote instills.

"Hey." Chad looks to the empty armrest and then to us. "I was watching that."

Rocks dumps the remote on my lap as though it's electrocuted him. "You're reading." I respond.

"And listening," he counters. I switch it back since there's only ten minutes left.

"Fine. But I get to pick the next show." I grin. It's been too long since I've sat here with him, and he nods before returning to the newspaper. Angling my head, I zone out the newsreader and focus on Rocks. Pretty sure watching TV is going to be a new favorite.

Rocks stares at the screen. I stare at Rocks. He's so cute when he's excited by technology or food. I'll never tire of witnessing it.

"Connie."

"Hmmm?"

"Look." Rocks jerks his head at the screen. The newsreader prattles on about the scene Enzo Ascari caused by appearing at court today for the commencement of the Vipers trial. I stare back at Rocks confused and raise my eyebrows. "Look at *him*," he whispers.

The story switches to a video of a cat riding a surfboard and not appearing at all fazed about being soaking wet. Rocks acts like he sees that sort of thing every other day, grabs my hand and pulls me back up to my room.

"What?" I ask as he shuts the door. Every muscle is tight across his back.

He points to the laptop. "I need you to do the googling."

I don't correct him. "What do you want me to google?"

"Enzo Ascari. That man from the television."

"Ok-ay, then." I do as he instructs, filling the screen with results.

"Can you make that man bigger?" Rocks points at a thumbnail of a man in a dark suit.

A few clicks and after a moment the page loads.

"Ascari leads the Mob to a new high," the headline reads. A picture of a middle-aged man in a suit leaving an Italian restaurant is below the headlines.

Rocks moves closer to the screen. I scroll down to read about the drug territory war between the Hong Kong-linked gang and the Ascari family. The article questions whether Ascari will take over more territory if the Viper's boss winds up in prison.

"Go back up," Rocks says.

"What is it?"

"Look at him, Connie. *Look*." I look at Rocks and not the screen. The tone of his voice is making me nervous. "He's got blond hair."

"So?" It's obvious that the man didn't know the photo was about to be taken. He's following another suit down the few stairs to the sidewalk. If I had to describe his mood, I'd say content but not exactly happy. It's the set of his eyes and mouth—there's just a hint of a smile, but no teeth are visible.

Rocks grabs the Polaroid and holds it next to the screen. "I think it's the same man," he says.

Rocks has clearly lost his mind.

"Look at his eyes—don't focus on his glasses, just his eyes. Connie, stare at each facial feature. Compare them. It's him." My heart begins to pound. It can't be. This man cannot be my biological father. Rocks keeps talking, as I focus on each part of the man's face. "Enzo Ascari— E.A."

"Uh-uh, no." I try to swallow, but my throat appears to be full of razorblades. "Please, no." His hair is longer—almost shoulder length and the dark rimmed glasses make it difficult—but there's no doubt it's an older version of the same man.

A gentle hand runs up and down my back. His touch helps, and I take a gasp of needed air as I fumble for my inhaler. "Can you search for more photographs of Enzo Ascari?" Rocks asks.

I nod and return to Google, but my fingers are shaking so much that they're not even close to hitting the right keys. Rocks turns the laptop toward him and follows my instructions to bring up hundreds of images, from newspapers clippings to mug shots, of Mr. Enzo Ascari.

Flopping back on the bed, I cover my face with my hands. I'm related to one of the biggest drug dealers on the East Coast. My real dad is a criminal. I hear Rocks typing. I need to calm down. I lean closer and breathe in through my nose and concentrate on the clean forest scent. It helps a little.

"Look," he says softly. Rocks' fingers pry my hands away from my face. He's enlarged a single black and white newspaper photo of Ascari. It's dated 1990 and is so similar to the man in the Polaroid that they could be brothers.

A strangled sob escapes me, and the tears flow unleashed from the depths of my emotional pit. "This is a nightmare," I cry.

Rocks pulls me under one arm against the side of his chest. His other hand strokes down my ponytail. "I got you," he whispers. "It's going to be okay."

How? How is the fact that my father is a wanted criminal—probably responsible for thousands of drug-related deaths—ever going to be okay?

But one thing's for certain. The father that I had tried to imagine is definitely not a hero.

14
Thanksgiving

PULLING THE COVERS over my head, I sigh. I've made it through the last two days of school and am on vacation. The days are a blur, the only memory standing out is seeing Rocks point to a picture of Enzo Ascari on my screen.

My father is a drug lord.

My father is a wanted criminal.

My father is an evil murderer—or at the every least, he's the man who gives his henchmen the command to kill.

Each time I try to convince myself that he might not be my dad, I take a look at the photos. Each time, there is no doubt that the man holding the baby in the Polaroid is a young Enzo Ascari. So if I'm the baby, then he's my dad—the end. And that makes perfect sense with Josie's warning about not wanting to know his identity. Of course, she wouldn't want me to discover I'm the offspring of a monster.

After Rocks left the other night and I stopped crying, I read as many articles on Mr. Enzo Ascari as I could stomach. What that man has allegedly done is sickening. One newspaper columnist had the balls to say he thought the guy was a genius due to the fact that his empire has dominated the market after less than twenty years in the game. Game? Who is this freak that calls himself a journalist? Selling drugs to kids, money laundering, and silencing people to get away with it is no game.

Oh crabapples, I'm beginning to sound like Chad.

I think about how my life would be if I hadn't been given up for adoption. Does Josie still see Enzo? Why is she living in that dilapidated house? Maybe she's hiding from him. Was I just an obstacle? Did he force her to give me up?

Questions buzz though my brain, and I can't answer or even logic out an explanation to any of them. I haven't eaten, and when my stomach rolls, I wonder how I'm going to force enough food into me later to appease mom.

My parents.

Parents V1.0 suck! Parents V2.0 I don't deserve.

I've been so angry and frustrated at them, and they turn out to be the best parents a girl like me—daughter of a drug lord—could be given. The elevator has broken down somewhere between my fourth and fifth rib. I rub my chest.

Do they know the truth? Is that why they're willing to lie to me for a lifetime about my adoption?

The pit widens and deepens simultaneously. The mix of emotions I'm adding to it is seriously out of this world. If they know, I can't blame them for wanting to keep me safe. In fact, that makes me want to run to their arms and hide there forever. But if they do know about Enzo, then maybe that explains why they were so strict when I was growing up. It wasn't about protecting their precious child, but about squashing any tendencies from my paternal side.

Ugh! I don't know. Finding my parents was supposed to clear my confusion. I don't think I want to know where I belong now. I expected that finding my parents would make me feel happy and relieved to know the truth. I didn't expect to feel fear. Fear of what I have to lose. For the past four months, I haven't appreciated how precious Parents V2.0 really are. What if I tell them and they don't know? What if what I discovered makes them not want me anymore?

ROCKS SENDS THE boys to do aeronaught protection duty for both my work shifts. A text Monday morning surprises me.

Can I bring the boys for a visit today? Please ask your mom.

All my girlfriends are in the TV room having a *Fast and Furious* marathon. Tiff forgets all about the guys on screen and their crazy stunt driving when she finds out who wants to visit.

"How's my hair?" Tiff asks, sitting up from being sprawled all over the couch. Brandy reaches over and messes it even more, and the two of them end up on the floor in tangles.

I find Kelly on the back porch watching Mini ride her toy pony round in circles.

"Can Rocks bring some friends over?"

"Friends? Hungry friends I hope. Of course, he can." She's glowing. For some reason, it makes me sad. I text him that they better be hungry—like those boys ever aren't.

"Girls, I'm going to need your help," she calls from the kitchen. When we go to investigate, we witness a rare phenomenon—Kelly is in a fluster. "Did they say what time? How many friends? Oh goodness, what should we bake?"

"We?" I repeat in alarm. Not exactly what the girls and I had planned. We're only up to movie three and have our marathon carefully timed. But my friends are always keen to sample Kelly's baking so we follow her orders without question. Once the oven is packed to capacity and there are trays of cookies waiting for oven space, we head to my room.

"Okay, Brandy and Lou, you work out if Rocks is into Connie like I think he is. Okay?" Tiff announces.

"No. There will be no monitoring of us." I groan.

"Come on. You're hopeless when it comes to signals, look at Parker. You were convinced he couldn't possibly like you," Lou adds. Reminding me of Parker is not helping my mood. Parker had texted me a happy vacation message, and I know I didn't give him my number.

"Did you give Parker my number?" I eye Tiff. All she does is smile, showing all her teeth. It's a little scary. "You're evil."

A knock on the door empties my room in a millisecond. By the time I make it down the stairs, I'm greeted with the sight of Rocks holding Mini and staring wide-eyed at the semi-circle of women. There are three frozen figures behind him, each looking equally nervous.

"Tiff," Rocks greets quietly.

There's a collective sigh—which includes one from Kelly—and I know I need to take charge. I'm pretty sure Rocks' tattooed arms are what have the girls caught in a state of delirium. Some days it amazes me that the Camazotz can be seen in public and yet keep their secret identity hidden. They draw attention without even trying. It will be interesting to hear how Brandy and Lou describe them later. Will they notice anything mysterious about them?

Ezra, Decker and Jeremiah are all in attendance, and I can't wipe the smile off my face at seeing them perched on stools around our kitchen bench. Way too much dark denim and leather is keeping the girls entranced and hopefully not focusing on me at all. Rocks is off to the side throwing Mini in the air, and her squeals are the only sound—other than chewing. The boys don't know where to look and are keeping their mouths full of cookies, cupcakes, quiches and pie—I'm guessing in an attempt to avoid conversation. The girls haven't eaten a single bite and are staring in a way that's making me uncomfortable—Kelly included.

I seriously wonder if it's a Camazotz mojo thing, and if I was this embarrassing when Rocks and I first started hanging out. My burning ears answer that for me.

I re-load the boys' plates and corral everybody into the TV room. Silently thanking up above that we didn't opt for the *High School Musical* marathon, I hit play. The awkwardness evaporates as Brandy starts explaining what they've missed. Seeing the awe on Ezra, Decker and Jeremiah's faces when the cars drift around corners during the first high speed chase is priceless. Rocks follows me out of the living room, watching the huge screen over his shoulder as we go.

Once in my room, I get his full attention.

"We need to watch more movies together," I say.

He nods and grins, his eyes sparkling. "I'm so sorry. I didn't know you were entertaining."

"Pfft, you've made their year. I won't hear the end of this for quite some time." I smile, grabbing an envelope off my desk and handing it over.

Rocks never expects gifts, so each time I give him something—regardless of how small—he acts like the earth has stopped spinning on it's axis. It's an event. It's embarrassing, but it makes my heart flutter all the same. He pulls out a high gloss photo of us from our photo booth session. I printed off a couple of my favorites yesterday at the mall.

Rocks tries to suppress a smile and lets his hair fall over his eyes. I can tell he's trying to hide from me. "Thanks," he says to the photo in his hands. I bend my knees and get down into his line of sight.

"You're welcome."

Rocks pulls out his wallet. "Did you know?"

Now my ears change color. "Yep."

Nothing more is said. I watch him pull out the tattered paper image and replace it with the glossy wallet sized one I ordered. I admire the ink work on his arms before finally looking up at him.

"You look tired."

He nods. "Three more deaths. The Sire's beside himself."

"What?" I grab his arm. We're standing face to face. "Another attack?"

"Yeah, that's why the boys are with me today. Connie, it's … I just … " He slumps down on my bed, resting his elbows on his knees and covers his face.

"Your family?"

"No, none of ours or the boys'. From one of the anti-aeronaught wings that I don't get along with. That doesn't change the fact that they're still part of the colony, and it's still a hit to our numbers."

I sit next to him and wait. We make a pair. I have a family tree I'd rather bury, and Rocks is burying members of his family tree at an alarming rate.

"There was a Fold vote two nights ago on moving. It was rejected this time, but the numbers dying are getting harder to ignore. We have to do something."

"You said moving wasn't an option."

He explains that some of the Fold members requested it, and the Sire decided to put the decision to a vote. It would be selfish of me to tell him that he can't leave me even if it endangers his life, so I don't. The hole expands a little further. Wanting my friend safe should be my priority, but I want him close more. I do what Rocks does when I'm sad or upset. I rub my hand up and down his back. He glances at me sideways from under his hair, and I catch a glimpse of a smile.

Tiff pokes her head around the doorway, and her eyes bug out of her head. She regains her composure before Rocks looks up. "Sorry."

We both stand. "We're coming." Rocks leaves my room first and Tiff hangs back.

"I have an idea," she informs me. I'm not even sure I really want to know.

Back in the kitchen, the boys are eating while we take a movie bathroom break. "So what schools do you go to?" Tiff asks.

Eyes flick back and forth nervously. Rocks answers, "We're home-schooled together up in the mountains."

That gets the girls buzzing and questions fly, but Rocks handles them all in his stride. I notice how he manages not to lie. It's impressive. He could teach the Phillips family a thing or two.

"What a pity you boys miss out on the fun of high school dances. Surviving them is like a rite of passage," Tiff adds. I freeze. She wouldn't dare.

Brandy and Lou explain to the boys about themed school dances and all that's involved. Ezra asks if school dances are similar to the club Rocks has obviously told them about. My skin tingles with memories of dancing body to body with him in the darkness, feeling his heat, and his hips guiding mine in moves I never knew I could do. The mind reader must know, and when I steal a quick glance in his direction, he raises one eyebrow at me. Goodbye breathing.

Tiff continues, "Oh, not as hot and steamy as those club encounters. I've seen what Rocks gets up to outside that club." All eyes are on Tiff—the boys included. "Guess that's what Connie is looking forward to with Parker in a few weeks time." She winks at me, and then laughs, acting as though she hasn't just dropped a bombshell.

"Making out behind the gym is part of growing up," Lou explains to the boys. "I should be so lucky." They all look at Rocks. I want to punch both my friends—hard. I chance a look, but he angles away from me.

"Guess we do miss out then," he states, "since we don't even have a gym." His voice is cold. He stands tall. "Come on, we should be going."

Rocks leaves without saying goodbye to me. I retreat to my room, and my friends make it in before I can lock them out.

"He likes you," they all sing in chorus.

"So?" The eel is back making my gut churn in an unnatural way. "Doesn't mean anything is going to happen!"

"I'm just giving you options," Tiff informs me.

"Tiff, this isn't a romance novel!"

THANKSGIVING IS A total write-off. The memory of Rocks storming out with a cold look in his eyes haunts me. It wasn't my fault, but guilt clings to me because maybe I should have told him I was going to the dance with Parker. If we really were just friends, then I would have told him. The fact that I didn't bounces around in my head. I stay in bed as long as I can get away with. Mini needs entertaining while *the mom I'm so glad I was given* finishes preparing a feast fit for a King, Queen and all the royal court.

To avoid interacting and to give me time to sort out this catastrophe in my head, I take Mini to the park. She'll sit on a swing for hours so long as she's being pushed. I take my position behind her cute little butt and launch her skywards. She squeals with delight, and the rhythm helps me to relax.

The girls are all convinced he likes me.

The girls don't know crap about Rocks or the Camazotz.

Rocks is pissed about the dance.

The only thing that confuses me more is why I didn't tell him myself. The guy I'm trying to bury my feelings for can change into a bat.

A bat. A freaking bat!

And the cherry on top is that my real father is a drug-dealing scumbag murderer.

When did my life become such a freaking freak show?

The cold November breeze flicks my ponytail across my face. I look around and notice that most of the other kids have left the park. A bird chirps from the shrub near the swings. A glance at my watch tells me I'm going to be in trouble. Grabbing Mini, I double-time it back home.

As expected, there is a slightly irate woman waiting on the porch. "Where have you been? You didn't take your cell. We're supposed to eat in ten minutes, and you're not even dressed. Give me Jasmine."

I skip showering and pull on my floral dress and cardigan, re-do my hair and race downstairs. I really didn't plan on pissing her off today.

Chad is seated at the table in his dinner jacket, no tie. I expect a frown, but instead he glances toward the doorway before speaking.

"I know that kid never wants to come home once you get her on the swings," he whispers across the most impressive feast. Table magazine should really be here to photograph it.

"She'd sit there all day and night if you let her," I say, waving my own olive branch.

We sit in silence, and the aromas of each dish slowly mingle in the air. Maybe I am a little hungry after all.

Kelly appears with Mini in her new dress. It's apple green with white trim, and I know it will be covered in food shortly. "Pie," she says, pointing her chubby finger at the golden disc in the center of the table.

Kelly leaves and reappears carrying the fattest turkey in history. We'll be eating that thing for a week. Once it's safely joined the other masses of food, she takes her seat.

We give thanks. Chad starts and lists all of the things in this world he's thankful for from the past twelve months. My eyes dart to his when he lists me as a precious gift. Kelly continues and I'm not surprised that Rocks has made the cut this year. She's sorry he couldn't be with us to share our Thanksgiving meal, but grateful that he has blessed our lives. I listen to the rest of her list. Halfway through, I catch myself about to make a mental snarky comment. But she doesn't deserve it. I'm a liar as well. And her lies, at least, were for my protection. That's the thing about lies—they're evil and insidious. They remind me of weeds. No garden is without them, but if you're not careful, they'll take over and choke out everything else. Some weeds even look like flowers and will fool you into believing they're the real deal.

I can't speak. I don't know where to begin. Am I thankful for that fateful letter that has changed the way I see my whole world? Am I still the girl that sat at this very table last year? How can I be when all I've done is lie lately? My eyes fall on Mini. Her innocent, sweet self is oblivious to the evil in our world. She smiles, baring her handful of teeth, and it melts even my tainted heart.

I understand why my parents wanted to spare me the horror of my real identity, but I wish they would've trusted me with the truth. I think over my actions and attitude for the last four months and know I've probably confirmed to them that I'm too immature to handle it.

"Mom. Dad. I'm thankful for you both." Those words are hard to spit out considering the circumstances. Two tears run down my cheek before I can stop them because it's actually the truth. "I'm sorry—" I want to say for all the lies, but don't "—but I am thankful for you." I want to ask when they think I'll be old enough to handle the truth, but don't. Instead I get up and walk to Mom's side. I hug her over her shoulders from behind.

"Oh, darling. You know I love you too." She holds my arms.

Next is Dad but he stands up and hugs me tight to his chest. His cologne is familiar, and I realize just how long it's been since I've been close enough to smell it on him. I kiss Mini's head and return to my seat, wiping my eyes.

This meal is going to be a Phillips' affair. The Hendersens and Ascaris are not welcome here today. I want a break from feeling lost, angry, and unsure. I want to be the girl who sat here last year with not a care in the world.

ROCKS HAS BEEN 'busy' all week. He won't reply to my texts. I thought we'd be hanging out heaps during the day since he's safe from nocturnal owls, but he doesn't show once. My vacation sucks. My guilt over the dance has morphed into anger. How dare he be pissed off at me? It's not like he's ever asked me on a date. I need to get out of the house.

Friday, Kelly has to work so I'm stuck with Mini. I pack her into my car, and we hit the road. My gut is screaming at me that this is the worst idea I've ever had, but I ignore it. I'm not listening. I know what I need to do, and I'm doing it. I'm closing the door on the chapter of my life that I never should have opened in the first place.

Pulling up outside the run down house, I have a moment of doubt. This might be stupid, but I'm here now. I pull Mini onto my hip and we head up the path.

Josie is not amused. "I told you to forget about me," she hisses through the screen door.

Holding up the photograph, gains me entrance. In the lounge, Mini is happy on the floor with her books. Josie sits perched on the edge of the chair, just like last time, nursing a cup of tea.

"I knew you'd taken it. I just couldn't work out how," she says.

I look away. "I'm sorry. He did it for me, but I've come to return it. I don't want it."

She takes the photo and sips her tea. A cold breeze flows through the open window with the promise of fresh air. I eye the stale carpet and wish I'd brought Mini's baby blanket.

"You know then?"

I nod.

"I told you not to dig, didn't I? Not exactly the fairytale I'm sure you told yourself was waiting for you."

"Look, I don't need a lecture from you. You started all this with that stupid letter. I know now, and yes, I wish I didn't, but I do. So it's done. I'm the spawn of Satan. I get it, thanks, *Mom*!" I move to pick up Mini. I won't stand an ear bashing from this woman who didn't want me. I'll accept lectures from Kelly because she at least has better taste in men.

"I'm sorry. I don't know what else to say except I'm sorry. He's—" she starts.

"Don't!" I stare at her. "Don't you *dare* start to tell me stuff about him now. I don't care if he's got a caring side that you fell in love with. He's an evil monster. How could you?"

"It's complicated."

I. HATE. THOSE. TWO. WORDS.

"No, it's not. There is good, and there is evil. And he is evil. Pretty simple. But don't worry because I will be staying as far away from *Dad* as possible."

She sighs. "Thank, God. He's more trouble than even you can imagine. Forget he exists."

"Already have." I pick up Mini and gather the books around her one-handed.

Josie opens the door and peers out before she lets us pass. Is she expecting to see someone lurking in her overgrown weed bed? The only other vehicle is a telecommunications van across the wide street. Digging up ghosts even spooks adults, I'm learning.

The whole drive home I memorize and catalogue the things I noticed about Josie Hendersen. I know I'm never going to lay eyes on her again, and even though I'm disappointed about whom my real mother is, I don't want to forget a single detail. She's my flesh and blood, even if I'll never admit that fact publicly.

Mini dozes for most of the way. I hate waking her before she's had enough sleep so I drive slowly down the back streets near our house. I figure each extra minute of rest is a bonus for her. A block from my house, the van in my rearview mirror is wearing my patience thin. I pull over briefly to let it pass and the sound of my indicator blinking on and off must wake her.

"Truck," Mini says from behind me.

"It's a van. If only they would teach their drivers not to tailgate, huh, cutie?"

15
Piercing

THE TRIP TO return the photo has me mad—raging bull on the streets of Spain mad. Josie's lips were sealed shut when I wanted to know who my father was, but the instant I discover that fact on my own, she's ready to tell me all about him. No thanks. I know too much already, but the hypocrisy is not missed.

Bun Lovin' Barn is the last place I feel like being. The sight of Tiff has me breathing fire. She never should have mentioned the dance or Parker. That choice should've been mine. I can't even think about Rocks. That hurts too much. The boy with perfect manners would never leave without saying goodbye—unless he was angry. But *we* aren't dating. I'm free to go to the dance with whomever I please. I think about having asked Rocks instead and what my night would entail. I squeeze my eyes shut for a second before opening the wiener pot. The tongs miss every dog I try to grab—slippery suckers. Once I have one firmly in the bun, I slam the lid. It clangs in the confines of the van.

"Don't be mad," Tiff says, loading up her dog with onions.

"I didn't wreck your vacation," I say to her quietly.

"I didn't wreck it."

"Well, why has he been avoiding me?" I eye her quickly before handing the dog out the counter window. The look on my customer's face tells me my smile is more menacing than friendly.

"He's just jealous. He'll come around."

"You make him jealous, and I pay the price. Hardly fair!" Having stewed on it all week, I'm mad at myself. If I'd told him about the stupid dance, he wouldn't be avoiding me.

Once our rush is over, I retreat to the back corner of the van and check Twitter.

"Oh shit!" Tiff says.

I'm not going to fall for her diversionary tactics to get me back on her side again. I need to focus my anger because she started this whole mess. I don't care how many hot guys she can see.

She bites her nail and keeps glancing at me and then out the window.

"Stay there," she says. That's it. I'm looking now. Joining her at the window, I scan the street. A few drunks are milling about, but nothing out of the ordinary. Her line of sight zeros in on the club.

"Sugarplums!" I turn away. That is not a sight I want to witness. I squeeze my eyes shut as tight possible.

The momentary flash of Rocks in the dark alley making out with some blonde girl is burned into my eyelids.

"I'm sorry," she whispers.

"Happy now?" I return to my corner.

Tiff follows. "It's just stupid boy jealousy."

"Yeah, he's so jealous of me that he needs to measure her tonsils with his tongue." Tiff winces and walks back to the window to serve a waiting customer. I press my nails into my palms as hard as I can. I will not cry.

When customers swamp Tiff, I'm forced to help her. My eyes are drawn like magnets to the alley, but I force them on the customer at the window and nowhere else. I focus on buns and dogs and condiments. The smell of sauerkraut hits me as I heap spoonfuls across a hot dog.

The next customer enters my tunnel vision. Rocks. Tiff is hovering, and I know she will save me from serving him if I give her any sign at all.

"What do you want?" I cross my arms.

"Whatever you'll give me, I guess. That's how this works, isn't it?" His eyes are dark.

I lean closer to the window. "What's that supposed to mean?" I hiss. The guy next in line frowns at me.

He shrugs. "You tell me."

There's a fire incinerating my internal organs. My blood is boiling, my hands are shaking, and I imagine my eyes are glowing bright red. I narrow them at him.

"Fine." I grab a bun and slap a dog in it before shoving it out the window. It's the bare minimum I can get away with. "That's three dollars!"

Rocks halts and his gaze burns back at me. "Fine!" He pulls out his wallet. Inside it, there's a photo of us sharing a happier moment, and that memory cuts me to the core. He lets the bills fall to the counter and storms off.

Watching his retreating back makes me feel like I'm Mount Vesuvius in the making. If I could get away with hurling hot dogs and squirting sauce at every customer in line, I would. Instead, I leave Tiff with the line of hungry clubbers and race outside. Rocks is around the back eating his poor man's dog. My feet stomp across the sidewalk.

"Listen, I know who my stupid parents are now, so I won't be needing your help any longer. Thanks and goodbye!" The words burn my throat, but I'm not going to watch him with other girls. The Camazotz plagued me enough without random girls from the club joining the equation.

He stops eating. "What?" I'm waiting for a yelling match, but he just frowns. It just pisses me off even more. I want to throw something.

"You and me are done. I see you've found a new aeronaught to teach you things, so get her to bring you into this century."

"Connie—"

"Rocks, we're done."

"But we're friends." I can't look in his eyes. All I see behind mine is him kissing that girl. Kissing the girl that should be me. How did we end up here? I like him. The girls are convinced he likes me, but here we are nonetheless.

"Friends come and go. There's no *blood* between us," I spit. "Go home. I don't need your escort services any longer!"

The van shakes from my rage as I slam the door. Tiff has started our clean up routine. The serving window is closed, and I don't fight the tears that spill down my cheeks. I ignore the fact that I'm crying, and after one glare, Tiff follows suit.

The walk home is freezing. Tiff offered me a lift, but she's on my sugarplums list, and I hope the walk will calm my filthy temper. I need to remember to bring a thicker jacket. My spine tingles and I rub my folded arms. I spare a glance over my shoulder. Dad would kill me if he knew I was walking home alone—again. Halfway there, I catch the outline of a bat under the streetlight. I'm not alone. The tears from earlier threaten to start again, but I will not cry in front of him. I hold my head up and double my stride.

On the porch, I turn around and look up to the heavens. There's no sign of him, but I know he's lurking close. "I'm serious, Rocks. This is it. Goodbye."

SATURDAY, MY MOOD worsens after Kelly—Mom?—Kelly begs me once again to go with them on the McNamara's reunion weekend after Christmas. I'd rather invite the Camazotz girls over for a nail night. Josie and Enzo are *not* my parents, but the guilt I feel for poor Chad and Kelly in the adoption gene lottery is intense. What are the chances of adopting a mobster's spawn? I mean really. Part of me feels that I should distance myself from them now in case the truth ever comes out. Bet the McNamara's wouldn't be so keen on me babysitting then.

I shove my wool jacket on the coat hanger behind the van door. Tiff hands me my black apron to tie around my hips. I need to make peace before we go back to school.

"I'm sorry. I'm still pissed, but just so you know, I told Rocks not to come around anymore." I hold up a hand. "No, I do not want to discuss it."

"I'm sorry too." She hands me some tongs, and we prepare for our night.

The first thing I do when it's time to head home is scan the sky. I spend a good few minutes using all my senses the way Rocks always talked about. I can't see a thing, but human eyes can trick you. The wind cools my face as my ears search out bat tones—nothing. I listen to my gut. The previous night, I had a feeling I was being watched. It's a creeping feeling that I've sensed a bit lately. I'm now paranoid as well as friendless. The coast seems clear. I had thought about driving tonight, but parking is impossible and having to explain why Rocks wasn't going to walk me home to Kelly was more than I had the strength to tackle.

Five minutes later, I discern the soft flap of wings. I smile automatically before I catch myself. He should not be here. Looking up, I spy one lone bat high above. The dark skies don't reveal any other protection program members tailing him. I pause and wait for him to lower to eye level. He must have something to say.

"Rocks, I told you no more. And you shouldn't be out alone," I state. He flits around my head in slow circles staying well above eye level. "I mean it. You shouldn't." I try to follow him with my eyes but stop when slight dizziness takes hold.

He flaps hard and ascends into the dark sky. "Just flip already!" I call up into nothing. I hear loud, sharp screeches somewhere above me and keep walking. I'm in no mood to play bat hide and seek. There's a small park a few blocks ahead, and I'm guessing he'll meet me there if he's going to flip. I walk along, keeping an eye out. Why did he come back when I told him not to? My elevator can't decide on up or down.

At the park, there's no sign of him. Alone, I would never enter this place at night, but sometimes Rocks and I cut through it to save a couple of minutes heading home.

I scan the skies. "I'm going to go in since you're here, but it's against my wishes. No use wasting time though." I'm glad nobody is nearby to witness the crazy girl talking to thin air.

The grass absorbs my footsteps as I head right and toward a cluster of small trees. The bat comes shooting out of the branches like a canon ball and nearly hits my head.

"Hey! What the fudge?" I shout. I look around to see why he would come at me at such speed. Was that a danger warning? I scan the shapes in the surrounding garden bed for anything vaguely human. Maybe there are some homeless he wants me to avoid.

Annoyance joins the other emotions swirling around in the pit. "Just. Flip." I scowl. I'm sure he has a clear view my face with his superior bat vision.

Instantly, there's a dark figure inches from me. I jump back with a small shriek. "Stop being a—" I gasp. It isn't Rocks. "Who are you?" I take three more steps back, but he's stepping toward me each time. I can't get any distance between us.

The darkness of the park makes it hard to get a good look at his features. He's taller than me, but isn't one of the boys I've seen—I don't think. His features don't have any tattoos or disfigurements. The only part I can focus on is his largish nose—nothing else out of the ordinary. I want to look over my shoulder, but I can't risk taking my eyes off the looming figure coming at me. "Who are you? What do you want?"

He chuckles. "Not so keen now little naught, but you invited me to flip."

"I thought you were someone else." I stumble but catch myself. I'm back on the path that heads toward the pool, but the trees are blocking me from the street. This is not good. My hackles are standing on end.

"Disappointed? I'm not. You look good enough to eat." I watch him lick his lips. His eyes flick to my boobs.

"Get away from me." I shudder. I am not going to be a meal.

"Or what? Rocks isn't here to help you now." He rubs both his hands together.

I will not be a victim to some sadistic Camazotz freak. I brace my feet apart and make two fists. In my head, I list my options. Aim for the eyes, or the groin. Hit hard and run. I will not give up without a fight. His eyes flicker to my hands causing him to halt.

"I have a message. Playing with Camazotz is a dangerous hobby for a girl who walks home alone after midnight. Don't come back to the market. If you do, your little sister will need rabies shots too."

Horror Movie girl awakens in me. How could I forget her? I scream and scream and scream and scream. My lungs sing out to the surrounding world, and the boy full of threats runs off into the darkness. My vocal assault prevents him from flipping, but at least he's gone. How dare he threaten Mini with an attack.

It takes an extra minute, but my shaking fingers eventually hit the right letters.

Tell the colony we're done!

Stop the threats.

You don't know anything about that, do you? If a bat threatens me again, I won't be held responsible for my actions!

I shove my phone in my pocket and run through the park faster than Rocks can flip. Three blocks from home, a loud thump on the path behind me makes my heart feel likes it's about to somersault out of my rib cage.

"Connie, stop. It's me," The familiar voice—that's slightly out of breath—helps calm my thundering heart. I stop running and bend over to catch my breath. "I swear to you," he pants. "I didn't send anyone to threaten you. I swear, but I need to know who it was."

My lungs are burning. My fitness is shameful. Looking at him hurts, but I force myself not to look away. "Get away from me. I don't know who the hell it was, but endangering Mini will bring out *my* claws."

A deadly rage fills his eyes at the mention of a threat to my little sister. Seeing him so enraged helps me calm down. He's innocent. My gut knew that all along, but I'm not sure who to trust these days. The Enzo revelation has put me on guard, and the fighting between us is blurring all the lines.

Rocks' presence calms me down enough to walk the rest of the way home. I explain every detail of the encounter and my big nose description is useless. We find ourselves outside my house in no time, but I don't want to sit and chat. I block his entry to the porch.

"When are you going to learn to recognize me?" he asks from the lawn.

I huff. "I don't have x-ray vision all right?"

"Try harder," he commands. He takes two steps back and holds out his hands. "I'm sorry. Listen, I know you don't want to be friends, but I can't walk away after a second threat to you. I can't and I won't."

With that he takes two steps back and flips in front of me. The conversation is clearly over.

Being back at school was supposed to dissolve the funk I've fallen into and distract me from my dark thoughts. It hasn't. Parker has almost finished his Economics assignment. We were in the library for over three hours before Principle Skinner eventually kicked us out.

December days are too short, and the sun has already sunk below the horizon. Winter is my least favorite season, although the Christmas lights do make December worth it. My knitted beanie could be an inch longer to save my poor ears. Parker walks me to the parking lot. His car is next to the building since he gets here for practice before I'm even out of bed.

He runs a hand down my arm. "Thanks so much. Sorry it's so late, but it was nice hanging out."

When Parker isn't being a wrestling jerk, he's kinda nice, sort of. He's learning that I don't need stupid stunts to impress me. But my heart's a bit over boys. Boys turn girls into uncontrollable freak shows, and I'm sick to death of being one.

"Yeah, I better go. I'm parked on the street. The lot was full. Slept late," I explain. He raises his arms, but I turn before my brain processes that he was about to hug me. Even though I turn back toward him, he's dropped his arms again, and now I don't know what to do. In the awkwardness that follows, he raises his arms but pats both my shoulders instead. It's weird, and we both know it.

"See ya tomorrow." I exit faster this time. I cut through the parking lot, jumping over the fence. I'm a block down and the only other car on the street is a van—another one. I squint but can't see the logo from this angle.

Footsteps on the pavement send me spinning around. Rocks, Decker and Ezra are walking out of the school grounds.

"What are you doing here? Following me again?" My nerves are frayed. I'm an elastic band stretched to the limit.

"Studying late?" Rocks walks up to me beside my car, but the boys hang back on the sidewalk. "That your new boyfriend?"

"What's it to you?" I puff up, trying to make myself bigger. I'll take you on buddy, I think to myself. His eyes roam over my body, and he snorts.

"I'm a lot bigger than you," he says, leaning down. "I don't want to fight. I just came to show you this." He points to the red metallic bar piercing his left eyebrow.

My eyebrows rise in response.

"It's so you can recognize me in the dark." He looks down the street toward the van.

"What?" I ask, following his gaze.

"Thought I heard something." He frowns.

I take out a pen and paper from my purse and copy down the numbers.

"What's going on?" He grabs my hand as I try to stuff the paper in my bag.

"Nothing. Let go."

"Why are you writing down license plate numbers if nothing is going on?" he growls between gritted teeth.

I know that look and let out a sigh. I miss my friend who knows all my deep, dark secrets. I miss the safe, secure feeling that Rocks gave me by just being there. "It's probably nothing, but … I think I'm being watched or followed. I don't know. I get this creepy feeling." I shiver. It only started after I told him we couldn't be friends. It's probably just confirmation of my insanity.

Rocks goes to touch my arm but stops. "You know I'm following you. Not all the time and mostly only after sunset. Maybe it's just that."

"Maybe. Do you know who came after me?"

He shakes his head and looks away. It gives me time to study his new piercing. It suits him. I would never have wanted anything to mar his features, but the red bar looks good. I want to touch it.

Rocks notices. "You like it?

I allow just one side of my mouth to rise. "Yeah, it looks really good." Hot, I think, but I'd never say, and that realization makes me feel even worse.

When I get out of my car at home, the creepy feeling is still lingering. I can't shake it, and it's starting to add to my constant state of being pissed off at the world. Parents V1.0 are gangsters, I'm fighting with Rocks, and now, my intuition is on the fritz. *Awesome.*

A short, sharp squawk, high in the trees in our front yard, has me squinting into the darkness. I walk up the porch steps and look out.

The beating of wings makes me jump again. I grab my chest. A bat has flown in under the porch, over the swing. It comes up to me at head height, and I see clearly a little red metal bar over its eye. The turmoil within dissolves instantly.

"Oh my God, that's adorable. Bat piercings. Who knew." I bite the inside of my cheek. His little face looks so freaking cute with a bad ass piercing. A second later, I'm peering up into Rocks' human one. He flicks his hair and I stare at the piercing some more. It's the perfect distraction from my mood.

"Easy to see, right?"

"Yeah. Thank you." He nods, his eyes serious.

Rocks walks down the porch steps and stands tall in the middle of the lawn. He scans the trees branch by branch.

"What is it?" The cool night air is adding to the creepy feeling that hangs over me.

"That bat call before wasn't me. Or the boys."

"What?" The hair on my neck has gone haywire. "What are you doing?" I whisper.

"I'm hoping for a communication, and if I don't get one, then I know it's whoever has been attacking you." He's silent again. His body language is fascinating to watch. He stands straight and tall, making himself appear even bigger than he is, but it's the way he uses his senses that I'm intrigued by. Rocks subtly sniffs the air—a long slow inhale that other people wouldn't think was unusual. I know he's combing the air for clues and scents. He cocks his head to the left—his ears searching out higher frequencies. At this moment, I recognize the animal within him.

A dog barks a few houses away, but that's the only sound the evening gives us. Rocks turns around and strides back toward the porch.

"You need to come with me tonight. I can't stay here, and you aren't staying here without me either," he states. "There's a presence lingering."

"Are you out of your freaking mind? I can't go with you. I have school tomorrow and my parents are inside. You're being absurd!"

"Don't argue with me. I don't know who that Camazotz is, and you aren't staying here without protection." He crosses his arms over his chest.

"We are not having this conversation. I'll lock the door and won't leave the house, but I'm not going to the colony. They'll eat me alive!" One thing I am certain of is that I'm not welcome there. I'm creeped out here, but up there, I'd never sleep a wink because I'd be worrying about that threat on Mini.

"Ugh," he throws his arms up. "We aren't seriously back here again, are we? You are *not* a menu item," he spits out. I get the feeling that his anger is simmering just below the surface like mine these days.

"I'm not meaning they'd *eat me* eat me, but then again, if you weren't there, I wouldn't be so confident. I'm just saying they hate my guts. If looks could kill sort of thing."

"Don't be absurd."

"You were inside your shop, the last time I visited. You didn't see the death stares and threats I received trying to get to you. Ask Scar—Zabreena."

"Is this a jealousy thing?" he asks, his hands now on his hips. "Are we back to that again too?"

I roll my eyes. "No! It's an 'aeronaughts are the devil's spawn for showing you human ways and luring you away' thing."

He stands shaking his head. Seriously, if he hasn't noticed how the other bats look at me, then his eyesight is worse than mine.

"I'm going inside and I swear that's where I'll stay. Go back to the colony. *That's* where your responsibility lies."

His angry features are the last thing I see before locking the door.

FRIDAY MORNING, I grab my lunch bag and race out. Arguing makes me restless and sleep didn't claim me until after three—just what I need to enhance my delightful mood. It's cold on the porch as the sun hasn't had a chance to warm it yet. I drop my keys fumbling with the lock.

EEEK!

My heart flips, but I know that sound. "What are you doing here? I told you to go home!" Glancing up, I spy the bat roosting in the top corner of our porch ceiling. I walk over and stand under him, the red bar gleams. "Rocks, I mean it. This is ridiculous. Now you're putting yourself in danger. What the hell?"

It's more than my nerves can handle. I should've known he would never leave me in danger even if it dumps him in it. I don't want to be worrying about him out alone as well. The energy to say all this fades. I can't argue anymore. My shoulders slump. I just want to go inside and crawl under my quilt and hide from the world—forever. "Whatever. Just do whatever." I turn and trudge to my car without a backward glance.

For three days, the black bat is perched in the same corner of the porch above the swing. Day or night, whenever I check, he's there. The red piercing makes his identity unmistakable.

The only time I know he leaves our porch is during my Bun Lovin' shifts. On Friday night a male voice echoing inside my head made me almost pee my pants.

I'm here.

I hadn't thought I was calm enough for him to be able to communicate with me. The previous times, I'd been distracted. I would have thought my failure at effective anger management would have been a block, but the voice was clear.

SUNDAY, *THE MAN who prides himself on home defense* finally notices the little creature that's become a resident.

"Kelly," he hollers up the stairs. "Get the long-handled broom and keep Mini up there."

I'm trying to decide what to paint on my nails. Bright, happy, colorful images make me want to demolish my room. I've done a black base coat and am waiting for that to dry.

"Which broom?" she calls back.

"The red one with the long handle. We've got a situation on the porch."

Fudge!

I fly down the stairs and out the door before Kelly has time to arm the love of her life. Chad is standing with his hands on his hips, studying the bat. My less than graceful arrival makes him turn around.

"Go indoors. The last thing we need is you getting attacked again." Too late, I think.

"No, give me the broom. I've just finished my shots. I'm the only one that's *safe*." I eye the bat.

"Out of the question."

My brain kicks into gear. Kelly isn't so good with furry creatures. If she screams …

I race back inside and find her in the utility closet. "Is this the one?" she asks, thinking I'm her protector.

"Yes." I grab the broom as she looks out of the closet at me.

"What are you doing?"

"Nothing. Go check on Mini. There's a bat on the porch." As predicted, she let's out a small wail of alarm. I head for the front door.

"Give it to me."

"No." I tighten my grip. "I know how awful those vaccinations are. Do you really want to experience that too? They might give us a family discount."

The standoff lasts another five minutes, and Dad only relents due to the shrieks for an update coming from Mini's room. I'm guessing half the neighborhood knows we have a roosting bat.

I upend the broom and stand by the swing. Checking the front window, the coast is clear, but I know he'll be back to monitor my progress.

"You need to go."

EEEK! EEEK!

"No? Rocks," I hiss. "The broom will be phase one. Phase two will probably involve copious amounts of bug spray, and I'm sure that's not healthy for bats either!"

His little eyes stare down at me. I've never seen him upside down before and am impressed by how small he can fold himself up considering he's such a long, lanky boy. My head hurts and I long for a peaceful night's sleep. The fighting and my frayed nerves are doing my head in.

"Have you seen or sensed anyone following me?" I ask. I wave the broom nowhere near him in case I'm under surveillance.

EEEK! EEEK!

"Me too." I sigh. I think I'm losing my mind. "Finding out about my father—" I whisper, "—probably just made me paranoid. I'm okay. Really. You need to go home and check in with what's happening there."

I wait for a response, but if I know Rocks, that will not be adequate enough for his liking.

"If I feel any tingle of suspicion, or if one single goose bump forms on my arms, I'll text you. Deal? I'll also take extra special care. I promise." I rub my fading scar. "Do you think I want more of these?"

I close my eyes. Air comes in through my nose and exits though my mouth. I do it again.

Promise?

"I promise." I draw a cross over my heart. Rocks lets go and swoops low over my head. I don't even flinch as the air moves my ponytail. It makes me smile. Cheeky Camazotz! "Got it!" I yell and am given a hero's welcome when I venture back indoors.

THE SMELL OF brownies reaches me the second I'm through the door. I've been at the mall with the girls looking for the perfect outfit for the dance—those are Tiff's words.

Crabapples.

I forgot to warn the baking queen that Rocks wouldn't be visiting this week. He hasn't been keeping his Monday/Wednesday visiting schedule for weeks now, but I guess she lives in hope. Then again maybe the brownies are for me—yeah, right.

"You're late," she states. I open the fridge and peruse the offerings.

"Sorry, at the mall looking for a dress." Distraction deployed.

"Oh, for the dance." She beams. "That's right. Did you find anything?"

I shake my head and open the brownie container, picking at the crumbs.

"What's that boy's name again?"

"Parker." I weigh up if I can make it to my room without further inquisition since I did technically start this topic.

"You must bring him around." Over my dead body, I chant.

Mr. Evening News enters the kitchen, holding the newspaper open. His head is buried in the pages.

"Two officers dead protecting key witness in the Viper trial," he reads, before lowering it for a second to look at us. "I told you I wouldn't go up against a drug dealer no matter what."

I slowly walk to the other side of the kitchen island. Kelly is on my right, and Chad and the newspaper are on my left. I wish I had two sets of eyes so that I could monitor each of them for the mere hint of weakness.

"What do you think of Enzo Ascari?" I ask, flicking my eyes back and forth between them.

He looks at me. "He's a criminal that should be locked away for eternity. Selling drugs to kids—everyone knows he's behind it, they just can't catch him—that's unforgiveable." He shakes his head. "Evil man. Bet he's never done a decent thing in his life."

His comment stings like a wasp. Does that include me? Maybe he doesn't know? But if he does, then he'll get the Academy award for not cracking a sweat or giving me any sign he knows I'm onto them.

"You don't know anyone silly enough to try drugs, do you, sweetheart?" Kelly asks. It sounds like an honest question. Am I reading way more into this than is really there? Where's the line drawn? My lies know no limit these days. I keep telling them to get what I need and it works, but my parental discovery has made me petrified of telling the truth.

I'M LATE STARTING my shift on Friday night. Parker wanted me to give his final essay one last read over. Does that boy type with boxing gloves on?

"Sorry," I say, throwing my bag in the corner and grabbing the apron.

"No sweat." Tiff's a trooper. The van is ready to go, and she's already got a customer. "You okay?"

"Parker." I roll my eyes. She grins and pockets the tip money.

"At least he's not being a dick these days," she says, leaning a hip on the counter.

I riffle through my handbag and bring out a sealed bag with the worst excuse for a blueberry muffin I've ever seen. Saying it resembles a stress ball is being polite. I hold it up.

"Ew, what's that?" She steps back.

"A gift from Parker."

"Bet you're glad he didn't ask you to eat it while he watched. I'd donate all my tips to see you trying to choke that down." Her laughter echoes in the van.

"I don't know whether bringing him a cupcake on Monday will be cruel or kind." I don't want to replace feeding one boy with another, because the first boy is one of a kind, but I also don't want any more 'edible' gifts from Parker either.

A group of hungry boys makes a line. Tiff and I get moving, making up their orders. Handing over the last dog—the guy wanted triple pickles and lashings of hot mustard—I watch the passersby. Working here has given me a new insight into college life. Tiff was right. I did need educating. A girl, further down the street, is laughing or imitating a donkey—it's hard to know which.

Tiff snorts. "Charming."

"You or her?" I ask, smiling. I watch donkey girl's friends. One punches her and the others imitate her distinctive laugh, then trips, and almost falls off the sidewalk in front of a van.

"SUGARPLUMS!"

In a flash, I'm below the counter and crawling on all fours to my bag in the corner.

"What the—" Tiff mumbles.

I dump the contents of my purse on the floor, spreading it out. Grabbing my phone, I fire off a text before I force air into my lungs.

That van is here.

16
Blood

"CONNIE, WHAT'S UP? You're a bit pale," Tiff says, bending down to my level.

"I'm being followed," I whisper. I point around the window and down the street. Tiff wants to know my secrets, well, here goes.

Tiff gets up and peers out. "By who? Since when?"

"That van."

"Stop whispering it's just us," she says, looking from me to the van. "Do you mean the telecommunications van?"

I nod and stare at my phone.

"You forget to pay your phone bill?"

"It's not funny." I crawl back over to her side and kneel up, peeking over the counter to look again. It's definitely the same license plate. The next few minutes are spent explaining my van encounters. I omit the first time I saw the van at Josie's place. I can't be sure that was the same van, as it wasn't until the third time I saw it that I took down the plates.

Tiff squats next to me. "I'm really worried about you. I have been for a while." I look away. "I don't think they're following you. The companies have areas, and the van you're seeing is just servicing its area. Your house, the school, and here are probably all part of that van's area." I'm so glad I never trusted her with the truth. If she's having trouble with this, there's no way in hell she would've coped with the Camazotz.

Her logic is sound, but I've got goose bumps. My gut is telling me trouble is lurking—and close. I suck my bottom lip into my mouth. "Is the door locked?"

Tiff humors me and checks. It isn't, so she clicks it shut. My phone vibrates, scaring me half to death. Fumbling, I try not to drop it.

Stay inside. I'm on my way, but I'll be a while.

"Who's that?"

"Rocks."

"Of course, he knows about this." She leaves me on the floor and checks on our dog numbers.

A busy spike forces me back to my feet and at the window again. I try to stay out of sight as much as possible. I know Tiff's huffs and puffs are aimed at me, but she doesn't say anything else.

The bang on the door is so loud that I squeeze the bun I'm holding too tight and the hot dog shoots out, disappearing into the briny waters of the pickle canister. Tiff glares.

"I'm guessing that's for you." She takes the abused bun and throws it in the trash.

"Connie, it's me."

Opening the door, Rocks, Jeremiah, and another very large boy I don't recognize are standing on the pavement. "This is my cousin, Harland," Rocks says, pointing over his shoulder. The guy, with shoulder length hair, mumbles a greeting I don't catch. All I zero in on are the viper bite piercings adorning his lower lip. "We're going over. You stay here."

I grab his wrist. "No." My blood pressure is rising rapidly. Tiff's right. This is ridiculous. "It's probably nothing."

"And if it is, then there's no need to worry." Rocks sneaks a glance over his shoulder.

Harland steps in. "We want you to come out and point really obviously at the van. If they're watching you, we want them to know that you know."

I can't stop my eyes from going wide. "What? You want them to *know*?" I look at Rocks and he nods.

"That's right. I'm sick of my cousin risking his life for a nau..." — his eyes flick to Rocks— "for an aeronaught. Let's finish this now." Harland is standing in the arc of light spilling from the van's open door.

My skin prickles as I study his stance and clothing. He's darker—like his spirit floats closer to midnight or something—than Rocks and the other boys. Or maybe he reminds me of a night with a new moon, whereas Rocks is more akin to a night illuminated by a full moon. The word predator invades my jumbled thoughts. If Harland pulled a switchblade, I wouldn't be surprised.

Stepping down, I do exactly as the guys have asked. They make animated gestures to confirm the vehicle, before the two boys flank Rocks, and they stride down the sidewalk. Halfway there, the headlights of the van flick onto high beam. I wince and raise a hand to block the white light. The silhouettes of the boys tell me they are doing the same thing. Before they get any closer, the van pulls a hard left and the screeching tires tell me they've left.

I'm being followed.

My knees buckle, but I catch myself by leaning against the Bun Lovin' Barn. Rocks walks up, opens the van door and steps half way into it.

"Tiff, Connie's not well. I'm taking her home immediately." His words register in my head, and I try to get past one long leg that is still half on the sidewalk. He blocks my entry by pinning me against the door. "I'm really sorry, but she won't be working tomorrow night either. See you around." He's managed to shovel all the junk into my bag and hands it to me. "Let's go."

"My coat."

A second later, he stands behind me and guides my arms into the sleeves. "Who was it?"

Rocks grabs my hand and pulls me in the direction of home. "I don't know, but it's going to stop." His hand is so warm in mine. I clear my head and concentrate on our connection. Rocks squeezes my fingers twice, and I look up into his soft eyes. "I've got you. Don't worry."

At one a.m. my phone illuminates my bedroom. I wasn't asleep anyway.

The Sire has agreed to perform a protection charm. You'll be safe after that.

His message makes absolutely no sense. I text back as much and after ten minutes of a furious text battle—including me logging onto the phone account and adding extra credit for him—I understand, but wish I didn't.

The colony and their little witchy herb woman are going to perform a ceremony—involving blood—tomorrow night that I must attend. He has clearly lost his freaking marbles.

No way. Forget it. I'm not going anywhere near a blood ceremony.

Close to four, I'm searching the shadows in my room for creatures that go bump in the night—or drive telecommunication vans. The gusty wind outside is buffeting the house, making it creak and groan and cause far too many heart rate spikes.

Open your window.

My bed socks slide across the floorboards near my windowsill. The pierced bat enters and before my eyes can register it, Rocks is standing in my room. The urge to throw myself into his arms grips me. I need him. I'm scared. Instead, I slide back to my bed and pull up the covers.

"I know you're frightened, but this is a huge deal. The Sire is putting his reputation on the line, and he's doing it for me. For you too."

I pull the quilt up higher so it covers half my face and nose. Peeping out, I watch him sit on the edge of my bed. "We don't perform this lightly. If the other colonies found out, it could cause conflict. The protection charm is believed to protect all who partake from *all* others—Camazotz included. It will look as though we don't trust the others, and that'll be seen as a hostile move if they find out."

My voice has vanished. I can't even begin to understand what this means. But it's obvious Rocks is putting his neck on the chopping block for me. My stomach churns and the emotional elevator plummets to the darkest depths of the pit.

"You need to trust me. Come to the colony. Everyone will gather for the charm, and then you can come home again. That's all."

We sit and stare at each other. The wind whistles through the branches outside. I shiver even though I'm snug in my toasty bed. Rocks' hand rubs back and forth over my knee.

"There's just one thing."

There goes the elevator again.

"What?"

The pause indicates I'm not going to like it. This is one thing I've learned about Rocks—he hates telling me bad news. "Just tell me."

"We need human blood."

I flinch away from his touch. I want to kick myself when pain flashes across his face briefly before I control my nerves.

"Not much. But some." He rests his hand back on my knee. "I can get it elsewhere, if you'd prefer." He looks away.

"But—"

"Connie, you know I don't drink from humans. You know that. But that doesn't mean your blood isn't the most powerful substance on the planet. I'm going to ask you once more—to trust me."

I bring one hand out of my blanket cocoon and link my fingers through his. I can't remember the last time I was lucky enough to witness my favorite smile, but right now I'm blinded by it.

SITTING BEHIND THE wheel of my car, I send a quick message to Rocks. I know he'll be anxious to hear from me.

Leaving now. K and C think I'm going to Tiff's before work.

Come straight to my shop. Drive safely.

The drive to the market doesn't seem to take as long as last time. Maybe it's because I feel as though I'm one step closer to the gallows with every mile covered. None of the baked goodies in our kitchen were able to tempt me to eat today, so my head is spinning a little. I can do this. I can be brave and not embarrass Rocks in front of the whole freaking colony.

Pulling off the highway, I follow the gravel trail to the Sanguine Mountain Market parking lot. The dilapidated old van sits in the same spot I swear it was last time. My heart races as I head up the path through the trees. All I can think about are the menacing stares and sneers last time I walked this same track. At the information sign, Decker and Ezra are standing laughing. Decker punches Ezra's arm and he howls like Mini, rubbing the spot where the fist connected. They both laugh and Decker successfully ducks out of the way from Ezra's retaliation.

"Hey, here she is," Decker announces, walking toward me. "Rockland asked us to meet you. He's with the Fold for a bit. Wanna see where I work?" His friendly demeanor allows my heart rate to slow.

Instead of turning left to Rocks' shop, we go right and head slightly downhill. The first building is the dairy, and I can hear and smell the cows even though I can't see them. The shop front has giant wheels of cheese stacked on top of each other; some have holes, others appear to be covered in mold. I look in the doorway as we pass because that's where Rocks gets his phone charged. She mustn't mind his interaction with an aeronaught.

Passing the tanner, Decker points to the Tin Smith shop.

"I bet you thought I was going to be a roofer, huh?

"What?" I don't have a clue what he's talking about.

"My name Decker means roofer, but I work with tin instead," he explains. I frown. "Didn't he tell you about each wing?"

Just a bit, I think. Decker goes on to explain that each wing has a naming convention, and all babies are named for their father's bloodline. His line is named for trades and lead by the Fold member— Judge.

"So in my bloodline there's Pilot, Ranger, Mason, Weaver, Taylor, Harper. You get the idea."

I look to Ezra. "My wing is Hebrew names or stuff that sounds like it's from the bible. Our Fold member is Levi, but not all wings have a Fold member. Only the seven wings that are voted into power are represented in the Fold."

We walk into the dimly lit shop. I never realized how much we rely on electricity to illuminate places in the modern world. It never occurred to me that history is full of so much darkness, and I'm not referring to the Camazotz kind.

The shop takes my breath away. The ceiling is covered in embossed tin, 3D light covers shaped like stars. Only three of them are lit up, but the light twinkles through the holes punched in the metal. Most of them have twelve points coming out, but some have so many points I can't count them all.

The wooden walls are smooth and stained with a dark varnish. It's so fancy compared to Rocks' raw wooden boards. The difference is that his is a workshop and selling space whereas this is just a display shop. The metal work is done out of sight.

The first bench is covered in Christmas decorations—tall angels, more stars and a collection of smaller decoration you could hang on your tree. The far wall is filled with mirrors of different shapes and sizes. Each mirror has an elegantly embossed tin frame. My eyes roam over the patterns punched into the metal.

"Those are gorgeous," I say, pointing at the table holding rectangular jewelry boxes. Decker's chest puffs out, and he opens a medium-sized box. It's lined with dark purple velvet and has a mirror inside the lid.

"Thanks. I made this two days ago," he says, running a hand lovingly over the lid. "But the light fittings are the biggest seller." He pulls a face. "My cousin, Jet, makes those."

Like Rocks, he seems to be able to read the thoughts swirling around in my mind. "His wing is named for gem stones."

"Cool."

I meander around the shop, running my fingers over interesting pieces. The boys trail behind patiently.

"Can I buy something?"

Decker stands tall, his smile owning his entire face. "Of course. How may I be of assistance, Miss?"

Ezra shakes his head and walks out laughing. I buy the jewelry box he made this week. The embossed pattern creates a starry night sky over the surface. It reminds me of small creatures that fly up near those stars.

We sit at a bench carved from a massive old tree, soaking up the fading afternoon sunlight. The boys are both wearing sunglasses but don't seem to mind the warmth on their skin. I stare at the red mountain peak logo on the paper bag.

Sanguine Mountain ... My mind ticks over. Optimistic Mountain? Cheerful Mountain? That can't be right, I think. I stare at the little red peak once more. Cheerful and optimistic are not exactly how I would describe the colony. I slide out my phone, trying to be discreet about it, and check my knowledge of the English language in my dictionary app and immediately wish I hadn't. My blood curdles. I swallow and look at the boys chatting quietly.

Sanguine also means blood-red. Blood-red Mountain? I'm glad I'm sitting down. I guess it's going to literally be blood-red soon.

"So you ready for tonight?" Ezra asks.

I try to swallow but can't speak. If I think too much about it, I'll be back on the highway. The boys share a look I don't understand. At this point, I figure the less I know the better. Ignorance is bliss. It really is sometimes.

"Rocks is a pro. He'll suck that blood out, and you won't feel a thing," Decker states.

"Suck WHAT?" I sit up straight, looking from one boy to the other. "Sucking? He never mentioned sucking."

"Oh, hell," Ezra says, shaking his head. "He didn't tell you, did he?"

"Such a chicken," Decker adds. They eye each other again.

"Tell. Me." I stand up and pace in front of them. The warmth from the sun is too much suddenly, and my skin burns from the heat trapped within me.

"He has to suck the blood from you directly, Connie. Usually the neck is the best place. Occasionally vampire myths get it right."

I grab my forehead and take a seat before I embarrass myself. I suck air in, but the oxygen isn't enough. "Drink from my neck?" I don't think I brought my inhaler.

They both nod. "If I was you, I'd head up to his shop. Let him do it in private before the gathering." Ezra says quietly.

"Yeah," Decker agrees. "You don't want everyone watching that."

I grip the edge of the wooden bench. Splinters are the least of my worries.

My head is still spinning about Rocks drinking from me so I hardly notice the little black bat that flits past the dairy, does one lap around Ezra and heads back the way it came.

"Rocks is ready for you," he says in a solemn tone. I'm thankful that I didn't eat earlier.

Jeremiah, Harland, and a middle-aged woman are talking to Rocks on his shop porch. The boys escort me past a group of not so friendly looking youths, but their stares aren't in the 'if looks could kill' category. They're closer to the 'if looks could maim' kind. None of the Camazotz girls are in sight and that calms me a little.

Rocks gives me my favorite smile. I wipe my hands on my dark jeans—at least this time I didn't try to impersonate a sunflower—and approach the group.

"Connie, I'd like to introduce you to my mother, Zada. This is my friend" —his eyes flick to mine and what I see wounds me— "Connie."

We need to talk—yet again. Now that I'm here, the anger I felt toward him over the dance fiasco has entirely evaporated. He will always be my friend. I honestly don't think I could live without him, and I need to tell him as much.

Zada is not what I was expecting, but in truth I don't know what I thought she would be like. Her hair is dark, dark, brown, messy and waist length. Sections are braided to keep it out of her eyes, but the rest moves with the slight breeze. Even though I haven't seen a tattoo shop, there must be an artist in residence. Her neck is covered in brightly colored flowers and seems at odds with the rest of her dark attire. She is dressed from head to toe in black, except for a silver ribbon that secures her corset. I imagine introducing her to Kelly and Chad and bite my cheek.

After one thorough glance, she speaks, "Well, now I understand." She leans over and gives me a soft hug, barely touching me. I think of butterfly kisses from my old Gran.

"It's a pleasure to meet you, Zada." She smiles, and flips, flying high up over the shop and out of sight. Rocks takes my hand and leads me inside. He lets go once we're through the door and walks over to his workbench.

"Doesn't she like me?"

"It's not you; it's just her. She flits here and there the second the impulse strikes her. That's just her way."

My heart is beating in the back of my throat. My mind races with dozens of questions. Will he feel the pace of my pulse? Will he know I'm scared and excited at the same time? What will I taste like? Before I pass out, I walk up to him.

After the deepest breath, I unwind my grey scarf. My black jacket covers my throat so I remove it as well and toss them both on the seat inside the door.

"I'm ready," I announce. Rocks turns and studies me.

I pull my black sweater away from the left side of my neck and step closer to him. I bare my neck in offering and close my eyes. "The boys told me how you'll do it. I'm ready."

A small chuckle fills the room. "Did they now?" he says ever so softly. His tone makes me think he's smiling. I can feel his body so close to mine. He moves in until we're touching. His hand runs up one arm as his long fingers slide over the exposed skin of my neck. I shiver. I want to open my eyes but can't find the courage.

His chest rubs against mine as he leans over me. I hold my breath. I feel a hand splay across my back and pull me even closer. Rocks is everywhere. My senses are on overload. The scent of the forest surrounds me, and I shiver once more in his arms. His lips briefly make contact with my flesh. I gasp because I was expecting a bite not a gentle caress. He kisses my skin once, twice, three times, and then opens his mouth and devours my neck. Still kissing me but more forcefully. His tongue swirls across my exposed skin. I moan and grab his waist with both fists—he's my anchor as I float adrift on a sea of sensations and emotions electrifying my body.

My brain is trying to focus. Is he relaxing me before the bite? His lips leave my neck for a moment and I'm shattered. I want to scream for him not to stop.

"Oh, Connie," he says, before he kisses my neck again with an intensity that curls my toes. Kissing has never felt like this ever. I feel his teeth graze the skin, and he bites me softly once before sucking the skin below my ear. I quiver. This is it.

But he pulls away. Rocks' lips have set fire to my entire system. I slowly open my eyes. "When are you going to do it?" I ask, confused. I sound breathless, but I don't care.

The backs of his fingers slide down my cheek and ghost across my lips. He frowns. "Later. At the gathering."

"Oh, no, please not there. I just wanted it to be us." I bend my head back again, exposing more flesh to him.

Rocks takes a step away from me, and I miss his touch. He looks at the floor and then out the window. When he meets my gaze again, his cheeks are flushed pink, but he looks away quickly.

His body language causes the tingles to fade as my suspicion grows. "What?"

"Um." He shuffles his feet. "You know I don't drink blood in human form. I told you that."

I blink. My brain skims over all the Camazotz information crammed up there.

Fudge me! I'm an idiot.

He's right. Bats drink. Humans eat.

"But … What? The boys said … Aaagh!" I step away and pull my sweater into place. I've been played—and thoroughly kissed. The pit inside me erupts, and I barely manage to stay standing.

"How could you?" I hiss at him. "Those little creeps!" Stupid should be my middle name. My hands are shaking so much that I half strangle myself trying to get my scarf back on. I need to cover myself. I want to crawl under the shop in the dark and stay there.

Rocks looks at me, and I notice his eyes are darker than normal. He shrugs. "How could I resist you?" he says in way of explanation. "That neck was too tempting."

I want to be mad, but his words make my heart skip a beat. Tempting. The inferno rages for an entirely different reason. I pray for the day when my emotions don't conflict each other one second after another.

"You shouldn't mess with people's feeling, Rocks." I turn away. Tears are filling my eyes, and I blink furiously. I don't know what's wrong with me. "That's not funny."

He steps up behind me. I can't have him touch me. Not now. I'm so confused. I want him so much, but I don't know what to do about it. Did he set the boys up to this stunt? Am I just a game?

"I'm sorry. I really am. Please don't be mad."

I grab my coat. "I'll be in my car," I say, leaving the shop. His kiss has awakened a deep longing, but does he feel the same way, or is this him being a jerk like Parker?

The doors click locked and the tears erupt. I don't know why I'm crying. I feel so much, and I can't explain any of it. I was so nervous and tried to be brave, and now I just feel like an idiot. A stupid, hormonal teenage girl surrounded by boys that play games. So often Rocks makes me feel like a little kid. He's so levelheaded and mature. I watch him with Mini and think he'd be the perfect dad even though he's just as young as I am, but he's older somehow. I didn't know just how much I wanted him to kiss me until I felt his lips caress my throat. I don't know why he did that. I need Tiff to translate.

The last rays of sunlight have vanished. The sky turns from orange to pink and darker blue. It's time.

I wipe my face and apply more foundation. That red nose has to go. Just as I complete Operation Girl Wasn't Crying, Rocks walks down the path. A little girl with a pink seahorse tucked under her arm is holding his hand. Her outfit is in colors of grays and reds and makes me think of a miniature emo fairy.

I grit my teeth and get out of the car. It's now or never. Rocks' brows are furrowed, but I focus on his little friend.

"I love my Bean's babies," she says in a loud voice. No shy little girl here. "Thank you, Miss Connie." Her smile chases away the lingering feelings of ridiculousness that were spilling out of the pit.

I kneel. "Hello, Bailey." I try not to focus on the white gauze covering her eye and half of her tiny head. I want to hug and protect her from any creature that would dare lay a scratch on her.

She lets go of his hand and throws the arm that isn't hugging her seahorse around my neck. "Do you have any more little babies with you?"

"Bailey," Rocks admonishes. "I told you not to ask that."

I laugh. "I'm sorry, but I don't today. I promise to bring you one next time though. What kind of animal would you like?" I take her hand and describe the dozens of new babies she could adopt. Rocks leads us off the path and into the forest.

He offers me his arm, but I shake my head. I can't be that close to him yet. He'll know how I feel, and I'm still too embarrassed. I can't believe I moaned when he kissed me.

His shoulders slump, and he leans in and whispers, "I know I said I was sorry, but I'm not. Now, I will always know what it feels like to kiss you, and I'll never be sorry for that." He walks ahead, clearing a safe path for Bailey and me through the underbrush. My eyes swim with tears and goose bumps cover my arms, but I'm distracted by a tug on my hand.

"Do they have butterflies? I love things that can fly like me. Tell me about flying babies."

We walk until the light fades. I trip and stumble repeatedly, making Bailey giggle. "Even I can see better than you," she says, smiling up at me.

Two little figures appear, and I hear muffled voices through the trees. The boys smile and whisper to each other pointing, unashamed to be staring at my hair.

Rocks grabs the smaller one, throwing him over his shoulder, tickling his ribs. "I told you not to stare. Don't be rude, boys."

"That's our brother, Moonshiner," Bailey informs me. "He's nine and a half, and the only member of the Moon wing." I nod at her. Rocks had told me Zada had a child with a male from another colony. The boy has no paternal relatives here. It's the only way to strengthen bloodlines, but very lonely for the first member of the wing.

Baxter is introduced next and waves hello. He takes Rocks' hand but walks staring at me over his shoulder. Each time I wink at him, he blushes and looks away for a few seconds.

The clearing is different from the one used for the carnival. It's a strange shape. A long rough oval that's sort of pointy at one end, and there are seven raised wooden platforms filling the space—three on one side and four along the other. One long thin platform, similar to a boardwalk runs up the middle. I recognize the Sire standing on the boardwalk. Hundreds of people mill around, appearing and disappearing from the surrounding forest. Screeches from above tell me the low branches are full of roosting bats. Rocks walks us to the middle platform on the far side and the hum of conversation ceases when I walk through, stepping over the boardwalk.

"Don't worry," says Bailey. "They just want to look at your pretty hair." I would kiss her if all eyes weren't currently on me.

I try not to stare back, but it's hard when you're at a Goth's Anonymous meeting. I wouldn't even know where to begin if I wanted to find clothing that would blend in. I catch flashes of tattooed flesh as people walk past. I shiver at the sight of so much exposed skin on a December night. Rocks helps me up onto the platform. Harland is on the other side and nods at me. The girl he's talking to turns around and glares. She's pretty and reminds me of Rocks.

"That's my sister, Graceland," he says close to my ear. I jump slightly. The darkness and creeping movements in the shadows is putting me on edge. His hand rests on my lower back, and he guides me to the long wooden bench lining the back of the platform.

"I'll only be a minute," he says and before I can protest, he picks up Bailey, throws Moonshiner back over his other shoulder and pulls Baxter with him.

The crowd seems to thin wherever he heads. People take a step or two out of his way. I get the sense that the colony is serious about him becoming a leader one day if his aeronaught love doesn't get in the way. Bailey and Baxter get ushered up onto the platform to the left. Moonshiner gets left by a tree in between the two stages. Rocks kneels down and speaks with him for a few minutes. The boy nods, looking more serious than any nine-year-old I've ever met. If the McNamara twins were that controlled, I'd happily attend my parent's reunion.

My eyes scan the other platforms. Scarface is standing on the platform to my right and waves with a sneer. I look away pretending not to see her and hope that her vision isn't good enough to see how much my chest is heaving up and down. Rocks returns to me, sitting down. His whole body is touching my side. I resist the urge to pull away because he's my anchor once more. Part of me wants to look back at Zabreena and see her face now. Rocks is with me, not her. I resist and instead watch a tall boy jump up on our platform near the trees.

"Oh my God, it's him."

"Who? Malachite?"

"That's the guy that threatened Mini." I sit ramrod straight, and my hands clutch the scarf protecting my throat.

Rocks looks over in time to see the boy lick his lips salaciously in my direction. I sink back out of his sight, using his body for cover.

"Oh, fuck no." He covers his eyes with one hand, and after a moment regains his composure. "I'm sorry. I apologize for my language, but are you sure?" He leans forward, resting his elbows on his knees to block the stares from the far side of the platform. Harland wasn't exactly friendly the other night, and now I know Graceland definitely isn't a fan either.

"Positive. Why?" I think I'm going to be sick.

"Damn it. He and Graceland will be together once they come of age." Rocks sighs and gets up.

He dodges around two little girls that have stepped up for a closer look at the blonde circus freak and stops in front of Malachite. They exchange words before Rocks grabs him by the neck and pushes him backward off the dais into the trees. The night swallows them and only Graceland and Harland seemed to have noticed. They both slink after him.

Holy crabapples.

My heart can't take much more of this place. It's beating triple time, and I'm seeing little flecks of light in my peripheral vision. Breathe in. Now out. Repeat.

"Where's Rockland?" Decker asks, looking around. I didn't even notice him approach. The darkness is pressing in as the sun has long set.

"He dragged that Malachite guy, who threatened Mini, off that way." I point. My ears burn. Does he know his little setup paid off for Rocks?

"Oh, hell!" Cupping his mouth, he calls across the gathering to the far platform. "Jez, come with." Looking at me, he commands. "Stay here. Ah, shit."

The last thing I'm doing is staying here alone when something is going down with Rocks because of me. Jeremiah jogs over, and they both vanish into the trees behind our platform. I follow.

Tripping over a root, I land on all fours. The earth is soft, and the smell of pine needles reminds me of the Christmas tree in our living room. I listen and hear cracking branches up ahead. Getting up, I half run toward the sound.

"You go near her again and I'll—"

"You'll what, big man?"

"Rockland, let him go," a girl's voice joins the argument. "You're hurting him."

Several dull thumps follow before they come into view. Rocks still has Malachite by the throat up against a large trunk. His feet can hardly be touching the ground.

Decker is up close to his brother, one hand attempting to pull him off the other boy. "Don't do it. It won't win you votes. Think about this long term, brother."

Rocks turns on his smaller sibling. "You think I give a damn about votes?"

"Decker's right. You don't need another enemy. Think of your Sire." Jeremiah adds. He pushes his way between the pair, and Malachite gets out of grabbing distance the instant his throat is free.

"You be careful, naught lover. You'll end up like that crazy sister of yours!"

Decker and Jeremiah block Rocks as he lunges at the sneering boy. I hear the air leave their lungs as his body collides with them hard. He just misses grabbing Malachite a second time.

"Don't you dare mention her!" He looks from the boy to his sister, shaking his head. "How could you? We're blood."

Light reflects in the streaks on her cheeks. I'm pretty sure she's crying. "I did it *because* we're blood," she sobs. "I can't lose anyone else."

The boys yank hard on either side of Rocks and pull him in my direction. It's too late to hide because Decker is already frowning at me. I attempt a smile.

Seated back on the platform, Rocks is silent. He body is rigid, and I try not to stare at him. The corner of his mouth has a slight darkish flush. The thumps make sense. The fact that he takes Mini's safety so seriously makes me want to hug him, but I don't want to be the cause of fistfights.

Bats fly low overhead and flip before my eyes. It's so routine now I don't even flinch. More people are gathering and distinctive groups are starting to form around the platforms.

"I'm sorry," I say, watching the ebb and flow of the Camazotz.

"Don't be. It's not your fault." He huffs out a big breath. "The gathering is shaped like a wing. It's easier to see from above." I scan the space and notice he's right. A scalloped bat wing is taking shape as people fill it.

Rocks explains that each platform represents a Fold Wing and the other smaller wings are making groups between them. Wings that are in alliance or have strong blood bonds side together and vote together. I look at the people surrounding our platform and wonder how long they will support the Land wing if I'm involved. The earlier altercation shows that the Land Wing itself is divided where I'm concerned.

Left, where Bailey is sitting, Rocks points out Judge. To our right, I see Zada. She's sitting on the edge of the platform, swinging her legs, a little girl is sitting on her lap. Rocks nods to her brother and leader, Zander. I ignore Zabreena again, but notice her eyes are on the boy next to me. Next to the Z wing—at the tip of the wing shape—is the Hebrew Wing. Following his finger down the underside of the wing is the group named for Gemstones. Carnelian, their leader, paces the wooden boards. He's not as old as the others—maybe thirty.

Rocks lowers his voice. "The last two wings don't see eye to eye with us. The Mac wing, lead by Macallister." He points to the furthest dais. "And that's Cypress. Males are named for trees and females for flowers, but all are named after plants. Don't ever mess with them." Cypress isn't wearing a shirt under his leather vest.

That wing is large. The members are dressed more deadly and sinister than the other wings. A young guy is calling the members down from the trees and when he turns my way, I notice the fangs tattooed on his lip.

"Who's that?"

"Ash. Not my favorite colony member." The gentle Rocks I'm so used to watching in my room isn't present. Our neighbor's dog gets upset every time the UPS guy visits. His hackles rise before the man even opens their front gate. Rocks reminds me of that dog. I'm his to defend and his duty has him on high alert.

I look away and my eyes land on little Moonshiner standing all alone—the only member of the newest wing.

"My father's ready for us," Rocks announces, looking at the center of the crowd.

"Your father?"

17
Attack

ROCKS IS STARING at the Sire.

"The Sire is your father?" I swallow, tasting bile. Rocks failed to mention that when he explained his family tree. I want to slap my forehead for not asking the right questions. He told me his father was Strickland and that their Fold member was the colony Sire. I just put two and two together. I was too focused on his mother's crazy relationships to focus on his dad, and now it turns out the colony Sire is his sire.

I can't muck this up. I stand and walk tall toward the end of our platform. Rocks overtakes me in one step and holds up his hand to help me. The feeling of his strong hand reassures me that I won't fall on my face. A procession of boys and girls holding lit red and gold paper lanterns enters the clearing. An old woman, with grey hair and a dress that drags along behind her, follows them. She's pulling a tethered goat and its bleats echo in the clearing. I'm grateful for the light the lanterns bring, but my eyes have almost adjusted. The moon is just peeping over the treetops. It's not quite full, maybe a few days off, but its presence calms me. It is light to the opposing darkness that surrounds me. The moon is on my side.

Rocks doesn't let go of my hand as we walk to the middle dais. I'm unsure whether that's a good or bad move for him after the stares I receive from across the clearing.

"Connie," Strickland says. He looks at his son.

"Let me assist, Sylvana," Rockland suggests. Strickland nods. And I'm grateful Rocks won't be leaving me here alone.

Rocks joins the old woman and takes the goat from her. It leans against his leg, seeming calmer as his fingers rub between its horns. The kids with the lanterns form a circle around us.

Next, the Fold members Rocks pointed out earlier join us. I keep my eyes on Strickland and focus on breathing in and out.

"Eeee-yaak-yaak-yah-eeeh!" Sylvana yells at the stars.

I jump to the left and bump into Judge. Looking up, I gasp because in the darkness I hadn't seen the massive ragged scar running down the full length of his face and neck. He smiles and I step away, trying not to shake. Do not be scared, I chant. His sons and daughter are so open to me that I know it's just his gruesome look that's making me edgy.

"We gather in secret to protect our blood," yells Strickland. He addresses the entire gathering with an air of authority that none other present possesses. He talks of the unidentified attacks, the deaths, and announces that even I have shed blood in recent weeks. This is news to many members because a murmur stirs through the sea of watching faces. Strickland calls for order and begins a blessing.

Sylvana's intermittent shrieks catch me off guard every time. Judge steadies me twice, and I manage a smile.

Rocks appears in the center of the circle holding a carved granite bowl. The witch dances left and right, her skirt forming an arc around her before she produces a knife. My eyes flick to Rocks. He winks, but it doesn't ease the turmoil in my stomach.

Sylvana takes the goat and makes an incision down its neck. Rocks catches the thick spray of blood in the bowl. Swaying, I feel Judge's hand on my back. His eyes are kind when they meet mine. I think of Chad—they can't be far apart in age.

Strickland steps up and slices the knife across his palm, adding to the blood collected. Each Fold member follows until Judge is standing before me with the knife. I don't know if I can cut myself. Rocks stops before me, holding the dark swirling liquid. I can't look at what's in the bowl and am thankful I need to look so far away from it to meet his eye.

"Hold out your hand," he says.

Judge grabs my wrist, and I hope nobody notices how much I'm shaking. "Ready?"

I nod. The pain is sharp and fast. I look back at Rocks for the moments it takes to add my blood to the mix. The bowl is taken from my sight and Judge wraps a crimson handkerchief around my palm. He's so kind to me that I feel bad for the fear that gripped me moments ago because of his scarred face.

"Thank you."

"It's my pleasure. You've been so gracious in accepting us." Pain stabs my chest. I think of all the times I hurt Rocks when I'd overreact about what he is. I recall throwing books and holy water and cringe.

Rocks places the basin on the grass and Sylvana chants and shrieks some more. He stands beside me and takes my injured hand. Ever so delicately, he unwraps the cloth, checks my wound and then meticulously re-bandages it.

I watch fascinated as the woman produces a large vial of liquid and adds it to the mix in a series of small drips timed with her twirling dance and shrieks at the moon.

"It's colloidal silver," he whispers. "For healing."

Next the substance is stirred with different collections of herbs before a fine powder is sprinkled over the surface. The moonlight glimmers across the still moving liquid.

"Ground ruby. For added protection and passion. It boosts life-force energy and is said to cleanse one's blood."

One last shriek silences the forest, and the potion is done. The basin is lifted onto the wooden dais. Strickland kneels before her. She dips all ten fingers into the dark concoction, her lips moving in a silent chant, and smears the blood across his face.

Strickland takes her place and the six Fold members all kneel. He dips three fingers of each hand and smears their faces. The substance is a rich red against their skin. I don't want to think about it.

The blood is poured into seven smaller vessels and each of the Fold fan out and bless every member of their wing and associate wings. By the time the entire colony is marked, the moon is shining high above us.

"Connie, you're next," Rocks says, when Strickland has marked his last follower.

Sylvana ceases her dance and steps between Strickland and I. The scent of rosemary and something that reminds me of bad eggs emanates from her. "She is not of our blood so she cannot partake in blood blessings."

Rocks goes to argue, but I grab his arm and shake my head. I'm not upsetting the medicine woman. The last thing I need added to my woes is a blonde voodoo doll, stuffed with pine needles. Rocks ignores me, and the three of them enter into a hushed argument. It ends abruptly with Sylvana's announcement to the whole gathering.

"Danger is present." She points a ringed finger at my chest, stabbing the air repeatedly. "Her presence will tip the scales weighing the survival of the colony." Spoken clearly and loud enough for all gathered to hear.

I'm the dangerous one? I'm surrounded by dozens of people who remind me of emo serial killers, and I'm dangerous.

Strickland brings the gathering to order and closes the ceremony. All eyes are on me and Rocks. And now the murmurs about the aeronaught freak have an added tone of disgust at the mention of danger.

"Are we done?" I ask. He nods. I know he's angry because he hasn't taken his eyes off his father, and a muscle in his cheek is twitching. The celebration begins. A fiddle and tin whistle start playing, but the scene is slightly macabre with the blood-streaked faces glowing under the moonlight.

Strickland looks at his son. There's a line of people waiting to speak with him, but before he sees to them, he speaks to us.

"I'm sorry, son, but what she decides must not be broken. I should have consulted her first."

"Our isolation and fear of change is going to be our downfall," Rocks replies and the venom in his voice shocks me.

"Leave it." Strickland turns to the first two men waiting—Cypress and Macallister.

I pull Rocks away. The tattoos that cover the bare flesh visible on Cypress show various animals and humans gushing blood from neck wounds. My stomach can't take much more.

"Give us permission to go after that naught of Celand's," Cypress says.

Rocks freezes.

"Not now," his father answers.

"Not now? I hope not ever." Rocks has returned to the men. Despite his lean frame, he towers over them all and looks menacing in his own right.

My eavesdropping is prevented by the arrival of Bailey and five little mini emo fairy friends—all smeared with blood. One Beanie baby is securely tucked under each girls' arm until my eyes land on the last little fairy who is empty-handed. Bailey performs introductions that Kelly would be proud of and then I'm bombarded with questions about how many more babies I can bring next time.

"This is why we need more babies, Miss Connie," Bailey says, pointing to the forlorn, empty-handed Odelia. The blood dripping down their faces seems all kinds of wrong.

It appears I've got my own fan club of five-year-olds. I kneel down and ask if Odelia would like to touch my hair. It's the right move because her face lights up in awe of my offer. The girls all crowd closer and watch her stroke the length of my long golden ponytail. It's the least I can do since she's didn't get a baby to love. The colony fascinates me as much as it scares the daylight out of me. I can't imagine Mini handing over four toys to her friends willingly, especially when they are the only toys she's likely to ever receive. Sharing is ingrained, and it takes me back to the brownie gobbling fiasco.

"He knows nothing! I swear to you," Rocks yells.

"Maybe not about Celand, but what about killing us slowly? What does he know about owls?" A group has gathered around the men.

"Father, I beg you. Do not allow them to question him. Murder is not what this colony represents."

Cypress laughs. "But we do understand an eye for an eye."

"It's not him!" Rocks yells at the crowd. I watch as he makes fists with his hands and stamps a boot into the soft grass.

"Enough!" Strickland shouts. "Rockland, you are forbidden from going to him. Cypress, Macallister, come with me." The crowd moves away, and Rocks curses loudly. He turns and apologizes to the girls, who giggle and swamp him, hugging his legs. The sight is so sweet, but I can tell by the set of his shoulders that he's barely holding onto his temper.

A bat flies in and does one low circle around Rocks and the five girls. They let go of his legs, flip, and follow the bat slowly toward the dark forest edge.

"Thanks, Mom."

Rocks locks his hands behind his head and tips it back to stare at the moon. "I know you're going to ask, Connie, but please don't. I don't want to talk about it."

I don't respond. Exhaustion has engulfed my whole body. I never win arguments with Rocks and know that the Celand topic is a particularly sore point. The last thing I want to do is start another fight.

Decker, Ezra, and Jeremiah join us, but before we leave, a tiny girl that barely reaches Rocks' waist tugs on his vest. The strain leaves his face when he sees her.

"Ireland, baby, where have you been?" He's picked her up. I think back to his family tree and remember that Strickland has a child with another woman. The eight-year-old wasn't raised with Rocks because she lives with her mother. She throws her arms around his neck.

"I've missed you so much." Another besotted fan. "Connie's pretty, and I don't think she's dangerous at all, do you?" She looks at me and then at her big brother. He kisses her cheek.

"I knew you were the smart one. I've got to get Connie home so I'll see you in a bit."

I don't argue when his elbow is offered for the return trip. I'm also glad the forest blocks most of the moon's light. Looking at him with streaks of blood—my blood—running down his face is unsettling. The darkness lets me forget.

"I can't believe they wouldn't bless her," Decker says. He's behind me and I hardly even hear his footfalls.

"Don't start me up again," snarls Rocks. "I am sorry though. So sorry, Connie."

I can't tell him that I'm glad they didn't "bless" me with blood. "It's fine."

"It's not. It will protect you. I know you think it won't, but it will." Rocks explains that blood and magic created them, so blood and magic can protect them too. He believes it will protect him the same way humans believe in guardian angels. When I argue, he rebuts my point by asking me to explain how simply smearing some of his blood on his belongings makes them vanish and show up again wherever he travelled to. And that phenomenon I can't explain.

He also tells me that even though Strickland said I could be blessed, it wasn't his call to make. Sylvana enchants the blessing and therefore decides who can take part in it.

"Hey, it doesn't matter. We know who attacked me now, so if you keep your eye on Malachite, I don't have to worry anymore."

"He can't drive."

"Oh, so he wasn't in the van?"

"No. But I'm starting to get the impression that I'm not the only one with aeronaught friends."

"Friends with an S?" I ask, trying to distract myself.

He stops walking. "Well, I just assumed Tiff." I smile at him because I know he can see it.

"She would be honored to be your friend."

"How is Tiff?" a voice I'm not used to hearing asks.

"Well, Jeremiah," Rocks says, turning around, "I never knew you cared."

The only answer he receives is a grunt and mumbled cuss.

"I'll tell her you said hi." I add, trying not to laugh. Another grunt.

Back at the market, there are people milling around everywhere. For some reason, this surprises me until I realize they can fly back a lot faster than I can walk in the dark. The boys were kind to accompany me and Rocks the whole way.

"You left your jewelry box in my shop," Rocks says, when I turn down the path to my car.

Arriving at his shop, there's a gang of mostly girls waiting on the picnic table nearby. The moon helps my eyes find Zabreena, Rebekkah, and the whole posse that visited Bun Lovin'. Just what I need to end my night.

"It's going to be one hell of a party tonight," Decker says, rubbing his hands together. "I wonder how many pups will be born after this?" Rocks punches his arm. "Ow. What was that for?"

Oh fudge crabapple sugarplum sundae!

His fan club is waiting to party Camazotz style. I storm into the shop to get my stuff. When I return, Rebekkah is leaning against his side, looking up at him with a look in her eyes that makes me want to vomit again.

"Come fly with us, Rockland. It's been too long. I miss you."

My knees threaten to give out from under me. I can't show weakness in front of these girls. I bite the inside of my lip and head for my car. I count my steps, trying to focus on anything but the thought of Rocks' lips on a neck that isn't mine. Images of him kissing all those voluptuous girls with their blood-streaked faces overload my brain.

"Ugh!"

"Connie, wait. Slow down." He's behind me but I'm almost at the signpost. I'm almost free. I don't stop, but he grabs my arm.

"Don't." I pull away so he steps across the path. "You going to go get your *bat* on with half of those girls?" Tears are filling my eyes, and I know he can see them.

He growls. "You still going to that dance with the freak that wears ladies under garments in public?"

"Yes!" I push past him without another word and leave.

MY EXAM PREPARATION is a nightmare. I read a paragraph of my biology text, and all I can see is Rocks and those girls in my head. The feel of his lips on my neck is plaguing my every thought night and day.

I contemplate telling Tiff to get her opinion on the matter, but there's no lie big enough to explain why I presented my neck to him like one of his goats at dinnertime. Without the Camazotz background, she would tell me I got what I deserved throwing myself at him the way I did. She would also know that I would never throw myself at a boy. We'd be back to square one with her knowing I wasn't telling the whole truth, and I'm not going through that again. I think back to before the letter when my life was so simple, and I didn't ride my emotional elevator fifteen times a day. Back then, my elevator only seemed to go up. How naive.

If Chad reads one more headline about Enzo Ascari, murdered police officers or the Viper's trial, I'll spontaneously combust. I don't want to know about it. Why do murders involving a man I've never met, make my conscience feel tainted? How is that even fair? The curiosity that gripped me about who he was has completely dissolved. I don't want to know.

Mini wanders into my room.

"No, Mini, I can't play today. Go see Momma."

"Rocks." She smiles. "Rocks today."

I bang my head on my desk, making her giggle. "No, baby girl. No Rocks today. I'm sorry. No more Rocks."

Taking her downstairs, I hand her over to *the people that brought her into this world and that I wish brought me into it too.*

"Rocks visiting tomorrow after school?" she asks.

"Ugh, no!" I shout before I can stop myself. "I have this little thing called exams to prepare for so that I can go to a college that will get me a job. Sound familiar?" She gives me the eye that tells me I'm pushing the limit. "I told him not to come so I could study. Please be so kind as to explain that to your daughter as well."

The scary thing is I've lost count on my lie tally and don't have a clue what number I'm up to, and they're definitely flowing easier and faster from my lips. Does this mean I'm an adult now?

If I can survive one week of school, four exams, and the dance, Christmas vacation will save my sanity. I hope.

SCHOOL LETS THE seniors out early the three days we have exams. Wednesday, I'm home alone and am surprised by a knock at the door. Rocks and the boys are standing on the porch. He tells them to wait outside, and I promise them cupcakes before we head to my room.

When I look at him, all I can see is the look in Rebekkah's eyes when she asked him to fly with her.

"Enjoy your bat party?" I can't help myself, but at the same time I want to slap my own face for being such a bitch.

"Counting down the minutes until you get behind the gym?"

I turn away and head to my desk. He doesn't sit down. "Look, I didn't come to fight with you. I wanted to tell you that Malachite didn't attack you."

I spin around to face him. "He did so. I recognize him."

"No, the first attack. He didn't give you that scar."

"Oh, crabapples. Ash? I know he hates me."

Rocks shrugs and says he'll confront him. Graceland asked Malachite to scare me away, but they never intended to hurt me physically.

"I also wanted to show you something. I got another piercing to make it even easier to know it's me." I stare at his face, but only the red bar is visible.

He flips. I swing around on my chair and face his little floating body. He angles his wings and moves in closer, opening up his chest. There on the left side is a silver ring. I lean in closer for a better look and cover my mouth with my hand.

Rocks has gotten a nipple ring. The thought of Rocks with no shirt, those tattooed arms, and a nipple ring makes my ears flame to a new intensity, but when I look at the little ring sticking out from his black fur, I can't hold myself together a second longer.

I explode with laughter, and the noise sends him backward before he flips again. I can't look at him. I cover my face with my hands and try to rein in my guffaws, but the little shiny ring on his little batty chest is burned into my brain. I hear him huff and chance a look.

Rocks is glowing red and trying to hide behind his hair. "I take it you don't like it."

"Haha, do you even have little batty nipples there? I mean, really? Do you? Do male bats have nipples?"

He crosses his arms over this chest and doesn't say another word. I laugh again because I just can't stop seeing the image in my mind. The laughter feels good. All the stress and turmoil dissolves from within. It's been too long since I've laughed.

"Guess I'll be on my way then." Rocks leaves my room, and I have to hold the railing or I'm sure I'll topple down the stairs. I grab the cupcake container from the kitchen and join the boys on the porch.

Decker and Ezra are grinning from ear to ear. Rocks walks to the middle of the lawn with his back to us. I offer them the container.

"Guess you agree with us on the ridiculousness of his latest piercing then?" Decker asks, taking a cake in each hand. I burst out laughing, holding my stomach. "I told you she'd laugh her head off," he yells across the yard.

I pat my jeans for my phone. "Hey, Rocks, can I get a photo of that?"

EXAMS ARE DONE. School is finished. I just need to survive the dance for a few hours, and I'll be free of all things school related for seventeen glorious days.

Kelly had tears in her eyes when she photographed Parker and I on the porch earlier. A high ponytail is my standard, and I don't wear a lot of makeup so I guess seeing me dressed up for once with curls cascading over my shoulders got her all emotional or something. She was surprisingly well-behaved.

Parker has been the perfect gentleman—for once. He opened the car door at school and held my hand until we got inside and found his friends. The wrestling team and I aren't going to be BFF's, but they aren't as bad as I had previously thought. Although, Wrestler Tom does have a flask of something that smells a lot like moonshine. Tiff needs to get over her attraction to him. Even with Jeremiah's silence, he's far better boyfriend material—minus the whole Camazotz thing of course. I promised myself I wasn't going to think about any boy other than Parker tonight. I owe it to him.

Walking in on his arm did earn me a number of snickers and stares from the more gymnastically flexible and academically challenged female population. I feel good in the black dress the girls helped me buy. The fitted bodice and three-quarter length sleeves are keeping me warmer than some of the girls present. It flares out at my waist to just above my knees. The only thing I wasn't too happy about is the V-neckline. My boobs do not need any advertising, but even I have to admit they look good in this. After Parker's initial bug-eyed look, he hasn't given them a second glance.

Tiff and Brandy drag their partners over to dance near Parker's group. I keep my distance from Parker at least for all the faster songs. The second a slow one starts, he pulls me closer and places my hands around his neck. My stomach rolls and heaves and not in a good way, and I don't know where to look. Rocks is convinced Parker is my boyfriend so I'm sure that's given him lots of 'options' with the Camazotz girls. I push the thoughts from my mind and rest my head on Parker's shoulder. His hands slide down my back, and I stiffen.

The first slow song is followed by another straight after, so I tell him I'm thirsty. Fresh lemonade never tasted so good. We take a seat away from his friends.

"Is it true you got one hundred on your Accounting test?"

"What?" I spit lemonade on my chin. "Who told you that?"

"Well, is it?"

"Who told you?" I hiss.

"So it is true. Wow. If I got a one hundred, I'd make sure the whole school knew about it." He laughs.

"Parker, the whole school already knows everything you do. You got an eighty-five, right?"

"Yeah, but it's not a perfect score."

"It's still a good score." Accounting has always been easy for me. I hardly even study it. The figures always just made sense; it's hard to explain.

"You need to believe in yourself more. That's something to be proud of."

I look away. "Thanks, Parker."

"Wanna go for a walk?"

Oh fudge. I gulp half my lemonade and try not to choke as I swallow three ice cubes whole.

This is a chance for a normal relationship with a boy that's just a boy. He's good looking, relatively intelligent when he's not surrounded by other wrestlers that turn him into a jerk, and has a body that I'll never get tired of looking at. Plus, he actually likes me. It's an even playing field, and there is not a drop of blood involved.

"Yeah, that'd be nice."

We exit through a side door that I didn't even know existed. Parker takes my hand and pulls me around past the parking lot to the dark alley behind the gym. It's already occupied, and the other couple is going for it. I have to look away and hope they aren't giving Parker ideas.

"You been back here before?" he asks when we find our own space beside a cage of basketballs.

"No." My fingers twist in knots.

"So, your first time?" I can see his white teeth in the dim light. My chest pinches and I can't help thinking of the boy that jokes about firsts.

Parker moves closer, and I step back until I hit the gym wall. He places his hands on either side of my head. "Got you now, pretty girl."

He kisses me.

I freeze.

Parker is a good kisser, but the tingles that fired through my body when Rocks' lips touched my skin are missing. Not one single firework zings through my system. He stops for a second and looks at me, his hands sliding down my arms to my waist. His lips push against mine once more and I respond. It feels nice, but that's all. It's not magical the way Tiff always described from her mom's books. It's not magical because it's not the boy my heart wants me to be kissing.

The kiss deepens, and he moves in closer. I'm suddenly feeling a part of him that I'm not ready to feel against me. I try to move back but I don't have any place to go. I wriggle but then stop when it occurs to me that it's just making matters worse. My hands push his chest until he stops.

"What's up?" He hasn't moved away, and I'm painfully aware of his anatomy.

"Um," I wriggle. He smiles. "Can we just take a break for a second?"

"Do you want to go to my car?"

WHAT? I want to go back inside. We are not doing anything in his car. I can't decide if I want to kiss him again let alone anything more. "No. No, I don't. Can we just go back inside?"

"We will in a few more minutes. There's just one thing. Just one."

His hands slip around both sides of my neck, and he bends my head to one side. I know he's going to kiss below my ear and the thought makes my chest ache. Some strange part of me doesn't want him kissing the place I offered to Rocks. He leans in, and his lips suck along my neck. But he moves lower and lower and one hand slides down and squeezes my breast. I get the distinct impression that was the ultimate goal.

"Parker, please stop. That's enough." I shove him. He moans and keeps kissing and massaging my sensitive flesh. "Parker!" I say loud enough for the next couple to surely hear and he stops.

Flapping and screeching fills the night air. My hair blows off my face from the force of their wings. Bats—three of them—are bombarding Parker's head and shoulders. They dive and swoop, taking turns hitting their target. I stay perfectly still against the wall and watch. Parker ducks and swats, yelling for help. He steps back, and the bats continue their aerial assault, following his every turn.

"Help. Help me. Ow. Shit." He turns and runs into the darkness. Two of the bats take off in pursuit, but one—minus a nipple ring—pauses for a moment.

"I'm okay."

EEEK!

He flies off to continue the torment.

I take a breath and smooth my dress out before heading back inside. There's a massive commotion by the door, and Parker is already retelling his horrifying attack to a gathering crowd. There's not a scratch on him. At no stage does Parker even look for me. He's too busy entertaining his audience. The girls are drowning him in sympathy, but I manage to push into the middle of his adoring fans.

"I'm going home. That's freaked me out a bit."

For once, I'm telling the truth.

18
B.N.F.

THREE WHOLE DAYS and all I can think about is Rocks kissing me, going behind the gym with Parker, and the Camazotz showing up. I need Tiff so badly, but that's just not an option. She did send me forty-seven texts—felt like that many—regarding the coincidence of Parker being attacked too. I know Parker was attacked—I was there. What I don't know is why Rocks was there? Is this protection duty? Maybe I should read more of Tiff's books. Maybe the answer is hidden in those pages of crazy romance. Maybe I'm kidding myself.

Kelly insisted I text Rocks and invite him to Christmas Eve dinner. I'm sitting at my desk touching up the chips on my nails. My red and white Santa hats took a beating helping Kelly prepare the feast.

"Are you mad at me?" a voice asks close behind me.

"Shi—sugarplums!" Jumping, I grab my chest. I didn't hear him come in. Spinning around, I notice my door is still closed, but the window is half open. I've made a habit of leaving it open when I know he's due. "Don't sneak up on me like that. God. You scared me half to death." The red and white hat on my middle finger resembles a snowstorm. I put the polish brush back in the bottle.

"Sorry." The velvet vest has come to dinner. He's quiet. Reserved. He straightens his vest for the third time in a row.

"Well, are you?" His boot kicks the leg of my chair. He hasn't taken his usual residence in my armchair, and it's making me uncomfortable.

"No, of course not."

He peeks at me from under his long hair. "Sure?"

"Yes." I swivel around fully and point to my bed or his chair.

Air leaves his lungs in a great whoosh and he smiles.

"Oh, thank God," he says, flopping down. He lies across my bed, resting up on one elbow. "I didn't know if ... well, if I was ... interrupting ... or not. I thought you might want to scratch my eyes out for ruining your make out session." He says make out session as though it burns his throat.

"I didn't want to be touched like that exactly," I tell him quietly. "Thank you."

He gives me the shyest smile I've ever seen on him. It's a long way from his happy smile that I've grown accustomed to witnessing in the kitchen.

"Guys shouldn't treat girls that way." His voice is louder now, but I can tell he's still restrained. He sits up and swings his legs toward me.

"I would never touch you ..." He coughs and looks away. "I mean, a guy should never touch a girl he cares about that way if she says no."

Our eyes meet, but only for an instant. I re-inspect my Santa hats.

The jackhammer has started up again in my chest. I glance down sure I'll be able to see it pounding through my flesh the way it would pulverize concrete. Is it possible that I don't need to compete with the Camazotz girls? That Rocks really *likes me* likes me? Is it possible that just being my sunny, light self is what he wants?

The tension in my tiny room is weird. I'm too chicken shit to ask him what I really want to know.

"Why did you come in my window?"

He looks at me and the mischief in his eyes is back. "Wasn't sure if you'd be spraying me with holy water or bashing me with bibles. Needed a quick escape."

"I'm never living that down, am I?"

"Nope."

"I have three words for you —B–N–F." I grin.

"They're letters." His eyebrows disappear under his hair.

"Not sure you can handle the actual words." I smile wider. "Bat. Nipple. Fiasco."

The smile that was on his face vanishes. He scowls, and I let go of the laugh I'm barely in control of. Just thinking about his little batty self with the nipple ring never fails to bring tears to my eyes. He stands up with his hands on his hips. He's towering over me but hiding behind his hair, and I catch the tiniest hint of a smile threatening to ruin his intimidating demeanor.

"I'll meet you at the door," I say, wiping tears of happiness from my eyes. We're okay. It's not weird, and he's not mad at me for kissing another boy. It's the best Christmas present I could ask for.

I bring Rocks into the kitchen. Mini is in the corner, standing at the playpen fence her parents were forced to erect around the tree to save the presents being demolished before Christmas morning.

"Stop!" Kelly shouts, holding her flour-covered hands in the air.

What the …

She's standing on the far side of the island, smiling in a way that reminds me of a creepy serial killer when he spots his next victim.

I glare. She starts pointing upward repeatedly. Following her gesture, I want to die.

"Mistletoe," she announces.

Oh sugarplums.

"So it is," Rocks agrees. "What's it doing up there?"

Bless him and his colony upbringing.

Kelly reminds me of a wet firecracker. I try not to laugh. "Oh, you don't know what that means?"

"Santa visits houses with mistletoe?" Mini's ears prick up at the mention of the man of the moment.

"Tanta. Tanta. Rocks." She points over the barricade at the jolly man in red amongst the presents. Rocks goes to take a step in her direction.

"Wait!" I'd give anything to take Kelly's blood pressure right now. Her devious plan isn't going quite the way I'm sure she envisaged. "It's tradition that you kiss the girl standing next to you under mistletoe."

It's the second time tonight Rocks' eyebrows have vanished. He looks at me wide-eyed and then back up at the mistletoe. I'd sell my soul to know what he's thinking.

Dad clears his throat in the other room. Kelly waits. Rocks bites his lip.

"I'm sorry," I whisper.

"So I'm supposed to kiss Connie?" He points from the mistletoe to me.

Kelly nods and clasps her hands in front of her chest. Chad moves from the lounge to his wife's side; he's frowning, and I know he will put an end to this madness. I make a mental note not to let Rocks drink the eggnog. Kelly must have taken taste-testing too far.

Rocks turns to me, his eyes flick to my ears. I'm confident they match Santa's outfit thanks to my conniving mother.

"It would be an honor." He places a soft kiss over my scar. He pauses when his lips make contact, holding them against my skin. The only part of my body that's alive is where his lips touch. I slip my fingers into his and squeeze. Always the gentleman.

Chad visibly exhales, and Kelly floats across to the oven, smiling. We stand for another moment under the mistletoe both of us fidgeting.

"Rocks!" Mini is a lifesaver and breaks the tension.

Dinner is not quite ready so we retreat to my room. Rocks stops just inside the door.

"Was the whole forehead thing disappointing?" His voice is soft and warm.

I face him. "Kelly will take what she can get, but I'm sure you've stepped up in Chad's eyes."

He twists his fingers together. "Were you?"

"Me?"

He nods. I swallow. It's now or never. If I don't tell him, he'll never know, and then I won't be able to blame him for 'flying' with the Camazotz girls.

"Yes."

Rocks looks up and his mouth drops open a little. "Does that mean you want me to kiss you?"

"Yes."

He steps closer. I can feel him invade all my senses. My heart rate rockets causing my pulse to pound like the bass drum at the dance club. He smells so good—so safe—so Rocks.

"You're nervous?" he notes.

"I am, but it's not what you think. It's not about the Camazotz thing. It's about being a disappointment."

"Connie."

"No, I'm serious. I never know if you hang around because I know your secret or because you like me."

"You don't think I like you?" He gives me the evil eye. He's been spending too much time with Kelly.

"As more than a friend, I mean." I shrug. "I don't even compare to those colony girls."

"You're right. You don't." His fingers stroke down my cheek. I look up and we're so close I notice how dark his eyes are. The blue is so dark it reminds me of a deep ocean before a storm. "It wouldn't be fair to compare them to you. You're everything they aren't. You're what I need, Connie. *You* are the girl I choose. The question is who do you choose?"

"You."

"A guy that can't even pick you up in his car and take you on a real date? A guy that's never even been to a movie theater or any place you take a girl?"

"Yes. I want a guy that wouldn't even hesitate to risk his life for me."

"I'd die if something happened to you." There is pain in his eyes, but it leaves as fast as it appeared. I feel exposed watching his eyes roam my face.

He lowers his head. I stand up on tiptoes to meet him half way. His lips are so warm against mine. He smells so good. Rocks hesitates and pulls back. I give him a little smile and wrap my arms as far around his shoulders as I can reach. He kisses me again, but this time doesn't hesitate to deepen it. His tongue tickles mine. I'm in heaven in his arms. All I can feel is Rocks. His body is so strong, secure, and lean. I could stay against him forever. This must be what Tiff goes on about. If I thought him kissing my neck was explosive, it's nothing compared to the feel of his lips against mine.

"Connie. Dinner's ready."

Crabapples.

Rocks is seated opposite me. Mini is in her highchair between him and Kelly. I can't take my eyes off the beautiful boy who told me he has chosen me. I want to dance on the table. I want to run around the backyard without my coat on, howling to the moon. I want to be back upstairs with Rocks—alone.

After too much food, we take down the tree barricade. Kelly has decided presents will be done while Rocks is here. Rocks suggests leaving so he doesn't intrude on a family moment but is quickly told that he's practically part of the family. I don't want to be sad on Christmas Eve at the mention of family. Between Thanksgiving and now, all I've done is obsess over the tainted blood in my veins. Do Kelly and Chad really know who I am and what it all means? I haven't a clue, but what I do know is the people here *are* my family. It feels so freeing to finally think of them that way again. I can't help where I ended up, and I need to forget the two people I secretly discovered in order to move forward and repair the bonds I've damaged with the ones that I love.

"Mini, give this to Rocks."

"Mini?" she asks, eyeing the present in her chubby hands.

"No, Rocks."

"Mini?"

I point. "Give it to Rocks."

She waddles over, but before she parts with the red box, she checks again. "Mini?" Our laughter makes her grin.

Rock grabs her around the waist and blows a raspberry on her cheek. She surrenders the box and heads back over to claim one she can keep.

He rests the box on his lap and watches the gift distribution. Mini is learning the art of giving, and it's becoming harder to get her to deliver gifts to their intended recipients. Rocks is stunned when a total of four gifts have his name on them—mine, Mini's, one from my parents—calling them that again makes me smile—and Santa has left him a little something here as well.

"All this? But ... "

My heart stutters twice. The boy that flew into my life is so generous of heart it astounds me. He never thinks of himself first, and he doesn't see himself clearly. He always moans about how he's not the right man for the colony job, but he's a born leader—smart, caring, considerate and utterly selfless. The colony would be lucky to have him lead them into this century.

I know he's worried that he hasn't bought gifts for us. I 'helped' him pick a gift for Mini. Handing it to him, I point to the gift tag. The look in his eyes makes my heart skip a beat, flip over backward and flutter to a stop. I want to kiss him so badly. Pulling out my phone, I send a quick text.

Christmas another first?

I'm rewarded with my favorite smile before he texts back. When I glance at Mom, she's glowing. Thankfully, Dad is inspecting his new abseiling helmet.

Another first I'm honored to share with my girl.

Pouncing on Rocks in front of Dad would not be a wise move considering they're leaving me home alone for three nights. It's best we don't draw any attention to ourselves.

I like the sound of that.

He beams, slips the phone into his back pocket and pulls out a velvet pouch from his vest. Mini is eventually persuaded to leave her stash and deliver the pouch to me. He apologizes to Mom—who waves him off with a flick of her wrist, claiming that letting her feed him was his gift to her—and starts unwrapping his stash.

I watch him tackle mine first. It's not new, but I know he'll love it. Dad wasn't using it since his upgrade anyhow, and I've added data to his plan.

"A smart phone," he exclaims, pouring over the cubed box. "Connie, you didn't."

"It's not new." I shrug one shoulder.

"But it's my very own connection to the Internet." I shift my eyes toward my parents. Internet access these days is a given. He follows my lead and puts down the box, but his eyes don't leave it as he starts unwrapping the next gift. Santa got him an iTunes gift card; Mini got him a jumbo carton of Milk Duds and the eReader is from my folks. I haven't felt this happy or free in a long time.

Rocks' fingers slide over each gift on rotation. He can't stop touching them, and if I know him, he's using all restraint not to rip into their packaging.

The pouch contains a necklace, which I put on immediately. Resting over my throat is a silver filigree bat—his mark. The metal swirls and twirls to make exotic delicate wings. I'm never taking it off and can't wait to thank him properly in my room. It's breathtaking, just like the boy that created it.

"ARE YOU SURE you don't want to come, Sweetheart?" Mom asks for the five millionth time.

"Positive." I'm doing my best not to shove them out the door and slam the locks into place. *Just go already*, I think to myself. Rocks is due in twenty minutes and they were supposed to be on the highway by now.

The reunion weekend has arrived at last. They will be away for four days between now and New Year—two travel days and two days of drinking and remembering their youth. Thank God I'm not going.

"The fridge is stocked."

"Lock the doors," Dad commands—again. "Rocks visiting?"

"Oh, you know, he might pop in." I force myself to maintain eye contact. *The man that I'm sure would feel strongly about a boy spending the night* doesn't need to know a boy is indeed spending the night.

Rocks insisted that I shouldn't be alone, and I didn't put up any fight whatsoever—shortest text message conversation ever.

"Well" —Dad looks at Mom, but she's putting Mini's bottle in her handbag— "behave yourself."

"Don't worry about me." And finally, they're gone. Flying upstairs, I rip off my winter pajamas. My wardrobe looks as boring as ever. What to wear when you're home alone with your new boyfriend? I consider texting Tiff but that would eat up the last minutes I have to get ready. In the end, my jeans and a V-neck sweater win. I just have to be myself. I don't have to dress to impress the way the Camazotz girls seem to do. Rocks has already picked me. The thought chases the butterflies from my stomach.

Opening the door, Rocks is sweating slightly. His damp skin causes his hair to stick to his forehead.

"You okay?"

He looks kind of puffy. Blushing, he explains that he couldn't carry a bag and is wearing four shirts, three pairs of underwear, six socks, and two phones. It's a big load for a little bat. I show him to the guest room so he can shed the extra layers while I go investigate the contents of the fridge. He didn't kiss me when he came inside, and I'm wondering when that's likely to happen again.

"Connie." My name echoes down the staircase. "Got a second?"

He's been up there for a good ten minutes. I leave the spaghetti revolving in the microwave to go investigate.

Walking into my room, my eyes instantly fly to my ceiling. Well, it resembles my ceiling except for the mini mistletoe forest that Rocks has hung all over it. My window is open, and there are leaves and berries littering my windowsill. The forest fills my senses.

"I had to fly with this load too." He stands in the middle of the room and slides his hands into his back pockets. Moving in front of him, I study him. He can't contain his grin and bites his bottom lip. "It's mistletoe, and we both know what that means."

I laugh. He's the cutest boy on the planet, and he's in my room wanting permission to kiss me.

"I hadn't noticed." He pulls a face like I'm crazy for not noticing the extra greenery. "Remind me what it means again?"

He hooks two fingers into my belt loops. "I get to kiss you."

"If you want to kiss me, you don't have to go to so much trouble or even ask. Just pull me close and do it."

His eyes darken and his fingers pull on the loops, following my instructions until our bodies touch. I watch the tip of his tongue flick out but disappear back between those gorgeous lips.

"One thing," he says, looking at my hair. His fingers find my elastic and gently pull it free, allowing my hair to cascade around my face and shoulders. "So beautiful."

And then he kisses me hard. His hands cup my face. There is no hesitation like a few days ago. Rocks devours me. He wants me and he's letting me know. I could die right here and I'd die happy. I match his intensity and soon we pull apart, needing air. Rocks blushes. "Wow. I've wanted to do that since the very first night in the forest. You hugged me, and all I could think about was kissing you."

"No way." He smiles and nods. "So why did it take you this long?"

"I wanted to so many times, but you seemed to emit a no vibe at me. I just got the feeling you didn't want me like that. Am I right?"

"Sort of. I could never believe that a guy as hot as you would want to kiss me—a boring run of the mill human when all those g—" A long finger moves over my lips interrupting my admission. He's grinning from ear to ear.

"You think I'm hot?" He wiggles his eyebrows. "Am I good-looking in your opinion, Miss Connie Phillips?" His lips are hovering over mine but tantalizingly out of reach.

"Yes! Yes, I think you're crazy good looking all right?" I'm rewarded with a kiss, but it's soft and sweet and makes my stomach flip.

I turn my head and rest it against his satin vest. His heart is pounding and I smile, glad to know I'm not the only one reacting to our kisses. He wraps his arms around me, and I fold into him. Bliss—warm, safe, bliss. "I can do that anytime without asking?"

I nod. "Connie. I've never felt like this before." He strokes my hair all the way down my back. The inferno inside me has ignited with force. I hold him tighter around the waist. "I'm so happy. I feel like something terrible is about to happen because I'm never allowed to be this happy without there being consequences."

He places a kiss on the top of my head. I shiver and Rocks closes my window.

"Hey, Beans—"

"Stop calling me that, " I say between gritted teeth. I love my nickname, but our ritual involves me feigning irritation, and it's been too long since that's happened. "It makes me think of whether I need to fart or not."

My ears burn. I can't believe I just said that. I'm so relaxed for the first time in a while it's making me forget myself.

The twinkle of mischief that I both love and am wary of appears in his dark eyes.

"WHAT? GIRLS FART? NOOOOO!" He covers his ears, then his eyes and then clutches at his chest as though he's having a heart attack. "OMG," he says, mimicking Tiff, "you've shattered my image of you." The window lock clicks, and he sits on the end of my bed opposite me.

I roll my eyes and command the corners of my mouth to not curve up and encourage him.

He suddenly gets serious and leans toward me to say quietly, "No, seriously. Camazotz girls—do—not—fart. It's scientifically proven. Impossible."

"Ugh, I hate you."

I throw my old bear at him, but he just lounges back laughing.

It's familiar. I've missed us just hanging out and not fighting.

Rocks pulls out both his phones. The lesson begins with inserting the SIM card and powering up. He already knows about apps from playing games on mine. We sit grinning at each other as the phone powers to life and connects.

"So let's start with searching on your phone. It's the same as the laptop." I tap Safari. "What do you want to know?"

He blows air out through his mouth. "So many things. You pick."

I start typing. Do male bats have—

Rocks is watching over my shoulder. "You don't need the Internet to answer bat questions, Beans."

"I do because you never told me." He frowns and I type the last word of my question in the tiny box.

—nipples?

"Do male bats have nipples?" I read loud and clear, hitting search, but my eyes are on the blushing boy beside me.

"Oh, not that again."

"Well, do they?"

He pounces and those long fingers seem to be able to tickle way too much surface area. I fall back onto the bed, and Rocks is everywhere. There is just too much boy for me to have a hope of winning. My shrieks and laughter fill the whole house.

"Stop," I scream. "Okay, okay, it's a nipple embargo."

His tickling intensifies. "Swear on it."

"I swear. I swear," I yell. Rocks stops tickling for a moment. I'm out of breath. He's half on top of me and looks down into my eyes. Suddenly, he springs off the bed and is upright faster than he flips.

"Shit. Sorry." His eyes are wide. "Um …"

I curl my finger at him. "Come back here." Patting the bed, I move over. I can't explain why I feel so confident with him. But being alone with Rocks is easy. "Please."

Rocks lies down next to me, but he's balancing on the very edge of the bed. I scoot down the end and pull off his enormous boots. Grabbing our phones, I lift his arm and snuggle into the crook of his shoulder. My head rests over his heart and my sock-covered feet play with his leg—his feet are too far away.

His huge exhale let's me know he's okay with our closeness. I rest both phones on his chest, and we stare at the mistletoe canopy. He must have stripped every tree for miles.

"Hey, look. Mistletoe," I say.

My head bounces up and down as he laughs. Leaning up on one elbow, I kiss him. Rocks pushes the hair off my face and curls his fingers around my neck. I swear the skin he touches will never be the same again.

We don't leave my bedroom for the rest of the day, but it's sweet and innocent and leaves me thoroughly wanting him even more.

ROCKS BEHAVED AS only a nineteen-year-old from 1865 would if the parents of his girlfriend were out of town. He left my room late and slept down the hall.

The smell of burned pancakes is slowly being sucked into our range hood. Rocks pours more batter into the pan. The bacon is warming in the oven, and I've set the table. He walks over and leans down for a kiss. The poor boy is going to do his back in with our height difference.

Again, I swear he can read my mind. His hands circle my waist and lift me onto the kitchen island. He smiles. "Ah, that's better." I can look him in the eye. I drag my fingers through his hair pushing it back off his face. It falls back when I let it go. The space between us disappears. I waste no time throwing my arms around his neck and his lips meet mine. He tastes of raspberries. Time stands still when he kisses me. Nothing else matters—until the smell of burning batter forces us apart.

"Damn it." He races to the stovetop, and another pancake casualty gets added to the trash.

Breakfast is a long affair, and afterward I send him up to my room while I get rid of the evidence that I wasn't home alone all weekend. Detective Dad will look for the tiniest clue that Rocks was here. I know it.

Dragging the loaded garbage bag down the path, I feel eyes on me. Rocks is watching from my bedroom window. He offered to put the trash out, but I told him we'd be back making out even sooner if I handled the recycling instead. That's a lesson for another day and Christmas recycling is out of control. Plus, I need to earn my allowance, and when Dad calls tonight and asks if I put the trash out, I won't have to lie. I blow Rocks a kiss. Who am I? My heart flips when he catches it out the window. Who knew I'd turn into the soppy-in-love girl.

Love?

I turn away, stumbling down the path, the wine bottles clanking loudly in my ears. I need to breathe. Is this love? The first person that enters my brain each day is Rocks—even when we're fighting. When he cancels his visits, my mood swings could alter the earth's rotation. The tingles that erupt over my skin when his fingers glide up my spine are like nothing I've ever felt in my eighteen years on this planet. The times I sit and stare at him when he's distracted by technology. The one person I cannot bear to lie to, and only one I ever want the very best for is Rocks. My lip aches from the pressure of my teeth.

I'm in love.

My body hums with a strange energy. I'm in love with Rocks. I giggle and turn back around, but he's gone. How did I get this lucky? I want to get back inside and kiss him again. Opening the huge bin, I dump the first bag inside. I'm grateful for Dad putting them on the sidewalk, or we would've missed the collection for sure. Recycling might be good for future generations, but it pisses off the current one. The bottles and cans always get stuck in the hemp tote Mom stores them in. I dump it upside down over the bin and shake hard, doing my bit for the planet.

Clash. Clang. Crack.

I shake it again, freeing two more wine bottles from the long handles. Tires screech behind me. Between my trash dumping and their lousy parking skills, we're going to wake the whole street. Hands grab my biceps, pinning them to my side. I look over my shoulder, but darkness engulfs me.

"Hey!"

Without my vision, I panic. Fabric has been shoved over my head. The covering reeks of stale cigarette smoke and mold. I struggle, but the iron grip on my arms tightens. Before I can let loose my best Horror Movie Girl scream, a hand clamps tight over my mouth, and I'm pulled against a human brick wall. The fabric is rough against my face, and the air leaves my lungs. My feet lift off the pavement. I kick and struggle, but before I make contact with the shins I was aiming for, my body is slammed down on a cold, hard surface. A dead weight lands on my lower back. My arms are trapped by my sides. I can't see. I can't breathe. I can't move. My breathing is shallow and fast, but it's not enough air. I think a man is straddling my body. I pray I'm wrong. What's happening? My lungs aren't cooperating. I whimper.

The hand leaves my mouth, and I scream but hear the door of a van slide shut with a thud. My cries for help echo harshly around me.

"Get off me! Let me go!"

"Shut it, or you'll be sorry," a gravelly voice growls.

I try to lift my torso, but it's completely useless. I need air. I need my inhaler.

"Help! Rocks!" I yell and the weight on top of me pushes on my lungs. I can't breathe or make any sound at all.

"You keep quiet, and I won't have to crush you, Sophia." The weight lessens but not enough. "Understand?"

"Who's Sophia?" I say softly. My boobs are throbbing from his weight. The floor beneath me is ribbed metal and it's digging into my chest and cheekbone. I'm pretty sure I'm in the back of that van.

He lets out a harsh chuckle. "So that's how we're going to play this, huh? I had a feeling you'd be a feisty one. Do you prefer Soph?"

"Oh, God, you've kidnapped the wrong girl. I'm not Sophia. Let me go. Please." I whimper again. Tears are filling my eyes. It's starting to make sense. I've been abducted by mistake.

"Well, you match the photo I got of Sophia Ascari."

I gasp and try to swallow the bile in throat. Ascari. It can't be a coincidence.

"Who the hell is Sophia Ascari?"

19
Crushed

THE VAN DRIVES for so long that I have no idea how much time has past since I was blowing a kiss at Rocks. The constant whirring of the tires on the asphalt tells me we are on a highway and have been for hours. I'm a long way from home.

Rocks.

He wasn't in the window when I last turned around, and the noise I was making with the trash may have dulled the van screeching to a halt. I pray that he's hot on my captors' heels, but then again, if they are linked to Enzo Ascari, I hope he's as far away as possible.

"Next exit," the voice beside me commands. After tying my hands and feet, he sat beside me but has kept a hand against my back the entire trip.

"I know," replies the man up front.

The pair argues about the driver's poor sense of direction, and I monitor every word looking for clues to my location. Nothing.

I slide forward until a fistful of my sweater is grabbed as the brakes engage. More arguments ensue about driving skills and competence. The four letter words being spewed back and forth indicate my captors respect for each other. A series of turns, a couple of stops and starts, and the vehicle pulls off onto crunchy gravel.

I try to stay calm, despite the thundering in my chest. My breath is hot inside the stale bag. Logic tells me that panicking will not help my situation. The uneven terrain suggests we're in the country. I focus on the senses that I know Rocks would be relying on if he were in my position. I listen. I sniff the air, but the cover over my head masks any clues.

Two hands pull me out of the van and onto my feet, but with them bound, I wobble around. "Ow!" Fingers try to catch me by my biceps to prevent me from toppling over, but they come too late, and I land hard on my side. The cover flies off, and I squint as the harsh sunlight directly overhead blinds me.

"You idiot, look what you've done," the driver yells. My feet are yanked in the air, and the cable ties cut off with a switchblade.

"Get up, Sophia."

"I'm not Sophia," I repeat, struggling to my feet. My eyes roam my surroundings left and right. It's an abandoned farm—a huge rusted shed on the right, runs back further than I can see, and on the left is a wooden house that has a porch half fallen off. I listen for a familiar squeak, but all I hear is the wind rustling the leaves. I wish for my coat when I see patches of snow in the shadows, but I've got bigger problems.

"Save it for Joey. You're old friends." The driver's voice belongs to an extremely rotund man. Relief floods me that he wasn't the one to sit on my back. I chant their descriptions to myself—five foot something, sandy hair, tiny eyes that make his fat cheeks seem even bigger. I memorize every detail for the police.

I turn and see the one that grabbed me is a runner-up in the Mr. Universe competition. His muscles bulge under his shirt. I don't think my fingers would fit around his neck if I tried. Baldy, Mr. Universe grunts at me, and I look away. His fingers remind me of hot dogs cut in half. Disgusting. He grabs my neck and shoves me toward the shed.

Now that the filthy bag is off my head, the smell of manure hits me the closer we get to the building. Feathers and grain litter the dirt near the small side door.

"Tony, get the door," hot dog hands commands.

"Don't use my name." He steps in front, and the hinges whine in protest.

"Why? You the only Tony in Georgia?"

Relief that I haven't left the state floods my system, and my eyes close in thanks. Inside the shed, the smell intensifies, and there's a second odor that reeks of decay. If I could cover my nose, I would. Near the door is a large caged area that narrows to a funnel near massive amounts of machinery with hooks hanging from conveyor belts. I get pushed closer to the machinery, and I notice a massive blade. When operational, it spins and beheads whatever poor creature is hanging from the hooks.

"You give us trouble, and we'll start that up. Got it?" He grunts. I sense he's not kidding. I can't look at the rusty metal saw blade a second longer. Threat understood loud and clear.

I want to be sick, and the world spins until I remember my phone is in my hip pocket. If I can get to it, I'm saved. We head across to the house, and the entry is more decayed than it looks. Tony's foot goes through the first step, but his size may be responsible. The house is musty and dank. Black mold creeps up the walls and piles of leaves rest in the corner of the first room.

I'm taken to the basement, which is thankfully dry, and cable-tied—hands and feet—to a metal chair. Sitting on my phone is not going to help. Exposed pipes line the ceiling and stacks of rotting boxes litter the space. Sunlight pours in the high window at ground level and allows for a hint of fresh air.

Hot dog hands begins, "Tell us what you know about the trial, and what time do the Feds expect you to check in?"

I hear Tony lumbering about above and pray the floorboards hold his bulk.

"I'm not Sophia Escari. I have no idea what you're talking about," I plead.

He glances at his watch. "Listen, I'm not one that likes to smack young girls around, but I will if necessary. Will you answer if I call you Samantha Foster?"

"Who's that?" My voice is raspy. I need water.

"It's what the Feds call you, or have you forgotten your new identity already?" He sneers.

"I swear to you I don't know what you're taking about."

"Convenient amnesia. If only you could suffer from that on the stand."

Our conversation continues in this manner until Tony joins us. The stairs creak and moan with every step. More talk of the FBI and whether they're fools thinking I could be hidden with a suburban family. He informs Mullins—so Mr. Universe has a name—that Joey will be arriving after dark. They both stare at me knowing my game will be up once "Joey" arrives and clamber back upstairs.

Furniture is dragged across the boards, and from the loud commotion, I gather they upset a sleeping raccoon. I will not panic— not yet. The basement has absolutely nothing of use. No weapons, no escape.

My brain is scrambling for answers. Nothing is making sense. Why would Enzo come after me after eighteen years? Was it because I visited Josie? What on earth has the FBI got to do with it all? Aren't they trying to arrest him? I close my eyes and think of all the times I ignored my dad reading out the news of the day. My real dad who didn't just raise me as his own but loves me and would rescue me if he had any idea that I have been kidnapped.

Tears well up as thoughts of Mom and Dad fill the hole in my chest. They're in West Virginia. Day one of their reunion is coming to a close. I imagine them laughing and reminiscing with their friends, Mini running around with the other toddlers. The tears spill over and run down my cheeks. I ache thinking of how terribly I've treated them since that letter arrived. They never did anything to deserve my anger. I just want to tell them how much they really mean to me. My sobs echo around the empty basement.

What time is it? Looking over my shoulder, the window alerts me to the fact that the sun has gone down. During Georgia winters, the sun is gone by five thirty usually. The basement is dark and growing colder. My eyes have adjusted. The only source of light is shining down the stairs.

Rocks should have arrived if he followed me. How fast can a Camazotz fly? So many questions I never got the chance to ask him. I rest my chin against my chest. Crying is pointless and a runny nose will make my situation worse. I take three deep breaths, will my tears to cease, and start to count—one thousand and one, one thousand and two. I will monitor the time if nothing else. There are three thousand six hundred seconds in an hour. Focus.

Buzzing on my butt cheek has me jumping the mere inch I can move. In two seconds, my stupid annoying ring tone will follow the vibrating. Fudge! It fills the basement and I wince when loud footfalls run to the stairs.

The men appear at my side arguing about whose job it was to check me for a phone.

"If I don't answer it, my parents will know I'm in trouble!" I yell. Then my brain kicks in. I *don't* want to answer so they *will* know I'm in trouble. My only lifeline and I screw it up. Why did I pick this moment to tell the freaking truth?

Those disgusting fingers bring out my phone, and the picture of Dad in his new abseiling helmet fills the screen.

"Tell him you're at the movies," Mullins orders, pulling a revolver from his jacket. I stare down the dark barrel. Frozen in place.

All I can do is nod.

I wish speakerphone was never invented. Hearing my Dad's voice hurts me. He's happy and he wouldn't be if he only knew. My eyes never leave the gun.

"Connie, sweetheart, you missed the best day up here." His voice is so relaxed and excited. I can hear laughter in the background. I will not cry.

I follow my order and tell him all is well and of my movie plans. He asks if I'm getting sick because my voice sounds strange, and the knowledge that he knows me so well cripples me. How could I ever think that man didn't love me as much as Mini? I fight more tears as Mullins ends the call.

The phone is switched off and dumped on a stack of boxes. Alone again. My fingers are stiff, the plastic cuts into my wrists when I make fists to get the blood flowing. I keep seeing the gun pointed at my head. These men mean business. I don't want to die. I sit and wait and listen. I start to count and another hour passes.

My hair blows across my eyes and movement flashes in my peripheral vision. I scream into the darkness. My nerves are on a very short fuse. The sound hurts my ears as it bounces off the hard surfaces. I was so focused on counting each second that whatever it was startled me.

When I run out of air, I look around to my right, but there is nothing there. I know I felt something. My eyes move down and what little air was in my lungs leaves it.

Rocks.

He must have flown in behind me, and now his little bat body is flat across the floor behind the boxes. My throat is closing up, and I can't get enough air. What have I done?

Boots thunder to the stairs, and all my practice lying is suddenly put to the test. The bare bulb above flicks on and I blink.

"Shut it!" Tony hisses in my face, whiskey fills my nose. "Why did ya scream?"

"I'm going to wet my pants." Those months of lying have come in handy. His nose screws up, and he takes a step back. "You think Joey will be impressed if he has to question me standing in urine?"

By the looks of Tony, he isn't too bright, and the thought of upsetting a bigger fish clearly has the cogs in his brain trying to turn. The knife appears, and I'm freed and dragged upstairs. When I return to the basement, I slide the chair forward in line with the boxes before I sit down. Tony secures me and Rocks remains undiscovered. His little body hasn't moved.

I focus on the pounding pulse in the side of my neck. I have to stay calm. I begin to count. Rocks will be out for eighty or ninety minutes.

Close to thirty minutes later, a car door slams and softer footfalls enter. The men explain that I'm not cooperating, and a voice as cold as steel laughs. A thinner set of legs in black jeans start down the stairs.

Squinting in the harsh light, Tony, Mullins and ... the creep from the colony that knows Scarface.

"What are you doing here?" I can't help myself. It's the Hispanic guy from the colony. His mirrored aviators are still on his head. He swears colorfully and loudly before twisting around and grabbing Porky Pig by the throat.

"It's not her, you stupid bastard." His fingers tighten around the pudgy flesh. Camazotz are lean and strong. Their hands and arms the strongest parts of their body from the workout they get flying. Tony gurgles and turns slightly purple.

"Hey man, you said 'it's her,'" Mullins states.

"I said it *isn't* her!" He growls. "This is not Sophia Escari. Don't you buffoons read the papers?"

He lets go and Tony's coughing fit is the only sound. Joey paces in a circle around his henchmen.

"She's just like the photo, and how come she knows you?" Mullins is slow, but he can at least join the dots.

Tony interrupts, not listening at all, and Joey finally orders them both to go and get the photo they keep mentioning. Their footfalls leaving the house make me shiver. I don't like them one little bit, but I trust this bat even less. Why is a Camazotz connected to my father? What are the chances?

"How did Rockland's little pet end up in the middle of all of this?" He stops in front of me, and his eyes wander down my body. "Where's your boy, huh?" Immediately, his eyes go to the open window. "Oh, no, he won't." He leaves my vision and I hear the window creak closed.

I need to create a diversion, but I've got nothing. "Who are you?" I scream over my shoulder. I still can't see him. I need him to focus on me. "Answer me. I know they've got the wrong person. What are you doing here?" My voice is harsh and loud.

Cold laughter sounds directly behind me. I pray.

"What do we have here? Oh, it's little lover boy." My emotional elevator has broken free and is plummeting into darkness.

I watch Joey looming over Rocks. "How convenient for me." His evil eyes meet mine for a split second before he lifts a boot and stomps on Rocks' right wing.

My scream is useless. He steps away, laughing and walks around the boxes to stand in front of me again.

"No rescue for you."

I can't take my eyes off Rocks. His wing is crushed.

"You broke his wing?" I screech. My gut heaves at the thought of the pain he'll be in when he wakes up. It's all my fault.

"Ah, well, they won't be able to charge me with murder this way, even though it's a death sentence," he sneers.

"What?" I gasp. My eyes flick from him to Rocks and back again. "What are you talking about?" I half whisper. Fear is snaking its way up my spine, and I know, in this moment, I have to be strong. The predator in him will eat me alive.

"Look at you sitting up tall," he taunts. "Appears you don't know all there is to know about your boyfriend, does it?" Joey says. A smug smirk replaces his earlier sneer. "You know he's all that's coming for you, right? There are no reinforcements."

My lips purse together. He shakes his head. "You think his friends like you, don't you? You think your golden locks dazzle them. That they'll worship you too." He points in Rocks' direction. "He's almost been kicked out because of you, and that suits me just fine."

The men return and Joey doesn't say another word about the colony. He studies the photo and frowns.

"See?" spits Tony, rubbing his neck.

"Who are you?" Joey moves closer and shoves the photo in my face. I see myself—but not quite. Her hair is shorter but also up in a high ponytail. Thinner lips smile with an uncanny likeness. She's possibly a size smaller in the waist, but her chest is identical.

"Who is she?"

"Sophia Escari."

I blink and my mouth falls open. "Tell me what you know!" he roars, making not only me but the other two men flinch as well. Without waiting, Joey moves around behind the boxes again. "Tell me or he loses the other wing."

Dumb and Dumber make a move to join Joey's side to see what he's talking about. He commands them to stay in place. "This doesn't concern you idiots."

"Leave him alone, asshole." My brain is in gear. I won't be responsible for any more injuries to Rocks.

The story spews from my lips. How I ended up at Josie Hendersens's house after Thanksgiving. I don't realize I'm crying until I taste the salt on my lips. "I think that's my sister," I finish.

Joey smiles and the angle of the overhead light makes his teeth appear pointy and sharp. The men leave and I'm left alone. My head is swimming. I have a sister. It's the only explanation of why we look so much alike. A memory stirs of Dad reading about a key witness—a daughter. She works for Enzo so has to be older than me. How did I not put this together before? A daughter with his wife—the baby in the photograph wasn't me. Josie's warning rings inside my head. *I'm the secret.* I'm who she was trying to protect by putting me up for adoption, and then insisting that I don't go in search of my biological father when I came of age.

Enzo Ascari doesn't know he has a second child.

I stare at the steps as Joey trudges down them. He's holding a small metal cage, and white feathers flutter to the floor when he dumps it next to my phone. I watch as he picks up Rocks and throws him in the cage, securing the door with four cable ties. His body is on top of his crushed wing. Joey notices my stare and laughs. "You really don't know shit. He can't flip now." He takes a bow and leaves.

Rocks can't flip if he's in a cage? I don't know anything about the boy I was making out with this morning. This morning? It seems like days ago since I was sitting on the bench surrounded by pancake batter, kissing Rocks. My brain is too scattered to concentrate on counting. He'll be conscious all too soon.

I listen to the muffled voices above. Someone else is coming to decide. I think to decide what to do with daughter number two. It dawns on me that my value has dropped. I'm not the witness they were after.

High-pitched screeching prevents me from eavesdropping. Rocks is awake and trying to straighten out his wing from under his body. It's heartbreaking to witness.

"Don't move," I whisper. "He broke your wing. I'm so sorry. He's knows about you." He pants on the bottom of the cage and slowly lifts his head to look at me. "Oh, God, I'm sorry. It's my fault." Tears make tracks down my cheeks again. My sweater is still a little damp from earlier. The cage rattles as his other claw hooks onto a cross bar on the side. He's trying to lift himself off his wing. His screech feels like it rips my chest open. The pain must be unbearable. He drops down onto his broken wing again and closes his eyes, panting harder.

"Are you okay?" It's a stupid question.

EEEK!

His answer makes me cry harder. "I know you're not," I sob. "I know you're not." I turn my head away so he doesn't have to watch me cry. My tears will pain Rocks as much as it pains me to witness his agony. When I finally get control, I face him. "I'm going to calm my mind, if you want to tell me anything." Why didn't I think of this sooner? He's probably yelling at me, and I haven't heard a word.

I close my eyes, ignore the biting pain in my wrists and start to count the seconds. It requires all my focus and after six minutes it works.

Decker.
Jeremiah.
Outside.
By now.

"No! They have guns." I hiss at him. "Can you tell them from here?"

Three squawks. "What?" The choice is yes, no or … . "You don't know?"

EEEKK!

I nod. Rocks confirms he can't flip while in the cage, and I tell him that Zabreena knows the Camazotz involved with my kidnapping.

More cars arrive overhead. It's late, but I'm wide awake. The bigger fish has just entered the pond. I expect a conversation, but the footfalls indicate he's coming to me directly.

"I don't blame you, Joey," he says, entering the basement. "But this doesn't help my brother or Ramirez get out of the slammer."

A group of six or so men crowd the basement. I stare at a middle-aged man in a suit. The fabric pinches around his belly, but I wouldn't describe him as overweight. I soak in every feature, but there's nothing out of the ordinary. He could be any man at my dad's workplace. He doesn't scream criminal and that makes my hands sweat.

"So you're the sister," he states. "But Enzo doesn't know about you, does he? Makes you not worth my time." I freeze. He's confirmed that not being Sophia is deadly. "Mullins, take care of this for me. Send me photos so at least I can remind that Ascari pig who he's dealing with."

"Could we ransom her?" Joey asks.

"He doesn't even know she exists. She's worthless."

"But—" Joey is silenced by his boss's outburst.

"I said no! I don't want his money. I want his number one daughter's silence!" His neck has turned bright red. He wipes spit off his chin.

I watch as they file up the stairs and the light clicks off. Darkness swims around me. I'm blind.

Don't worry.

"I want to believe you." My voice is weak. "Whatever happens, I'm sorry, Rocks. I'm sorry about your wing and getting you mixed up in my mess."

I hear the cars drive off and know it's only a matter of time. By the sounds above, only Tony and Mullins are left. They argue and I try not to listen since the topic is how and where I should be taken care of. The more the men argue over my demise, the more I want to tell them not to worry. My lungs have gone on strike, my throat is imitating a roadblock, and the white dots in my peripheral vision are turning into shooting stars. I won't be alive long enough for them to kill.

I picture Mom, Dad, and Mini. I remember our Christmas dinner, all around the table together with Rocks. "Rocks?" I can't see a thing, but I look vaguely where he should be. "I-I love you."

His squawks fill the darkness, and I hear his claw hitting the metal. The cage rattles and the cry changes to ones filled with pain. "Stop moving. It's okay. Please don't hurt yourself," I whisper and he settles.

Raucous yelling and stomping booms above our heads. The men are either fighting for the honor or dancing a polka in concrete shoes. The house creaks, and I duck out of instinct.

"Get away," Tony screams.

"Ow, shit." More cries and then two earsplitting thunder cracks ring out. My chair jumps at least three inches in the air and I nearly fall. "You nearly shot me, you fat bastard."

The herd of stampeding bulls head to the door. I listen harder searching for a hint of what is causing the chaos. The muffled yells and cries fade away.

"Connie?" A voice sounds inches from my face.

"Shit!" I yell, blinking at the darkness. I know that voice. "Decker?"

"Where's the light switch?"

Light floods the room, blinding us all. Jeremiah half falls down the stairs. "Come on. I've locked them in the shed but not for long."

Once I'm released, I grab my phone and the cage and follow the boys through the house. They flip the second they're outside and start screeching, flying back toward the shed. The van door is unlocked, and the universe definitely wants me to reach nineteen because the keys are hanging from the ignition. Rocks squawks in pain when I dump the cage on the passenger seat.

"I'll get you out as soon as I can, but we've got to get away from here."

ROCKS IS LYING across our couch. He's hugging his right arm to his chest with his eyes shut. I've wrapped all the bags of frozen vegetable we have in tea towels and placed them over the swelling in his arm and hand.

The trip home took half the night. Once we were far enough away from the chicken farm to reach civilization, I pulled into a gas station. The boys showed up out of the darkness soon after and helped me free Rocks from the cage. Cable ties hold better than I would have believed. Decker placed him gently on the seat and spread his injured wing out flat. Rocks never made a peep, but my fingernails nearly drew blood across my palms just watching.

The boys decided it was safer to have an aerial escort, than to ride in the van and agreed to meet me back home. The looks I caught them give each other did nothing to alleviate my fears.

Rocks flipped not long after I found the highway. His groan of pain and scrunched up face caused me to veer onto the wrong side of the road. There was not a single thing I could do to help him. After several minutes, he slouched back; blowing air out of his mouth in short gusts, and positioned his arm across his chest.

I asked him why he didn't stay as a bat, and his answer almost forced me to pull off the road. Driving and crying do not mix.

"I couldn't wait any longer to tell you that I love you too," he said. He reached across the console to give my hand a quick squeeze. In the madness of our evening, I'd forgotten my declaration. More tears leaked down my face, but the accompanying elevator was definitely going in a positive direction.

Once back home, the boys had taken the van to the park and left it in the handicapped space.

I brush the hair out of Rocks' face. He's burning up and soaked in sweat. Grabbing a wet cloth, I lay it over his forehead.

The boys are standing together mumbling in hushed tones. "I'm going to take him to the hospital."

"You can't," Decker says. Rocks opens his eyes, and the pain is too great for even him to hide from me. "If he flips, that's it. Game over."

I look back at them. "He needs a cast." They look away. The fear that I felt in the basement has returned tenfold. I don't understand the defeat on their faces. I leave the boys and return to the kitchen. The peas have defrosted. I bag up crushed ice from the fridge dispenser. The first aid course from school is coming back to me. The girls and I laughed more than not, and if I had have known I'd be using it for real, I would've paid better attention.

Leaving the kitchen, Jeremiah slips out the front door and when I enter the living room, I understand why.

Decker is crying. He's not doing that guy thing where they pretend they aren't crying and being tough. He's openly sobbing. A sharp pain cuts down my center at seeing his anguish. Tears are running down his face, and he rubs them against his sleeve.

He kneels on the carpet and grabs Rocks' good hand. "Goodbye, brother." He looks down and sobs into his chest for a moment. "I love you, man. I just don't know what I'll do."

"Decker, look at me." The pain in his voice is breaking my heart one beat at a time. I have to get him to the hospital. "Look after Zada and keep an eye on Moonshiner. We're all he's got. Make sure the other boys don't tease him too much." Decker nods his head. "You'll make a just leader."

"No, I won't. That's your job." He sobs loudly and covers his mouth with his hand.

Why are they talking like this? Has Rocks been kicked out like Joey said?

"No, it's up to you now." Rocks winces. "I've only ever been a disappointment to Strickland. You can live up to Judge's expectations. I know you can, brother." Rocks closes his eyes and breathes slowly for a couple of minutes.

Jeremiah sticks his head around the doorway. His eyes are red as well and that makes me really start to panic. I can't even imagine Jeremiah feeling enough to laugh out loud, let alone cry. "Decker, we need to be home before dawn," he says softly.

Decker's face crumbles under the words. He moves and gives Rocks a half hug even though he knows he's hurting his brother with the contact. And then he strides out the front door.

I follow them onto the porch.

"Decker, I swear I'll look after him. It'll be okay. You'll see him soon," I say, resting my hand on his forearm. He wipes his eyes and looks at me. The tears I've been holding inside spill over when I witness his sorrow. His pain becomes mine mixed with fear of what I don't understand is happening.

"No, I won't. You don't understand. He's not going to survive this."

"Don't give up on him. I can help. It's going to be okay."

"Connie, Rocks isn't going to make it back to Blood Mou—"

"Decker, what the hell? What are you doing?" Jeremiah interrupts. The tension between the boys changes to something I don't recognize. I don't think it's about Rocks right this second.

"I can drive him back to the market. That's easy."

"I'm not talking about Sanguine Mountain Market. That's closed now till spring anyway. I'm talking about—"

"Decker, don't!" Jeremiah grabs his arm, and I can see from the white outline of his hand just how firm his grip is on his friend.

Decker rips his arm free. "She has a right to know where the attack is going to come from. And you know as well as I do that she's going to pay in blood for this."

Pay in blood ... I sway on my feet. I can't worry about what that means until Rocks is taken care of.

They stare at each until Jeremiah turns his back on us and walks out onto the lawn.

Decker meets my eye, and I can see the worry on his usually calm face. "Rocks needs to return to the *real* Blood Mountain, Connie—our roost."

Thank you for reading.

Glossary

Aeronaught: an ordinary human that cannot fly.

Camazotz: a human with the ability to shape-shift into a vampire bat. Any offspring born of a Camazotz will also have the ability to shape-shift.

Fledgers: name given to Camazotz aged fourteen to eighteen years of age.

Flip: the involuntary shape-shift from human to vampire bat that occurs thirty-six hours after their last shift. This prevents the Camazotz from choosing to stay in their human form forever.

Naught: a derogatory terms for a human.

Pups: name given to young Camazotz from birth until thirteen years of age.

Roost: the top secret location where the Camazotz live as bats.

Shaman: someone who can cast spells or curses of great power. They can summon good or evil spirits and were labeled witches throughout history. The Camazotz rely on the shaman for healing.

The Fold: the members of the ruling council that create the laws and decide the fate of the whole colony. There are seven members in the Fold. They are usually the heads of the most powerful wings, but are voted onto the ruling council by all adult and fledger colony members.

The Sire: the leader of the colony voted into power by the Fold members. The Sire will rule indefinitely until he decides to step down or is challenged by another Fold member. This usually consists of a fight to the death.

Wings: family bloodlines within the colony. Each member sees themselves as part of a wing rather than part of this family or that. Members born into each wing are named for that wing to identify their father's bloodline.

About The Author

Sanguine Mountain—Book One in the Camazotz Trilogy—is the debut novel of Jennifer Foxcroft.

Jennifer was born and raised in Australia. She spent her youth dreaming of far away lands and the crazy critters that inhabit them. When she wasn't swimming in the backyard pool or training the family pet to ride a bicycle, she would visit those magical lands and accompany her characters on their exciting adventures. Even as an adult, her daydreaming of fanciful lands never ceased. To this day, she regards herself as a teenager trapped in an adult body. This series is a glimpse of the characters and places she often visits.

For more information about the author and her series, please go to www.jenniferfoxcroft.com Sign up for her newsletter when you visit.

Twitter: @MsJenFoxcroft

Facebook: facebook.com/jenniferfoxcroft.author

Help An Indie…

Indie authors need you!

Yes, we need your amazing book reviewing skills. If you enjoyed reading Sanguine Mountain, Jennifer would greatly appreciate a review. And you already know how obsessed with technology Rocks is. Imagine his smile when he checks the review count on his new phone and sees one written by you. You'll make his day.

Reviews are welcome on Amazon, GoodReads, iTunes, and Barnes & Noble.

Thank you so much. You helped an indie author today.

www.ingramcontent.com/pod-product-compliance
Lightning Source LLC
Chambersburg PA
CBHW020959120726
47905CB00009B/2759